Cape May Christmas in July

KIMBERLY BRIGHTON

PRAISE FOR KIMBERLY BRIGHTON'S
CAPE MAY SERIES

"Brighton skillfully weaves together a heartwarming romantic comedy filled with alluring chemistry and poignant moments...from the bustling courtrooms of Philadelphia to the tranquil sandy shores of the Jersey Cape, Brighton's tender yet humorous Cape May series explores the power of choice and fate and the complexities of love."

– *Prairies Book Review*

"The perfect light romance novel for summer beach reading at the Shore...these Cape May-based dramadies have all the twists and turns to set your heart aflutter."

– *Main Line Today*

"This fun read fully embraces its Love Actually-inspired plot, featuring enthralling vignettes which take their protagonists through the ups and downs of love and life."

- *Reedsy Discovery*

Kimberly Brighton depicts each couple's perspective in vivid detail. The unpredictable plot kept my interest, as every page gave another piece to each puzzle. The Way to Cape May will appeal to romance readers who enjoy stories that give a realistic view of individual progress in love.

– *Readers Favorite*

"A heartwarming tale with a strong sense of place and relatable characters, brimming with complicated relationships, delicious romantic chemistry, and a touch of human drama. Brighton's mastery of complex yet endearing characters shines through as the tensions between each couple reach a boiling point before finally simmering down. With her astute understanding of human psychology, she weaves a story that is both heartwarming and full of passion and vulnerability."

– *Prairies Book Review*

BOOKS BY KIMBERLY BRIGHTON

The Way to Cape May

A Cape May Kind of Love

Cape May Ever After

Copyright @ 2025 by Kimberly Brighton

Readers Guide Copyright @ 2025 by Kimberly Brighton

Cover design by Diane Meacham and book design by Jessica Kleinman

All rights reserved.

The scanning, uploading and distribution of this book without permission is theft of the author's intellectual property. If you would like permission to use material from the book (other than for review purposes), please contact CapeIslandPublishers@comcast.net. Thank you for your support of the author's rights.

Published in the United States of America by Cape Island Publishers

CapeIslandPublishers.com

Library of Congress Control Number: 2025908973

Printed book ISBN: 979-8-9879070-8-5

Ebook ISBN: 979-8-9879070-9-2

This is a work of fiction. Names, characters, places, and incidents either are the product of the author's imagination or are used fictitiously. Any resemblance to actual persons, living or dead, business establishments, events, or locales is entirely coincidental.

To the ocean and all its lovely creatures, and people like Max who work to protect both.

Kelsey

FIVE HOURS. THAT'S ALL.

Just five more hours, and Kelsey Grace would finally be free. Free from the glare of spotlights, the grit of Hollywood, the heat of LA.

Free from her attention-craving costar, Jaxon Quinn.

Not that she minded having one of *Celeb Mag*'s "Top Ten Swooniest Bachelors" around, but lately, he just served as a reminder of things she regretted. After spending months together filming their most recent romantic comedy, she was ready for a break. Not so much from Jaxon himself, but all he represented.

Mr. Swoon himself came charging headfirst into her dressing room, pointing to his scalp. "What's this?" he demanded as he pulled on a strand of hair. "Tell me this isn't what I think it is."

They'd spent so much time working together over the past few years, Kelsey could read his mind as if his thoughts were tattooed on his forehead. Knowing what was causing his current strife, she decided to have a little fun. Running her fingertips through his sun-kissed waves, she feigned inspection and gasped.

"What?" Jaxon yanked his head up, eyes filled with terror. "It's happening, isn't it?"

She ruffled his hair and laughed. "Relax. You're not turning gray."

"But I *am* turning thirty. Not out of the realm of possibility."

"As they say, thirty's the new eighty."

"Feels like it."

"We'll get you into assisted living tomorrow," she said as she rolled her suitcase to the door. One step closer to her vacation.

"Where you goin' again?" Jaxon asked, eyeing her luggage. "Maybe I'll go with you."

"Tahiti. And no, you won't."

"Come on, KG. Just you 'n' me, the sand and the sea—"

"Just me...solitude and serenity."

"You can't leave me. I'm having an existential crisis." He plopped down on her couch.

"Didn't you just have one yesterday?"

"Comes with the age, Kelse. I'm sad."

"Everyone gets older, Jax."

"Not about that. I'm sad you're leaving. Who's gonna entertain me once you're gone? I know—do the trailer again. That'll make me happy."

One night, giddy from a long day of filming, Kelsey entertained him with her version of a trailer for their upcoming movie. She wasn't in the mood to do it now, but if that's what it took to get Jaxon Quinn out of his existential funk—and her dressing room—she'd play along.

She grabbed a hairbrush-turned-mic and dropped her voice to movie-trailer register. *"No man on earth could send shivers down a woman's spine like Jaxon Quinn."*

"Yes!" Jaxon clapped, fangirling.

Kelsey continued in her James Earl Jones voice. *"All he had to do was peer into her soul with his jade-green eyes. One sweep of his long lashes, a nibble of his supple lip, and she had no choice but to melt into a puddle at his feet."*

"Oh, Jaxon!" He gave a falsetto cry as he fake-fainted onto the couch.

"No one knew this better than Jaxon Quinn, himself. He'd practiced the move so often in his mirror, he practically puddled at his own feet."

He pointed skyward. "Facts."

"*But not Kelsey Grace, the only woman who could withstand his oozing charm.*" She paused for effect. "*Or could she?*"

Summoned for their scene just then, they hustled down the hallway to the set.

Kelsey continued. "*Coming soon to a movie theater near you. Oh...and men? Hide. Your. Women.*"

"You're a nut." Jaxon laughed as he gave her a noogie. "But you're my kind of nut."

TWO HOURS LATER, FILMING COMPLETE, KELSEY AND Jaxon crossed the lot with their publicist as a studio tour approached in the distance.

"Shall we give 'em what they came for, Kelse?" Jaxon asked. "One last hurrah before you leave me?"

"Go for it, guys," Verna said, pulling out her cell phone. "Cue the fauxmance."

Jaxon grabbed Kelsey's hand, swung her out and swooped her back into his arms. Just like Fred Freaking Astaire. *He peered into her soul with his jade-green eyes, gave a sweep of his long lashes and a nibble of his supple lip.*

And...nothing. She didn't puddle at his feet. She was Kelsey Grace, after all—the one woman on earth who seemed immune to his "oozing charm."

Much to his dismay.

She looked at him with feigned adoration as the crowd of tourists cheered. If he didn't know the truth, he'd almost believe he had a chance with her. That's how good she was.

"Don't leave me," he stage-whispered, loud enough for the crowd to hear.

"It's only for a short time," she said, giving him a teasing glance through mile-long lashes, her wide smile bracketed by the cutest dimples Jaxon had ever seen, despite having a pretty cute set of his own. A mane of silky espresso flowed down her back in waves, falling softly around his hands as they encircled her waist.

Jaxon dipped her slightly backwards and brushed his lips against her neck. The crowd went wild. It was the little things that made people scarf up his Oscar-worthy displays of public affection. If he weren't such a card-carrying member of the F-boy club, he'd be the perfect boyfriend for someone. Kelsey, in particular. No other woman made him want to rescind his membership.

She gazed at him with those eyes—decadent pools of melted dark chocolate he could drown in if he wasn't careful. Jaxon didn't normally go for the sweet, vulnerable type. Or brunettes in general—preferring the sexy, self-assured blondes who lined the Southern California coastline. But Kelsey's intoxicating combination of sweet and heat made him reconsider. It was no accident she'd been dubbed "America's Sweetheart" by the tabloids, with her wholesome girl-next-door persona.

Jaxon was the lucky man to have plucked her from the market, or so their fans believed. Their fauxmance was a shrewd publicity stunt to promote their upcoming rom-com.

"Marry me, Jaxon!" a fan screamed.

"I saw him first," yelled another.

Risking fandemonium, he turned to face the adoring crowd. "I'm honored, but I'm already taken with this one."

Publicity stunt, maybe, but not exactly a lie.

Jaxon loved women and women loved Jaxon. They ogled him, slid into his DMs, lunged at him. But Kelsey was a different story, an enigma. She wouldn't be caught dead doing any of the above. He just wasn't sure if it was Kelsey herself who was so alluring, or simply the challenge she posed.

Verna appeared in his periphery, telling them to wrap it up. Jaxon leaned back, his hands trailing down Kelsey's outstretched arms until only their fingertips touched.

The crowd roared with delight.

This may have been the best performance of his life. If Jaxon Quinn didn't watch it, he was going to win an Academy Award right then and there. That, or fall in love. With Kelsey, maybe. Himself, definitely.

In fact, he may have just done both.

Kelsey

KELSEY GAZED AT JAXON LIKE A WOMAN IN LOVE. AT least how she imagined one would look. She wouldn't know, having never been in a serious relationship. But she'd seen enough movies—heck, acted in enough—to know how to pull it off. It's what she did best. Fake it till you make it, a skill she excelled at onstage and in life.

To everyone watching, she was the luckiest woman in the western hemisphere. She'd snagged the unsnaggable Jaxon Quinn, or so they believed. To Kelsey, though, it was just another example of the facade that had become her life.

Gazing into his sea-green eyes brought thoughts of Tahiti, where she was about to spend a month in sweet solitude. Where a beachfront bungalow perched on a white sand beach next to the azure waters of French Polynesia would become her sanctuary—devoid of film crew, studio producers, Jaxon. An unprecedented opportunity to break from the never-ending stream of roles she'd been playing, a chance to know herself again. Assuming she'd even recognize her.

Her mouth slid into a smile, until she remembered they

were supposed to be sad to be leaving each other. *Waah,* cue the sorrow.

Channeling her inner diva, Kelsey's lip quivered, and a fat tear rolled down her cheek. Her voice rose a decibel as she bid her final farewell. Overacting? Maybe, but the crowd was far enough away that their little show of affection required the projection of a Broadway musical.

"I'll miss you!" he cried out.

Talk about overacting. The man couldn't help himself. Not that it mattered. He could give the worst performance in all of celluloid history, and he'd still have women fainting in his wake.

The son of two beautiful Hollywood stars, Jaxon Quinn had been thrust into the spotlight at the tender age of three. Adorable from the first take, he soon became the fresh-faced teen heartthrob splayed across tabloids and teen walls, including those of Kelsey's younger sister, Sarina. To say Sarina once had a raging crush on Jaxon Quinn was an epic understatement. Fortunately, adult Sarina had long since moved on—which was good. Kelsey would never go after someone else's crush, as evidenced by her past.

Jaxon blew her a final kiss, and she caught it. The crowd applauded the cute exchange, the same one they'd done on their first date, strolling in Santa Monica. Just the two of them, a film crew, and millions of live social media viewers, invited to witness their first date in the ultimate publicity stunt. Kelsey found it ridiculous, not to mention over-the-top attention-seeking, but went along with it. As she did most things in her life. She understood that, in a world fraught with hatred and violence, fans yearned for love in all its hope and glory. It's why they mobbed theaters when their rom-com movies were released and cheered on their budding "real life" romance, desperate in their need to ship them.

Verna had suggested the ploy one night as they sat around

the pool at Jaxon's Malibu mansion. Their most recent movie, *My Trucker Romance*, hadn't brought in the reviews they'd hoped for, with most critics claiming the plot was weak.

But the chemistry is fire between these two, one critic noted. *They should date in real life—people won't be able to stay away from their future flicks.*

From that moment on, Verna pushed the idea as a brilliant marketing tactic to help promote their next flick, to be released that fall.

"Fauxmances have been the literary rage since the beginning of time," Verna had said. "If it works in novels, why not real life?"

"Because it's dishonest," Kelsey had responded.

In the end, Verna and the studio won out, as they promised it would only involve a few public sightings. Some social media posts. And...a creative publicist, a scripted plot, and a written contract binding them to terms of the fake romance, executed in the conference room of a law firm. Talk about romantic.

The last thing Kelsey wanted to do was give the studio a reason to think twice about her future roles. It was the greatest lesson her dad had taught her: Be a good girl. Do what people ask, and you'll be fine. So far, that strategy had worked.

"Just until the movie comes out," Verna promised. "Then, you'll discover he's cheating and move on to someone else after nursing a broken heart."

Kelsey recoiled at the suggestion. "Why can't I be the cheater? Why is it always the woman having to nurse a broken heart?"

"Welcome to reality," the publicist quipped. "This is how it happens in real life."

How would Kelsey know? She'd never been in a serious relationship. Guys tended not to stick around that long.

Her sister Sarina once postulated that men perceived her

to be out of their league. While Kelsey liked that excuse, she knew it wasn't the real reason. She had no problem attracting guys, until they discovered *just plain Kelsey* lurking beneath the makeup and glam clothing. Shy, sometimes tongue-tied, often klutzy despite her surname suggesting otherwise. Once they learned the truth, that she was nothing like the image she portrayed, they took off for greener pastures.

At least, that's how she saw it.

Kelsey eventually went along with the charade because she understood fans' fascination with romance and comedy, the combination of which made them forget everything else, at least for a couple hours.

Bonus—the fake romance kept fans from discovering what a dateless doofus she was.

If she were honest, the rom-com thing was getting old. She wanted to break from her four-movie streak. Tired of being typecast as a whimsical woman in love, she longed to land more dramatically challenging roles, yet each time she asked, her agent told her to ride the wave as long as she could.

"Soon, you'll be too old," she said. "Enjoy these roles, and those looks of yours, while you have them. Before you know it, you'll be cast as the old lady in the grocery store pushing four cats in a stroller."

So Kelsey acquiesced, grateful for any opportunity to grace the silver screen, knowing it could all be taken away in a second if she said or did the wrong thing. She'd seen too many other celebs lose it all over one infraction.

"Good job, guys," Verna said as the tour moved on. "I'll post these tonight. Jax, maybe you could join Kelsey in Tahiti so we can grab shots of you two frolicking in the waves, rubbing sunscreen on each other, and—"

"*Hell* no!"

Oops. The stunned look on their faces told her she must have voiced her thoughts aloud. "Sorry, I need a break from—this." She waved her hands in the space between her and Jaxon.

"No offense, Jax," he joked.

"I just need to get away for a bit. Alone."

This was the part of her job she disliked the most, the fakeness of it all. Pretending she was in a relationship with Jaxon Quinn, of all people! As if she could ever land such a perfect specimen of a man if they weren't being tethered together by a studio contract. As if the reality of her single life wasn't embarrassing enough, the man was literally being forced to "date" her in a legally binding sort of way. As well as her so-called friends (also paid actors) as they spent Saturdays romping on Rodeo Drive, lounging in La Jolla, dining in Del Mar. Truth was, she didn't have many friends, and the ones she had weren't that glam.

But America's Sweetheart had an image to uphold—that of a perfect twenty-eight-year-old, sought after by men, surrounded by friends, living the good life. In reality, she spent weekends alone, binge-watching reality dating shows. The only thing that would make it more tragic was the addition of a cat or two and a tub of Ben and Jerry's. Guilty on the second count, often practicing her lines on their cardboard faces as she dug into the pint.

It was the comedic tragedy of her life—the woman known as Hollywood's most sought-after bachelorette wasn't sought after by anyone—man, woman, friend, or feline.

"Glad that's over with," Jaxon teased as they headed back to the studio. "I'll warn you, though—if you don't stop looking at me like that, I *will* fall in love with you. For real."

Kelsey smirked. "Thanks for the warning. I wish I could say the same."

"My heart!" Jaxon stumbled backwards, grabbing his chest as he flashed a perfect white smile. "Say you don't mean it."

"Mean it," she teased and stifled a giggle. "You're too old

for me, anyway."

Most straight women couldn't resist falling for Jaxon Quinn, but somehow, she had. While she appreciated his objective beauty, she knew Jaxon wasn't her person.

He followed her back to her dressing room and flopped on her couch.

"Make yourself at home," Kelsey said. "Can I get you a drink? The paper? Your slippers?"

"Funny." Jaxon picked up her TV remote and started flipping channels.

Kelsey ducked behind a room divider to change. "Seriously, Jax, I need to get going. My airport ride is—"

"Cape May!" Jaxon proclaimed, turning up the volume. "Your hometown's on the Weather Channel."

Donning her robe, she perched on the couch next to Jaxon.

"Fortunately, the storm spared most of the Cape," the announcer reported. "The beaches suffered significant erosion, but that's nothing new for this area. Bad news for shops and restaurants, though. Summer is when these business owners earn their living. With the storm canceling July Fourth celebrations and thwarting tourist visits, profitability has suffered. Hopefully, they'll be able to recover those losses in the second half of summer."

Kelsey's family had already shared news of the storm's damage, but hearing it on national news made her stomach knot. Thankfully, there were no deaths or serious injuries, and Kelsey's sister's café had been spared. Nestled in the middle of Washington Street's outdoor pedestrian mall, it was blocks from the beach on slightly higher terrain. But the town's beloved arts center wasn't so lucky. Housed in a centuries-old wooden barn, it had withstood many coastal storms throughout its lifetime, but this one had proved too much. The center was where Kelsey and her sisters had developed their affinity for the arts. It had played an important part in shaping their lives.

"Sorry about your hometown," Jaxon said.

"Thanks," she said, a sadness creeping through her as she disappeared behind the screen again.

She had just finished dressing when her sister Molly FaceTimed her. Emerging, she held up her phone to indicate she was taking a call. Jaxon gave her a quick kiss on the cheek and ducked out.

"Hey, girl!" Molly said as she and Sarina popped into view. "Coming to you live from the world-famous Sunrise Café!"

Molly panned around the room so Kelsey could see.

"Hey, ladies, I'll have to make this quick. I'm leaving for the airport."

"Wee! Are you coming home?" Molly, the youngest of the Grace sisters, squealed with enthusiasm.

"Sorry, Moll. I'm heading to Tahiti."

"Why, when we have the world's best beaches here?"

"Or, used to," Sarina deadpanned.

"We just finished filming, and I'm heading out for vacation," Kelsey said. "What's up?"

"As you know, I've been helping with storm cleanup," Molly said, "and Sarina's been offering free coffee and food for the workers. But what the town really needs is money for supplies and labor, not to mention a boost in morale. I want to put together a fundraiser for Cape May, like a celebration of sorts, and we need your help."

Kelsey felt her skin prickle, as it did whenever she was asked to do a favor she didn't want to do. "I'm not performing in Grand Lillian's play, if that's what you're about to ask."

Grand Lillian, as she insisted on being called, was their grandmother and family matriarch, who ran the local arts center. Every summer, she directed a community play. Occasionally, when she couldn't find an excuse not to, Kelsey gave cameo performances in one of her productions.

Not this time.

"The play's already cast, so you're off the hook," Molly assured her. "We'd just love for you to come home and lend your famous face to our efforts. You know, do a little promo thing."

"When is it?" Kelsey asked, giving one last glance around her dressing room as she headed for the door.

"Next weekend."

"Sorry, kiddo. I'd love to, but I have nonrefundable travel plans." Then, to add more credibility to her story, she threw in a lie. "Jaxon's coming, so I can't disappoint him."

"You could always bring him," Sarina said with a smirk. "It would be nice to see the two of you together. In person."

Kelsey didn't love Sarina's cynical tone. She made a mental note to never let Sarina see her with Jaxon. Her shrewd sister likely wouldn't be fooled by the fauxmance if she witnessed it in person. Not because she was jealous, or still in her teen crush era, but because she tended to pick up on things others didn't. Like when people weren't exactly being honest. Thanks to the studio's nondisclosure agreement, Kelsey wasn't at liberty to tell her family the truth.

Molly gave a little clap. "Yes, bring him here! I'd love to meet your bae."

"Not if Sarina's walls are still covered with his face," Kelsey teased. "I can't take a chance she'll try to snag him."

"Please," Sarina sighed, rolling her eyes. "I'm not thirteen anymore."

"Oh, snap! What I wouldn't give to see the two of you brawling over Jaxon Quinn!"

"She can have him," Sarina said emphatically. "At twenty-five, I think I'm beyond celebrity crushes. Besides, he's too squeaky clean for me."

"So you're not able to come home for the fundraiser, Kelsey?" Molly asked, sounding disappointed.

"If it's money you need..."

"It's not just about money, although raising it is my endgame. First and foremost, I want to bring the community together, have us work collaboratively to rebuild what needs to be rebuilt, including our town spirit."

Kelsey chuckled. "You sound like a Hallmark movie."

"Maybe so, but I haven't forgotten what it was like to be raised in our hometown, and while I'm stuck here without a job, I have to do something worthwhile."

Molly was right. They'd been blessed to call Cape May home. The exhaust fumes of LA must have clouded Kelsey's thoughts.

"We figured it was a stretch, but thought we'd try anyway." Molly sighed with resignation.

Kelsey hated letting her sisters down, but swaying palms were calling. It wasn't often she had the opportunity to do something just for herself. Most days were spent at the mercy of her schedule, her publicist, and all that came with being a public persona. A solo trip meant a break from the lie that had become her life.

She spotted the limo waiting for her in the studio lot, apologized to her sisters, and blew them a kiss.

"I'll be in touch. Say hi to Grand Lil for me. Can't wait to see you when I see you."

"When'll that be?" Sarina asked.

"Hopefully Christmas."

Sinking into the buttery leather seat, Kelsey tried to relax as the car made its way toward LAX. But something gnawed at her.

Cape May, her sweet hometown, had been beaten down by a vicious storm. Beaten down, but fortunately, not broken. Kelsey could relate. This fake life of hers, this image she had to uphold, the lies she had to tell her family—it was all becoming too much. She, too, felt beaten down.

Maybe she didn't need a shiny tropical vacation with swaying palm trees. Maybe she needed a few days in Cape May, her beloved hometown.

She closed her eyes and gave it some thought.

Nah. Swaying palm trees it is.

Colton

COLTON BANKS STRODE TO THE COUNTER OF THE CAPE May General Store as a slight breeze whispered through a screen door, providing a whisp of respite from the sweltering summer afternoon. He'd forgotten how hot East Coast summers were, and that some Victorian buildings in town hadn't yet joined the twenty-first century by installing air-conditioning. He rolled an icy bottle of Coke across his forehead to cool his hot skin when a tabloid headline caught his attention.

"Kelsey Grace: America's Sweetheart Snags Her Prince."

Grabbing the magazine, Colton plunked down a twenty, told the clerk to keep the change, and shoved the rolled-up tabloid into the waistband of his jeans. He thought his t-shirt would hide it, but when he climbed into the driver's seat of the pickup truck, his brother Max called him out.

"What's that, a weapon? Don't tell me you just held the place up with a magazine."

Busted. "Just an article I want to read," he mumbled as he tossed it in the back.

Max swiveled his head, following the trajectory of the rag mag as it landed on the seat with a thud. "Hey, Kelsey's on the cover." Then, "*Ohhh.* I get it."

"Get what?"

"Why you bought it. Gotta keep tabs on your high school crush. You know, there is such a thing as social media." Max grabbed the magazine from the back seat. "Not like—whoa, fifteen bucks? Dude! The internet's free." Max punched him playfully in the arm.

"Ouch!"

"Sorry man. I forgot. How are you feeling?"

"Better before you slugged me," Colton said, wincing as he rubbed his shoulder. His million-dollar shoulder, the one that had catapulted him to NFL quarterback fame before a devastating injury ended his career.

While the physical aspects had healed for the most part, the emotional wounds of all he'd endured hadn't. Still reeling from the jarring life changes that had plagued the last eight months of his life, he was struggling to come to terms with the finality of it all.

"I just don't mean how you're feeling physically—"

"I'm fine," Colton snapped. He felt bad for cutting him off, but didn't feel like getting into it just then. Or ever.

The brothers had returned to Cape May after their father had succumbed to a heart attack two months prior. Despite the circumstances, they were fortunate to have the time to come together and give their family property the rightful farewell it deserved. Max, who'd just graduated from college, had the summer free before he was off to grad school. Colton, who'd lived in California since he was drafted six years ago, was no longer needed there. While Cape May wasn't exactly where he'd choose to be, it was only temporary until they sold their family property, consisting of a farmhouse, barn, and a 100-acre vegetable and fruit farm that had provided their family a livelihood since the nineteenth century.

Max pressed on. "Is Kelsey the reason you bought the magazine?"

"Nope. Got it for another article."

"Right," Max said, in a tone suggesting he knew better. Reading the cover, he smirked. "Lemme guess which one. 'Man Finds Severed Finger in Chili?' Or I know. 'Hollywood's

Top 10 Ugliest Babies.' Yep, that must be it."

"Don't be a dick," Colton laughed.

"You guys keep in touch?" Max asked.

Colton's jaw tightened. He and Kelsey hadn't kept in touch, but he knew if he said as much, Max would want to know why. Colton and Kelsey had once been best friends, but he'd never shared their falling out with his brother.

Max flipped to the article, reading aloud. "'America's Sweetheart, Kelsey Grace, has finally landed her prince.' Wow, that seems sexist. Who's the prince?"

Colton ignored him.

"Oh, says here it's Jaxon Quinn. Yep, that tracks—he could be my prince, too. This makes it sound as if she needs a dude to rescue her, though. Pure junk."

Colton turned on to Lafayette Street, his eyes instinctively drawn to the gazebo in Rotary Park. The one he tried to avoid looking at whenever he passed this way.

It once held sweet memories of childhood and Kelsey Grace. Now, it was nothing more than a painful reminder of the night she walked out of his life for good. Yet there it stood, in all its glory, bathed in the glow of a setting sun.

A sea breeze blew through the truck's open windows, bringing with it random notes of a band's warm-up. On summer nights, the gazebo became a stage for the town's summer concert series. People were scattered around the lush lawn, waiting for the show to begin, as kids played tag and lovers snuck kisses.

For a moment, Colton was transported back to that fateful night. It was the last time he'd see Kelsey, but he didn't know it at the time. In the ten years since then, their paths hadn't crossed once, despite both living on the West Coast and occasionally returning home for family visits.

That didn't keep him from going to the movies every once in a while, just to see her face again. To remember what it was once like to be in the presence of his childhood best friend, his first crush, the one who always made him feel like something he wasn't. Strong. Smart. Secure. Nothing and no one—not even football or family—had ever made him feel like he belonged in the way Kelsey had.

Whatever. It wasn't meant to be. He just wished someone would tell his heart, so he could finally move on. Which was exactly what he planned to do as soon as he and Max finished wrapping up their family estate. Now a free agent in every sense of the word (except, ironically, with the NFL), Colton could go wherever his heart desired. Like the woods of Montana—off the grid and far away from there, with nothing but him and his dog. All so he could finally be free from what tethered him to Cape May.

He just wasn't sure if it was the farm...or his ex-best friend.

Molly

"WELL, WE TRIED." MOLLY SHRUGGED AS SHE ENDED the FaceTime call with Kelsey. "I knew it was a long shot."

"It's okay," Sarina said. "We can pull this off without her. Woulda been nice, but I guess that's what we get with our sister in such high demand."

They'd grown accustomed to not seeing her much, after Kelsey landed her first big role six years ago and moved to LA.

It was hard for Molly to believe her sister was her age when she made it big. She was jealous Kelsey had not only known what she wanted to do with her life at twenty-two, but had made it happen. Something Molly wouldn't know, as evidenced by the myriad applications she'd strewn throughout

New York's five boroughs in the two months since graduating college. Most of which had boomeranged right back in the form of rejection letters. With a boyfriend living in Manhattan and an impending proposal, she couldn't wait to get a job and join him.

"Is Brennan coming this weekend?" Sarina asked.

"Probably not," Molly said.

"Too busy for his girlfriend's big event?"

Molly shrugged, hoping to appear nonchalant. "He's got a lot going on, getting accustomed to city life."

"Accustomed?" Sarina scrunched her face in judgment, emerald eyes cast in disbelief. "What, is there zero gravity there? Lower levels of oxygen or something? What's there to get 'accustomed' to?"

"I don't know." Molly waved off her sister's wry humor. "I guess he wants to get the lay of the land."

"Well, tell Lewis and Clark I admire his gumption—navigating the wilds of Manhattan with nothing more than GPS, Wi-Fi, and the billions who've gone before him. Wish him luck."

Molly tossed a sponge at her sister.

True, it was a bit weird for Brennan to need get "accustomed"—his word—after landing a cushy job making serious bank with a global investment firm right out of college. Their original plan was to move to New York and find a place together, but the firm had wanted him to start right away, so they put him up in a company-owned studio apartment until the two of them found something on their own. In the meantime, Molly stayed in Cape May, working in Sarina's café when she wasn't applying for jobs. All packed and ready to go, she hoped an interview opportunity was imminent.

And then the storm hit.

As Molly rode through town on her beach cruiser the following day, dodging tree limbs and debris, she was shocked by the sheer force of Mother Nature and the random destruction she'd left in her wake. Some buildings had large swaths of missing roof tiles, while others, immediately adjoining, were left fully intact. Flood waters rushed into some streets, but spared others. Chunks of beach were sheared off in places, while blocks away, dunes remained untouched.

In one particularly hard-hit section of town, Molly leaned her bike against a tree and helped neighbors remove rubble, lug limbs, and sweep sand from the streets. It was cathartic, seeing the direct results of her labor. The destruction left in the storm's wake felt a lot like her current goals, scattered and uncertain.

For the next week, she'd delivered free coffee from Sarina's shop and offered her assistance with cleanup, often not crawling into bed until after midnight. It was a calling of sorts—stuck in Cape May without a real job, she had nothing but time and labor to offer. Despite the grueling physical demands and little sleep, it gave her a sense of purpose.

And that's when she came up with the idea of creating a combination celebration and fundraiser to assist with restoration efforts. She'd hoped her oldest sister would lend her fame to their efforts—photo ops of her helping to prepare for the event, maybe some meet-and-greets. Even just her presence at the event. While she was disappointed Kelsey had declined, Molly was confident they could pull it off without her.

The tinkling of the bell on the café's door heralded an incoming customer, bringing her back to the present. Peeking around the corner, she saw a former classmate lingering in the doorway.

"Hello?" he called out as he ran a hand through his thick, dark hair and adjusted his nerdy-cool glasses.

"Hey, Bunsen!" Molly sang out. It was the name she'd given Maxwell Banks in eighth-grade science class.

He laughed, his cheeks turning crimson.

"Hi, Max," Sarina called out. "Thanks for stopping by."

"No problem," he said, giving a small wave. "Hey, Molly."

Molly and Max had been in the same graduating class but ran in different circles in high school. He was a quiet, geeky sort; she, an outgoing cheerleader. He was also their class valedictorian and a recent Harvard grad, which meant he'd be doing something amazing with his life. Meanwhile, Molly, of less prestigious post-secondary schooling, career-less and without direction, was stuck in Cape May.

But only temporarily.

"I'm here to see what you need for the week," Max said as he pulled out his phone to take notes.

Max's family owned the farm that sourced Sarina's café with fruits and veggies. This was the first time seeing him since they graduated four years ago. She assumed his return home was only temporary, as well, especially after hearing his dad had recently passed, and he and his brother were selling their farm.

As Sarina discussed the items she needed for the week, Molly tried to keep herself busy, but saw Max occasionally looking at her. She couldn't help noticing how much he'd changed. He didn't appear as geeky as he did back then, but she wasn't sure if that was because he'd grown into it, or she was less judgmental (probably the former). Nor was he as skinny as he once was, now appearing more toned and muscular. His smile was bright, and his dark eyes lit as he joked around with Sarina, just before tossing glances at Molly.

After Max left, Sarina flipped the sign on the door to "Closed."

"He's got a crush on you," she said matter-of-factly.

Molly laughed. "How would you know?"

"One, he kept looking at you. Two, I saw you looking back. I do believe I saw sparks."

"The only sparks you're gonna see from this girl are the

ones flying off Brennan's two-carat engagement ring." Molly held up her left hand and wiggled her fingers.

"Oh yeah? And when's that gonna happen?"

"Soon. We've been talking about it, and with my birthday next week, it would just make sense."

Brennan was her first love. He'd come along just when she'd needed him, a source of strength and a beacon of attentive light, helping shield Molly from shame after her dad left their mom and absconded from their lives. After dating for six years, engagement was the inevitable next step. They both agreed Molly's job hunt had to take priority over moving in together and planning a wedding. Another reason for her job search desperation—to leave post-graduation-solo-life purgatory and get on with married-in-Manhattan bliss.

Despite that, Sarina's comment about Max intrigued her. As someone who never turned down positive attention—actively sought it out, in fact—Molly enjoyed the rush she felt when people, especially men, noticed her. Not because she was looking for someone else. She was just wired that way, accustomed to being someone's central focus as she'd been for her dad, before he left, and Brennan, thereafter.

But recently, Brennan's attention had been focused on his job. He hadn't been home since graduation in May and had lately been busy on weekends when they'd usually see each other. Most of his plans involved golf outings or other work-related events. While she understood it, she didn't love it.

There was something about Max that gave old soul, with a quiet confidence and calming reassurance that was enviable. Even if he was a major nerd—or at least was one back then. Or maybe it was the feeling of having a guy look at her the way he had, especially when it had been a while since a guy—since Brennan—had given her a look that made her feel...something.

Something that felt like hope.

Max

MAX'S HEART WAS POUNDING AS HE LEFT THE CAFÉ. HE hadn't seen Molly Grace since high school, but the exhilaration he once felt in her presence came rushing back, as if he were still standing at his locker, mesmerized, as she walked by with her gaggle of girlfriends. While they never acknowledged him, Molly always did, even if it was just a smile, or a "Hey, Max." Sometimes, if he was really lucky, she'd fist-bump him as she passed.

It was hard not to crush on Molly. She had a bubbly personality and a smile that lit up any place she occupied. Her smooth skin wasn't besieged by teen acne like that of their classmates, Max included. Her long chestnut hair, now in its summer era—sun kissed to a lighter shade—naturally curled at the ends and bounced when she walked from the spring in her step. The way her hazel eyes gleamed as she teased him smacked him right in the feels. To this day, he couldn't recall her friends' names—for all he knew, she could have been surrounded by a pack of wild dogs. He couldn't even look at other girls in high school, that's how infatuated he'd been with her. He hung on her every word, the times she paid him attention, and thought about her every night as he lay in bed, heart thrumming in a way that made his ears ring and his head swimmy as he conjured images of all he wished he could do with her. Kiss her rosebud lips. Wrap her soft hair around his finger as he breathed in her natural honeysuckle scent. And oh, so much more. There wasn't a speck of Molly's outward appearance Max hadn't committed to memory during those formative years.

But it hadn't always been that way. It was in eighth grade when he first became aware of Molly in that way. Up to that point, she was just the sister of his brother's best friend, existing merely in his academically focused periphery. Having nothing in common, Max was disappointed when he was paired with the vivacious girl in science lab, hoping instead to be assigned a more serious student, one who'd help ensure they earned an A.

But on that first day, Molly flashed him a smile, unleashing a tempest of feelings he'd never felt before. A simultaneous burst of joy, a breathless rush, while at the same time a desperate hunger, a yearning like no other. No girl had ever smiled at him or laughed at his jokes, like the ones he made about Bunsen burners.

"That's it. From now on, I shall call you Bunsen," thirteen-year-old Molly announced as Max adjusted the gas. "Careful, Bunsen. Don't burner your buns."

Max didn't know if the nickname was a compliment or an insult, but he'd take it. No one had ever bothered to give him a nickname, especially someone as pretty as Molly.

Pimpled and slight of frame, Max hadn't yet developed like the other boys who'd started sprouting facial hair and developing deepened voices. To add insult to brace-face injury, Max was painfully self-conscious about his appearance and hid behind his oversized glasses. Colton assured him he'd fill out one day, just like he had, suddenly growing taller and adding muscles at fifteen. Max wasn't so lucky, not hitting six feet until college.

Molly was kind to him during those painful years, and for that, Max was eternally grateful. His mom had died when he was eight, so his emotional growth was largely shaped by the men in his life, who had their own way of dealing with grief in a more stoic, silent way than how Max was wired. He longed for a softer touch, an outlet to share his emotions—something his brother and dad couldn't provide. As a result, he'd learned to flat-line his feelings around them.

But Molly opened up something in him. Although he never shared it with her, there was just something about being in her presence that allowed him to *feel*. She always had something kind or funny to say that made him smile. Her playful teasing provided the levity he was missing, reminding him there was more to life than loss and sadness. She made him feel like he belonged to an elite club, even if it only existed in his mind.

In fact, she was a lot like his mom. Sweet. Caring. Fun.

Fortunately, Molly was as smart as she was bubbly, and they earned an A+ in science lab that year, along with rare accolades from their tough teacher.

In high school, things changed. Molly made the highly competitive cheerleading squad and was swept into the clique of popular upperclassmen, including the arms of perpetual prom king, Brennan Sloane. Max veered off in the opposite direction, joining robotics and math club, fading into the background. Molly would still smile or wave when she saw him, when no other girl in school would give him the time of day.

Max's phone buzzed, bringing him back to the present.

"Did you get Sarina's order?" Colton asked when Max answered the call.

"Yep, she needs it by tomorrow. Big order, but I can handle it."

"That would be great. I'm off to meet with the lawyer but can help with delivery tomorrow."

"No problem," Max said. "Good luck."

"Yeah, thanks. The sooner we settle the estate, the sooner we get outta Dodge."

"True," Max said, even though he didn't feel the same urgency his brother did to sell their family's land and leave town. "Tell me again where you're going, that you can't wait to get there?"

"Wherever the wind takes me, baby bro. I'm thinking Montana."

Max recoiled, as this was the first time Colton had mentioned it. "Why there?"

Colton shrugged. "It just appeals to me. Off the grid, and lots of space for Cadence to run free."

"How's the old girl doing?" Max asked, referencing Colton's dog.

He sighed. "She's good. I just miss her like hell, but I didn't want to have her move twice. Another reason to get where I'm going, so I can get her settled in her new home."

Max was disappointed in Colton's plan to flee Cape May as soon as he could get away. Colton was the only family Max had left, and he'd been looking forward to some brother bonding as they undertook the grueling task of preparing the property for sale. It was hard enough losing their father, and he'd hoped their time together could help ease the grief he'd been experiencing. But Colton refused to talk about his feelings or take it deeper than surface-level discussions about estate settlement, which left Max feeling as if he were losing his brother as well.

Then again, there was a part of him that felt he'd already lost Colton. Ever since he'd gone off to college, he'd become a stranger to Max, which was only exacerbated when he'd been drafted to the NFL. Over the years, football had seemed to consume Colton, but not in a good way. On the outside, he looked healthy and productive, appearing as fit and trim as he'd ever been, but on the inside, something had changed. On the few occasions they'd seen each other over the years, Max had barely recognized his brother. Gone was the funny, sensitive kid. His eyes no longer lit up over their shared jokes, and he'd long since stopped sharing things with Max.

With both parents now deceased, Max longed for a connection to their past, to the Colton he once knew. He secretly hoped it would take a while to sell their land, to give them more time to reconnect, and for Colton to be reminded of who he was.

Tucking his concerns aside, Max picked up his pace. He needed to get to work on Sarina's order. Now that Molly Grace was back in town, he felt something stir within him he hadn't felt in a very long time.

Something that felt like hope.

Sarina

SARINA WAS EXHAUSTED BUT THANKFUL FOR A BUSY morning. Business had been slow since the storm but was beginning to pick back up.

Molly went to the back to wash dishes while Sarina sank into a chair. Closing her eyes, she rubbed her temples when she heard someone come in.

Her ex.

Sarina and Luke had broken up a month ago but had remained friends. Still, he found reasons to stop by on a daily basis. Perhaps because he hadn't seen the end coming—Sarina initiated it—after setting his heart on spending his life with her. But she only had room for one love in her life and Sunrise Café was it.

"Hey, Sarina." Plopping down at the counter without waiting for an invitation, he gave her a sad smile. "I have bad news."

"If it's about Mike Trout not coming to Philly, I already heard it."

"No. It's worse than that."

"Tell that to Phillies fans."

It was true. The region still wasn't over the fact that their superstar South Jersey-bred center fielder had chosen to remain on the West Coast.

Luke ran a hand through his perfect blonde Ivy League cut, his dark eyes clouding over. "A development company is looking to bring Cape May into the twenty-first century. Among other things, they want to bring in a *Jolt!* franchise. They're looking for a location and an owner."

Her pulse roared. "You can't be serious."

Jolt! was the country's leading coffee chain. For some reason, people went batshit crazy over it. Sarina was convinced they put narcotics in their beverages. There was no other way to explain the viral obsession with their coffee, which tasted like it had been drained from someone's car battery.

"I *am* serious," Luke said. "Sorry."

"Can't you tell them to pound sand?"

Luke, whose family owned one of the largest real estate companies on the Cape, gave a sympathetic chuckle. "I'm afraid real estate doesn't work that way."

"Yet Cape May has somehow managed to keep chain companies from moving in since the beginning of time. Why is it suddenly different?"

He shrugged. "The times are a-changing."

"No offense, Luke, but you've had your license for fifteen minutes. You're hardly a reliable source of trending real estate."

"But if you add the fifty years my family's been in the business, I think I know what I'm talking about."

This was not good. A chain like *Jolt!* moving into the Cape was the last thing she'd wish on her sweet, mom-and-pop shop hometown. And her café. Her brand of freshly roasted coffee had been well-received and was gaining popularity with residents and visitors alike. She hoped it wasn't just because of its location on busy Washington Street Mall. She wanted her success to percolate from her creative curation of full-bodied coffee beans and the exotic flavors she conjured. Starting her own coffee line was a passion project, and a modestly lucrative one as well. Knowing how crazed people were about the national chain, if one opened up within a ten-mile radius, it would ruin that part of her business.

"You've got to find a way to stop them from moving in," Sarina pleaded. "I've got a good thing going here, and I don't want that to change."

"I'll try to talk them into finding another shore town, but I just wanted to let you know, in case you wanted to get ahead of it."

"How would I do that?"

"Maybe you'd want to consider a franchise arrangement, where you make *Jolt!* your official coffee. You may have to buy into it, but that will keep a competing owner out."

Sarina laughed out loud. "Luke, I'm barely—" She stopped herself before admitting she was barely making ends meet.

The café was coming up on its first anniversary. While she did well last summer, she hadn't anticipated how slow the off-season would be. She'd developed a small group of regulars, but with her reasonably priced offerings, she wasn't buying up boardwalk hotels any time soon.

Once spring came and tourists returned, she'd done better—until the storm hit, just before July Fourth. It caused a major disruption in cash flow that typically flooded the town in summer. She'd further strained her budget with post-storm donations of coffee and snacks to volunteers. Probably not the smartest business move. But it had felt like the right thing to do.

Sadly, benevolence didn't pay the bills. She was scraping the bottom of her bank account, her rent was two months in arrears, and another payment was soon due. She'd successfully availed herself of the landlord company's good graces, citing the storm as a cause for her tardiness. They'd given her some time to get it together, but that wasn't going to last forever.

She'd never admit her financial issues to anyone, because that would only confirm their beliefs she wasn't suited to run a café. That, and her lack of experience, were the reasons her grandmother had shot down Sarina's original request for a loan.

"Maybe try working in a café first, to see how you like it," Grand Lillian had suggested. "I'm not handing out my hard-earned money to someone until they've proven themselves."

"I've already worked in cafés," Sarina insisted.

She wasn't lying, although the European cafés she'd worked in were nothing more than glorified bakeries, not full-service meal establishments. Her grandmother's lack of faith in her was unsettling, even if she intended it as tough love.

Luke, too, had tried to talk her out of risking her life savings, but when he realized she was forging ahead with her plans one way or another, he offered her half the upfront money in exchange for joint partnership. She'd considered it at first, based upon the fact he both made, and came from, good money. Until he started in with his ideas for the café's layout and menu offerings, all of which were in diametrical opposition to what she envisioned. She wanted cool and eclectic, he wanted cookie-cutter and boring. But there was another reason. Knowing she and Luke weren't in it for the long haul, she hadn't wanted to become financially reliant on him.

That left her with no other choice but to get a small business loan, the first time she'd ever borrowed money. It was the only way to do her café the way she wanted, indebted to no one but the bank.

"The developers seem pretty serious about wanting *Jolt!* to go in somewhere," Luke continued. "They're intending to bring in other chains—all part of the packaging they do with new mixed-use residential and commercial builds. They know what works when certain stores are put in together."

"Well, we should spread the word, so no landowner sells out. That kind of development would kill the Cape and destroy its historical significance as a Victorian resort town."

Even as she said the words, she knew she was appealing to the wrong audience. If the developers used Luke's family's real estate business to broker such a deal, they'd stand to earn a shit ton of money in commission. But she had one ace up her sleeve...

The fact that she still had his heart.

She placed her hand on his. "Luke, I don't want to lose my business to a national chain, so please, find a way to stop this from happening. I'm begging you."

She felt bad tugging the emotional strings still attached on his end, but there was no way she was going to allow a chain to come in and ruin her business.

The bell on the door tinkled again as Grand Lil breezed into the café. Didn't people read signs? Then again, no amount of signage would keep her feisty grandmother from doing what she wanted.

"Well, if it isn't my favorite future grandson-in-law!" she sang out.

"Grand!" Sarina exclaimed through clenched teeth. "You know we're just friends now."

"Well, an old lady can hope, can't she?"

"Besides, I'll be engaged before she is."

Sarina startled to hear Molly's voice. She'd forgotten she was in the back.

"I'm pretty sure Brennan has the ring already," her sister said.

"Phooey," Grand Lillian exclaimed. "You can do much better."

"What do you guys have against him?" Molly whined.

Sarina smirked. "How long do you have?"

Grand Lillian ignored the squabbling siblings and poured

herself a cup of tea as Luke rose from his stool.

"Well, ladies, I'm off. I've got a property to show."

"As long as you're not showing it to you-know-who," Sarina said.

"Who?" Molly asked.

"Never mind. Inside joke," Sarina said. She didn't want to tip anyone off that their predictions about her café's viability may well come true.

After Luke left, Lillian took his place at the counter. "How are plans for the fundraiser coming along?"

Molly chewed her lip. "They're...coming."

Sarina tried to hide another smirk. Plans may be coming, but not Kelsey. Just wait 'til the old bird got wind of that.

"Good," Lillian said, "because we need to raise enough money to keep the arts center where it is."

"Where's it going?" Sarina asked.

"A little birdie told me someone purchased the arts center land."

"I thought it was owned by the city," Molly said. "Who bought it?"

"I'm not at liberty to say."

"Why, or you'll have to kill us?" Sarina asked.

Lillian's proclamation of a tattling "little birdie" was laughable. No doubt, she'd crawled up a tree and shook the living shit out of the bird to cough up any and all gossip it had. News didn't just find Lillian Grace. She swooped on it like a vulture.

As always, Grand Lillian ignored her sassy comment.

"If the new owner sells the land, God knows what will become of the Cape."

"Are you saying that raising funds to help rebuild the arts center may be pointless, if the land's gonna be sold anyway?" Molly asked.

"Not if I can help it," Grand Lillian said. "That's why we need your sister here, to remind people how crucial the center is for Cape May's culture. Raising funds will only sweeten the deal by helping to pay for the rebuild. How did your call go, anyway—will Kelsey be joining us?"

Molly shot a look at Sarina, eyes wide as she twirled a caramel-colored curl with her finger. "Go ahead, tell her."

Sarina was the only one brave enough to deliver bad news to their grandmother, as the two were more similar than either would like to admit.

"She can't come," Sarina said abruptly as she turned to stack coffee cups. Brave, perhaps, but she didn't need to face the firing squad of the feisty matriarch head-on.

"Can't? Or won't?"

She paused before delivering the bad news. "She's going to Tahiti for a month."

Sarina turned to see her grandmother raise the teacup and take a slow, thoughtful sip. Dabbing her lips with a napkin, she neatly tucked it under her cup. She rose, looming larger-than-life, despite having a frame so petite she'd have a hard time getting on rides in Wildwood. "We'll see about that."

Sarina blinked, and she was gone. She looked at Molly.

"Uh oh. The plot thickens," Molly said.

Sarina nodded. "Something tells me we'll be seeing our sister sooner than we think."

Kelsey

As the exit 0 sign whizzed past the window, Kelsey wondered how she'd found herself careening down the Garden State Parkway in New Jersey, instead of a runway in Tahiti.

Alas, her current status could be summed up in two words: *Grand Lillian.*

Her grandmother's text had come through as Kelsey was about to enter security at LAX.

> CALL ME - URGENT

Kelsey tried to remain calm as she dialed her grandmother's number, knowing the family matriarch was a smidge prone to drama and exaggeration now and then. But she never texted in ALL CAPS. Something was wrong.

"What's up? Everyone okay?" Kelsey demanded, dispensing with formalities.

"They're fine." Her grandmother's voice quivered. "But I'm not."

"What's going on?"

"I'm hurt." Grand Lillian paused and shuddered a deep breath. "In my feelings."

"Oh, for the love of Pete." Kelsey sighed with both exasperation and relief, having momentarily forgotten the octogenarian was a former actress of both stage and screen. Steadying her voice, she asked, "What's really going on?"

Her grandmother explained that the lead in Cape May's annual summer play had run off to Vegas with her boyfriend for a surprise wedding. "Which, mark my words, won't be a surprise now," she threatened. "I have *Cape May Magazine* on speed dial."

"You'll do no such thing, Grand Lil."

"I make no promises. I don't know what she sees in him. I've seen rats more attractive in the dumpster behind Acme."

"While I'd love to discuss this, I'm about to—"

"I've heard," she said, her tone icy. "How can you?"

"How can I what? Take a well-deserved vacation?"

"You can first come home to help your sisters and the town that made you."

Kelsey rolled her eyes. It wasn't the first time her grandmother had used this type of ploy to elicit her assistance with a fundraiser.

"Can't, Lil. My boyfriend's expecting me." She flinched at telling yet another lie—to her grandmother, no less. When would it stop?

"Oh yes, Jaxon Quinn." Grand Lillian's voice took on a softer tone. "Your hunka burnin' love. Can't say I blame you there."

"Okay, Elvis. Take it easy."

"Will he be wearing a Speedo?"

Kelsey ignored her.

Her grandmother continued in a mousy tone. "Can you pretty please come home for a couple days and help us with this teeny-tiny play?"

"What about one of the local actresses—can't one of them fill in? Yvonne maybe?"

"Poison ivy, head to toe. Looks like she's covered in barnacles, as if she washed ashore from the storm."

"*Oh*-kay. How about Fergie?"

"Shark attack."

"Come on—"

"Yes, it was a sand shark, and it was last summer and only a flesh wound. But she's still so traumatized, she had to winter inland and hasn't returned to the Cape since."

Kelsey gave a frustrated sigh, knowing where this was heading.

"Won't you *please* do your old grandmother this one final favor, Kelsey Jean? Consider it my early Christmas gift, in case I die before then."

Kelsey called her bluff. "You won't. You're as strong as an ox."

"True. But I need you. Be a good girl and give in to your old grandmother."

Kelsey cringed upon hearing the words, the same her dad had repeatedly said to her throughout her childhood, designed to play upon Kelsey's natural people-pleasing tendencies. *Be a good girl and clean your room. Fetch me a beer. Tell Mom I was here all night.*

As the oldest sister, it was her lot in life to be responsible. Not Sarina, the feisty middle child, who'd stand up to Dad with a sarcastic comeback. Or sweet Molly, who'd cry and get her way. No, Kelsey was expected to fall in line. Show up, shut up, set a good example.

Not this time.

"I can't. I have to—"

"Break an old lady's heart?"

Kelsey was stubbornly silent, despite the guilt slicing through her like a knife.

"Fine," Grand Lillian said, in a tone suggesting it wasn't. "If this boyfriend is more important than your old grandmother, go right ahead."

Victory! Kelsey was about to end the call when the dramatic woman rambled on.

"If I have to call off this play, the arts program will fail, and it'll all be on your shoulders."

"What are you talking about?"

"I didn't want to tell you this until you were home." Kelsey could hear the sudden shift to seriousness in her grandmother's voice. "But the arts center was so badly damaged, it can't be repaired. If we don't raise enough money to rebuild it, the program will be gone with the wind that destroyed the building. The very program that catapulted you to fame and fortune." Pausing for dramatic effect, she added, "Not that you owe it anything."

And there it was. If anyone should get a Golden Globe for guilt trips, it was Grand Lillian. Kelsey could picture her regal chin, thrust in defiance as she soldiered on.

"But Tahiti, well, it's not like you can jump on a plane any day and go there," she continued. "Oh wait, you can. I forgot you make the big bucks now."

Kelsey rolled her eyes, anger roiling within her as she felt herself falling back into her old appeasing ways.

Grand Lillian was tougher than grit, a force to be reckoned with. Hurricanes had nothing on her. Kelsey knew, if she didn't do her this favor, she'd never hear the end of it. Especially if she wasn't exaggerating about the arts program. Maybe it was more important to give back to her beloved hometown than bask on a South Pacific beach.

"I'll think about it."

"I knew you'd say yes!"

The battle was over. When the family matriarch wanted something, she got it. Especially from Kelsey, who never fought back.

"Thank you, my dear. You won't be sorry. You'll be helping save all of theater. At least in South Jersey."

"You're not really dying of anything, are you?" Kelsey asked, just to be sure.

"Yes," she said, sounding serious until a giggle broke through. "I'm dying to see you!"

"Oh, God," Kelsey sighed. "Meryl Streep has nothing on you."

"The compliment is all hers," Grand Lillian said. "Oh, and your flight leaves in an hour."

For the first time in her life, Kelsey hung up on her feisty, award-winning actress of a grandmother, knowing a text with her flight details would be forthcoming. All due respect to Meryl Streep, but Grand Lil really did have a thing or two on her. Not that Kelsey would ever tell her that.

Despite the beckoning of distant tropical shores, Kelsey had made peace with her decision to return home. Even if it had been the result of matriarchal masterminding and not her own free will.

As the Cape May sun beamed through the car window and danced on her skin, the plastic shell of her Hollywood life began to melt away. Despite her fame, the residents of Cape May left her alone for the most part. Everyone was friendly, but no one *from* there chased her down for autographs or selfies and, instead, came to her defense when visitors tried. While it wasn't Tahiti, Kelsey was confident she'd get some alone time—taking early morning walks, riding her bike on the quiet back streets of the Cape, hitting the less-crowded beaches in a floppy hat and sunglasses. There was nothing like lounging in a beach chair on the Jersey coast, a soft breeze cooling her sunbaked skin as she watched the waves crash.

She couldn't wait for those moments to actually reconnect with herself. After so many years of being in the spotlight, feigning being someone she wasn't, she hardly knew who she was anymore. She'd lost sight of all that mattered to *her*. What *she* wanted for her life, not just what others expected. In fact, the last time she saw a glimmer of her true self was in Cape May. A return to self was long overdue.

It also felt good knowing she was here to help with the

town's restoration, as the remnants of the storm's damage, still evident weeks later, rolled by her windows—colorful Victorian cottages with missing shingles, old trees torn in half, debris lingering on lawns and side streets.

Passing the gazebo, the heartbreak she'd experienced a decade ago came rushing back as if it were yesterday. It was where she and her childhood best friend had played as kids. Where they pinky swore as five-year-olds to be besties for life, where they hung out after school and did homework together. As teens, they'd sneak out in the middle of the night and meet up there to share gossip or lend shoulders to cry upon. It was their place, until that night—the night he walked out of her life and into someone else's. The last time she'd laid eyes on Colton Banks in person.

Kelsey turned her eyes back to the road. There was no use thinking about that now. She was only home for a week and would soon leave those memories behind. No longer plagued by what was, what could have been. Her only saving grace was knowing Colton wouldn't be here. The last she'd heard, he lived not far from her in California, with someone he was likely to marry.

Minutes later, she burst into the café, singing her arrival. Her sisters and grandmother greeted her with hugs. Sarina flipped the sign on the door to "Closed" and poured coffee for everyone. The women caught up until they heard a man's voice at the back screen door.

"Delivery for Ms. Sarina!"

"You guys wanna give me a hand?" Sarina asked as she went to let him in.

"Be there in a sec," Kelsey said, before slipping into the tiny bathroom to splash some water on her face and clean up a bit after her trip. She checked her reflection in the mirror. Yikes. A little rough, but that's what happens after a six-hour, red-eye flight. At least she wouldn't be seeing anyone but family today.

Until she opened the door and stepped into the path of an oncoming man.

A man holding a box. Make that, *was* holding a box, until it went airborne. Hail Kelsey, full of grace, fruits and vegetables all over the place.

"Sorry!" Kelsey exclaimed as she knelt down to grab a wayward watermelon at the same time he did.

"My fault," she heard him say as his fingers brushed hers. A surge of electricity shot through her, and she looked up—into the pale-blue eyes of her childhood crush.

Colton Banks.

"Oh my—" Kelsey's voice caught in her throat.

"Are you *serious?*" Colton exclaimed, sounding incredulous.

Kelsey, flustered, could barely find the words to respond. He sounded happy. Or annoyed. Maybe both.

Along with time, they stilled, fruits and veggies rolling around them. They slowly rose, not taking their eyes off one another. A second passed, then another, then as many seconds as years had transpired since they last stood face-to-face.

Finding her breath, she exhaled his name. "Colton."

"Kelsey," he whispered back. "I had no idea you were in town."

No one had told her Colton was home. If they had, she might not have given in so easily.

But there he was, in the flesh. And there she was, looking as if she'd clung to the wing of the plane instead of sitting pretty in first class.

She tried to cast her travel-weary appearance from her mind. Just looking at his face, she felt ten years of hardened feelings beginning to soften.

"Come here," he said, pulling her close as he wrapped his arms around her.

She breathed in his still-familiar scent and felt the *thud-thud-thud* of his heart racing against hers as she was transported back to their youth. Memories of them together flashed like a choppy home video of all the times he'd held her like this. When her beloved dog died. When she tanked the SATs. That night in the gazebo, just before he broke her heart.

His embrace lasted longer than it should have, but the draw was magnetic and Kelsey was powerless to end it. She sank further into him, feeling more real, more at home, more *her*, than she had in a long time.

"I've missed you," Colton whispered into her hair.

Tilting her head, she looked up at him. His lips parted, and the unmistakable look in his eye served as forewarning they were about to relive history.

Suddenly, he stiffened and recoiled. Instinctively, she reciprocated.

"Sorry," he said. He cleared his throat, his expression hardened, and his voice took on a businesslike tone. "How long are you in town?"

She was confused by his sudden sober mood, until she remembered he belonged to someone else.

"A week," she said.

"Great," he said, bending over to pick up the remaining produce. "Well, I...better help unload."

With that, Colton disappeared through the back door.

Kelsey sank down on her heels to keep her legs from giving out completely. Stunned couldn't begin to describe how she felt. She wasn't expecting to see him or to have the feelings she thought she'd squelched come flooding back.

When she finally mustered the strength to stand, she headed to the kitchen and began unpacking boxes as Colton brought them in, careful to avoid further eye contact. Easy, since he didn't look at her either. Still, his presence in the café commandeered all her senses.

"Hey, everyone, I have an idea. I want to get your thoughts," Molly called out after the boxes were unloaded.

Max and Colton headed to the back door to leave, but Grand Lillian stopped them.

"Now, boys. You can't just deliver your goods and leave." The matriarch ushered them back inside. "Sit, have coffee."

"I'm in!" Max said.

Everyone took a seat except Colton. Leaning against the wall near the back, arms crossed, he looked like he'd rather be anywhere but there. He'd barely changed in his outward appearance—still the same fair-haired, All-American quarterback with a soft, youthful face, welcoming smile, and dreamy blue eyes. He'd lived a charmed life. Talented beyond belief, he'd been sought after by so many—scouting agents, coaches, team owners, fans, women.

One woman, in particular.

But aside from his physical features, there was a negative aura about him, so different from the last time Kelsey saw him at eighteen when he was filled with eager hopefulness, ready to take on the world. No doubt due to his injury and his dad's recent death, which she completely understood, but there was an edginess she'd never seen in the sweet boy she'd once known.

Kelsey felt her own guard going back up, as the sting of his long-ago rejection returned. Whenever she envisioned how it would be when they ran into each other, she never pictured him looking tortured.

"Next Saturday is July 25, also my *birthday*," Molly said, singing the last word. "I thought it would be fun to do a Christmas in July–themed celebration and fundraiser. Grand Lillian's play is that weekend, and now that Kelse is filling in, we can charge more for tickets. We'll ask businesses to set up sidewalk sales and donate a small portion of their proceeds to the cause. Special events will be offered at a nominal cost, including kid craft stations and visits with Santa. I'm envisioning a town-wide Christmas dinner that night, with a long

Grinch-style table like they had in Whoville, and ending the night with fireworks on the beach. How does that sound?"

Max was the first to weigh in. "Sounds great!"

"Sounds expensive," Sarina said, brow furrowed. "I thought the idea was to raise money, not spend it?"

"Molly, it's a fabulous idea," Grand Lillian said, overruling her cynical middle granddaughter. "We'll get donations of food and supplies to keep costs down."

"We'll tap in to the holiday spirit, which Cape May does so well during the real holiday season. Y'all in?"

Colton spoke first. "I'd love for Max and I to help, but we're busy with the farm, tying things up before the sale."

"Certainly, you could spare *some* time," Lillian said, eyebrow raised above an icy stare.

"Sure we can," Max said, turning to Molly. "You can count on me."

Colton's forbidding brow told Kelsey he would rather *not* be counted on. He pulled a buzzing phone from his jeans pocket. "Gotta take this," he said, excusing himself as he went to the hallway.

"Sorry, he hasn't been himself," Max said, then turned his attention to Molly. "About that dinner, Colton and I can construct some smaller tables that could be arranged end-to-end, to create the illusion of a long one. Just food for thought. No pun intended."

Everyone laughed, the tension in the air waning. Until Colton returned.

"We gotta go," he announced.

Max got up dutifully.

Grand Lillian placed her hand on Colton's arm. "I know you're busy, and this is a tough time for you boys. But don't forget where you came from," she said, giving him a measured look. "We could really use you, and I know your dad would want you to help your town in any way you can."

Colton's eyes softened as he looked down at the tiny force majeure, the tentacles of her masterful manipulation obviously extending beyond family as she channeled her inner helpless old lady.

"We'll see, Grand Lil," he said as he turned to leave, but not before he glanced over at Kelsey. Then, as if everyone else in the room evaporated, he nodded at her. "Take care, Kelse. Good seeing you again."

Kelsey was relieved when he left. She could breathe again.

Just a week. She could avoid anything for a week.

Including the guy who—judging by the way it raced—still had her heart.

Colton

"WELL, THAT WAS SOMETHING," MAX SAID AS THEY climbed into the truck after leaving the café. "Kelsey Grace, back in town. Did you know?"

Colton ignored him.

Max changed the subject, apparently getting the hint. "I think it would be nice to help out with the fundraiser. Grand Lillian was right. Dad would want us to do our part."

The last thing Colton wanted to do was see Kelsey Grace more than he already had. Once was enough. It was all his heart could take.

Passing the gazebo once again, Colton felt the breeze through the open window carrying more memories. He closed it to keep them away.

"Forgot to tell you," Max said, breaking the silence. "I saw Luke Martin today. He asked you to stop by Monday afternoon."

"What for?"

"To purchase Girl Scout cookies."

Colton laughed, reminded of Max's humor. "Funny guy."

"Thanks, I'll be here all week. Wild guess, but as our Realtor, I'm thinking he wants to talk about the land sale?"

"Great. I want to get this thing wrapped up by next week."

"Tell me again why you're in such a rush to get this place sold?"

Colton frowned. "Nothing for me here."

"That's not what it looked like back at the café."

Once again, he didn't respond, too afraid to let his feelings show, for fear he'd expose something he wasn't ready to share—that he was broken, unfixable. After a lifetime of hurt and disappointment, rejection and abandonment, he'd lost every single thing that ever mattered to him. Except Max. And his dog.

Cape May only served as a reminder of all he'd lost. Once Max left for school, there'd be nothing left for Colton here. But moving on to parts unknown would allow him to go off the grid, take off the mask, be alone with his dog, feel without drowning in sorrow. This time, his loneliness would be by choice, something life's traumatic events had robbed him of.

"Is it about money?" Max asked, interrupting his thoughts. His voice took on a teasing tone. "I know you swindled the NFL out of millions, but have you also gotten caught up in something nefarious, like gambling debt?"

Colton chuckled. "No, baby bro. Nothing like that. Speaking of money, how are you set for school?"

"I took out a loan, so I should be fine."

"Shit, Max!" Colton exclaimed. "Why on earth didn't you ask me for the money?"

"That's your money. You'll need it to live until you figure out your next chapter."

"I've got plenty to support us both."

Thanks to aggressive investment of his funds, Colton could

survive on his NFL earnings, even if he never took another job. While he respected Max's decision not to ask him for money, there was no way he'd allow his little brother to go into debt over school. Even if Max wouldn't accept a handout, his half of the money from the property sale would support him nicely. A development company had shown interest in the farm, and Luke had suggested they'd be able to name their price.

"That's kind of you," Max said, "but I wanna do this on my own."

"Well, then, another good reason to sell this land as soon as we can. You can give back that loan before it earns interest and use the proceeds of the sale to keep yourself afloat until you graduate and find a job."

"Speaking of which, I've got to get to mine. Do you mind dropping me off?"

As he awaited the start of grad school, Max had resumed the same summer job he'd held since high school at the Marine Mammal Stranding Center. Ultimately in furtherance of his goal to become a marine biologist.

"You don't have to be working this summer, Max. I've got you."

"I don't mind it. I'm gaining work experience in a field I love. It also keeps me busy, and my mind off...you know."

Colton squeezed Max's shoulder in grieving solidarity over their father's death. "I know."

After dropping Max off at work, Colton returned to the house to find a shoebox on the kitchen table with a note from Max saying he'd found it in the barn. Its presence caused Colton's heart to skip a beat. He'd forgotten all about it since he'd hidden it in the rafters when he returned home from college one summer.

Not wanting to face its contents just now, he stashed the box in his bedroom closet. He decided not to look at it until the night before the settlement, at which time he'd light a bonfire in their backyard pit and burn its wretched contents, along with a few other mementos he no longer needed. A rite of passage before he moved on to his new life.

    Later that night, after Colton was certain Max was asleep, he pulled out the magazine article about Kelsey. He'd outright lied to Max as to why he bought it—of course it was to find out her latest news. Even if it did involve another man. His heart sank as he read about Kelsey's new romance, but he couldn't stop himself. He had to know details so he could drench himself in the reality that she belonged to someone else and to keep his embattled heart from hoping for a different outcome.

    According to the article, they'd met on set and made a few movies together before realizing there was more between them than friendship. Jaxon took her to dinner in Santa Monica one night, and they strolled the pier afterwards, where he kissed her under a sky of fireworks and asked her to be his real-life leading lady. It went on to explain—in excruciating detail—how they spent their weekends roaming through outdoor markets, cruising the coast, and lounging poolside at Jaxon's beachfront house in Malibu.

    More so than the words, though, were the pictures that struck Colton in the feels. Photos of Kelsey looking up at Jaxon with undeniable affection. Her big, soulful eyes, the windows to her soul, gleamed with adoration as Jaxon gazed upon her with a hunger Colton knew all too well. It was why he couldn't look at her in the café earlier that day, afraid his face would show the truth he'd been hiding for so long.

    The article drove home the point that she was in love with someone far more interesting than he. Someone gainfully employed—someone whole.

    "Stop," he said aloud to derail his thought train. He tore the magazine in half and shoved it into a wastebasket. Another thing he'd need to burn. "Enough, now."

Except, in the dark, he couldn't get the image of Kelsey out of his mind, looking up at her "prince." Max was right, how utterly sexist. Those who knew Kelsey well, like he once had, knew she waited for no man, prince or otherwise.

The Kelsey he knew in high school would have mocked such a concept into oblivion. She knew who she was and never faltered for a man, including Colton. He wished she would have, every once in a while. Like other girls—following him, putting notes in his locker, and painting their faces with his jersey number on gameday. But that's not who she was. She was easily unimpressed with his newly found high school fame. Waiting patiently while the girls crowded around his locker, she'd mock them, making teasing, lovesick faces behind their backs, which always cracked him up. She would come to the games and cheer, but never do anything to call attention to herself. Most of all, she kept his ego in check if it ever ventured beyond the lines of acceptable self-glory.

In so doing, she had every bit of his attention. And his heart. She just didn't want it.

As he drifted to sleep, thoughts of their chance meeting in the café crept into his head—the way she looked up at him as they grabbed for the fruit, and later, as they hugged. Perhaps it was his wild imagination, or maybe just wishful thinking, but it wasn't too different than the way she looked at Jaxon in the pictures.

Stop being delusional, asshole.

Sarina

AFTER SARINA CLOSED THE CAFÉ, SHE INVITED HER SISters to happy hour to celebrate the rare occurrence of all three being in town at the same time. They agreed to meet up at Delaney's Irish Pub.

Settling into a booth, they toasted their bonus time together.

"Tell me about this new man of Mom's," Kelsey said.

Sarina groaned. Molly gave a little clap.

"Don't listen to her," Molly said. "He's dreamy."

"More like nightmarish," Sarina said, sipping her wine.

She was joking, mostly. As the only Grace sister still living in Cape May full-time, she'd met their mother's new boyfriend a handful of times. He seemed nice enough, but Sarina was wired for suspicion. Especially toward the eager men who'd recently tried to date their beautiful mom. It had been six years since their father left, and she'd just started putting herself out there.

"What makes him so 'dreamy'?" Kelsey asked, ignoring Sarina.

"He just whisked her off on a ten-day yacht cruise around the Caribbean, so there's that..." Molly said.

"In other words, he's just like Dad," Sarina joked.

Except their dad hadn't so much as taken their mom on a ride around the block in their beat-up minivan. He hadn't given her shit in all their years together. No family vacations, no jewelry, not even a stinking Valetine's Day card. But if she'd been hoping for drunken fights, lonely nights, and single parenting woes, he'd given her the world.

"She sounded happy on the phone," Kelsey reported. "She's sad to be missing our fundraiser, but she's coming to LA next month, so I'll see her then."

"I'm glad she's found someone," Molly said. "She deserves it, after raising us alone."

"Raising *you* alone," Sarina corrected. "Kelse and I were already out of the house when Dad left. He actually spared you."

"He wasn't *that* bad," Molly said, pouting.

"Not to you, his little princess who could do no wrong,"

Sarina said. "Meanwhile, I could do no right. I spent most of my childhood imprisoned in my room for 'being a smartass.' His exact quote."

Kelsey laughed. "Because you were. But you didn't see his expression as you marched indignantly up the stairs, spouting about injustice. I think he loved when you fought back. He once said you reminded him of himself. He definitely enjoyed your humor."

"That's because I was 'the funny one.' Remember?"

Sarina hated the way her dad had labeled each of the girls, even if he wasn't far off the mark. Humor was Sarina's go-to, the thing that got her out of uncomfortable situations. Like her childhood.

"And the one most like him," Molly said. "Not just in looks. You also have his snark."

"He seemed to be proud of that," Kelsey noted. "As the oldest, all I got from him were orders. Be a good girl. Help Mom. Set good examples for your sisters. While you spent your childhood in your room, I spent mine in boot camp."

"He *was* really hard on you," Sarina said. "But I think most older children will agree that's the case."

"You know what he said to me once when I was being bullied at school?" Kelsey asked. "He told me to fight back, like Sarina would. 'You don't see her getting bullied. Molly either, but she's too cute to be bullied.' Basically telling me I was fair game for bullying because...I wasn't tough enough? Cute enough? Kinda shitty to say that to a kid."

"He definitely did a number on your self-esteem. That's why I fought back. I wasn't gonna let him have that part of me."

"Which explains why you're so self-assured."

"So where did that leave me?" Molly asked, eyebrows raised in curiosity. "Where did I spend my childhood?"

"On a throne," Sarina and Kelsey said simultaneously.

Laughing, Sarina held up a fist and Kelsey bumped it with hers.

"That's not true. Once you guys left for college, he basically ignored me."

"Ah, it all makes sense now!" Sarina said, snapping her fingers. "That's when you started dating Brennan, wasn't it?"

"What do you mean?" Molly asked defensively.

"You needed a daddy figure!" Sarina said, casting a taunting grin at Molly as she took a sip of wine.

Molly pouted. "He's six months older than me. Hardly a 'daddy figure.'"

"Dad leaving when he did had to be the hardest on you, Molly. What were you, sixteen?" Kelsey asked, her soulful brown eyes filled with compassion. "I was graduating college at the time and heading off to LA, and Sarina was—"

"On a quest to travel the world," Sarina said.

"Ah, that's right. Backpacking around Europe. Another goal cut short."

Sarina had left school halfway through her second semester of freshman year after discovering college wasn't for her. But backpacking through Europe? Right up her alley. She'd been saving for years—working before she was of legal age, socking away her under-the-table cash earnings—to one day take off for the wild yonder. Once in Europe, she buttressed her savings by working whatever odd jobs she could find, stayed in youth hostels, and hiked instead of paying for public transportation when feasible.

And then, eight months into it, she woke up one day and decided she was done. She'd seen the countries she wanted to see, made lots of friends, and developed skills most people would never learn. Grueling labor and hard mattresses had taken their toll. She missed Cape May, her family, and surfing the South Jersey coast. She was ready to return home and start on her next goal: becoming an interior designer. That lasted six months. Then, it was to join the Peace Corps, a goal even shorter-lived.

"Another example of you not being able to finish things," Kelsey teased.

"What?" she asked, trying to hide a guilty smile. "I finish things."

Kelsey counted on her fingers. "College. World travels. Remember how you were going to become a party planner?"

Right. She'd forgotten about that one.

Sarina knew Kelsey's teasing was in good fun, but it rankled. After all, her reputation for not finishing things was one of the reasons her family thought her café would fail.

Kelsey thought for a moment. "I know I'm forgetting things."

"Luke..." Molly added.

"Hold up," Sarina said, setting her wine glass down with emphasis. "I'll give you all that other stuff. But Luke...that's uncalled for."

"What happened there?" Kelsey asked. "Luke was good for you. Down-to-earth, kind..."

"Cute, wealthy..." Of course, Molly would add those two attributes. She had a lot to learn about what makes for a solid foundation in a relationship.

"Too suffocating," Sarina said. "He asked me to marry him—"

Oh. Shit.

Molly gave a little scream and a clap as Kelsey exclaimed, "No way!"

Well. It was out now. "Way."

She hadn't told her sisters about it, because what was the point, when she'd turned him down? He'd brought it up casually one day. So casual, she almost missed it. He wasn't down on a knee with a ring thrust in the air or any such bullshit like that. Probably because he knew her well enough to know she'd have drop-kicked him into next week. Romantic hoopla was so not her jam. But, yeah, in his own Sarina-informed way, Luke Martin had softly suggested they get married.

She'd met his suggestion with a hearty guffaw.

"It doesn't have to be a big deal," he'd quickly said, upon seeing her reaction.

"Marriage *is* a big deal. Sorry, friend, it's a pass."

Thinking back on it now, she felt bad for how she'd responded. She just wasn't ready for that kind of commitment, and definitely not with Luke. The attributes her sisters had pointed out were all correct, he was everything most women would want in a man. And, not to give Molly's two cents more than it was worth, but *yeah*. Hot and loaded. For whatever reason, he just wasn't for Sarina.

Truth be told, she didn't know what type of guy *would* be right for her. If any. All she knew was, he'd better damn well be someone special.

Kelsey was right, if Sarina was anything, it was self-assured, confident in who she was. She knew her own worth. If she was gonna give it all up for a guy, he'd better match her in intellect, humor, and personality. And more. He had to be... exciting. Definitely not someone so squeaky clean. Even a bit edgier, with a tat or six. Motorcycle optional, as long as he was a badass.

Then again, Grand Lil would go into full cardiac arrest if she ever brought someone home who looked like he'd done time, so maybe not that edgy. Just...not Luke Martin.

Molly excused herself to use the restroom. Kelsey turned to her and asked how the café was going.

"It's going," she said, trying to sound positive.

"Okay, something's wrong."

"Nothing's wrong. Why would you think that?"

"I was wondering if maybe I could contribute to the cause," Kelsey said.

"Molly would love that."

"I'm not talking about Molly's cause. I'm talking about yours."

"In what way am I a 'cause'?" Sarina asked, hoping she didn't sound as defensive as she felt.

"Not you. The café. I know you have to be losing money after the storm hit, with everything you've given away, and now the fundraiser. Can I contribute?"

"I can't take your money, Kelse. I appreciate it, though."

It's not as if she hadn't considered it once or twice. Especially when she was opening, thinking maybe her sister could be a silent partner. But she wanted to do it on her own, to prove to everyone she could. She was headstrong that way, to a fault.

"Look. I'm just...worried about you, is all,"

Sarina laughed, perhaps a bit too loud. "Why are you worried about me?"

Kelsey sighed. "I don't want this to come out the wrong way, but as we joked earlier, you have a tendency to not finish things. I've always thought that came from a fear of failing. But now I wonder...could it be a fear of succeeding? Because being successful means shedding the bad-girl attitude. Being accountable and vulnerable, like knowing when to ask for help."

"Ooh, sounds fun," Sarina said. "Sign me up."

Kelsey ignored her snark. "If it's a fear of failing, I get it. A legit concern that rears itself not only in business, but in relationships. But let's face it, you're a runner. Always have been, both physically and metaphorically. Running from Mom and Dad as a kid. Running from college, relationships, and other things when they got tough. I just don't want to see you bail on the café from a fear of success, of your life finally working out the way you want it to."

"Who says I'm gonna bail on the café?" Sarina demanded, even though she'd been having those thoughts herself. Wondering whether it had been a bad move, opening a café with no business experience, and whether she'd be smart to sell it all off and move on to the next thing.

"*You'll* decide whether you bail. It's within your control."

As Sarina let her words sink in, Kelsey took her hand. "You're doing an awesome job. But I know all too well the script you've written for your life, that things don't work out for you. I think that's a big reason you don't finish things. You don't want to fail, but you also can't envision yourself succeeding. Because...what if you do? That means the comfortable narrative of your life has to change. And change is tough."

"Okay, Dr. Phil. I get it."

"I'm serious. Just promise me you won't give up on this dream of yours."

"I won't," she said defensively. "Love how you guys think I can't do this. Or that I don't have the fortitude to stay with it."

Molly rejoined them just then. "Sorry, ran into a friend from school. What'd I miss?"

"Nothing." Their simultaneous response differed only in tone—Kelsey's bright, Sarina's brooding.

"*Oooh*-kay," Molly said, glancing from one sister to the other. "Obviously something's going on. Typical, I'm always the last to know things."

Kelsey changed the subject as Sarina stewed. It was bad enough their tough-as-nails grandmother hadn't believed in her. But to hear Kelsey paint her as irresponsible and reckless was insulting. Sure, there were times in her life where she switched gears and went on to new projects, but that was a matter of choice. Not emotional immaturity, or an inability to finish what she'd started.

If she'd had any thoughts of accepting Kelsey's offer to donate to her "cause," they were gone now. Maybe she was being a stubborn ass, but she wasn't ready to admit she might have taken on more than she could handle, running a café with no financial backing other than her savings and a small business loan. Despite mounting debt, no one was going to see her waving that white flag yet. Her sister was dead-ass wrong, suggesting she was afraid of success. She'd show her if it was the last damn thing she did.

Kelsey

After happy hour, the girls returned to their childhood home. Kelsey went to her bedroom to unpack. There, a photo on a shelf caught her attention. It was of her and Colton on their first day of high school, taken from behind as they walked into the building holding hands. It was the same pose they'd recreated each year since their first day of preschool.

Apprehensive about their new adventure, the toddler friends had found comfort in their clasped hands while, behind them, Colton's mom memorialized the moment with the snap of a camera lens, a tradition that would be repeated annually for the next fourteen years.

Crossing the room, Kelsey picked up the rustic wooden frame Colton had made for her in ninth-grade woodshop. She ran her fingertips over the words he'd carved across the top, their sentiment tugging at her heart. *Best Friends Forever, K+C.*

Taped to the back of the frame was the note he'd written when he gave it to her.

Kelsey, wherever I go in life, I'll always be with you, holding your hand. Thanks for always holding mine. We got this high school thing (and beyond!). Just remember—you'll never walk alone.

Tears stung her eyes as she thought back to that first year

of high school, before everything changed. Seeing the picture made her long for those simpler days, when things between them were good. Before football. Before Ashley.

Sarina burst into her room just then, startling her. She shoved the frame back on the shelf in haste, hoping her sister hadn't seen her gazing at the picture.

"I'm heading back to my place," Sarina said as she hugged Kelsey. "Thanks for coming back. It means a lot to us. Me especially. It's been rough being the only Grace sister in town."

"At least Molly's back for now, until she finds a job."

"Yeah, I just don't know how long she'll be here with Brennan the Magnificent in Manhattan. I think the minute he invites her to move in, she's gonzo."

"I can't believe she's still with him," Kelsey said, shaking her head. "She's too young to tie herself down to one guy."

"Speaking of guys..." Sarina hesitated, her eyes gleaming. "Jaxon Quinn, huh?"

She couldn't tell if Sarina was being genuine or sarcastic. While Kelsey was a romantic by trade and Molly by heart, Sarina was more practical in her approach to relationships. She didn't believe in love at first sight, or the kind of boastful love Kelsey and Jaxon had been putting on for everyone. She wouldn't be surprised if her shrewd sister saw right through their act.

Too tired from a day of travel to keep up the charade, Kelsey looked away, her eyes catching on the picture of her and Colton.

"Hey, I remember this." Sarina, following her glance, crossed the room and picked up the frame. "Such a cute tradition. What year was this one taken?"

"Freshman year. Mom took this one, after Mrs. Banks—"

"Oh, right."

Colton's mom had passed away weeks before they started high school. Since preschool, she'd been the one to take the kids to school. Kelsey's mom was a first-shift nurse, at work long before their school day began. But that year, Kelsey had begged her to take off work for the morning so she could capture the memory in Mrs. Banks's absence.

"Heartbreaking," Sarina said, echoing Kelsey's thoughts. "So sad she never got to see what became of him."

Kelsey had no idea what it was like to be a mom, but whenever she thought about Mrs. Banks, her heart broke. She left this world when her boys were fourteen and eight, missing the most transformative part of their lives. She'd never get to see her shy, soft-spoken boy be recruited as starting quarterback for his high school team. She'd never get to boast when he was offered a full scholarship to play for a Pac-12 school. She'd never lose her voice during college games, cheering as he threw one smooth touchdown pass after another on national television, like he was born for it. And her heart would never swell with pride when her son became a first-round draft pick for the NFL.

Most importantly, she'd never get to know the man he'd become.

Colton Banks had achieved what most little boys could only dream of. Until that fateful day when, with the wrong twist of his shoulder, his career imploded before everyone's eyes.

The last time his mom had known Colton to pick up a football was when he was in the Mighty Mites league and his helmet was bigger than he was. One of his teammates had told him he had to be "mean" to play football. He'd cried to his mom after practice, claiming he didn't want to be a mean boy. It wouldn't be until a year after her death when he'd focus on getting himself in shape, attract the attention of a football coach, and discover a natural talent beyond anyone's wildest imagination.

His mom would be so proud to know what a great player he'd become—not because he was mean, but because he was good. A genuinely nice guy, Kelsey had to admit, despite what had happened between them.

Sarina interrupted her train of thought with another hug. "Hopefully you two can patch up whatever is going on there." Her sister gave her a poignant look as she turned to leave.

Dream on, Sarina.

Molly

"WHAT'S THAT LOOK FOR?" MOLLY ASKED THE FAMILY cat, who glared at her with wide-eyed feline judgment as she poured her second glass of wine. "I know I've just been out with my sisters, but they bailed on me."

Sarina had gone back to her place and Kelsey had likely crashed after jet lag got the best of her.

Following her to the living room, the cat meowed her displeasure.

"Sorry, girl. I know you were hoping to see Brennan this weekend, but he's got another work thing. It's just you and me. Again."

This time, it was a Saturday morning golf outing that kept Brennan from coming home for the weekend. But that didn't mean they'd have to miss their weekly FaceTime session, he assured her. She'd suggested they do it Saturday night after he returned home, wanting to make *sure* he returned home.

He answered on the first ring. By the tone of his voice, she could tell he was lying on the couch with the Phillies' game on in the background. Good.

"Any leads yet on the job front?" he asked.

"Just applied to twenty more. I should get an interview out of that, right?"

Brennan chuckled. "I would hope so."

"In the meantime, I'm organizing a fundraiser for Cape May."

"Really?"

"Why do you sound surprised?"

"Not surprised. I know that was your hobby in college."

"Hobby?" Molly laughed. "You do know I raised millions of dollars for several organizations."

"Yeah, sorry, I didn't mean it like that. I know you'll do well."

"Then what's up? You sound..." *Judge-y.* "Something."

He hesitated. "Don't you think you should spend that time finding a job instead?"

"Applying for jobs *is* my full-time job. I need a break every once in a while."

"I know, but a job's important, Moll. Gotta put your all into that search."

Easy for him to say, the guy whose college internship morphed seamlessly into a lucrative job, while hers hadn't. Instead, she was left to pick up the shards of her shattered expectations, piecing them back together with a plethora of applications, desperate to find a job in her field.

Brennan suggested she go into finance. It's how his family made their money. His passion (and starting salary) convinced Molly she also wanted to become a finance bro. She'd always been a hard worker, working three part-time jobs in high school, and knew she'd kill it in finance. Between their two salaries, they'd rake it in. At least until they had kids, when she'd dial back on the corporate world and do something less intense, something she was actually passionate about.

If only she knew what that was.

But after so many rejections, her enthusiasm waned. In truth, she had zero interest in the positions for which she'd been applying.

"I'm starting to think investments aren't my jam," she confided.

"Why does it have to be your jam? Just find a place that'll hire you and pay you well."

"Trying. No one wants me in finance."

"How about sales? With your looks, you can schmooze anyone into buying anything."

Molly flinched at his suggestion that her outward appearance should somehow factor into her success. Not her degree in economics, her knowledge of the market, her intern experience.

"Pharmaceuticals are the way to go," he continued. "Lots of money there."

"Why does it all have to be about money? How about passion?"

"When passion starts paying the bills, let me know," he quipped.

"A person can only take so many rejections. I don't think New York wants me."

"Why don't you look elsewhere?"

"Outside of New York?" Where *he* lived?

His silence was unsettling.

"You *do* want to me to move in, right?" she asked, panic flooding her voice. "I'm fully packed, and I've saved enough money to get me through the first month or so. I'm excited for us to start looking for apartments together—"

"About that." He sighed. "The company says I have to find a place by the end of the month. That's two weeks. It's hard to find housing here, so I've already started looking."

It felt as if he'd reached through the phone and slapped her. They were supposed to do that together.

"Can't you wait? I have a big weekend ahead of me with the fundraiser, but I can come up after that—"

"Sorry, Moll. I've gotta move on this. I'm running out of time."

"But if we're going to live together, shouldn't I have a say? I can move next week, as soon as this event's over."

He laughed. "How will you afford to live here? We don't know if you'll even find a job in NYC."

"I can work in a restaurant until something full-time comes along."

"That doesn't make sense. You have a college degree. Don't you want to use it?"

"I'm not using it now, working in Sarina's café."

He was silent for a moment. "Listen. I'll talk to the guys and get some leads. Maybe Jonesy can get you a pharma job. Gretz sells restaurant equipment and makes huge commissions. It's not finance, but it's something that'll bring in enough money to support the lifestyle we want."

She agreed, even though she had no interest in sales. Anything to get her to New York, and fast. It wasn't fair for him to be looking at apartments without her, when it would eventually be her home, too.

"So are we in agreement?" he asked. "I'll dig up some leads and start looking for a place, and we'll talk about you moving in after you get a job."

Ugh. "Okay…"

Something nagged at her.

"I get the feeling you're not excited about me moving up there."

He sighed. "I am, Molly, but we have to be practical. I can't wait to start looking for a place until you to find a job."

"I just thought it was something we'd do together."

"And we will. I'm just starting the process out of necessity. I won't make any decisions until you see the place."

"Promise?"

"Of course. Hopefully, the guys can help you find a good sales job." He laughed, adding, "We'll need two incomes to pay off your debt."

"What does that mean?"

She knew what it meant. She'd worked hard over the years, but her part-time jobs weren't always enough to support her taste in high-end fashion, designer shoes, and bags. That's when she'd learned the magic of credit cards—buy now, pay whenever you can. Better yet, have your boyfriend pay. It was part of their deal: she'd look good, he'd pay for it.

"I'm teasing," he said, his voice softening. "You know I love your expensive drip."

"Gotta keep your future 'trophy wife' looking hot, right?" she teased.

"Girl, you could wear a trash bag and still be hot."

It was a running joke between them, but as archaic and sexist as it sounded, there was something Molly loved about the idea of being a trophy wife. She couldn't help it if she'd been brainwashed by Disney movies into believing she needed a man to look after and protect her, while she, in exchange, made him look good. Over the years, she'd bought into the whole knight-in-shining-armor routine, hoping her handsome prince would whisk her away into the sunset. Although she'd never admit that to Sarina, who'd smack her in the head with a Calphalon frying pan and knock her right off Prince Brennan's valiant steed.

Maybe her sisters weren't too far off the mark about Molly being their dad's "princess." He'd been larger-than-life to her. Much like Brennan.

Her dad's leaving cut deeper for Molly, not just because she was suddenly without her "hero," as her sisters believed. It was because she was left to endure the emotional fallout, the only one buried in the rubble of her mom's shattered dreams. Falling asleep to the sound of her mother sobbing. Begging her mom to eat as she pushed away her food, whittling away to a mere shell of her former, vivacious self. It was too much to ask of a sixteen-year-old, becoming a caretaker for a parent at a stage when she was in desperate need of parenting herself.

Her only escape was Brennan. Going out with him allowed her to be a carefree teen again. He was a source of strength. Being in his presence, especially when he fawned over how great she looked, made her feel like herself. A princess—just like her dad had made her feel. Which was what she'd needed back then.

But now?

Maybe it was time she rethought her aspirations.

THE EPIPHANY CAME TO JAXON ON THE NIGHT OF HIS thirtieth birthday as he was partying in the back of a limo with his closest friends.

This wasn't fun anymore.

Not just the night of carousing with friends. The whole *single* thing. He wasn't sure if it was because he'd just entered the Decade of No Return, or whether it was because he couldn't get a certain costar of his out of his mind.

Kelsey Grace. He had no idea why she'd suddenly occupied his thoughts. How he would've loved to have joined her in Tahiti to see if he could get something started with her for real. She posed quite the challenge, and there was nothing Jaxon Quinn loved more than the chase.

Shame, too. He had a few weeks off before his next project and could've easily spared the time, had she seemed into it. Instead, she'd texted to say she was going home to Cape May to *save the town like a Hallmark main character*, which nixed the idea of exploring the real potential of their fake romance.

Unless...

"J-Quinn, my man." His buddy Fritz interrupted his thoughts as he extended his hand for a fist bump. "Where to next? Your choice, birthday boy."

"Guys, I think I'm gonna call it a night."

They all stared at him, stone-faced, then burst into laughter.

"Good one!" Fritz laughed, clasping him on the shoulder.

"I thought you were serious," another friend said. "You probably should back up your bedtime now that you're geriatric. Just not tonight."

"No, guys, I'm done. I need my beauty rest."

"Dude. No amount of rest is gonna fix that face," Fritz joked.

Fifteen minutes later, Jaxon found himself in the driveway of his Malibu beach house, waving goodbye to his friends. As they pulled away, someone popped up through the limo sunroof and yelled to him: "Don't forget to take your dentures out!"

Jaxon retreated inside and found a magazine propped up against an oversized centerpiece on a table inside his grand foyer. His housekeeper must have placed it there for him to see. Its cover featured a photo of Kelsey and her "prince."

"If only that were the truth," he said aloud, not sure what was more comical—him being referred to as a prince, or the two of them having a romance like the one described in the article. Maybe both.

Nonetheless, it appeared they'd fooled everyone. Even him. Maybe that was the problem—her acting was so good, he actually believed Kelsey Grace had feelings for him.

He flipped to the section showing pictures of them on their first date. No wonder he couldn't get her out of his mind—she was gorgeous. Despite their relationship being fake, she was realest person he'd ever known. And so were the feelings he was starting to feel for her.

Or was it just the idea of the chase? There was only one way to find out.

Cue the chase.

Jaxon heard the clicking of tiny toenails on his marble

foyer. He turned to find his housekeeper's Chihuahua running towards him.

"Taco, what are you doing up so late?" Jaxon scooped up the pup, dismayed to find the little guy sporting a tiny turtleneck with the word *Hunk* on it.

"I see I'm not the only one forced to parade around for others' amusement," he said. "I'm sorry, little dude. It gets better, at least I hope so."

Jaxon sat down on his oversized leather couch. Taco curled up on his lap.

"See this girl right here?"

Taco looked up. Cocking his head to the side, he yipped.

"Yeah, she has that effect on me, too. I'm thinking of going to her hometown and surprising her. Tell her I wanna make our fake relationship real. Thoughts? Comments?"

Taco cocked his head even further, and Jaxon could swear he furrowed his brows.

"I know. It's a long story, little man. Do you have the time?"

Taco rested his head on his tiny getaway sticks, his bulging brown eyes gazing at Jaxon with rapt attention, giving the impression he had all the time in the world.

"Oh, man—find someone who looks at you the way you're looking at me, right now," he advised Taco. "Take my advice, your life will be so much easier."

Jaxon proceeded to tell his little friend all about Kelsey.

"What do you think, do I take a chance and make a go of our faux?" Jaxon laughed. "See what I did there?"

Taco sat up and yapped his undeniable support.

"I'll take that as a yes," Jaxon said, tucking Taco protectively under his arm. "Come on, Hunk. We got some packing to do."

Together, man and beast headed for the long, curved stairs to his bedroom.

Beyond that, the sandy shores of Cape May.

Molly

MOLLY AWAKENED WITH A RENEWED PURPOSE AFTER Brennan forwarded her a few sales job leads. She got to work on cover letters, but as each job became indistinguishable from the next, her eyes glazed over and giddiness set in.

She dictated as she typed.

"Dear Boring Corporation. Give me a damn job, already. I give two shits what your mission and vision are, because you're just like every other greedy monolith out there. But you need to sell shit, and I need a job if I wanna—"

If she wants to...what?

"Move in with my boyfriend, so we can play house and overspend at Whole Foods. Have regular sex. God, how I miss sex."

"Uh...TMI?" Kelsey grinned from the doorway. "You okay?"

"Yeah." Molly giggled. "All this job hunting has gone to my funny bone."

"I'd wish you luck, but something tells me you won't need it, you sex goddess you."

Molly threw a pillow at her sister's retreating back.

Later, during a break in the café's morning rush, Molly and Sarina sat in the back room to plan the menu for the Christmas in July celebration.

"I'm thinking we'll start the event at eleven," Molly said, consulting her notebook. "We'll offer coffee, tea, and pastries in the morning, and later, boxed lunches—something easy and portable they can take to the beach if they want. What do you think?"

"I'm thinking how much this is gonna cost me."

"People can pay for food and drinks, and we'll charge a cover for activities. They shouldn't have a problem with that; it's a worthy cause. For dinner…what about the traditional Christmas fixings, served buffet-style?"

"I'll need to pull in some catering partners."

"Can you handle that part?" Molly asked, chewing on her pen as she regarded her ever-expanding to-do list. "So much to do in a week."

"Why don't you ask Max to help you?" Sarina teased. "I bet he'd do anything you asked."

Molly rolled her eyes. "I don't need some lovesick guy following me around all week."

"Suit yourself." Sarina stood and removed her apron. "Gotta run. I'm delivering coffee to the theater and need to start painting sets."

"I can't believe you have time to run a café and do set design. You're amazing."

"Well, when certain grandmothers put things a certain way, we find the time. Know what I'm sayin'?"

"What did she say to guilt you into it?"

"Oh, you know, the usual. 'It's important to have a play with good sets, you're the best artist on the island, the play won't be the same without you,' yadayadayada."

Molly laughed but wondered if Sarina was happy to have a break from all-things-café, a chance to get back in touch with her creative self. Designing sets for their high school plays was one of her sister's passions back in high school, but now she rarely had time to do anything non-café-related. Except when Grand Lil insisted.

"Can you swing by later and deliver lunch to the theater?" Sarina asked. "My staff will pack it up; I just need you to run it over, since I'll be up to my eyeballs in set construction."

Great, one more thing to do. "Sure."

The sisters walked out together. As Molly headed toward Grand Lillian's old golf cart, Sarina laughed.

"Oh God, you're not riding around in that time machine, are you? I don't think Grand Lil has used it since the '80s." Pausing, she added, "The 1880s."

"It worked just fine this morning," Molly retorted, shooting her a glare. "Don't jinx it."

Molly waved goodbye to her sister as she climbed into the cart. She couldn't wait to get moving with event planning, excited for the opportunity to practice her schmoozy selling skills. She'd set up several back-to-back meetings to discuss the event and solicit donations.

She fired up the old golf cart and took a series of backroads. Halfway to her first destination, the cart sputtered, jerked, and stopped. Molly employed the tried-and-true IT trick—turning it off and back on again—but all it did was make a strange retching noise. She tried it again a few more times, then decided to let it sit for a minute.

Panic swept through her as she realized she was still far from her destination. She reached into her bag for her phone to check the time, but it wasn't there.

Shit. She'd left it in the café.

Guesstimating the distance to her first stop, she wasn't sure she'd get there in time on foot. But she had no choice. She grabbed her bag and began walking at a brisk pace. Soon, she heard the soft crunch of tires on macadam and a voice call out her name. She turned to see Max rolling up in a pickup truck.

"Nice day for a walk, isn't it?" he called out.

Excellent. The last thing she needed was this guy engaging her in needless small talk. "Not really, Max."

"What's going on? You okay?"

"Just dandy."

Molly marched on as Max rolled along with her.

"Was that your golf cart back there?" he asked. "Did it break down?"

"No, Max. I just decided to walk and get some steps in."

Max chuckled. "Okay, enough dumb questions. How about you get in and I take you where you need to be?"

Molly stopped in her tracks. She had zero interest in hanging out with Maxwell Banks, but she did need to get places, and her feet weren't going to do the trick. It was her only choice.

"Okay, thanks," she said as she climbed into the truck.

"Where you heading?"

"Delaware."

Max shot her a look.

"Kidding. Although, next time you may want to ask before you commit to giving someone a ride."

"Oh, I'd take you to Delaware. Or Maryland. Heck, even F-L-A if you asked."

Molly blushed. It appeared Sarina was right—he might still have a little crush.

When they arrived at their destination a short drive later, she jumped out of the truck. "Thanks for the ride. See you later."

"I can wait and take you back," he suggested. "There's nowhere I have to be today."

Molly hesitated. While she didn't want to spend more time than necessary with Max and unwittingly encourage him, it *would* be a lot easier if he could wait and bring her back to town. Otherwise, she'd have to use someone's phone to call Sarina.

"If you don't mind, that would be great," she relented.

Minutes later, after a firm handshake and an agreement

with Lenny's Party Rentals, Molly returned to the truck.

"Success," she declared. "Lenny's providing whatever we need, free of charge."

"Alright!" Max offered a fist bump.

Reluctantly, she reciprocated.

"Where to next?"

"I have a 10:30 at Schmidt's, so if you don't mind dropping me off there, I'll have Sarina run over with her car and get me."

"Molly, seriously, I can get you where you need to go all day."

"No, that's okay," Molly said. While she appreciated his willingness to help, she was ready to rock-and-roll this event planning on her own. To assure him she wasn't an ingrate, she added, "I really do appreciate the ride. I'm trying to keep these appointments and be timely, so this is a great help."

"Not a problem," he said.

"By the way, were you serious about constructing tables for the event? I liked your idea of connecting smaller ones to make a really long one like in *The Grinch*. I want it to feel like everyone's sitting down to a holiday meal together."

"Of course," Max said. "As long as you don't ask me to wear antlers and play Grinch's dog, Max."

"You saw right through me."

"Good thing I just had my costume drycleaned, then. Yes, we can work something out for the tables. I'll see if I can get the lumberyard to donate scraps."

"That would be great."

"Do we need to get a permit to do all this?" Max asked.

"That's a good question," Molly said. "My boyfriend asked the same thing."

She'd been looking for a way to infuse the word into the conversation, to establish she wasn't up for shenanigans with Max.

"Are you still dating Brennan?" he asked.

She nodded, happy he remembered. "As for a permit, yes and no. We'll be using Grand Lillian's permits to satisfy state requirements. But I'll need to get a local permit and approval from Borough Council, which I intend to do tomorrow. Then there's the matter of getting buy-in from the other departments, like police and lifeguards, as well as Washington Street business owners to assure they're all in on it."

"You've really done your research."

"I was on the student fundraising committee in college. I've done a few events myself."

"Like what?"

Molly told him about her collegiate fundraisers—raising money for a differently abled playground, a scholarship program, pediatric cancer research. Max asked follow-up questions and seemed genuinely interested in her answers. Unlike Brennan, who never asked for details and often rushed her stories to "get to the point."

"That's impressive," he concluded. "You must be both creative and analytical to accomplish all that."

She'd take the compliment, even though she didn't feel it was warranted. She'd never seen herself that way

"Here we are, fair lady," Max said as they arrived at their next stop.

Molly giggled, as if she were being driven around in a carriage with a handsome prince.

Wait, did she just think that about Maxwell the Geek? And why did that name just pop into her head? Her friends had called him that back in high school, but she never had. He was a nice guy who didn't deserve to be mocked.

"Thanks. If you have other things to do…"

He shook his head. "I'll be right here when you're done."

"You really don't mind carting me around like this?"

"Of course not. It's my pleasure."

She was pleased to see Max hadn't lost his nice-guy ways.

Crush or no crush, he'd apparently given up whatever he was planning on doing that morning to help her. Something she wasn't accustomed to.

Kelsey

When Kelsey arrived at the theater that morning, Grand Lillian was already there, directing someone on set construction.

"Ah, there you are," her grandmother said as she handed Kelsey a script. "You'll probably remember much of it."

They were doing the same play Kelsey and Colton had starred in during their senior year of high school. Colton's debilitating shyness normally kept him behind the scenes as a set builder. But that year, he'd been cast as understudy for the romantic lead, who ended up contracting mono a week before the play. While Colton would have rather lain across the tracks before a speeding locomotive than perform, once he got into character, there was no stopping him. Even Kelsey, who'd been cast in plays and musicals since childhood, was blown away by his acting chops.

Especially when he went off script for their final scene and did something to shake the entire foundation of their friendship. Recalling it now...

She took a sharp inhale and shook her head to rid herself of the memory. Concentrating on the script, she was soon amazed at how quickly the lines came back to her. Relearning them in five days shouldn't be a problem.

"Hugh?" Lillian called out as she shielded her eyes against the glaring lights, waving to someone in the back of the theater. "Come here, I want you to meet your leading lady."

A diminutive, mid-fortyish man with a well-trimmed white beard jogged down the aisle toward them. Kelsey could tell, from a distance, she had some height on him.

"Um, he's shorter than me?" Kelsey spoke through the corner of her mouth. "And like a hundred years older?"

"He has a big personality," Grand Lillian said, from the corner of hers.

"The audience isn't going to buy the fact that I'd fall in love with Kenny Rogers."

"Don't worry, he's good. He played Don Quixote in his high school rendition of the play."

"When, the roaring twenties?"

Kelsey wasn't convinced of his leading man abilities. He was quite different from the prototype she was accustomed to after years of Jaxon.

"Pleased to meet you, Ms. Grace," he said as he gave a slight bow.

"It's Kelsey. Nice to meet you, Hugh." She was somewhat relieved to find that, up close, he was only a few inches shy of her.

Grand Lillian suggested they get started. Kelsey backed up to take center stage when she heard a familiar voice behind her.

"'Scuse us."

She jumped out of the way as Colton and Ralph, one of the stagehands, moved an oversized backdrop across the stage.

Wait. What was Colton doing in the theater? She shot him a look of surprise, but he quickly glanced away.

Good to see we're still doing this.

Kelsey and Hugh began running lines, but the image of Colton in her periphery was unsettling. There was no way she'd be able to concentrate on her lines if Colton Banks was taking up real estate in this theater. She told Hugh she needed to take five and found her grandmother in the green room, going through costumes.

"What's he doing here?" she hissed.

Grand Lillian cast an innocent look behind Kelsey. "Ralph? He's a stagehand."

"You know damn well I'm not talking about Ralph."

"Then, I don't know who you're referring to." She blinked innocently.

"Of course you do. Why is Colton Banks in this theater, moving sets?"

"I think you just answered your own question."

"Well, according to Colton himself, he's 'too busy' for a fundraiser. Now, suddenly, he has time to build sets?"

"It's amazing how a little guilt trip can change someone's plans."

"Oh, trust me, I know," Kelsey said, not sure if she should be relieved or annoyed that she wasn't the only victim of her cunning grandmother. "What did you say to convince him?"

"I've been helping the boys pack up their house, so I asked if he'd return the favor. I told him he's the only one who can pull this off in five days. You, of all people, know the talent that boy possesses."

Her grandmother was right. As lead builder on their stage crew back in high school, Colton possessed an impressive talent for set construction. Still, she didn't need to be seeing him every day.

"He and Max are going through a hard time right now. I'd appreciate you being kind to him. What ever happened with you two, anyway?"

Kelsey averted her gaze. "Nothing."

"You dated, right?"

"Nope. Just friends."

Grand Lillian gave her a disbelieving look.

"I'm serious."

Her grandmother merely nodded, but Kelsey wasn't lying. There was a big difference between wishing for something and it actually happening.

"Well, whatever happened, there's no time like the present to let go of this animosity between you," Lillian continued. "I don't want this theater filled with bad vibes. Got it?"

"Got it."

Another lie. As long as Colton Banks was rude to her, she'd show him the same treatment. While she felt bad for him, losing his career and then his dad, it wasn't fair for him to treat her as if she were to blame for their falling out.

Returning to the stage, she began running her lines with Hugh, as Colton pounded nails in the background. It seemed whenever she spoke, the pounding became louder. Kelsey raised her voice until she was practically yelling.

Bring it on, buddy—two can play at this game.

Colton

COLTON COULDN'T HELP THE FRUSTRATION ARISING within him, but pounding nails helped release some of it. He'd often wondered what it would be like the first time he saw Kelsey again, but didn't expect the rejection and heartbreak to be as fresh as the day it had happened.

After their unexpected encounter the day before, Colton had vowed to stay as far away from her as possible. He was already on grief overload from the death of his father, the grueling task of packing up, and saying goodbye to his brother and the only home his family had known. He couldn't add Kelsey to the already burdensome pile.

But then, he received a text from Grand Lillian early that morning, telling him to meet her at the theater. Colton knew the feisty woman to be dramatic, but she'd never texted him in ALL CAPS. He figured it must be an emergency.

According to the Grand Dame, Ralph needed Colton's help and expertise with the set. He couldn't refuse, not after she'd been such a help to him and Max these last few weeks as they readied their property for sale. It would just be a couple days of his time. Then, he could walk away from the theater, and all it represented, for good.

Colton continued pounding away in an attempt to drown out Kelsey's voice, which was taking him back to days he was trying like hell to forget.

"I really appreciate your help on this," Ralph said over the hammering. "I'm not great at construction design. Lillian said you're the best."

"No problem," Colton muttered. "I loved doing this in high school."

If it weren't for Kelsey's presence in the theater, he'd be enjoying himself. Building something with a visual endgame made him feel good. Instant gratification. It was his passion, and before sophomore year of high school, building things was what he'd planned to do with his life. Something where he could use his hands and his mind, like construction or architecture. Maybe both. But then his hands were needed for passing footballs. Before long, constructing things was no longer in his playbook.

Nor was standing there onstage as Kelsey ran her lines from the play they did in their senior year. Colton could still remember what happened at their final performance like it was yesterday. The big finale on closing night—which was completely unscripted. The ending called for the characters to gaze longingly at each other, suggesting the promise of a kiss to come, as the curtain fell.

But on closing night, without planning to, Colton had thrown the script out the window and done something he'd wanted to do for a long, long time. He grabbed his best friend's face and kissed her like he'd never kissed anyone before—or since.

He could feel Kelsey's body tense for a split second, her mouth still under his, but within moments her lips softened, tongue engaged, and she was no longer the recipient of an unexpected kiss, but a very willing participant.

To the audience, it may have appeared as though they were just acting out the script, but to Colton, it was real. The stuff dreams were made of.

The kiss went on as the curtain fell around them. Colton felt as though they could have kept going forever—until he felt a clap on his back and the director's voice in his ear.

"Break it up, guys."

Kelsey instantly pulled away, her face flushing a bright crimson, her eyes darting everywhere but at Colton.

The director's laugh rattled around them. "You're lucky I've always hated that ending. I should be pissed at you for you going off script like that."

"Sorry," was all Colton could muster through his thrumming heartbeat. A wave of nausea hit him as he realized what he'd done.

Shaking his head, the director walked away. "You may want to work on that approach, Casanova."

Colton, mortified both by his actions and the clumsy execution thereof, wished the stage would open up and take him with it. Play or no play, he'd crossed unspoken lines, unexpectedly and without consent. Having no idea how Kelsey would take it, he hoped it wouldn't prove fatal to their friendship.

"I'm sorry, Kelsey. I didn't mean to do that," he spit out, taking a deep breath and exhaling the guilt that had besieged his chest. "I...just got caught up in the moment."

"The moment?" she asked.

Her tone was one Colton couldn't detect. Was she disgusted? Amused? Perhaps a bit of both. She stared at him and time stood still.

Now was the moment he'd been waiting for, to tell her how he'd been feeling about her. He debated whether he should come clean with his feelings, or let it go, pretend he'd just been caught up in his character. His eyes riveted to their surroundings, the hustling stage crew moving sets and yelling directions to one another, before ultimately landing on Kelsey's relentless gaze.

Thinking back on it now, he could kick himself for what he'd said next, but in the awkward moment he'd believed it was the only way to save face.

"The moment," he mumbled, shrugging. "It just seemed like something the character would do. Nothing more."

She held his gaze, her expression unwavering. Finally, she nodded. "Got it."

She turned and disappeared into the blackness of backstage before her name could reach his lips.

He felt like a colossal fool, letting her walk away, not telling her how he felt about her, that most of his thoughts were of her. How he desperately wanted to take their friendship to the next level. But under the glare of stage lights, with the crew hustling around them, and the fear of destroying their friendship if she didn't feel the same way churning in his gut, he just couldn't do it.

In the week that followed, he didn't see her much. He didn't know if it was purposeful on her part as a result of the kiss, or that she was legitimately busy. Either way, the divide was excruciating and he knew he had to confess his feelings to her.

But when he'd finally mustered the courage to tell her how he felt a week later, she'd thrust him into the arms of someone else before he could even get the words out, telling him all he needed to know.

Their kiss meant nothing to her.

"Colton, what about this piece here?" Ralph's voice jarred him back to reality. "I think Lillian wants this to be the skyline, but I'm not sure."

"Let's consult with the designer when she gets here."

"I'm here!" Sarina breezed down the aisle with a cardboard tray of take-out coffee.

"Good to see you, Colt," she said as she handed him one, eyebrow raised. "Just a little surprised, with all you have going on."

"Yeah, me too. But you know how convincing some people can be." He gestured towards Grand Lillian, who was holding court backstage with the costume team.

"Say no more, my friend," Sarina laughed as she patted him on the arm. "I appreciate you doing this. It'll make it a lot easier for me knowing you're on the job."

"Just like old times, right?" he said, referencing their high school stage crew days.

Colton was relieved to know painting wouldn't fall on his shoulders. He didn't want to be here any longer than necessary, especially now that Kelsey and Hugh, in character, were looking at each other as if they were falling in love for real. Obviously, all part of the act, but he didn't need to see it. Her acting skills were amazing, and it was a bit much for Colton to bear.

Yet, as hard as he tried to concentrate on set-building, he occasionally found himself focusing on his periphery, where Kelsey and Hugh rehearsed their scenes. He could almost recite Hugh's lines, that's how indelibly burned into his brain they were from when he played the part.

He also tried not to notice their playful banter as they laughed over misconstrued lines. Her laughter filled Colton with simultaneous joy and pain. Joy, because her laugh had always made his heart soar. Pain, because he hadn't heard it in so long.

Two days. He should be done with the sets in two days, and then he could go back to the farm and tend to the business of moving on. Physically, and emotionally.

Kelsey

During a break in rehearsal, Kelsey sat in the back of the theater going over her lines. As she got to the last scene, her thoughts drifted to the last time she'd performed this very play—with Colton as her co-star. It had taken Kelsey by utter surprise when, without warning, Colton had gone off script and kissed her.

She'd never been kissed by a boy until then. Despite practicing on pillows during sleepovers with her friend Ashley, she wasn't quite certain of the mechanics. But this one was nothing like in the movies—slow motion and dreamy, dramatic music building to a crescendo—the way she'd always envisioned her first kiss to be. Instead, it was sudden, messy, and more than a little clumsy. Still, his mouth revealed feelings she'd realized, in the moment, she'd been fighting for a long time.

As his tongue swirled against hers, she gave herself over to those feelings, reciprocating eagerly. His velvety kiss sent her skyrocketing and she wished it would never end. Until the director shattered the magical moment and they pulled away from one another as if they were on fire. She couldn't hear the man's words over the buzzing in her ears, but his sudden presence sent her crashing back to earth even as her mind remained in the clouds, trying to make sense of it. Why he did it. What it meant.

But then, thoughts of Ashley, her dear friend—her only female friend—hit her like a glass of cold water to the face. In the past year, Ashley had developed a crush on Colton and was unable to talk about anything else. How nice he was, how funny and smart. How in love she was with him.

Kelsey instantly felt guilty about the kiss, even though Colton had initiated it. She shouldn't have enjoyed it as much as she did. A good friend—a good girl—wouldn't do that to a friend.

Still, she was compelled to ask him why he did it. When Colton told her he'd been caught up in his character, she was relieved, if slightly disappointed. But most of all, relieved. Not wanting to feel either emotion in front of him, she bolted backstage, insistent on believing he was telling the truth. That the kiss had nothing to do with them, and everything to do with the characters.

Because to think otherwise could potentially be the end of the only two friendships that mattered to her.

Molly

Returning to Max's truck after her most recent stop, Molly was ecstatic.

"Looks like you scored big again," Max said.

"I'm killing it with these donations. I think we may just pull this off."

As they approached Cape May Point on the way to their next stop, Max spoke in a deep baritone. "On our left, ladies and gents, you'll see the Cape May Lighthouse. It's 199 steps to the top. Will you make it?"

Molly laughed. "Did you just issue me a challenge?"

"If that's how you want to see it, then yes, I challenge you to a lighthouse climb."

"Maybe after my meetings. I don't want to be late."

He returned to his baritone voice. "And she's rejected the challenge!"

"Oh, I didn't reject it. I just postponed it. I'll *race* you to the top."

Molly was confident in her counterchallenge. While Max was decidedly more muscular than he was in high school—most likely from all that farming he'd been doing during their college summers—she assumed he spent most of his school year burrowed in a library carrel. She, on the other hand, was an athlete who cheered competitively in high school and was on her college's dance team. She could take the likes of Maxwell Banks any day.

"You got yourself a deal, li'l lady," Max joked through a crooked smile that, for some reason, made Molly feel squishy inside. While Max wasn't outwardly her type, there was something disarmingly charming about him. Understatedly, which only made him more attractive.

She pushed the thought away out of deference to her boyfriend, who was the opposite of Max looks-wise and beyond. Fair-haired with light eyes, Brennan was not only her physical type, his financial sitch was a major bonus. Especially after living through her family's financial fallout after their dad left. Molly had worked three jobs in high school, not only to contribute financially, but to afford her expensive tastes. She worked her ass off to create her own drip. Look where it had gotten her—she'd caught the attention of the school's most popular boy. Now here she was, six years later, about to be his fiancée.

While there was no comparison between her beau and this farm-bred local, there was nothing wrong with objectively noting that Maxwell Banks had become—for lack of a better word—*hot*. In a geeked-out, Clark Kent kinda way.

After she returned from her final meeting, Max offered some good news. "I have a friend who knows his way around golf carts. I asked him to take a look at yours, and he just called to let me know it's back in working order."

"That's great! What was the issue?"

"It's kind of difficult to explain."

"You don't think my female brain can handle it?" Molly challenged. "How about you try me?"

"How long do you have?"

"All day, now that you mention it," she said, crossing her arms. "But only if you keep it simple and draw me pictures so I can fully grasp the complicated concepts you're about to lay on my feeble mind."

Max sighed, all serious. "Motorized engines require a lot of physical components. Gears, shifts, and so on. Are you following me?"

"Wait, what's a motor?" Molly asked, wide-eyed.

He ignored her sarcasm. "One of the most essential elements required to make a motor run is a type of fluid that powers the engine."

"Are you talking about gas?"

Max laughed. "Yes. There was nothing mechanically wrong with your little jitney, friend. It was simply out of gas."

"You jerk!" Molly said, pretending she was mad. She gave him a playful punch in the arm and was met with a rock-solid muscle. Her eyes widened involuntarily at the sheer mass.

Dropping her head into her hands, she groaned. "I can't believe I didn't think to check the gas." She lifted her head back up to him. "I feel very silly right now."

"It happens to the best of us. I once ran out on my way home from college last Christmas and had to walk two miles in a blizzard to find a station."

"Thanks for making me feel better. How much do I owe him?"

"Nothing. It's on me."

She peered over at him. "Why are you so nice?"

"My mom," he said quietly, with a shy smile. "I didn't have many years with her, but that's the one thing she drilled into us. 'Just be kind' was her motto."

"I'm sorry you lost her at such a young age," Molly said as she laid her hand on his arm. "And now your dad. How are you doing?"

"Hanging in there," he said. "It was just so unexpected, you know?"

"I do know. I lost my dad when I was young. Not as young as you when you lost your mom, and not to death. He just left."

"I remember that," Max said softly.

"You knew?"

She was shocked. She'd gone to great lengths to lie to her classmates about her dad's sudden disappearance, telling them he'd taken a new job requiring extensive travel around Europe. The lie stuck among her high school friends and fellow cheerleaders, probably because their school was regional and they all hailed from different shore towns. Most of her friends were from Avalon and Stone Harbor, and they never got to know her family. Molly always found reasons not to invite them to her house. The lie was even easier to perpetuate in college, where the only one who knew her ugly little secret was Brennan, who was sworn to secrecy.

"My dad told me. Our parents were friends when we were younger."

"Huh." Molly thought about that for a moment. "Is that why you were so nice to me in high school?"

"I mean, it wasn't the only reason," Max said, appearing to blush. "And I was nice to you before your dad left. But after that...I knew what you were going through, having lost my mom."

"It was a really pivotal time in my life. I was *sixteen*," she said, her voice cracking. "My sisters were already out of the house, so I was left to deal with everything. It was dark there for a few years. Thank God for Bren—" She cut herself off.

Max chuckled. "I often wondered if you guys got together because of that."

"Because my dad left?"

"Well, yeah. I'm guessing he probably helped you get through it."

Hmm. Kind of like what Sarina suggested, only in nicer terms. At least Max didn't use the words *daddy figure.*

"I'm sorry to be comparing my situation with yours," she said. "Your parents didn't have a choice. My dad did. He could've pretended he cared and stayed until I left for college. It was such an important stage of life, and it would've been nice to have his guiding hand. Instead, I got the middle finger."

It had been six years, but Molly was surprised by the vitriol their conversation dredged up. She hadn't felt this way, or talked about it, since she could remember. It was a part of her life she'd squelched, so she could carry on. Pretending to be happy-go-lucky was her survival tactic, and so far, it had served her well.

For once, it was nice to wipe away the smile and be real.

"I'm so sorry you had to go through that."

"No, Max, I'm sorry for droning on. What you've been through is nothing like my situation. I'm sorry to carry on like it is."

Talk about a plot twist. She hadn't seen this one coming, spilling her guts all over Max. God, how self-focused was she? Here was a guy who'd lost his mom when he was a young child. She'd had her father for twice the time. And now, his dad was gone too.

"You're not droning on, Moll. Different circumstances, but a parent's absence, however it happens, is tough to take."

Molly was blown away by his support, for once feeling connected to another human who understood loss. Most of all, she was amazed by her own openness about the situation. Other than with her sisters, she never talked about her dad leaving. Max just brought it out in her, as if they'd known each other intimately for years. Unknowingly, he'd created a safe space in the cab of a pickup truck for her to remove the veil of stoicism.

"Thanks for that," she said, placing her hand on his arm again. "Nice to talk to someone who understands. I don't really have that."

"I got you. Loss is loss, and it sucks."

Molly nodded, no other words necessary.

They rode along in silence until they pulled into town.

"I have one more favor to ask of you," Molly said.

"You want me to let you win the lighthouse race?"

"Heck no, I got that one in the bag already."

"We'll see."

"I promised Sarina I'd deliver lunch to the theater. Would you mind helping me?"

"Will I get a free lunch out of it?"

"Maybe, if you keep our little 'Molly doesn't know cars need gas' secret to yourself."

"I don't even know what you're talking about."

She smiled. "Thanks. I really appreciate you driving me around all morning. You didn't have to do that."

"Again, it was my honor."

"Don't let it go to your head."

"Oh, trust me," he said, giving her a lopsided grin, "it already has."

Colton

COLTON COULDN'T BELIEVE HOW FAST THE MORNING had gone by when Molly and Max arrived with lunch. Deciding that was enough free labor for one day, he was about to cut out when Max asked him to stay.

"It'll be fun to catch up with everyone," his brother promised. Easy for him to say. Of course, Max would find it "fun" to catch up with the Grace sisters. Meanwhile, Colton would rather undergo open heart surgery without anesthesia. Which was exactly how the morning had made him feel, being this close to Kelsey, who seemed to be avoiding him as much as he was her.

Famished from the morning's labor, Colton gave in to Max's request and joined the circle of bodies seated on the floor of the stage. With Kelsey directly across from him, he kept intense focus on his meal to keep from stealing glances at her.

"Everything okay over there, Colton?" Sarina teased from across the circle. "You're eyeing up that sandwich as if you're about to kiss it."

He coughed and sputtered. "This has to be the best sandwich I've ever had."

Which wasn't a total lie. Sarina had proven to be as much a food artist as she was a talented painter, but his hyper ham-on-rye focus was merely a ruse to keep the others from discovering his true focus. Directly across the stage from him, Kelsey was recounting humorous anecdotes from her movie shoots. He didn't want to appear to be taking in her every word, even though he couldn't help doing just that. And he *definitely* didn't want to hear the words Ralph spoke next.

"Is your boyfriend coming to see the play?" Ralph asked. "My wife wants to know. She saw that article about the two of you and is hoping you brought that 'hot hunk' with you. Please tell me I have nothing to worry about."

Colton shot a look at Kelsey, awaiting her answer. He couldn't help himself. Their eyes met as she looked up at him.

"No. He's in LA." Although she was talking to the group at large, her words felt as if they were meant for Colton alone. Wishful thinking on his part, perhaps. Although, he was pretty sure he didn't imagine the way her cheeks turned crimson as her gaze locked with his. "You have nothing to worry about."

Colton was relieved he wouldn't have to face Kelsey and her "prince." With any luck, Colton would be long gone before she brought the douche around. The sooner he got out of here, the better.

It felt as if his life depended upon it.

Max

MAX WASN'T EXACTLY BEING HONEST WHEN HE TOLD Molly he had nowhere to be that day. He had a lot to do to prepare the property for sale. But spending the morning in the presence of Molly Grace was well worth forgoing his responsibilities, especially knowing he might have helped her just a tiny bit as they discussed their losses.

He was famished by the time they got to the theater and happy to dig into Sarina's delicious lunch offerings. But more than that, he enjoyed hanging out with the cast and crew, especially sitting next to Molly as she regaled everyone with tales of her job-hunting fiascos. She was bubbly, a natural storyteller, and Max found himself wishing he had half her confidence. At one point, when the group dynamic broke off into individual conversations, she looked at him, golden eyes shimmering with what looked like genuine interest.

"So, Maxwell Banks, I hear you're off to grad school. For what purpose, may I ask?"

"To study marine biology, specializing in cetology."

"Which is?"

"The study of whales, dolphins, and porpoises. I'm working part-time job at the Marine Mammal Stranding Center, assisting with rescue, rehab, and release of stranded animals."

"Very cool," Molly said, then gave him a coquettish smile. "Must be nice to have a *porpoise*."

"It is. I just figured, I love them so much, I might as *whale*."

She gave his arm a playful shove. "You're funny, Maxwell Banks."

He laughed, his heart doing the triple flip. As she twirled one of her curls and gazed at him with those sparkling eyes, Maxwell Banks felt *himself* getting more and more wrapped around Molly Grace's finger.

After having lunch with the actors and stage crew, Molly went off to do more errands, and Max returned to the farm to pack up.

Among a stack of boxes burrowed away in the attic, he found one labeled, "For My Boys" in his mom's handwriting. He'd never seen this one before.

Inside were two smaller boxes, each labeled with their names.

Opening his box, Max found trinkets from his childhood—a lock of baby hair, a first lost tooth, a notebook in which she'd recorded first words and funny things he'd said as a toddler. She must have done this after her cancer diagnosis, knowing she wasn't going to see them through adulthood. The thought made his heart ache. At twenty-two, he'd already spent most of his life without her, but one never gets over the death of a mother.

He sat cross-legged on the floor and set the box down on his lap. His mom had so lovingly put these items together for them, and he wanted to give them the time they deserved. Losing her at such a young age, and now their father as well, made the discovery even more poignant.

Max smiled at each memory his mom had recorded. The label affixed to a baggie containing a lock of hair read: *Max's first haircut, age two. He asked the bald barber if he wanted to borrow it.*

The one relating to his first lost tooth read: *Colton accidentally threw a football intended for Dad but hit Max instead. Colton burst into tears, insisting he wasn't a mean boy.*

Max laughed out loud. Their mom would love to know how Colton's football throwing skills had improved, earning him national recognition and several titles. And, to the best of his knowledge, no additional lost teeth.

He flipped through the journal to where she'd recorded notes about his first words, not surprised to learn *fish* was one of them. Max loved fish as a toddler. His parents had given him an aquarium for his room when he was three, filled with fish he learned to take care of.

His mom had written a note about this, too.

Max loves sea life. All kinds, even those that aren't real. One day, I gave him fish sticks, and he asked how they could see to swim since they didn't have eyes. I had to run from the room, that's how hard I laughed. He's going to be a marine biologist, I just know it.

Max was amazed at his mother's prognosis. Reading on, he found a page with a note addressed to him. The tears began flowing again.

Max, my dear sweet boy. You just turned eight last week. This will be the last birthday I get to share with you in person, but please know I'll be there for every birthday you have for the rest of your life—in the pretty ribbons on your gifts, the flickering flame of your birthday candles, and all the wishes you'll blow at them. From the moment I met you, I knew you'd be a smart boy. I bet, in ten years, I'll find out you were valedictorian!

His mom was wise beyond the years she'd been given. He *had* been valedictorian. He'd graduated at the top of his class with a perfect GPA, earning himself a full-paid scholarship to Harvard.

Please don't ever lose your sensitivity and caring nature. Your silent strength, calm confidence, ability to make people laugh, and your sweet, loving nature will serve you well. You'll make someone very happy one day. Just keep looking until you find the person who makes your heart do a little flip whenever you see them. Be good in school, live an honest life, and continue helping our planet and the animals you love. They need you.

I love you to the end of time, and although I won't be here to see you grow old, I will always and forever be in your heart, and in all the goodness around you. When you see a cardinal, that'll be me checking in with you. When the sea breeze blows, it's me wrapping you in a loving embrace. When a butterfly flaps its wings, it's me, stopping by to say hi. Stay you, sweet boy, be kind, and never forget how very much you are loved. Forever, Your Mom.

Max clutched the letter to his chest as he wiped away his tears. "I know you're with me. I love you."

He reread the part about finding the person who made his heart flip.

"I may have found her, Mom," he said, sighing. "Except she's in love with someone else."

Despite that harsh reality, his heart more than flipped when he looked at Molly. It commandeered all his senses, judging by the lustful yearning that slammed into him like a tsunami as he'd driven up behind her that morning. He recalled the determined swish of her ponytail, the sway of her hips. Her sundress clung to her in all the right places, accentuating her narrow waist, the thin fabric unable to hide the perfect shape of her cute bottom. He'd had to quickly adjust himself before she climbed into the cab, bringing with her the scent of honey and sunshine. Her grumbly mood wasn't enough to bring him down, especially as it lightened with each successful stop. He felt honored to assist her in achieving her goals, even if all he did was drive her around. He wasn't kidding, he'd take her anywhere.

Something caught Max's attention just then, something outside the kitchen window.

A monarch butterfly swirled in the breeze, flapping its wings. Stilling for a brief moment in time, it paused at the window before soaring off.

JAXON FINISHED MAKING HIS TRAVEL PLANS AND reached out to Verna to let her know what was going on.

"As the song goes, I'm 'On the Way to Cape May,'" he told his publicist. "I'm gonna make this thing real."

"What thing?"

"The thing between me and Kelse. Turns out, I've caught real feels for her. I want to make the *faux*-mance a *go*-mance." Jaxon laughed at his joke. "See what I did there?"

"I saw," she deadpanned. "Are you sure this is what Kelsey wants?"

"There's only one way to find out."

"You sure this is what *you* want? I've never known you to settle down, which is why the fauxmance works well for you. We can make the whole thing go away, whenever you say the word. That's not the case if you make it legit. Things get messy when they're legit."

"I'm pretty sure she's the one. She's the realest person I

know, dude, and you know how hard it is for me to find that."

"But you're also besties. You sure you want to mix pleasure and business this way? If a girlfriend is what you want, we can arrange for that. But it doesn't have to be your costar."

"I can't stop thinking about her," he said.

"Her, or the challenge she poses? I know how intriguing it must be knowing you can't have her."

"Let me put it this way...I've never found anyone like her, and while she may not be exactly what I'm looking for, I think she's the closest I'll ever get. Anyone closer would be downright perfect, and we all know that doesn't exist."

"Okay." Verna sighed with resignation. "Keep me posted, especially if you change your mind."

"Trust me, V, I won't be changing my mind. Cape May, here I come!"

Kelsey

KELSEY, FIRST TO ARRIVE IN THE THEATER, WAS PERCHED on the edge of the stage, reading her script, when Colton came in.

"Hey," she greeted.

He stopped dead in his tracks like a startled deer, as if surprised by her presence. Their eyes met for a quick moment before he dropped his head, gave a quasi-wave, and hustled past her. "Hey."

Kelsey turned her attention to her script, until she saw him in her periphery lifting a board from the ground, his toned muscles apparent through his t-shirt. She was surprised he was able to lift such an object after his shoulder injury. Dude must have been doing something to stay in such shape. She could barely peel her gaze away.

Of course, that would be exactly when he turned around, his eyes finding hers. She swore he was about to smile, until his face slid into the same unenthused expression he'd worn since their chance meeting at the café.

It saddened her that they weren't communicating better, and that he was treating her so differently than the others. She'd heard him joking around with Sarina and Ralph as they worked on the sets yesterday, while successfully avoiding eye contact with her at all costs. She felt bad for all he'd endured but had no earthly idea what she'd done to make him so mad at her when she was the one who'd been hurt all those years ago.

Watching him work, her heart softened. He'd always been close to his parents. Losing his mom as a teenager, and now his dad, had to be tough. It was just the two of them in the theater, and the silence between them was deafening as the former best friends worked hard to ignore each other. She decided to take the high road.

"Hey."

Colton looked over, his expression at first hopeful before melting to feigned disinterest.

She forged on. "I'm sorry about your dad. I know how close you were."

"Yep," he said, facial muscles tightening. "Thanks."

"How are you doing?"

He turned and held her gaze, profound sadness seeping through his forced facade. She knew a lot about facades, having lived behind one for so long. But Colton wasn't a trained actor, and try as he might to hide it, his grief shined through like a beacon.

"I'm fine."

"I have the best memories of your dad," she continued, unfazed by his brusque response. "Especially his humor. Remember whenever we did the Hokey Pokey as kids, he'd ask, 'What if the Hokey Pokey is *really* what it's all about?'"

Colton gave a reluctant smile. "Oh, man. I forgot all about that." He then chuckled, mimicking his dad's voice. "'If all it takes is to put your right leg in, shouldn't we all be nailing this thing called life?'"

"The king of dad jokes," Kelsey said.

"Before they called them that."

"How about the time he put a huge rubber cockroach in your lunch box?" Kelsey teased, recalling twelve-year-old Colton's antics when he discovered the unwelcome pest.

Colton laughed out loud. "'Kill it! Kill it! Kill it!'" he said, mimicking his younger self as he jumped around that day.

Kelsey cracked up, recalling how she'd bravely reached into the lunchbox, grabbed the rubber insect by the leg, and flung it at the kid who'd earlier taunted Colton in gym. The kid fell backwards in his seat, earning him a concussion, and Kelsey and Colton an extended stint in detention.

"Wasn't the first time you saved my life," Colton said.

"Or the last."

He paused and held her gaze for a moment before pointing to the sets. "Well, guess I'd better..."

As he strode across the stage, Kelsey felt the very tip of the ice between them begin to melt. Grand Lillian was right. This was a hard time for him, having to sell his family's farm in the wake of his dad's death and a career-ending injury. She should show him some grace. Forgive him for their past.

Hugh arrived and they began running their lines. As they rehearsed, she could occasionally see Colton, backstage building sets with Ralph, mouthing the male lead's lines. He mustn't have forgotten them, either. At one point, she broke character and shot him a look. Realizing he'd been caught, he made a funny face at her. She laughed.

"Oh sorry, did I get that line wrong?" Hugh asked.

"No, it's just—" she pointed at the stage crew, "—they're being silly back there."

During a break, Kelsey was scrolling through texts when she caught another glimpse of Colton onstage. This time he was lifting a heavy set piece with Ralph but obviously doing most of the work. Kelsey found herself mesmerized by his strength, the contours of his ripped trapezoids, the tone of his biceps. She also noticed the masked pain on his face as he worked through it, reminding her how strong Colton was.

It made her think about that night before sophomore year of high school, the first time she'd become aware of his strength. It was two years before their stage kiss. She'd been away at theater camp all summer and had texted him the night she returned home. He insisted they meet in the gazebo. There, she found a guy she barely recognized. Now a good foot taller than she was, he was toned, tan and...*well*. Lordy be.

"I'm here to meet Colton Banks. Have you seen him?" she'd teased.

He'd lifted her up, and she instinctively wrapped her legs around his waist in a move that was entirely uncharacteristic for her. She couldn't help it—something had compelled her.

He held her there longer than a platonic friend would, his muscular arms supporting her.

"I missed you," he breathed into her hair, squeezing as he spun her around.

"Wow," she said, looking up at him after he set her down. "You're—*wow*."

"Go ahead, punch me in the stomach. I know you want to."

She giggled. "I'm not punching you in the stomach."

"Seriously, you have to feel how solid my gut is."

Kelsey cocked her head at him. "Can I just touch it, instead?"

"Fine, Burger King. Have it your way."

He lifted up his t-shirt and, in the soft glow of gas lamps, she could see his defined ab muscles. She finally understood what was meant by the term *six-pack abs*. She wasn't aware Colton even had muscles, much less ones like these.

"Go ahead, cop a feel. I won't press charges."

Timidly, respectfully, she reached out and poked three fingers, softly, into his torso. He was right, it was rock solid.

"What *is* this sorcery?"

"Worked out all summer," he said, beaming as he lowered his shirt. "And I worked every day on my dad's farm, lifting stuff and strengthening my core. Made bank, too. Just call me 'Abs, bucks, and dirty fingernails.' The girls won't be able to resist me now." Colton laughed at his own joke.

Kelsey's heart did a little jig. They'd been best friends forever, but if she was honest about it, she'd been seeing Colton in a different light since the end of middle school. She didn't care what he looked like, before or after his growth spurt. It was his sincerity, his kindness, his humor that she appreciated about him. But wow. She couldn't help but find her best bud, her playmate since infancy, had become...what's the word? Oh. That's right...

"Hot with a capital *H*!" Ashley had proclaimed at their next sleepover, after laying orbs on the new and improved Colton.

Internally Kelsey agreed, but externally she kept her mouth shut. It just didn't feel right to talk that way about the boy she'd known since babyhood.

Every day, after theater and cheerleading practices were over, the girls would meet up at the local diner where the high school kids gathered. Ashley would talk nonstop about her day, recounting the number of times Colton had looked at her, certain there was something there. Knowing Kelsey and he had been BFFs forever, Ashley grilled her on all things Colton. Including why she had never made a move on him herself.

"Gross!" Practicing her acting skills, Kelsey pretended to gag at the very thought. "He's just...Colton. I've known him my whole life. He's like my brother."

Yet even as she said the words, she wondered if they were born of old habits. After his impressive physical transformation, she didn't know how to look at him anymore as he began to feel less and less like a brother, and more like an actual guy.

In Ashley's words, a *hot* guy.

At first, the thought of ogling him like the other girls gave her the ick, but before long she found her own glances lingering longer than usual, timed so that he wouldn't notice. She'd never in a million years let him see it, and in his company she jokingly mocked the lovestruck girls to his apparent amusement. Yet the dynamic between them felt as if it was beginning to shift, ever so slightly...a slow, subtle blurring of boundaries that had always been certain. His presence felt as easy and as natural as it always had, but something about the space between them began to take on a heaviness that felt almost...electric. At times, when their hands would brush against each other, Kelsey would feel a charge. She wondered if he felt it, too.

Still, she kept it clean and never voiced any of it to Ashley, certain it was just a passing thing, the onslaught of teen hormones. Kelsey had been a late bloomer in the guy department but was starting to notice them now more than ever. Especially when Ashley would giggle and grab her arm every time a hottie passed them in the hallway.

"Oh, you guys would make the cutest couple!" she'd whisper excitedly after they passed. It seemed Ashley was as hellbent on finding someone for Kelsey as she was hot on her own trail for Colton.

Much as Kelsey was starting to notice other boys, though, no one held her interest like The Forbidden One.

She brushed her feelings away on the daily, reminding herself she'd never go after a guy her friend liked. Especially a friend who was there for her whenever she needed someone. She and Ashley had been good friends since middle school, since that fateful first day when a group of popular girls hadn't allowed Kelsey to sit at their table. Ashley had stood up, told her friends they were bitches, and gone to sit with Kelsey.

From that day on, they were nearly inseparable. Walking through town wearing matching Cape May hoodies, they'd share iPod earphones and listen to Taylor Swift's *Fearless* album, belting out the lyrics to "Love Story" and "You Belong With Me." Ashley made her laugh when her parents made her cry. When Kelsey sought refuge from her annoying little sisters, Ashley hosted her for weekend-long sleepovers. Next to Colton, Ashley was her ride-or-die, the friend to last a lifetime, and Kelsey convinced herself no man would ever stand between them. Or so she thought. But at the time, it meant that unless and until Ashley denounced her feelings for him and expressly waved a green flag for Kelsey to proceed, Colton would remain untouchable. In the battle between lust and loyalty, the latter would always win out. And had, to this day.

Well, almost.

"Watch it."

Kelsey was ripped back to the present by Colton's voice. He was talking to Ralph as they nailed together two huge pieces of plywood. Colton's arms stretched out, flexed with his grip on the pieces, and once again, the visual evidence of his brawn was apparent. She wondered if his abs were still as tight. If the rest of his body was any indication, she guessed they were. She also wondered if he'd mind her punching him in the stomach to find out. The thought made her smile. Just as he turned her way.

"What?" he asked, giving a nervous chuckle.

"Nothing," Kelsey said, trying to think of something funny to say. Then it came to her. "It's just—'the abs, the bucks, the dirty fingernails.' I don't think I can resist it all."

Colton looked at her dead-on for a second, and she suddenly regretted putting herself out there with such an intimate joke about their past. Chastising herself, she vowed to return to radio silence—

But then his mouth curved into a conspiratorial grin.

"I should let you punch me in the stomach for that one."

Kelsey was relieved. The ice she'd just skated on, while still there, wasn't quite as thin. As they held each other's gaze, Kelsey found herself wishing she could jump into his arms like she did that night at the gazebo.

But...no. Too much had happened since then. Plus, she couldn't jump into his arms while they were holding someone else. He had a girlfriend, Kelsey reminded herself.

She would, instead, take him up on his offer to punch his stomach. For leaving her. For letting football go to his head.

For picking someone else over her. Despite the intimate moment, she had to shut it down.

Just like the sets, she felt her walls going back up again.

Colton

COLTON WENT BREATHLESS FOR A SPLIT SECOND AS HE watched Kelsey cross the theater. Her joke about his abs brought him right back to that night in the gazebo after she'd returned from theater camp, when he couldn't wait to show off the physique he'd earned that summer. Looking back on it, his cheesy actions were cringe-worthy, but sixteen-year-old Colton hadn't known any better. Kelsey may have been his best friend, but she was also his first crush, and his woman-wooing skills were far less developed than his body. A fact that remained today, he realized, as he walked into a doorframe he'd just constructed, nearly knocking it over.

He had to stop staring at her if he wanted to get this job done and get out of here without breaking something. A set piece. An arm.

His heart.

Another memory of their youth came flooding back, this one from senior year, a week after their stage kiss. He'd asked Kelsey to meet him in the diner, excited to share his news. He'd been selected as a top recruit for his dream school. As he waited for her in their favorite booth, his heart nearly beat out of his chest. Not just about his selection, but about the question he was finally, *finally*, going to ask her after building up his nerve in the week since that life-changing kiss—how to recruit Kelsey from being his best friend to his girlfriend.

"So what's this big news?" Kelsey had asked, squirming

with excitement as if she knew it was good.

He told her he'd be signing a letter of intent to play for his favorite school. He repeated what the recruiter had told him, from what he could expect of his scholarship prospects to how much his life was about to change, being a quarterback for a Pac-12 school.

Knowing what he knew now, Colton would never let his eighteen-year-old self sign up for that life. But his dad had no problem doing so because, in the end, Colton's football career was his dad's dream. Not that he blamed the man. At the time, they just didn't know what they didn't know. Like how every nuance of his game would be broadcast, announced, hailed, scrutinized, criticized on national TV. Or how immense pressure would come down on him from all angles, including a decades-old global network of alumni who'd either cheer his name, or turn it into an expletive with every move he made, both personally and professionally.

Or how Kelsey would react when Colton repeated to her what the recruiter had said.

"After telling me I'm gonna have a spotlight on me, you know what he says? 'Get yourself a good-looking girlfriend.' I was like, what? And he's like, 'Yeah, the world's about to fall in love with that face of yours, and whoever you date will fall under that same scrutiny. So, get yourself a good-looking girlfriend.' Can you believe he said that?"

Colton sat back laughing, waiting for Kelsey to respond in kind. His fingers curled around the note in his pocket—the one he planned to present to her tonight. The one that read, *Hey, good-looking! Will you be my girlfriend?*

But instead of laughing, Kelsey excused herself and rushed off to the bathroom. Colton sat there, waiting, hoping she wasn't sick. He pulled the note from his letterman jacket and reread it. It was now or never. Fueled with confidence from his meeting with the recruiter, Colton knew that time was now. After neatly refolding it, he returned the note to his pocket but kept a firm grasp on it, ready to whip it out.

Kelsey returned, her eyes looking red.

"You feeling okay?" he asked.

She waved him off, giving him a forced smile. "Allergies."

Colton wasn't aware she had allergies, but he shoved the thought aside. His heart picked up its tempo once again as he ran his forefinger along the edge of the note, taking a deep breath.

"I have something—"

"Ashley Bancroft," Kelsey blurted out.

"What?" he asked, confused.

She sniffed and shrugged. "You want a good-looking girl-friend, she's the one."

Colton wasn't sure how to respond.

"Seriously, C," Kelsey continued as she placed a hand on his, "that girl has had a crush on you forever. And she's a cheerleader, so it's perfect."

He wrinkled his brow, not sure where this was coming from.

"Big famous football guy, perky blonde cheerleader," she said, making fireworks with her hands. "A winning combination."

If it was so perfect, why didn't it show in her eyes?

He clenched his hand around the note. "But I don't—"

"What? You don't like Ashley? Of course you do," she said, huffing as she waved him off. "All the guys do. I see you looking at her in the hallway when she passes."

Colton blinked, wondering how that mattered. Of course, all the guys stared at Ashley, him included. It was hard not to—the girl was a knock-out. But that didn't mean he liked her. His raging desire for Kelsey eclipsed any feeling of mild attraction he may have had for Ashley. Or any other girl in their school.

How had this suddenly gone so wrong?

He was about to reveal his truth—that Kelsey was the

good-looking girlfriend he wanted—but she began waving at someone who'd just entered the diner with a group of their friends.

Ashley appeared at their booth.

"Go ahead, Colt," Kelsey said. Her smile seemed forced, her sweet voice tinged with an undercurrent of bitterness. "Tell her."

"Tell me what?" Ashley asked, perfect blonde curls bouncing against her well-endowed chest.

Mouth too dry to speak, Colton looked from Kelsey to Ashley, not sure what he was supposed to say. His heart was starting to crumble in a way it never had before, taking his breath and all his words with it. He wondered if he was on the verge of a heart attack.

"Okay, if he won't say it, I will," Kelsey began, mimicking an overly patient kindergarten teacher. "You have a crush on Colton, and Colton has a crush on you. He wants to know if you'll be his girlfriend." Kelsey looked at him pointedly. "Right, Colton?"

Horrified she'd put him on the spot like this, Colton stared at her, dumbfounded. Her eyes were like two lumps of black coal, just before they glowed red with heat. He'd never seen her look like this.

It was then he knew. Kelsey had no feelings for him beyond friendship. She probably sensed he was about to ask her out, and this was her only way to dodge the bullet. Be mean and sarcastic, shove him at someone else.

Message received.

Grabbing her jacket from the bench seat, Kelsey jumped up. "Have fun, kids. You make a cute couple." Then, she turned to him. "Looks like your letter of intent is signed, sealed, and delivered, Colton. Now that you got yourself a *good-looking girlfriend.*"

"Girlfriend? Are you serious?" an exuberant Ashley

squealed as she hopped into the booth next to him and planted a kiss on his cheek. "I'm in!"

Kelsey turned on her heel and fled the diner.

He didn't know what to do. He wanted to jump from the booth and follow her, find out what that was all about. But not only was Ashley blocking his way, something else held him back.

Crushed confidence.

As it turned out, being able to throw a football hadn't erased the years of self-doubt, humiliation, and bullying Colton had endured throughout his childhood. The only one who'd bolstered him against all that was Kelsey. From his earliest memories, she reigned like a queen over his thoughts and feelings. He'd always looked up to her as being wiser than he was. He'd do anything she said. If she told him to lie in traffic, he'd do it.

She basically just had.

Her actions, the tone of her voice, the look in her eye, told him all he needed to know—she was repulsed by him. Probably because of the kiss, the *stupid* onstage kiss he never should have improvised. He could only assume she'd been grossed out by it, relieved when he hadn't brought it up, then saw what was coming and wanted no part of it. It was the ultimate blow-off, a perfect switcheroo to keep him from embarrassing himself by suggesting she become his girlfriend. Kelsey had spoken, in more ways than one, and he had to listen if it was the last thing he did.

He may have been a shining star on the football field, but as he sat there in that diner, befuddled and fumbling, he saw himself through Kelsey's eyes. Colton was still the awkward chubby boy others made fun of. That's how she'd always known him, and what he'd always be to her.

After she left, taking his heart with her, Colton gave Ashley a shy smile. He wished he could find the words to tell the girl how he really felt, but he couldn't bring himself to do it, because she seemed so excited and the truth would burst her bubble.

The truth: he was in love with Kelsey.

The other truth: he was too much of a wimp to tell her. Or anyone. It wasn't the first time, nor would it be the last, that his insecurities reigned over his true feelings.

Or the last time Kelsey broke his heart.

Fingers unfurling, he let go of the note in his pocket and, with the same hand, clasped Ashley's. Their fate...signed, sealed, and delivered.

Coming back to the present, his racing heart reminded him he wasn't ready to face his past with Kelsey. Not just that day in the diner, but the last time they saw each other. The night she left him in the gazebo, in the ultimate act of rejection. His heart had been too damaged by her, twice now, and he wasn't willing to get hurt again.

Just like the sets, he felt his walls going back up again.

MOLLY ARRIVED AT THE MUNICIPAL CLERK'S OFFICE FIRST thing on Monday morning to secure a permit for Saturday's event. While Grand Lillian had coached her through what she should say to obtain it, Molly worried she was too late. The ordinance required thirty days' notice, and she only had five.

The front desk clerk shot her down before she had even completed her sentence, reciting the requirement. "I'm not authorized to bend the rules."

"But...this is supposed to be a Christmas in July event."

"I'm sorry, sugar, but it's not my rule to break."

Molly was crestfallen as she exited through the heavy glass doors of the municipal building. Sinking down on the top step, she called Brennan to see if he had any solutions. When he didn't answer, she was about to leave a message when she heard someone call her name.

She looked up to see Becca Barnshaw, a former classmate, walking toward her.

"Molly Grace!" she said, giving her a hug. "What are you doing in town? I heard you moved to New York."

"I'm...in the process. What are you up to?"

"Working at the bank. Have you seen anyone else from high school?"

"Yeah, Maxwell Banks. Remember him?"

"Remember him?" she giggled. "I had such a crush on him in middle school."

Hmm...a crush on Max? She'd have to remember this factoid, maybe fix them up.

"I'm assuming you've seen Justine and Ava?" Becca asked.

Justine and Ava were Molly's closest friends in high school, but they'd grown apart. "No. We haven't really kept in touch."

"Ava just got married and Justine is engaged. I can't imagine getting married at our ages, but more power to them."

Molly was surprised that Becca, who hadn't been super close to them in high school, knew more about her former besties than she did. Then again, their lives had taken off in different directions.

"You should come out with us next time we go for drinks." Becca looked at her phone. "Oops, late for work. Give me your number so I can let you know next time we're getting together. Maybe ask Max to join us."

After they exchanged numbers and Becca waved goodbye, Molly returned to her woeful state, covering her face with her hands as she rued her poor planning.

"Oh no, out of gas again?"

She looked up to see Max taking the steps two-by-two.

"Something like that," she said as he plunked down next to her. "Out of gas and no more wind in my sails. I can't do it."

"That doesn't sound like the unsinkable Molly Grace I knew yesterday. What's up?"

"The ordinance requires thirty days' notice to secure a permit, but we have five, and the clerk won't budge."

"Is there a way you can still do the event without a permit?"

"Let's see." Molly pulled a notebook from her bag and consulted her list of planned activities. "No permit's needed for the play. There's a sand sculpting contest on the beach—"

"Which is a recreation department thing. I have a friend who works there, so not an issue. What else?"

"I was envisioning sidewalk sales by store owners, of course the food, but that would be taken care of by Sarina and other restaurant owners. Santa visits with kids—"

"Another thing that doesn't require a permit. I don't know, Moll, maybe you don't need one."

"Except I also wanted to do a parade, and I'll need approval to have tables set up in the mall area."

"True," Max said as he raked a hand through his hair. "Colton and I started building them last night, by the way."

"Thank you." That was so nice of the Banks brothers—she hoped they'd get the chance to make use of them. "I'm waiting for my boyfriend to call back. Maybe he'll have a solution."

Max shot her a look.

"What? He's a smart guy. He should have some ideas."

"Gee, if only we could find a smart guy around *here*..." Max stood up, holding his hand over his eyes as if looking out to sea. "I think I may have spotted one."

"Touché, Mr. Smart Guy," Molly said, laughing.

"I know I'm stating the obvious, but maybe there's a loophole. Do you have the ordinance on you?"

"What do I look like, a walking law library?" Molly joked.

"Yeah, never mind."

"Kidding. I have it here."

"Yep, there you go," he said, pointing to the document as they read it over. "'Upon application, the board has the right to waive any portion of the ordinance it deems appropriate.' If we can get them to waive the thirty-day requirement, we should be good."

Molly laughed out loud. "Wow, and I thought I was an eternal optimist. How do you propose we 'get them to waive' it?"

"Do we know anyone on the board?"

Molly shrugged. "I haven't lived here for four years."

"Me neither. Come with me."

Max grabbed her hand and pulled her up, continuing to hold it until they reached the door. His hand was strong, encouraging. It felt nice.

He held the door open. As they entered the lobby, Molly saw a sign she hadn't noticed earlier, notifying the public of the Board of Commissioners meeting that night.

"How serendipitous," Max said as they passed the sign. He led them to a plaque on the wall listing the names of current board members. Max tapped one with his knuckles. "George Solis. He knew my dad—he's our man. Walk this way." Max started doing a funny walk toward the office. Molly followed, grateful for his humor and levity.

"Hey there!" Max said to the clerk, extending his hand as he leaned over the counter. "I don't know if you remember me. Maxwell Banks. Gert, isn't it? We've met a few times at various functions."

"That's right." Gert smiled at Max, as if she was trying to remember. "It's good to see you again, Max."

"We're looking for George Solis."

"He's not due in until ten," Gert said.

"I see." Max nodded. "My friend Molly here is Lillian

Grace's granddaughter. I'm sure you're familiar with Lillian and all the good deeds she'd done for this community?"

"Oh, yes." Gert beamed at Molly. "I'm sorry, I didn't realize you were her granddaughter."

"No problem," Molly said, wishing she'd thought to drop her grandmother's name. Lesson one in schmoozing: use your connections.

"We have a situation, and I know you're the woman for the job. Molly is putting together an impromptu fundraiser on Saturday, to help the town and residents with cleanup and rebuilding costs. How did your house do in the storm?"

"We were lucky. Lost a few shingles, but that's about it. My neighbors, not so well."

"Heartbreaking how much damage a storm can cause, isn't it? Lillian was hoping we could rely on you and your passion for this community for help. We can't host the fundraiser without a permit."

Molly was awed by Max's schmoozing abilities. Soon, good ol' Gert would be eating out of his hand. Who knew Maxwell Banks could be so...what was the word?

Charismatic.

She turned her gaze to Molly. "Is that what you're seeking the permit for, the fundraiser?"

"Yes," Molly said, perplexed. She'd just discussed this with the woman minutes ago, but somehow, only Max's deep voice seemed to resonate with her.

"According to the ordinance, the board has the right to waive any requirements. If we can get my buddy George to agree to consider our application, will you put it on the agenda?"

"I'll see what I can do."

"Thanks, Gert." Max clasped his hands in prayer formation and bowed before her. "You're a godsend. I'm so glad to hear your house was spared. Beautiful place you got there."

"Thanks, Max."

"Amazing," was all Molly could say once they were in the hallway. She gave him a high five.

"Strap in," he whispered. "It's about to get even more so."

With his hand on the small of her back, Max guided her toward a man coming down the hall.

"George!" Max called out. "Speak of the devil. It's me, Max Banks, Roger's son. We were just talking about you."

"Maxwell!" George cried out as he shook Max's hand. "So sorry about your dad. He was a good man."

"He was." Max nodded. "He thought the same of you. Do you know Molly Grace? Lillian's granddaughter."

"Pleased to meet you," George said, shaking her hand. "Wow, I can tell you're related. You have the same twinkle in your eyes as your grandmother. Lovely woman, she is."

"Thanks."

"Right before she's about to rip your heart out, amiright, Max?" George bellowed a laugh, clapping him on the arm. "You about to rip someone's heart out, Molly girl?"

Molly grimaced. It was one thing for the fam to poke fun at Grand Lil, but not others.

"Ah, she's a lover, not a fighter," Max said, shifting his stance so he was standing slightly in front of her, most likely to keep her from taking a swing at the boisterous, full-of-himself man. Molly did not love this glimpse into the Old Boys Network at its finest.

"I'm joshing," George said. "What really brings you guys to municipal hall on this beautiful day?"

"We're here for a huge favor. Molly's working on a Christmas in July fundraiser to help with the storm cleanup efforts, slated for this Saturday. The permit ordinance requires thirty days' notice, and we're five days out from the event. Just wondering if you guys could add it to your agenda for the meeting tonight, and possibly waive the requirement?"

"What all does it entail?"

"Molly's the expert; she's the one to ask."

After she explained the planned events, George nodded. "Sounds nice. Is Lillian is involved?"

"Do you *know* my grandmother?" Molly teased, taking one for the team as she played into the OBN. "Only a maximum-security prison sentence would keep her from being involved."

George laughed heartily. "Very true. If you get us the application, I'll make sure we discuss it tonight."

"Already done, Mr. Solis. Thank you for your time," Molly said.

After handshakes, Max and Molly burst through the doors of the municipal building, containing their laughter until they were outside.

"Max. Well. Banks," Molly trumpeted after her giggles subsided. "I had no idea what a schmoozer you are. Your political future looks so bright I need shades."

"Hell no," Max said, shaking his head. "Politics are not for me."

"You mean, you stepped out of your comfort zone to help me? You really are a nice guy. A dying breed."

"Nah, there are plenty of us out here. You just have to know where to find us."

"How is it you know Gert?"

"Never met her before in my life."

"But wait, how did you—"

"Know her name?" Max gave her a grin and flashed his eyebrows. "I saw an email on her computer screen and took a chance."

They burst out laughing again.

"Tell me you know George Solis, though."

"Met him once, through my dad."

"And yet you acted like you've known him for years."

"It's the art of the schmooze, my friend."

"Oh, so we're friends now?" Molly teased.

"I think you're stuck with me."

"Good, because we've got a lot of schmoozing to do."

"You may want to take notes."

So noted, Maxwell Banks. Your kindness, charisma, and schmoozing charm are so noted.

Max

MAX'S HEART RACED AS THEY LEFT THE MUNICIPAL BUILDing. Not only because he was in Molly's presence—although that had a lot to do with it—but because he'd just pulled off the biggest batch of BS he'd ever perpetrated in his whole life.

Max was a rule-follower. He'd never schmoozed people, acted like he'd known them when he didn't, or asked for favors he wasn't deserving of. But "like" will make you do amazing things, and right now, he was so in "like" with Molly, he'd do just about anything for her. Scale Congress Hall. Stand in the middle of Washington Street, fully naked, reciting the Gettysburg Address. Pull the ferry across Delaware Bay with his teeth.

Or pretend he was some kind of hot shot who had an "in" with municipal government. Blow off yet another morning of work at the farm. And, most of all, get derailed from his purpose, the reason he went to the municipal building in the first place, to pay the water bill. Oh well, he'd do it later.

"Where are you dragging me today?" Max asked as he climbed into the golf cart next to Molly, uninvited.

She gave him a teasing look. "What makes you think I'm dragging you anywhere?"

"Uh, the fact you may need someone to bamboozle folks? As you can see, I'm a pro."

"I certainly *can* see that," Molly said as she turned on the cart and pulled out of its parking space. "You may even be a better smooth-talker than my boyfriend, who knows how to work people. It's part of what makes him so good at what he does."

"What does he do?"

"Finance."

Max bristled at the suggestion that *my boyfriend* was some sort of anomaly, a rare and coveted unicorn. As if every finance bro wasn't a natural smooth-talker. But he'd known Brennan in high school and, while he certainly knew how to win people over, he was also a nice guy. Max felt bad silently bashing the dude and struggled to keep his jealousy at bay.

Molly rattled off the list of stops they had to make before zigging around town. After bringing lunch to the theater and joining their friends for the meal again, they continued on their errands.

As Sarina was finishing up a productive day painting sets, Grand Lillian cornered her.

"How are you doing with all this event planning?" she asked.

"Fine," Sarina answered, knowing there was more to her question than met the eye. "What do you really want to know?"

Grand Lillian laughed. "You know you're my favorite granddaughter, right?"

"You're only saying that because I'm feeding your crew this week."

"Not true. It's because you have more of my *chutzpah* than the other two. And while you may not have gotten the same grades your sisters did in school, you're smart in other ways. Street smart, like me."

"Are you part of a gang I'm not aware of?"

"See, you have that quick wit, that take-no-shit attitude. I raised you right." Grand Lil squeezed Sarina's cheeks just like she did when she was a kid. "But that's also why I'm worried about you. I know how headstrong you can be, how hard it is for you to—"

"Sorry to interrupt." Colton appeared out of nowhere. "Lillian, can you come here? We have a question about the set."

As her grandmother excused herself to help the men, Sarina wondered what Grand Lil was getting at.

Her grandmother was right. She *had* had a lot to do with their upbringing—Sarina's in particular. Kelsey was always closest to their mom, and Molly was undoubtedly their father's favorite. That left Sarina, floating around parent-less in the favorites department, her wild tendencies running roughshod over her family. She was always taking off, challenging the system, giving their parents a run for their money.

Until Grand Lil stepped in. A middle child herself, Lillian took more time with Sarina, showed her more patience and understanding. Most of the time.

Lillian became a permanent fixture in their household, especially after her son left them. Watching her grandmother partner with their mom to raise the girls—rather than siding with her own offspring—was impactful for Sarina. Even though she and Kelsey were already out of the house, the women still provided guidance through their tough late teens and early twenties, when strong parenting wasn't only necessary but critical. Especially with an MIA dad. Sarina didn't know what she'd have done if they hadn't welcomed her when she returned from Europe, tail between her legs after dropping out of college and spending her up-to-that-point life savings. They'd given her a roof over her head and food on her plate, despite her parting words when she'd left for Europe, denouncing their "obsession with domesticated life," proclaiming to not need their help.

Of course, they *did* dish out some harsh judgment.

"Reckless child," her grandmother had taunted. "All that time and money, and where did it get you?"

"Umm, all around Europe?"

"And what do you have to show for it?"

"Let's see. I've been to places and experienced things most people won't in a lifetime. Global friendships. Out-of-this-world experiences. An expanded food palate and a kick-ass Insta page. Shall I go on?"

Now, five years later, she began to see her grandmother's point. It had been fun, but if she hadn't done the Europe thing, she'd have so much money now, she'd never have to worry about keeping the café afloat. She could've owned the building. Instead, here she was, her fledgling café in the throes of financial instability.

"I'm back," Grand Lil said, bringing Sarina to the present. "As I was saying, you know how much I was against you opening a café without business experience. Not your smartest move, and now I see you taking on even more. I worry about your common sense."

And, just like that, her grandmother sucked the air out of Sarina's sails like no one else could.

"I love you, too, Grand Lil," Sarina said through a smirk.

"How do you plan to do all you've signed up for? Now you've agreed to Molly's pie-in-the-sky demands of your resources, on top of being overly generous with the community. Which I appreciate," she said quickly, "but I worry you're stretching yourself too thin."

"Well, you needn't worry. Like your earlier assessment of

me, I'm smart. And unlike your later assessment, I *do* possess common sense. I've enlisted the assistance of fellow business owners in supplying food for the event."

Sarina turned away, in case the worriment that had taken up residence in her heart reflected in her eyes.

"I also know, because of our similarities, how difficult it is for you to admit when you need help," Grand Lil continued.

"See, that's where you're wrong. I don't need help."

Of course, she did. She just didn't want to admit it to her.

Grand Lillian gave her a skeptical glare. "I just hope this has been a good life lesson about how reckless it is to start something when you have no experience. Despite such folly, I'm here for you if you need help."

Oh, *fuck* no.

"Thanks for the offer, Grand, but I'm fine. I'll keep it in mind, though."

Like hell she would.

"I also have a nice boy who I'd like to—"

"No," Sarina said. "I am not looking for a nice boy."

"Obviously, judging by how you let the last one get away."

"That's right. I want me a *baaad* boy," Sarina said, carrying her sarcasm too far as she often did. She couldn't help it—she loved riling her grandmother up, especially when the woman was being so insufferable. "The badder, the better. Wild, covered with tats, a day-drinker, someone unemployed who only showers once a week."

Grand Lillian walked away, shaking her head. "There's no help for you, girl," she said over her shoulder.

"Good thing I don't need it, then."

Sarina's phone rang just then, and an all-too-familiar out-of-town number scrolled across the screen. She refused the landlord company's call as she had several times already, knowing it was about back rent. She still needed time to come up with a plan, and fast.

Back at the café, Sarina was about to crunch numbers in an attempt to reconcile finances when Luke walked in.

"What's up?" Sarina asked, trying to keep her annoyance at bay. "I'm busy, so if you can make this quick, I'd appreciate it."

"I have an offer I want to discuss with you."

"If this is about getting back—"

"It's about business. I just received an offer you should know about. The development company is interested in taking over this space for the Cape's new *Jolt!* location."

"Very funny, Luke. What makes them think it's available?"

"It's a legit offer, Sar."

"Well, I hope you told them to shove it right up their corporate ass."

He sighed. "Of course I couldn't do that. As a Realtor, I have an ethical duty to listen to their offer and present it to you."

"Funny thing is, you aren't *my* Realtor."

"But I am your boy—*ex*-boyfriend, and I care about you. I thought you may want to consider it."

"Are you insane? Why do you think I'd want to consider their offer?"

"Maybe hear what it is, first."

Sarina feigned disinterest, but curiosity won out. "*Fine.* What is it?"

"They know you're not the owner, just a tenant," he continued, "so if the landlord decided to sell this building to the developers, you'd have no rights."

"Gee, Luke, don't sugarcoat it," she said, her voice dripping with sarcasm. "I'm well aware of that, so what's your point?"

"My point is, they don't want to see you get squeezed out, so they're offering to buy your assets. Everything you put in here. The industrial-grade appliances, tables, chairs, supplies, you name it. Plus, a bonus as an incentive to relinquish the space. Together, we're talking tens of thousands of dollars, which will settle all your debt and give you enough extra to go on and do something new. Like that surf camp you always talk about."

"First off, why do you think I'm in so much debt that I'd even consider their offer? This was my dream, remember?"

"I do remember. I was with you every step of the way. I know how much you took out, how much you spent, and how slow this winter was. I also know you've been donating food left and right. Doesn't take a mathematician to figure out you can't be super solvent now."

"Things may be a little slow, but that doesn't mean I want to give this up."

Although, "tens of thousands of dollars" sure sounds enticing.

Lots of tens, knowing what she'd spent on everything. Luke was right—taking their deal would allow her to open the nonprofit surfing camp for differently abled kids she'd been mulling over for years. She'd hoped to get it started once the café was up and running.

He took her hands in his. "I just wanted you to know there's an option if you want to walk away from this."

Recoiling, she pulled her hands away in disgust. "What makes you think I want to walk away?"

Even though I just considered it myself.

He gave her a knowing look. "Walking away is your strong suit. Trust me, I should know."

"Well, not this time," she snapped. "And tell them to stay the fuck out of Cape May."

Kelsey

When Max and Molly showed up with lunch, the cast and crew gathered again in a circle on the stage. Kelsey was surprised when Colton sat next to her this time—until she realized it was the only spot open.

"Sarina's definitely found her calling," he said under his breath as he ripped into his bag. "I wasn't kidding yesterday when I said she made the best sandwiches. Probably the best I've ever had."

"Even better than Crosswind Middle School's chicken beak sandwich?"

He chuckled. "Oh man, you had to remind me." Kelsey had bitten into a hard object in their school's disgusting lunch offering, convinced it was a beak, and it had become a running joke. "Now I'm craving one."

"I can ask if she'll put it on the menu."

"You'd do that for me?"

"Of course."

He stared at her for a second, and she stared back, until awkwardness once again befell them.

Kelsey wasn't hungry so she passed on eating. Instead, she defaulted to the old tried-and-true passer of time, eraser of awkward moments—checking her phone—so she wouldn't obsess over Colton's proximity. He was so close she could feel the heat from the stage lights radiating off him.

That's when she noticed Sarina casting a curious look at her.

Raising her voice, she addressed her sister. "He was just telling me the bread is stale, and the meat is rancid."

"I made it that way just for him," Sarina quipped, her quick wit never missing a beat. "It's my new menu item. I call it 'So Last Month.'"

"Seriously, Sarina, delicious," Colton said. "You should really consider opening a café."

"OMG, why didn't I think of that?" Sarina exclaimed, slapping her forehead. "Colton, you're brilliant! Care to be my investor?"

"My checkbook's right here. How much?"

Colton and Sarina continued joking with one another as the rest of the cast and crew ate. Kelsey was jealous of their friendly banter.

Then again, Sarina hadn't stood in a gazebo with him, holding her breath because she thought he was about to kiss her, just before he told her he was in love with someone else.

Colton

WHILE THE SPOT NEXT TO KELSEY IN THE LUNCH CIRCLE wouldn't have been his first choice, sitting together felt more like a habit than a matter of limited options. It was instinctive. They'd sat together as toddlers, slept next to each other for kindergarten naps, and spent grades one through six at the same lunch table—until that phase when boys and girls parted like oil and water, only to resume commingling in high school. Despite their decade-long separation, old habits die hard, and he felt his walls come down a bit.

After lunch, Colton went back to work on the sets, hoping to get a lot done before he had to leave for the meeting with the real estate agent. As the day went on, he felt his guardedness dissipating more and more. Unexpectedly, he found himself enjoying hearing Kelsey and Hugh act out their parts, mostly for the good memories it brought back. He even took a break during construction to watch.

Sitting in the darkened wing where no one could see him, he was mesmerized as he watched her. It felt good to take down the veil of disinterest and just feel something for a change. She still had that effect on him after all these years.

Colton startled when a man called his name.

"Sorry to interrupt. We have the lumber you requested."

He went with them to help unload the truck.

"Can you handle it?" one of the guys asked. "You know, with your shoulder?"

"I'm good." Colton grunted as he lifted the heavy wood, knowing he probably shouldn't. Not that it mattered—he'd never again play pro ball—but he didn't want to add further insult to his injury. Yet, on some level, the physical pain felt *good*, as if it was providing an outlet for emotional pain. Given a choice, he'd choose the former over the latter every day.

As they carried the last of the lumber inside, Kelsey and Hugh decided to take a break. One of the lumber guys took the opportunity to approach them.

"Ms. Grace, do you mind if I get a selfie with you, for my girlfriend? She's a huge fan."

"Of course," Kelsey said, giving him her award-winning smile.

Colton marveled at how easy being in the public eye was for her. How natural. Meanwhile, whenever he'd been interviewed after games, he felt like he couldn't keep his size-eleven cleat out of his damn mouth. He'd end every media moment hoping the NFL and fans hadn't picked up on what an imposter he was. Maybe not on the field, where it was just him, the ball, and his teammates. But certainly off-field, where it was him and his lifelong tongue-tied awkwardness. Sacking him, every single time.

His phone alarm went off, reminding him of his upcoming meeting.

When he arrived in the Realtor's office a little while later, the bubbly receptionist jumped up from her seat.

"Good to see you again, Mr. Banks. How's your shoulder today?"

It bothered him when people only remembered him for the injury he'd suffered in the last game he played. It was months ago, but so many people still reacted as if it had happened yesterday.

"My boyfriend was your biggest fan, and he asks me every day how you're doing."

Colton was struck by her usage of the past tense. *Was your biggest fan.* It made him feel like a washed-up has-been at the ripe old age of twenty-eight.

Great career choice.

But then he softened. She was just trying to be friendly. Without fans, he and his fellow teammates were nothing but grown men throwing balls at each other. Even the lumber guy had meant well. Colton just needed to stop being so sensitive.

"I'm good, thanks for asking."

Luke Martin came out and offered a strong handshake. "Colton, good to see you," he said, as he ushered Colton to his office. "Please, sit. I've got some news. During a title search of the farm property, it was discovered your dad had purchased a plot of land on Cape View Drive a week before his death. I'm guessing you had no knowledge of this."

"None at all," Colton said, shocked. "What land?"

"The arts center property. He probably didn't have a chance to update his will to include the new land before he passed."

Colton raked a hand through his hair, perplexed by this news. "What would my dad want with that land?"

"I don't know. The agent who handled the transaction has since retired. Would he have confided in someone else? In any event, the company eyeing up the farm has been looking for commercial property to complement their residential development. They've currently offered on another property, but if it falls through, I'd suggest you include it in the sale and increase the asking price accordingly."

"Umm, yeah. I should probably talk to my brother first, but...I don't see why we wouldn't include it."

"Great. Why don't you get back to me after you talk to Max, so we can get the ball rolling if the other offer falls through."

Colton dialed Max's number the moment he left the office. "Did you know Dad bought the arts center land?" he asked as soon as Max answered.

"He *did*?" Max's incredulous tone confirmed his mutual surprise. "Why would he do that?"

"I have no idea," Colton said, his brow furrowed. "The development company may want it included in the sale."

"It's your call, Colt," Max said. "You're the executor. I'll go along with anything you want."

"I just wish I knew what Dad bought it for. Knowing that would make this easier."

"Luke didn't have any insight?"

"He wasn't involved in the transaction."

"What about Fred Smith?"

Fred was their neighbor, the man their father had called when he was having chest pains, who, in turn, called 911. They'd spoken to him multiple times since the funeral, but he'd never mentioned the land.

While there was still much to be done at the theater that afternoon, this was more important. He took a detour and found Fred in his office a few blocks away.

"Colton!" Fred got up from his desk and greeted him. "What brings you here on this fine day?"

"Did you know my dad bought the arts center property just before he died?"

"I did." Fred regarded him skeptically. "I'm guessing from your look you didn't know?"

"No. It was discovered during a title search. It wasn't in the will."

"Oh, man. I assumed he would have spoken to you boys about it or at least updated his will. Then again..."

Colton knew what he was thinking. A person in his early sixties in good health doesn't anticipate the immediate need for will updates, much less sudden death. Struck with a pang of grief, he swallowed hard.

"I'm sorry I didn't think to mention it."

"Not your responsibility. I'm just not sure why he didn't tell us. Did he say why he bought it?"

"All I know is, the city's upkeep of the property and building was becoming too challenging, and city council had been looking for a private owner to take it over." Fred shrugged. "For whatever reason, your dad wanted it. I never had a chance to ask him why."

Colton shook his head in disbelief. "I thought he was trying to ease up on the property maintenance stuff. He told me it was becoming too much, and was thinking about finding someone to help him run the farm, so he could eventually..." He choked up as he said the word. "Retire." Blinking, he willed away the tears and continued. "It just doesn't make sense."

"I'm sorry I didn't press him for more information."

"It's okay. I appreciate you sharing what you know."

He turned to leave when Fred added, "I've often wondered if that's what caused his heart attack."

Colton turned back. "In what way?"

"He was working at the center when he called me. He'd lifted a large piece of wood when he thought he pulled a muscle in his chest. He was having a problem catching his breath, so he called and asked if I'd take him to the hospital."

Colton shook his head in disbelief. "I'm guessing it wasn't a muscle…"

"No, and that was my instinct, too. He called me because he thought I was just next door at home, but I was here in the office, and knew I couldn't get to him fast enough. That's why I called the ambulance. By then…"

His silence told Colton all he needed to know.

When Colton had received the call, his dad had already died. He'd never asked for details about where he was prior to arriving at the hospital, or even whether he was alive when he got there. Whatever his dad had been doing there must have directly caused his death.

Suddenly, the idea of including it in the land sale was appealing. There was no way he'd want to keep the land if it had led to his death, but he wanted to share all the facts with Max first before they made a decision.

Back at the theater, Colton ran into Grand Lillian. Almost literally, nearly toppling the diminutive woman. The last person he wanted to see.

She stood firm, hands on her hips, giving him the side eye as she asked how his meeting went.

"Fine," he said, avoiding her steely gaze which, for some reason, appeared knowing.

She nodded slowly, not taking her eyes off him, before going on her way. She didn't say a word, but Colton assumed she must have known about the arts center land. Not that its ownership should matter to her, now that the storm had demolished the building. They could always move the arts center to a new location. Still, he hoped she *hadn't* heard about it, because if anyone would give him a fight over selling the land, it would be that eighty-four-year-old, four-foot, ten-inch ball of fire. Being blitzed by three-hundred-pound linebackers was child's play compared to dealing with the likes of her.

Jaxon

JAXON LEANED HIS HEAD BACK INTO THE PLUSH LEATHER seat of the private jet, trying to get some sleep. He'd opted for a red-eye so he could kill two birds with one engine strike—make his way across the expansive US while also catching a few z's.

But sleep didn't come easy, especially as he thought back to his conversation with Verna, and the unease he felt after she questioned his decision to make things real with his costar.

Was he ready for this?

It didn't take him long to realize...yes. Turning thirty meant it was time to take himself out of the game and settle into a one-woman sitch.

Finally, he drifted off to sleep as a dream emerged. He was on a beach in Tahiti and looked up to see Kelsey running toward him in slow motion. His heart swelled, confirming his belief she was The One.

But as she got closer, he realized it wasn't Kelsey. It was a blonde woman with light eyes and an athletic build. More like his usual type.

"Surf's up, Quinn!" the woman said, laughing as she looked up at him. Her hair was kissed by the sun, and her eyes gleamed the color of sea glass as she wrinkled her nose, dotted with freckles. He was a sucker for freckles. "Let's see what you got!"

There was something electrifying about her personality that simply drew him to her.

Suddenly, they were bobbing on the ocean on surfboards. She caught a wave, and he watched, mesmerized, as she rode it with effortless style, her tanned body, bathed in sunlight, bending and twisting in perfect harmony with the ocean. He was captivated by her skill as she executed every maneuver as if she and the wave were one.

His eyes flew open, as he realized his dream was no longer about Kelsey. Closing them, he tried to superimpose her image onto the surfing girl, but he'd already awakened. As much as he tried to force it, he couldn't return to that beach to see what would happen next.

One thing was clear, though. His dream girl wasn't Kelsey. What could this mean?

"Don't be an asshole," he said aloud.

"Excuse me?"

He opened his eyes to find the flight attendant standing next to him. "Is there something you need, Mr. Quinn?"

"Oh, sorry," he said, laughing. "I was talking to myself."

"Here you go. I brought you a gin and tonic, just as you like it." She chuckled. "They're known to take the asshole right out of a person."

"Thanks," he said, accepting the drink. "One can only hope."

Taking a sip, he wondered whether dreaming of someone else meant he wasn't that into Kelsey.

Nope. He'd come too far for it to be a mistake. A driver was on stand-by to take him to his Airbnb in Cape May. He was going to surprise her the following day, after the curtain fell on her opening night. The plan was in place, and he wasn't about to stop now.

SARINA HAD JUST FINISHED CLEANING UP WHEN HER phone rang with the same out-of-state number she'd ignored earlier. She'd come to know the number well.

"Shit," she sighed. She was tempted to let it go to voicemail but sensed her grace period on being nonresponsive was running out. She answered.

"Hello, Ms. Grace. It's Ed, from Riker Property Management. We're going to need you to pay your current rent balance by the end of the week, or we'll have to initiate an eviction process."

"By the end of the week?" Sarina cried out.

Where was this coming from? Up to this point, they'd been understanding of her situation. Maybe they'd found out about *Jolt!*'s offer and wanted to squeeze her out.

"We've given you more time than most tenants. We know you've just opened a business, but we have to consider ours as well."

What a dick. She was about to tell him as much, but realized she had some accountability in this. After all, she was the one who'd insisted on renting this space. It was owned by some millionaire who didn't live anywhere near Cape May, who hired an out-of-state corporate management company to do their dirty work—shaking down the little guy to get pennies to fall from their pockets. Had she rented from a local landlord, she may have been able appeal to them as a likewise-local business owner.

"I'm waiting for a loan to come through." Bold-faced lie, but she needed more than four days to figure it all out—to consider her options and muster the courage to admit defeat. "Can you at least give me a week?"

He signed. "We'll give you the weekend. But come Monday the twenty-seventh, that's it."

"Thank you," she said.

"Just a reminder—the owner's asking that you set up an annual inspection with the sprinkler company."

"That's my responsibility?"

"According to the lease, yes. As a food-service business, you're expected to coordinate a time when no customers will be present, since they'll have to shut off your water. You must then follow any recommended changes within your ability."

She made a mental note to do it next week, if she was still a tenant by then.

Hanging up, Sarina sat in the darkened back room, debating what to do about her finances. Asking family for money would bring her shame, proving she wasn't capable of operating a business without their help. But it would allow her to keep the café.

Then again, Luke's offer from *Jolt!* was an instant solution to a messy situation. Sell her assets, settle her debt, and move on to something new. She'd walk away proud to have fulfilled her dream to own a café, however short-lived.

Yet each option came with an assassination of her character. What would it be? Ask for money and admit folly, or quit and admit failure?

She was tired of thinking about it. Buying herself more time with the management company was enough accomplishment for one day. She'd figure something out tomorrow.

Now, it was time for sleep.

Kelsey

A STORM BREWING OFF THE COAST SENT WIND WHIPPING up the beach as Kelsey set out for her morning walk. The tide was higher than usual, as the angry ocean churned up past injuries and spit out fresh wounds. It was cathartic, walking along water's edge in solitude—a first since she'd returned home. She mulled over her past with Colton, her present life both on-screen and off, and where she stood with all of it. Her thoughts meshed with the tumultuous waves as she asked herself one simple question.

Who was she?

Who was Kelsey Grace, the person beyond the media focus, the fictional spin her life had taken, the many titles she bore? Actor, granddaughter, daughter, sister. *Good girl.* Friend to some, significant other to none. For once, she allowed her mind to wander, unscripted and without direction, as she peeled back the layers of her many facades and caught a rare glimpse of that person she once knew. Someone shy and introverted beneath an extroverted veneer. Insecure, despite an air of confidence. Seemingly self-assured and in control, yet easily swayed by others.

Like the fauxmance. Ditching her much-needed vacation. Forced into proximity with Colton Banks. None of which she wanted, all of which she believed she had no choice about. Always doing what was expected of her. Maybe that's why she'd let studio execs, agents, publicists—anyone with control over her career—push her into projects she wouldn't have otherwise chosen for herself. Her dad had really done a number on that part of her psyche, expecting her to always go along with the program. All in exchange for his love and acceptance. Conditional love at its finest.

Kelsey stopped dead in her tracks. Staring out to sea, she tried to remember the last time she'd seen him.

College graduation. Six years ago.

It dawned on her that she'd been operating under a set of standards set for her by a person who was no longer in her life. She'd allowed his outdated and irrelevant expectations to drive her behavior, not recognizing she was free to set her own self-expectations and bar for success.

Starting with being true to herself. Seeking her own acceptance, becoming the person *she* wanted to be—someone who could stand up for herself and go after what she really wanted. Like time by herself. More serious roles.

Colton.

Why did *he* come into her mind just then?

Despite a raging surf, the foggy walk had offered a quiet stillness, clarity, and a clearer reflection of her true self. She may not have all the answers, but maybe she wasn't meant to. Perhaps, at twenty-eight, self-discovery wasn't as much a destination as it was a journey.

Okay, enough introspection for one day.

Once again, Kelsey arrived at the theater before everyone else, armed with an ulterior motive having to do with a certain ex-quarterback. Hoping he'd arrive early again so they could continue reconnecting.

She'd just settled down to go over lines when he strode in with an amused expression. "Well, if it isn't America's Sweetheart."

She couldn't tell whether he was joking or being cynical.

Kelsey cocked her head to the side. "I hope you know I had nothing to do with that nickname."

Before he could respond, Ralph walked in. Colton disappeared backstage.

"I'm off to the lumberyard," Ralph called to him. "Anything else we need?"

"We're good, Ralph. Thanks for going."

As soon as he left, Kelsey heard Colton cry out in pain. She followed the sound and found him doubled over backstage, clutching his hand.

"What happened?" Kelsey rushed to him, alarmed.

He looked at her with a pained expression and held up his hands, one clasped over the other.

"I got myself with the staple gun." He winced, turning away, eyes squeezed shut. "I can't look, how bad is it?"

"Oh, my," Kelsey said, channeling her inner doctor. Not that she had one, but she had years of experience coming to Colton's aid over the many medical emergencies he'd suffered during his injury-prone childhood. "Let me grab some paper towels. I think Grand Lillian has a first aid kit too. Here—" she pulled a chair over and eased him into it, "—we don't need you fainting like you did in chorus."

Colton tried to smile. "I'm glad you haven't forgotten that."

Kelsey found the first aid kit, along with a bucket—Colton was famous for throwing up when he saw blood. She found an unopened water bottle and poured it out over his wound, then inspected his injury, finding two small puncture wounds.

Colton rocked in his chair with a look of profound nausea. Kelsey pushed the bucket closer to him with her foot.

"If you're gonna throw up, do it in there."

"I'm not gonna throw up," he grumbled.

"Does this mean you outgrew your famous vasovagal response?"

"Girl, playing football for as long as I have, you have to outgrow some things," he said, wincing. "I've seen guys' legs bend in ways they shouldn't. I've witnessed blood spurting from gaping head wounds, and—"

It looked as if he were choking back vomit.

"Bouncy cheerleaders, little kid fans, the roar of the crowd—" She tried to come up with the positives of the game to keep him from puking. It seemed to do the trick.

He swallowed hard and smiled up at her. "Thanks."

"Rough sport, but I bet there've been lots of highs along with it."

"Including having your shoulder ripped from its socket." He smirked. "Still haven't gotten over that one."

"I know," Kelsey said. It was the first time she'd acknowledged his injury. "I'm so sorry."

Colton was looking pale again, swallowing repeatedly.

"How's West Coast surfing?" Kelsey asked, once again trying to distract him as she cleaned his wound. "Better than East?"

"Definitely."

Colton had been surfing on the East Coast since he could walk. Same with Sarina, but the gene had missed Kelsey. The only surfing she'd ever done was during a movie shoot, with fake waves superimposed on the green screen behind her. Another fake-it-till-you-make-it scenario.

"What do you like about it?"

He reminisced about his California surfing experiences as she bandaged his wound. After a couple minutes, Kelsey noticed him going silent. When she looked up, she found him staring at her.

He gave her a half-smile. "You really missed your calling. Are you sure you're not a doctor?"

"No, but I played one onscreen."

"That's right. *Prognosis: Love.*"

Kelsey shot him a look. "You saw the movie?"

It was a Valentine's Day blockbuster rom-com, starring Kelsey as a doctor and Jaxon as a nurse who fell for each other in—where else?—the cardiac unit.

"Oh...I.." Colton stammered, as his cheeks flushed a

ruby red. "I saw the trailer on the internet one day. It just...started playing."

Dost thou protest too much?

"Alright, I saw it," he confessed.

"You did?" she asked, trying to hide a smile. "That's funny. I don't take you for a rom-com kinda guy."

"I wasn't, until my best friend started acting in them."

Her heart swelled to hear him acknowledge her in that way. "I'm touched, Colt." Smiling, she added, "I have to admit to catching a few games myself on TV."

"That's funny. I don't take you for a football kinda gal," he teased.

She was dying to ask if he'd seen all her movies but didn't. She was enjoying taking care of him and had dragged out his treatment session as long as she could, hoping she wasn't being too obvious about it.

"Okay, that should do it," she finally said.

"Am I gonna make it, Doc? Tell it to me straight."

"Too soon to know for sure, but I believe your chances of survival are pretty good."

"How good?"

"Eighty-twenty, as long as you stay away from those staple guns."

Their faces were so close, the instinct to kiss him so great, she had to physically back away to keep herself from doing it. Heart racing, passion coursing through her, she was instantly transported back to their unscripted stage kiss. She wondered if he was thinking the same thing.

He cleared his throat. "Thanks so much, Kelse. Appreciate you saving my life."

"It was touch and go there for a while. Thank God you pulled through."

"How can I ever repay you?"

She waved him off. "I think we're even. You certainly did

your fair share of caring for me over the years."

"Like that time you puked in the cafeteria?"

A reference to the time Kelsey had thrown up all over their lunch table in third grade. Everyone scattered, most screaming for dear life, but Colton had remained by her side, comforting her.

"You didn't take off like everyone else did," she noted.

"You were my friend. Friends don't take off on each other."

He raised an eyebrow at her, and Kelsey wondered if he was thinking about that night in the gazebo when she'd done just that. The night she took off on him, but with good reason.

She heard a door slam, reminding her this wasn't the time or place to get into it with him, despite a talk being long overdue.

He pointed to his bandaged hand. "Thanks for this."

"Alright, break it up," Grand Lillian's booming voice reached them before she did.

Mortified that her grandmother had witnessed their intimate moment, Kelsey's cheeks heated. She must look like a Jersey tomato—Colton certainly did. He took off in a flash, leaving behind veritable cartoon swoosh.

Molly

MOLLY ARRIVED AT MAX'S HOUSE THAT MORNING WITH coffee to thank him for his assistance over the past few days. And maybe to ask for more.

Pulling into the driveway, she saw him striding across the yard carrying a huge piece of lumber. The sleeves of his t-shirt revealed toned biceps, and his strong thighs strained against worn jeans as he set it down on a wooden frame.

She honked to let him know she was there. He strode over, removed his baseball cap, and bowed at the waist.

"Top 'o' the morning to you, Miss Grace. Mighty fine carriage you got there."

"This ol' thang?" Molly's pitch rose as she butchered a Southern accent. "Why bless your heart, Mr. Banks. It runs on something called gazzoleen."

They both laughed.

"Obviously, I'm not the actress in the family."

"No, but you're one heck of a golf cart driver."

"And delivery person. I brought you coffee." Molly handed him a cup and gestured to the wood. "Is that for one of my tables?"

"Yep, Colton and I started working on them the other day," he said, as he affixed his hat, this time backwards.

Oh boy. Molly was a sucker for a backwards baseball cap. She was taken aback by his eyes. It was the first time she'd seen him without glasses and didn't realize how dark they were. Like the black coffee she was drinking, almond-shaped with enviably long lashes. How had she missed this? Maybe Becca was on to something, crushing on him back then.

"*Mmm*, Sarina's coffee is the best. Beats that shitty *Jolt!* Any day." He took another sip as he placed his foot on the running board of the cart and leaned toward her. "Where are you off to today?"

Molly took a deep breath to ward off the warm feelings his look had stirred within her. "*We* are off to pick up the permit unanimously agreed to by the board last night. All thanks to you, Mr. Schmooze. After that, a Cape-wide hunt for donations, lunch at the theater, and finally the beach to stake out a place for the sand sculpting contest." She paused. "That is, if you can spare the time. I don't want to take you away from table-making."

"Not a problem, we're making good headway. I'm happy to

accompany you."

"Okay, then. Hop in, friend."

"So, we're still friends?" Max teased.

"I think you're stuck with me."

Molly was happy Max wanted to join her. Event planning was certainly more fun with him around. If someone had told her she and Maxwell Banks would become friends after graduation, she wouldn't have believed them. But they were simpatico, temporarily home for the summer, transitioning from a lifetime of institutionalized schedules to freewheeling in the big bad adult world.

Max climbed in and off they went, Molly smiling to herself over her newfound friendship.

Kelsey

After their intimate moment, Kelsey and Colton avoided making eye contact with one another for the rest of the day. Both proved to be good at avoiding physical proximity as well, which continued at lunch. Colton sat on the opposite side of the circle this time, concentrating on his meal like it was his last, not looking up once.

Except when Max entered from the wings, handing him his phone. "Your phone's ringing. You left it backstage. It's Ashley."

Kelsey glanced at Colton just as he shot her a look before scrambling to his feet. "'Scuse me, gotta take this."

Once again, Kelsey was reminded of their mutual childhood friend, the one who'd stolen his heart. They'd been in a serious relationship since. How foolish to assume her rediscovered feelings were being reciprocated.

Not then. Not now.

The memory of that fateful night in the gazebo brought back a flood of emotion. It was the night before he left their hometown for college football training camp, and they'd agreed to meet to say goodbye. She felt her heart drop as she approached the gazebo and caught a glimpse of him already waiting there, his toned physique silhouetted by the soft glow of gas lamps. She couldn't stand the thought that this would be the last time she saw him for a long time. Her childhood friend, her first crush. With all the media hype over the start of his college football career, she had no idea when she'd see him next. It didn't help that their schools were on either side of the continent.

"Hey." His expression was somber, his tone hinting of the same emotions she'd been battling all day.

Forgetting he had a girlfriend, she wrapped her arms around his waist and rested her head on his chest. He held her there for a while, his heart thumping against her ear.

"That's better," he said as he pulled away, his tone lightening. "I've missed you."

Since that day in the diner, she'd found ways to conveniently be busy whenever he suggested they get together. It was what a *good girl* would do. Now that he was dating Ashley, she felt it inappropriate to hang out with him as much as they once had.

Beyond that, she was having a hard time containing her feelings of jealousy and remorse over being the one who'd pushed them together. Those last few grueling months of high school were, perhaps, the first time she learned how valuable facades could be—pretending you didn't care when, inside, your heart was crushed.

"What gives?" he asked softly, aqua eyes probing. "Where ya been, friend?"

She shrugged. "I've just been—busy. Getting ready for

school, seeing fam, you know."

"I thought maybe you were mad at me for something."

She shook her head. Mad wasn't exactly the right word.

"You sure?" he asked. "I kinda feel like you've been blowing me off."

"Sorry if my life isn't revolving around you anymore," she joked, although it sounded meaner than she'd intended.

His jaw tightened. "Come, sit. Talk to me." He took her hand and led her to a bench. "How are you feeling about—you know. School. Leaving. *Everything*."

"Nervous. Sad, a bit. Mostly excited. How about you?"

"Same."

"How are Max and your dad doing with you going away?"

"Max has been crying all week, but my dad's totally pumped. Me playing college ball is his dream."

Kelsey wondered why his eyes clouded over. "Is it your dream, Colton?" she asked softly.

He chuckled. "It better be, seeing as I'll be running around USC's football field tomorrow afternoon."

Kelsey stopped herself from prying further. Like he said, it was happening whether it was his "dream" or not. "Promise me you're not going to let the fame go to your head."

"I won't. I'm just a South Jersey boy, playing ball with some friends."

"Every Saturday."

"Right."

"On national TV."

"Don't remind me."

Kelsey knew him well enough to know that, while he loved playing the game, he wasn't in it for fame and glory. She was worried about him being cast into a national spotlight in a way he might not be ready for.

"No matter what happens with your career, don't forget who you are and where you came from. Don't forget Colton

Banks, the boy I'm—" She stopped herself before saying the unthinkable. "The boy I know so well."

"Aww, Kelse..." He wrapped his arm around her. "I promise I won't."

She turned to face him. He leaned in so close she could feel his minty breath on her skin. He blinked, his expression going serious.

"*Kiss me.*"

It was so out of character for her, she wasn't certain if she'd actually said the words or just thought them. All she knew was that she wanted to feel his lips on hers one more time. It was horrible of her, she knew—he was with her *friend*, for goodness' sake—but she needed to know if he'd felt the same way she had after their kiss.

He curled a finger and lifted her chin. "Kelse..."

Their lips were so close, she could almost taste her name.

He suddenly pulled back. Exhaling, he pressed his fingertips to his temples. "I can't."

"Can't...or won't?"

"Our friendship..."

"That didn't seem to stop you on stage."

"I know. I'm so sorry about that."

She looked directly in his eyes. It was now or never. Praying for Ashley's forgiveness, she stepped off the ledge she'd been teetering on for months.

"*I'm* not sorry."

His gaze snapped to hers—so many questions contained within its depths. Sighing, he leaned back as he closed his eyes. His voice came out so faint, she hardly heard it.

"It was a mistake."

She recoiled. He may as well have slapped her across the face. "A mistake?"

He gave a frustrated grunt as he opened his eyes. "You know what I mean. I got caught up in the role. I shouldn't have done that to you."

"I wouldn't be asking you to do it again if I didn't want it."

"Oh, God..." He deflated, as if he were about to give in. Instead, he leaped from the bench. "No. I can't. I'm with Ashley now."

Thrusting his hands on his hips in apparent frustration, his back to her, he looked to the ceiling before he suddenly pivoted. "Isn't that what you wanted?"

It wasn't so much the words he said as his tone. Unmistakably harsh, laden with sarcasm, matching his pointed stare.

Of course it's not what she wanted. She'd only thrown Ashley at him because—well, lots of reasons. Ashley had liked him first, or at least had *voiced* her feelings for him first. But beyond that, Colton was out of Kelsey's league, and she knew it. He was handsome, talented, and could have any woman he wanted. Why would he want her? She was awkward, shy, and nothing like the type of trophy girlfriend who could land a handsome college quarterback. Isn't that what the recruiter had told him? *Get yourself a good-looking girlfriend.* A category in which Kelsey didn't belong, but which Ashley did.

But ever since the two had started dating, she'd been filled with regret, wishing she hadn't told Colton about Ashley's crush. Of course, he'd be interested once he found out. Who could blame him? She was beautiful, sweet, and fun to be with. It took them no time to become the most talked-about couple as they strolled hand-in-hand through the halls of their high school. As Kelsey had predicted: *famous football guy, perky blonde cheerleader. A winning combination.*

Yet the memory of their onstage kiss still haunted her, the feeling of his lips on hers still lingered. Despite Colton's assertion that the kiss was character-driven, Kelsey couldn't help but wonder where his character ended and he began. It had been too sweet a moment to have been just about the play.

"This *is* what you wanted, right?" he repeated when she didn't answer.

She struggled to take a deep breath. She wanted to scream, "No!" but she was hit by a tsunami of guilt. For betraying her friend, and for betraying *herself*. She wasn't the type of person to kiss someone else's boyfriend.

So instead of answering his question directly, she asked one of her own. "Are you in love with her?"

Not that she really wanted to hear his answer.

He looked down at his Nikes for a long time before raising sad eyes. His expression, cast in silent sheepishness, told her all she needed to know.

She jumped up and brushed past him. He reached for her arm but missed.

"Kelsey, wait..."

But her tears were well on their way to becoming full-fledged sobs. She took off running before he could see her reaction.

"Kelse, please—I didn't realize—I need to—"

She didn't catch every word as his voice was tossed by the breeze. What did it matter? Through his body language, the regretful tone of his voice, his message was loud and clear.

He was in love with Ashley. And she had no one to blame but herself.

Colton

COLTON COULDN'T BELIEVE THE CALMING EFFECT Kelsey'd had on him as she bandaged his wound that morning. She just knew how to make him feel better, like no one else ever had, despite everything—geographical distance, other partners, and not having spoken for so long.

She also knew how to make him want to kiss her.

He recalled that fateful night in the gazebo, before they'd gone off to college. He'd just started dating Ashley, at Kelsey's insistence. Which is what had made it all so confusing when she'd asked him to kiss her that night. Up to that point, she'd acted as if she wanted nothing to do with him romantically. She was the one who pushed him and Ashley together, making it clear she wasn't interested in him. Of course he'd wanted to kiss Kelsey in the gazebo, but he wasn't that kind of a guy. He wouldn't do that to Ashley—even if his heart had always belonged to her best friend.

He'd been caught off guard when Kelsey asked if he loved Ashley. On some level he did—he was, after all, a teen boy with raging hormones, dating the most popular girl in school. He'd gotten caught up in the stardom of it all, especially after being named *Cutest Couple* for their senior superlatives. They'd been friends since middle school. But friend love and romantic love, it turned out, were two different things. He just hadn't known that at the time.

When Kelsey took off, he'd called after her. "Kelse, please! I didn't realize you felt that way about me. Please come back—I need to tell you the truth..."

But she ignored him and kept going.

Later that night, he realized his feelings for Kelsey had been building for so long, they weren't going to simply disappear just because he'd started dating someone else. They were real, ingrained in him, born from a lifetime of knowing someone to the core. She clearly didn't feel the same, or she would have come back when he promised her the truth. The only way he figured he could move on was to get the feelings out, put them into words on paper and shove them away for good. He did just that when he got home that night—wrote them down and stuffed them into a lidded box under his bed—in hopes the physical act of putting them away would manifest emotional results.

Apparently it hadn't.

What he felt today, looking up at Kelsey as she bandaged his hand, was of the same intensity he'd felt back on stage when he kissed her. The urge came on like a freight train. Maybe because it had been the kiss of a lifetime. He knew, because he'd never felt such passion since, even with his girlfriend, in their ten years together.

Make that, ex-girlfriend.

Ashley had broken up with him shortly after his injury. For the most part it was mutual—they'd been together since the end of high school, and both agreed they'd long since lost the flame. More than anything, their relationship had become a matter of convenience, having attended the same college and moving to Cali together after Colton was signed to the NFL. But shared real estate was about the only thing they had in common.

That, and a golden retriever puppy they'd rescued right after he got signed. They'd named her Cadence, as a nod to the play call quarterbacks make before the ball is snapped. While he'd never admit it to anyone, Ashley breaking up with him was nothing compared to the heartache he felt having to leave Cadence in California.

Thankfully, it was only temporary. Both he and Ashley agreed she'd keep the dog while Colton settled the estate. There would be so much to do, Colton wouldn't have the time to tend to her, play with her, or walk her like he'd want to. Especially when he'd only be in Cape May for a short while before he moved on. Both agreed it would be traumatic to move Cadence twice—clear across the country, then up to Montana—especially because, as a rescue, she had a hard time adjusting to new situations. Still, it broke Colton's heart leaving her behind. As a result, Ashley agreed to routinely FaceTime Colton so he and Cady could "talk." Reuniting with his beloved pup was the other driving force behind him wanting to offload the property as soon as humanly possible.

Max was the only person Colton had told about their breakup. His buddies all found out when Ashley showed up at an after-party on the arm of their mutual good friend and teammate shortly after Colton's injury, proving what he'd suspected all along—Ashley was more enamored of Colton's football career than she was of him.

Her phone call during their lunch break had been unexpected and alarming. Normally, he wouldn't take her call, especially when hanging out with the theater crew, but Cadence had been sick lately, and he wanted to make sure she was alright. Ashley had called to say she needed surgery the following morning. He asked her to keep him updated.

Molly

MOLLY AND MAX ENJOYED ANOTHER PRODUCTIVE DAY of fundraiser prep. After lunch at the theater, they headed to the beach, where they found a crowd gathering around a dark lump at water's edge.

"Oh, no!" Max jumped from the cart before she even had a chance to park.

Molly ran to catch up to him. "Please tell me that's not a person."

"Worse," Max said, his pace quickening as he strode toward the gathering crowd. "Looks like a dolphin washed ashore."

He was right.

"Okay, guys, I'm gonna need you to stand aside," Max said in an authoritarian tone to the crowd, who appeared to be attempting to return it to the water. He knelt beside the struggling animal.

"Shouldn't we put him back in the water?" someone asked.

"No, they beach because they can't navigate out of the surf zone due to sickness or injury. If we send him back, he'll only beach again. He needs help before he's returned to the water."

Molly, too, believed returning the animal to the ocean was the humane thing to do. She was duly impressed by Max's knowledge.

"It's gonna be okay, buddy," Max whispered as he stroked the animal's belly with one hand and made a call on his phone with the other. "Hey, it's Max. I have a stranded dolphin on Jackson Street beach." After exchanging a few more words with the person on the other end, he hung up and turned to the crowd. "I work at the Marine Mammal Stranding Center. They're on their way."

Max asked if anyone had a beach towel to keep the dolphin covered. Several were offered up. Molly took them to the water's edge to get them wet and handed them to Max.

"Is that so he can sleep?" a child asked.

"It's to keep him from getting sunburned. Just like us, they need protection from the sun when they're on the beach."

"My mom has sunscreen! I can go get it if you want."

Max couldn't hide the smile tugging at his lips. "That's really nice of you to offer. They don't use sunscreen, but wet towels work well. If you'd like to help, how about filling a bucket with water so we can keep his towel from drying out?"

The kid took off running for a bucket, followed by several other children. Molly jumped in to help with the kid bucket brigade, while Max tended to the dolphin and answered questions. Before long, a rescue vehicle arrived filled with several trained volunteers, who loaded the wounded animal into a tank.

"I'm gonna go with these guys to help out. Wanna come?" he asked Molly.

Without hesitation, she joined him in the back of the truck. The only time she'd been to the Stranding Center was in seventh grade for a field trip. She was curious to know what they'd do for their dolphin friend.

At the center, Max and the guys lifted the gurney and took the dolphin inside to a waiting ICU tank. Molly waited in the lobby until he finally returned.

"How is he?" Molly asked.

"The vet seems to think he'll be okay."

"That's such a relief. Thank God you were there and knew just what to do. You saved his life!"

"Well, maybe. It's part of what I'll be doing with my degree, so it was good practice."

Molly was amazed by Max's cool and confident manner, combined with his obvious knowledge and dedication.

"Do you remember coming here in seventh grade?" Max asked. "Best field trip of my life. That's when I decided for sure I wanted to be a marine biologist."

"Coming from someone who lacks 'porpoise,' I'm not sure whether to be impressed or jealous. Maybe both."

"You seem to have quite a 'porpoise' when it comes to fundraising," Max said. "Look at all you're doing for this event. I'm the one who's impressed." Max held her gaze for a moment before he clapped his hands and rubbed them together. "How about a tour? I can show you what I'll most likely be doing after grad school."

"I'd love it. Is this where you hope to work?"

"Here or any marine facility that'll have me. But since I'm going to school in New England, I'll likely end up in that area."

"Oh." She was surprised by her disappointment.

Max led her around the center and showed her what each of the rooms was for. After their tour, one of the guys from the rescue team dropped them back off at the beach, where dark gray clouds swirled above. The waves stacked high, crashing violently against the sand as winds whipped in warning of the approaching storm.

"I'm in awe of the ocean when it's like this," Molly said as the wind lifted and tossed her long hair into a tempest of curls.

"Look, you're a modern-day Medusa," Max said, grabbing at one and missing.

"Hisssss!" Molly joked, shaking a curl at Max.

"Don't look at me!" he joked as he held his forearms in front of his eyes. "Please, don't turn me to stone!"

"Look at me, look at me!" Molly said, a monstrous tone to her voice. She pulled at Max's wrists, widening her eyes at him as if casting her spell, but something came over her. She found it hard to look away from his beautiful dark eyes, his wide grin, his perfectly straight teeth. It was as if he'd flipped the spell and turned *her* to stone. Damn backwards hat.

"Staring contest. Starting now," she challenged, blinking seconds later. "Aw, you got me."

"Don't ever take me on in a staring contest and think you'll win," Max said. "I'm the reigning champ of Harvard's Varsity Staring team."

"Sand got in my eye."

"That's what they always say."

They sat on the windswept beach in silence, watching the tumultuous sea display its graceful wrath.

"The ocean's sheer power never ceases to amaze me," Max said.

Molly glanced over, taking in his perfect profile. It was fascinating to watch him in his element—earlier, with the dolphin rescue, and now, gazing at the very thing he would dedicate his career to. He was deep, like the sea itself. Multifaceted. So very different from the alpha males Brennan and his friends presented as.

Molly had been thrilled to be invited into their inner circle, basking in the glow of being "Brennan's Girl." Spending summers in his family's oceanfront mansion in the dunes of Avalon, vicariously enjoying their wealthy lifestyle. It was a sweet life Brennan promised, full of opulence and grandeur, along with the security of being a part of something bigger and more glamorous than the life she'd been handed. He'd certainly fulfilled a deep-seated need she'd had at sixteen—a need for acceptance, a sense of belonging.

But now, on the cusp of twenty-two, she wondered if those needs still existed.

Dwelling in Brennan's shadow for so long, she'd never had the opportunity to shine her own light. Now, thanks to the distance he'd created between them, she was starting to see her life through a different lens. Discovering how her star could shine on its own, she basked in its glow.

The friendship offered by this simple man sitting next to her, devoid of pretense, certainly helped. It was so easy being in his presence, the way they bantered and laughed, the way she'd emoted all over him the other day, and now, how they sat together in comfortable silence. Giving her space to shine without overshadowing her, Max truly brought out the best in her.

She shivered against a sudden wind gust, and he leaned in, wrapping his arm around her. Laying her head on his shoulder, they continued to sit in silence, staring at the sea. Suddenly, a flash of light lit the sky, followed by a loud crack.

"We should bolt, before we get hit by one." Max stood and helped her up.

"I haven't felt this calm in such a long time," she said with a sleepy smile as they returned to the golf cart.

"I've thoroughly enjoyed myself today."

"Me too. I could get used to hanging out with you, Maxwell Banks. You make a nice friend."

He gave her a smile, his eyes shadowed in disappointment. "You too, Molly Grace," he said quietly. "A mighty nice...*friend*."

She understood the letdown in his tone.

Max

After meeting with beach patrol about the sand sculpting contest they were planning as part of the fundraising event, Molly and Max headed to the inner Cape for their next stop. They were passing a vineyard when Molly received a call.

"Hey," she answered. Pulling over, she turned off the engine and got out of the cart, walking away to continue the conversation.

From the tone of her voice, Max assumed it was *my boyfriend*. The smile she wore as she answered the call instantly chilled the warm vibe Max had gotten from their time together on the beach.

As hard as it was to peel his gaze away from Molly, standing there in her pale-yellow sundress, sunlight dancing off her honeyed hair as she chatted animatedly, he did so out of deference to her privacy. But he sensed a sudden shift in the nature of the call when Molly's voice rose. She was far enough away he couldn't hear her words, but he could pick up on her tone, which had gone from light and airy to annoyed and defensive.

He pretended not to watch as she paced back and forth between rows of grapevines, tension and frustration evident in her posture. Their eyes met, and she made a blabbing gesture with her hand. *My boyfriend* must have been on some sort of rant, judging by Molly's lengthy silences punctuated by animated gestures, like throwing her hand up in exasperation as she turned and paced in the other direction. Max looked away, not wanting to appear interested (gleeful?) that they were fighting.

When the phone call ended, Molly marched back to the golf cart, groaning as she climbed in.

"Everything okay?" he asked.

"I don't know."

"Wanna talk about it?"

"No."

Turning the key in the ignition, she peeled away. The sudden movement almost sent Max tipping out of the side of the golf cart, so he held on for dear life as she gunned the machine. Unfortunately for Molly and her need for rage-filled speed, the cart puttered along at twenty miles an hour—which didn't have the same allure as would speeding away at sixty miles an hour in an angry huff.

Half a mile later, she pulled over and flipped the engine off as she turned to Max. "Actually, yes. I could use the opinion of a normal, healthy male."

"I got a guy. Shall I call him?"

"You're about as normal and healthy as they come. You'll do just fine."

He'd take it.

"Let's say you've dated someone for six years, and you're about to move in together. Do you involve her in apartment hunting?"

"Of course," Max said without hesitation.

"Not *my* boyfriend. He just informed me he found a place."

"Without you?"

"Yep. Never mind the fact it's gonna be my home, too, since we'll be engaged soon."

Damn. Max had no idea they were close to engagement. She could have left that part out, for the gut punch it delivered.

"We were supposed to find a place together, but he's been too busy on the weekends, and he wanted me to find a job first. Which I've been trying to do. Then, suddenly, he goes out looking without me. He couldn't even wait until next week when I could get there. Not only did he find something on his own, but he put a deposit down."

"Refundable?"

"Non."

"Huh." Max pressed his lips together to keep from blurting out the words "red" and "flag." Instead, he set aside his incredulousness and tried to put himself in Brennan's shoes so he could give Molly constructive feedback. It seemed that's what she needed more than criticism.

"He probably knows you'll like it, and had to act immediately so he wouldn't lose it."

"You think?" Molly asked, her eyes wide as if trusting him to decipher the Manhattan rental market along with evasive male behavior.

"Maybe?" He shrugged. "What do *you* think? You know him best."

"I honestly don't know, Max. I feel like we're not on the same page. I looked forward to us finding a place and exploring city life together, but he's forging ahead without me."

"I would think doing that together would be fun."

Max could just imagine the fun he'd have with Molly, exploring a new city together. Heck, riding around on the golf cart in their hometown was the most fun he'd had in a very long time. He wondered if there was another reason Brennan wasn't eager for Molly to join him. It sounded like some bullshit, but he didn't want to alarm her. Especially since people tended to blame the messenger.

She signed. "In his defense, I know he's stressed about everything."

Max wondered how stressed one would have to be to make her feel like an afterthought. Never having been in a serious relationship before, Max knew little about the dynamics. But he did know the feelings he'd had for Molly for the past decade, and there was nothing that would stop him from wanting to be with her all the time, feeling grateful for her presence in his life, honored he got to wake up next to her every morning. Even if it was in a cardboard box.

"What's he stressed about?" Max asked, hoping his tone didn't convey his disbelief.

"New job, new city. I get that it's hard, with all this transition."

All this transition? What, was the guy going from Himalayan Sherpa to Manhattan businessman?

"I'm sorry to vent to you like this. I don't feel like I have anyone to talk to. My sisters don't like him."

"But *you* do, and that's all that matters." He couldn't help but ask the next question. "So, what is it you like about him?"

"I love him, for one."

"I mean *like* about him. It's easy to love someone you've been with for so long. But do you *like* the person he is? The person *you* are when you're around him?"

"On the surface, yes. He's just my physical type. And, you know—he not only comes from money, but he makes good money as well."

Max waited for Molly to put forth more reasons, but she remained silent.

Was that it? She liked him for his looks and money?

He shook his head, not so much from disbelief, but to keep the word *shallow* from echoing in his head. He didn't want to see Molly in that light, but...

"Looks are genetic, and money can be made," he said. "That says something about his family and employability, but what about *him*?"

"He's...smart. Not *you* smart, but smart enough to land a good job. He's nice, you know that. And he's funny. Not funny like you, taking mundane things and making them laughable."

"Like my love life."

"Stop!" Molly punched him playfully. "I think we need to

correct that. I have thoughts."

He waited for her to share her thoughts, but she was back on the Brennan thing.

"It's like there's been a huge power shift ever since he got this job in New York, and now he gets to pick our apartment and tell me when I can move in. Meanwhile, I'm down here slinging coffee and slapping pork roll onto bagels. I get he's this bigwig making six figures, but that's no reason to treat me like I'm not important."

"Wait. Can we go back to his salary? Six figures—are you for real?"

"Yes. Can you believe it?"

"Right out of college."

"Yeah."

"Hmph." Max looked skyward. "I am definitely going into the wrong field."

"No, you're doing something good for our planet."

"I could do a lot more with six figures. I should find me a Brennan."

Molly laughed. "Yeah, the money doesn't hurt. I know he loves me, and I love him. We've been talking about getting engaged for two years now. He said he wanted to wait for a special occasion and with my birthday being Saturday..."

The look on Molly's face just then shattered him. Full of hope, yet vulnerable and sad. While he'd love to encourage Molly to further question Brennan's motives, it wasn't in Max's nature to diss another person. He didn't have a competitive bone in his body, except for academics. Even then, the only person he competed with was himself. Most of all, he'd do anything to keep from making her feel worse.

"We're all facing a lot of changes right now, graduating college and heading into our new lives," Max offered.

"True. He has a lot on his plate."

Yes. A six-figure job, a new life in Manhattan, and a

gorgeous girlfriend who can't wait to spend her life with him. What a guy, putting up with all that.

"Just...trust the process," Max found himself saying. The *process*? What the hell could that possibly mean? Meet Molly, fall in love, spend the rest of your life with her. Seems pretty simple, no process necessary.

Molly sighed, sounding relieved. "You're right. Thanks, Max. I really appreciate you talking to me about this."

"It's what friends do, Moll. I'm here for you."

"Good," she said, casting a teasing glance his way. "I could think of worse things than that."

Max laughed. "Like?"

"Scabies, poison ivy, someone vomiting on your shoe," she said as she steered back onto the road.

"Very funny."

"Lice infestation, a mouse running up your pant leg, tsunamis..."

"Okay, smartass. I think we get it."

Later that night, as Max recalled their conversation, he felt uneasy. He'd always viewed Molly as strong, intelligent, in control. But he'd seen a different side of her that day. Not quite the self-assured version of her he'd come to know but, instead, vulnerable and trusting, perhaps to a fault. He hated seeing her question the feelings of a man she was about to spend her life with. She deserved better than that.

Both from the guy, and herself.

Kelsey

GRAND LILLIAN APPROACHED KELSEY THAT AFTERNOON. "I saw you and Colton warming up to each other this morning. I'm assuming you've resolved whatever's going on there?"

"He hurt himself and I was helping him."

"Well, I need your help, too."

"With what?"

"The arts center land was recently purchased by a private owner who wants to sell it to a developer."

"I thought the town owned the land. Isn't that one of the reasons for the fundraiser, to rebuild the center where it is?"

"Yes. That's why I need you to stop the sale."

"Me?" She laughed. "How do you propose I do that?"

"Ask him."

"Oh right, like I'm just supposed to call this stranger and beg him not the sell the land because we want to use it for our own recreational purposes?"

"He's not a stranger. It's the man whose hand you just bandaged."

Kelsey almost fell over backwards. "Colton Banks bought the arts center property?"

"His dad bought it, shortly before his death."

"Why?"

"Nobody knows. Roger called me the day before he died and asked if we could meet the following week to discuss the future of the center. Obviously, that never happened. You have to find a way to stop your beau from selling out."

Kelsey laughed out loud, envisioning herself strapped to the For Sale sign, screaming, *With God as my witness, this land won't be sold.*

"Why can't you? Has someone suddenly stripped you of your witch-like power over others?"

"Of course not. I just don't possess the same brand you do."

"I have no power over Colton Banks."

"That's not what it looked like to me." Grand Lillian raised an eyebrow over her steely gaze. "Please. It'll be more compelling coming from you. The two of you spent so much of your childhoods there, and I know how much it meant to both of you. Unless..."

"Unless what?"

"You offer to buy the land from him."

Kelsey's eyes widened. "I love the arts center, but I'm twenty-eight, single, and live in LA. New Jersey land ownership is the very last thing on my mind."

"Then you have some convincing to do."

Kelsey crossed her arms. "Pretend I was to go along with this plan of yours. How do I convince him not to sell?"

"Like this," her grandmother said, smiling. "Close your eyes. What are your best childhood memories of the arts center?"

Kelsey played along, summoning memories of summer camp and after-school programs. The center was where she'd learned to play piano and act, where Sarina had learned to paint, and Molly to dance. Eating homemade popsicles in the forts they built from sticks and sheets. Snow days and snowball fights. Holidays, making ornaments and learning to bake cookies. She could still smell them. The memories brought a smile to her face.

"My gosh, we did a lot there. It was so much more than an arts center. It was warm and homey, like—" Kelsey's eyes flew open. "Like a grandmother's home."

"Exactly!" Lillian clapped, her voice excitedly hushed. "It *was* my home, figuratively speaking. With any luck, it'll continue to be. *That's* how you convince Colton. You talk about the old times you two used to share there. You draw upon your inner actress like you just did. You're Kelsey Grace. You can convince anyone of anything."

She wished she had as much faith in herself as Grand Lil did. But yes, for the arts center and her beloved grandmother, she would talk to Colton and see if she could convince him not to sell. The arts center had made her the person she was, someone she'd long ago forgotten. It was time to give back to the place that had made her. Time to get back to *her*. The real Kelsey Grace.

Colton

AFTER LEAVING THE THEATER, COLTON WENT FOR A WALK to clear his head about everything that had happened in the past twenty-four hours—learning he and Max now owned the arts center land, Cady's upcoming surgery, Kelsey tending to his injury. Mostly that part. The warmth of her hands, the sweet smell of her. The way his heart beat faster than it had in months. Years, even.

Walking along the promenade, he saw a group of boys playing football on the beach. One of the kids called to him.

"Colton Banks! Hey, guys, it's Colton Banks, my favorite player!"

Suddenly, Colton found himself surrounded by a pack of tiny football players. One kid asked if he'd sign his football.

"Oh, man I don't have a—"

"I do. Hold on a sec," said one of the fathers, who went to his car and returned with a Sharpie.

Colton wrote a personal message to the ball owner while the other kids scrambled to find something of theirs he could sign. A baseball cap. A beach bucket. A seashell. Even the t-shirts they wore.

He was happy to oblige. It had been a minute since anyone had asked for his autograph.

The boys asked Colton to show them how to improve their techniques, so he gave them some tips. Afterwards, they gathered around and lobbed questions at him—what it was like to play for the NFL, how much money he made, and what kind of car he drove.

"You don't have to answer any of that," another father said as he joined them. "Although I'd love to know about the car."

"Chevy pickup," Colton said, giving him a smile. "Farm boy at heart."

The adults laughed.

Colton was happy to answer the questions of the eager crowd. It was the first time in a long time he'd felt bigger than his injury and his failed career.

Until one of the moms inquired about his love life.

"Are you still dating that cheerleader, the local girl you went to college with?"

Colton blushed. He was about to answer when a divine act of intervention occurred.

The ice cream man.

Like seagulls to an open potato chip bag, the boys fled toward the truck in mass pandemonium, screaming all the way.

"Sorry, I have to head out," he said to the parents who remained.

One man offered him a handshake. "Mr. Banks, I really appreciate you spending your time with these guys. It means the world to them."

"It was my pleasure," Colton said, meaning it. "They're a great group of kids."

"Are you back in town for good? We'd love to have you coach our Mighty Mites team. It would be our honor to have you work with them."

Colton smiled as he reminisced. "I remember those days. That's where I learned to play. Unfortunately, I'm not staying in Cape May. I'm—"

"Oh, of course," the man said. "Going back to California."

There was no way he was returning there, but he didn't need to share that with complete strangers.

As he climbed back into his truck, he felt validated. The offer to coach those kids had lit a tiny flicker in his belly. Of... something. Hope, perhaps. Interest in something other than the tragic trajectory of his life, something he hadn't felt for quite some time. Maybe there was a future for an injured ex-NFL player—helping to shape future ones. Minus the injured ex part.

Then again, that would require staying here in Cape May, something he wasn't willing to do. Perhaps there'd be a similar opportunity in his future hometown, wherever that may be, assuming he wasn't so far off the grid he'd have to travel miles to even find kids to coach.

When Colton got home, he found Max in the barn, going through boxes.

"Hey, I wanted to let you know I spoke to Luke," he told his brother. "The development company wants both parcels of land, badly. If you're truly okay with it, I'd like to close the deal."

"Have they made an offer yet?"

"Their starting bid for the farm was two million. I'm waiting to hear what they're offering in addition to that for the arts center property."

"Dude!" Max exclaimed. "Holy shit. That's over asking price for the farm alone. I never would've guessed it was worth that much."

"Dad kept the farm in good working order. God only knows what he was doing with the other property. According to Fred, that's where he was, lifting a heavy piece of wood, when his heart attack occurred. It was probably too much, caring for both." Colton felt a dagger of guilt slice through his own heart. "I should have been here, Max. I should have come home right after my injury and helped him out."

"You can't blame yourself, Colt. You weren't in any kind of shape yourself for manual labor. And we had no way of knowing that was going to happen. In all regards, he appeared to be totally healthy."

It was true. Their dad was in excellent physical shape and led a healthy lifestyle.

"I don't know what they'll offer for the arts center, but I've decided all the proceeds for both parcels will go to you."

Max laughed out loud. "You can't be serious."

"I am."

"We should split it, Colton. That's only fair."

"I don't want to split it. I'm set, financially. I want to make sure you are."

"That's more than I'll need."

"Then donate the rest to charity."

"Not a bad idea. This farm's been in our family for centuries. We should do something to honor that legacy. You know how passionate Mom and Dad were about the environment—maybe something in that vein."

"Whatever you want to do is fine with me. My job is to get you the most amount I can. Beyond that, it's up to you."

"Except..." Max hesitated. "How contradictory is that? Selling to a development company, who's gonna disrupt the environment, then donating to an environmental cause."

"Maybe that would help to lessen the affect?"

"I'll have to give it some thought," Max said.

"Alright. I'm meeting with the developers tomorrow, so I'll get more details then."

Kelsey

KELSEY DECIDED TO TAKE AN EVENING BIKE RIDE BEFORE the rain came. Riding through the backroads of the Cape's wooded interior was liberating. It was one reason she loved coming home—getting out in nature.

She ended up at the arts center. She'd purposely been avoiding it until now, but somehow her legs pedaled her there. As though they knew she needed to witness it for herself.

Big mistake. She was horrified to see just how badly the storm had damaged the building, snapping and tossing century-old wood, scattering it across the property. While part of the building remained intact, most of it was beyond repair. A tear rolled down her cheek as she recalled her conversation with her grandmother about all the good times she'd had there.

Something off in the corner of the property caught her eye. It was the treehouse swing set Colton had designed and built with his dad, the summer before he left for college. It was his parting gift to his hometown, a place for kids to play. The structure had remained standing, tall and proud, untouched by the storm.

She paused, contemplating her next move. Should she? Shouldn't she?

Compelled by her conversation with Grand Lil, Kelsey turned her handlebars toward Seashore Road and coasted onto the crushed shell driveway of Colton's farm. Noticing the screen door was open, she stepped onto the porch.

"Hello?" she called out.

"Kelsey?"

She turned to see Colton striding across the front lawn. He wore a confused grin as he took the porch steps by two. "What's up?"

"I was just riding by, and I wanted to see if you needed any help?"

Colton hitched an eyebrow, his eyes twinkling with amusement. "We're done working for the night, but you're more than welcome to... Here. Sit." He motioned to the large porch swing. "Can I get you something to drink? Iced tea, perhaps?"

He seemed nervous, uncertain how to act. It made her giggle.

"Only if it's your mom's famous sun brew."

"It's the only thing we serve here. Be right back."

Kelsey looked around the front lawn of the Banks farmhouse, recalling childhood summers spent playing there. A faded tire swing spun slowly from a branch of the grand oak tree. The patch of grass once worn away by children's feet had long since grown back. As had the shortcut path from the road—the one Kelsey made with her bike tires, unable to ride an additional three seconds up the driveway. She felt sad, seeing the physical evidence of just how much things had changed in the time since she and Colton had been in each other's lives.

A light breeze meandered across the lawn, lifting the hem of her sundress, sweeping through her long hair. Its cooling effect helped to calm her racing heart.

Colton returned with two iced teas, a bowl of grapes, and a box of Cheez-Its. Their favorite summer snack. "Didn't know if you were hungry, so I brought these just in case. Dinner of champs, right?"

"A.k.a. girl dinner," she said, chuckled. "You don't know how many nights this is what I eat."

There was something comforting about the combination. Maybe the past.

"Good memories." They both said it in unison. Laughing, they clinked their glasses.

He settled on the porch swing next to her as she nervously tapped her fingernails on the side of her glass. Colton gently rocked the swing back and forth, feet planted firmly on the ground. Kelsey tried to join in the swinging, but her toes barely reached the chipped-paint floor of the old wooden porch.

Dusk settled around them as the cicadas came out for their mating calls under the glow of fireflies. Suddenly nervous about his potential reaction, she searched for something benign to talk about before she launched into her pitch. It seemed strange to be here, in his silent presence, yet at the same time it felt natural, familiar.

"I can't believe your mom's flower garden is still going strong," Kelsey said, noting the patch of yard in which a bountiful rainbow of wildflowers grew.

"Thanks to my dad," Colton said. "I don't know if you remember, but the spring after my mom died, that whole patch was overrun with dead weeds. Max and I begged him to take the fencing down and plant grass so we could play baseball there."

"I remember."

"He refused, obviously." A slow smile crept across his face. "I don't blame him now, as an adult, because weeks later, the flowers grew back in full force. Apparently, she'd only planted perennials, knowing they'd return each year. Kind of like a parting gift."

They sat in silence until she broke it.

"You're probably wondering why I'm here."

"It's not for the Cheez-Its?" Colton joked.

"Oh, it's always for the Cheez-Its. And, well..." She breathed a heavy sigh. "I've been told you've inherited the arts center land."

"News travels fast, I see."

"Yeah. And I've been sent to appeal to your better, more artistic senses." She looked up and their eyes met. "In other words, please don't sell that land."

"Oh, man," Colton tittered, shaking his head in feigned disbelief. "And here, I thought you came to offer me a role in your next movie."

"Well, that too. But first things first. Is it true a developer may purchase it?"

"Yeah, that's the plan," Colton said, looking straight ahead.

"But if that happens, won't they use the land for commercial purposes?"

"I guess," Colton said, looking down as he squished a mosquito with his foot. "But I can't control what they do with the land once they purchase it, Kelse. You know that."

"That's why I—and my family—are asking you not to sell."

Colton's jaw tightened. "It's not that easy."

"What's not easy about it? Don't you think future generations of kids deserve the same experiences we had?"

"Of course they do, and they'll have them. Just in another location."

"But that's where it's always been, a perfect spot nestled here in the middle of the Cape, away from the touristy stuff. Perfect place for local kids to come and hang out, especially in summer, climb the treehouse you and your dad built, swing on the swings and play in the big yard. Just like we did."

"Kelsey, the building's been destroyed by the storm. Its remains will have to be torn down and the whole thing rebuilt, which'll cost a lot of money. Isn't it easier to move the program to an already existing building with more space?"

"No, because rebuilding it from the ground up allows us to put in whatever we want. I'm envisioning a state-of-the-art performing arts theater and a couple dance studios. Visual arts studios for painting, pottery, sculpting. And an industrial-sized kitchen for cooking lessons, so the after-school kids can learn how to cook for their work-weary parents."

He sighed. "I'm sorry, I just—"

"Let me buy it."

Her emphatic assertion came as a surprise even to her, having gone from *no interest in land ownership* to making her impetuous offer. But after seeing the arts center in its current state, there was no way she could let it go to someone else.

"Your tree house still stands, Colton," she continued. "Which is important in two ways. One, if you sell, they'll likely tear down the last thing you and your dad built together."

He tried, unsuccessfully, to mask a grimace. "And two?"

"Two...you know how to build things. If anyone could rebuild the arts center, making it bigger, better, and stronger than it once was, it's you."

Colton looked down at his feet and shook his head, his voice softening. "But I'm not gonna be here to do that, Kelse. I'm leaving town. Permanently. As soon as the sale goes through."

Kelsey sat with that for a second. The idea of Colton Banks leaving Cape May sent a shiver down her spine.

"Why so soon?" It was barely a whisper. "You're not playing football anymore, so...couldn't you stay for a little while, just until it's rebuilt?"

She tried to make it sound like an offhanded suggestion, but to Kelsey it was much more than that. Exposing her vulnerable side, the part of her that wanted him to stay and give her a reason to as well. To rectify their past.

Then again, he had another reason beyond football to return to the West Coast.

"I know you've been here for a couple months and need to go back, but even if you won't be the one building it, couldn't you stay for just a bit longer and help me design it?"

"No."

A gust of wind lifted her hair. She felt her skin prickle.

"Why do I get the feeling you don't care about this place anymore?" she asked.

"Because I don't."

She felt as if he'd slapped her. "But this is your home."

"*Was* my home. Not anymore."

"So, what, you sell and just...never come back?"

"That's the plan. No reason to."

Kelsey recalled Ashley's parents had moved out of town years ago. Without either of their families here, they had nothing tethering them to Cape May.

His proclamation that he had nothing to return here for obviously included her. Her heart snapped.

"Wow," she exhaled with sudden disgust. "I didn't realize how self-centered you'd become. You used to love this place, and the arts program. I thought you had a good childhood here. Don't you want other kids to have that same opportunity? Give back, by paying forward?"

"Like I said, they still can."

Colton was right. The arts program would survive a change in location, and could potentially be even better, as he'd suggested. But it was about more than just the arts center. It was about preserving a piece of her childhood. Their childhood.

Of Colton.

"It just won't be the same," she declared.

Colton tightened his jaw and looked straight ahead. "Well, things change."

"Tell me about it," Kelsey said, getting up.

Wild wind swooshed through tree branches, shaking the leaves in ominous warning. A gust of hot air lifted her hair, reminding her she needed to get going if she wanted to beat the rain.

She turned back toward Colton. "You know, the night you left for college, I told you not to let fame go to your head. But you did, and now all you care about is money."

"That's not true."

"No? The Colton I knew never would have sold out. He would have helped his community. He would have stayed, rebuilt the arts center. I know you have someone *waiting for you*—" Kelsey made a face, lacing the last five words with bitter sarcasm, "—but certainly not a *job*."

Oops. Once the words were out there, she regretted them.

Shock painted his expression. "Talk about changing," Colton spat. "I'm not the only one."

"What do you mean? I'm still the same person I've always been."

"Is that so, *America's Sweetheart*? Or have you finally, at long last, *found your prince*?" Colton mimicked. "The Kelsey I knew wouldn't stand for a nickname like that, being branded like some sort of damsel in distress who needs a man to save her."

His words cut her to the core. Tears stung her eyes, and she tried to blink them back. If only he knew the truth. About Jaxon. About her lonely couch nights. About Ben and Jerry. But he couldn't know the truth, because she was legally bound to a lie.

Dashing off the porch, she ran toward her bike as lightning lit the sky. She heard Colton calling to her, telling her it wasn't safe to leave, but she didn't care. She had to get out of there, and fast, before the truth spilled out of her. The truth about her faux life. About the fact that she'd never had a serious boyfriend. The truth about why.

She pedaled hard against the soggy driveway, relieved when she finally hit the macadam road. The skies unleashed, and within seconds, everything about her was saturated. Kelsey raced on, knowing, but not caring, how dangerous it was to ride a bike beneath a canopy of trees during a thunderstorm. She wanted to get as far away from Colton Banks as she could.

The road was almost impossible to see, between the darkened sky and the brackish combination of salty tears and fresh pellets of rain clouding her vision. A bolt of lightning provided one second of navigational respite, followed almost immediately by a crash of thunder. It was striking precariously close.

She became aware of the hum of a motor coming from behind her. Between claps of thunder, she heard someone calling her name. She turned to look back.

It was Colton.

Sarina

As Sarina returned to the café from the theater, a blackening sky roiled with whipping winds and bent trees, wearily bracing themselves for the oncoming storm. The café had been so busy today, it was late afternoon by the time she got to the theater, painting sets well into the evening. The increased business filled her with a hope she hadn't felt for some time—not since she'd first opened. It felt so good, she seriously questioned her earlier thoughts of quitting.

Sarina headed to the back room to do food prep for the following day, until a banging noise derailed her from her mission. Peering down the hallway, she noticed the screen door slamming open and shut. Dammit, one of the staff members must have left it open. As she rushed to pull it closed, a group of shrieking females tore down the narrow street behind the café.

"Are you sure it's him?" one woman yelled.

Another hollered back, "I'd know him anywhere!"

"I saw him first!" The fittest of them all sprinted ahead in an impressive burst of energy.

Sarina chuckled, wondering what could possibly make a group of grown-ass women give chase after some random, yet apparently desirable, object. It was too late in the day for the hot Fudgy Wudgy guy, the female townsfolks' latest heartthrob, to be peddling his frozen treats. Plus, he usually stuck to the beach.

Back in the kitchen, she began chopping veggies for a salad when she heard a loud *bam!* It sounded like it came from the freezer. Like a silly person in a horror flick, she set down her knife and headed down the hall, when she heard it again. She looked around for a weapon within arm's reach, not wanting to turn her back on a likely marauder to retrieve her cleaver. But the only thing she could find was a mop she lovingly referred to as Carl.

Whipping the freezer door open, she jumped in. It was dark, so she wielded the mop like a machete until it met with a solid object. An object that screamed.

"What the—"

"Aaaahhh!" Sarina shrieked. She swung harder at the moving target, pummeling it.

"Stop!" the object yelled. "I'm unarmed!"

"I'm not!"

"Wait!" The object—a man—grabbed the end of the mop. "Please stop! I'm not here to hurt or rob you. I'm just hiding out!"

Sarina screamed again and ran from the freezer, locking the door behind her. "You can work that out with cops!" she yelled as she dialed 911.

"Just open the door so I can explain!" he pleaded.

"You can explain yourself to the nice judge after they lock up your ass."

The operator picked up. "What's your emergency?"

"I have a man!" Sarina yelled, trying to catch her breath.

"Do you, now?" The female operator snickered.

"A man in my freezer," Sarina, still panting, tried to explain.

"What kind of a man?"

"Oh, he's the sensitive type, enjoys sunsets and long walks on the beach..." Resorting to sarcasm, even in the face of extreme danger, was Sarina's toxic trait. She huffed. "What do you mean, what *kind of* a man?"

"Can you describe him?"

"Blonde, I think. Tall. I dunno, I was too busy hitting him with my mop."

"It's really cold in here!" the man yelled as he pounded on the door.

"That's what you get for hiding in someone's freezer!"

"Ma'am? What's going on now?" the operator asked.

"He's trying to get out."

"Do you know this man?"

"Of course not. Why else would I call you? He broke into my café and was hiding in my freezer."

"Please, can you let me out? I'm not a threat!" Freezer Guy yelled. "I'm Jaxon Quinn!"

"And I'm the queen of England."

"Are you, now?" the operator asked. "Is Prince Philip there, or someone else I can talk to?"

"Oh, I get it. You think I'm nuts," Sarina said. She could see how comical this would be to someone who *didn't* have a serial killer hiding out in their café.

"I'm just trying to understand what kind of a man would fit in your freezer?"

"This is Sarina Grace, owner of Sunrise Café. My freezer is a walk-in."

"Oh," the operator chuckled. "I'm sorry, I pictured—"

"Seriously, can you send some officers? I'm fearing for my life, here."

Okay, maybe not, but if she'd learned anything from Grand Lil, it was that a little drama went a long way.

"I've dispatched a unit," the operator said. "By the way, love your café. Best coffee I've ever had."

"Aww, thanks," Sarina cooed. With the wildly popular, nationally revered *Jolt!* threatening to move into town, she'd gladly take all the kudos she could muster. "I appreciate that."

"I'm gonna stay on the line with you until the officers arrive."

"Great. I have no idea what this dude's capable of or why he's in my freezer."

"I'm here to surprise Kelsey Grace," the man announced.

Sarina whispered into the phone. "He claims he's Jaxon Quinn. Here to surprise my sister."

"Well, if that's the case, I'll call off the cops and send a bottle of champagne and strawberries." The operator laughed heartily.

Sarina instantly took a liking to the woman, unafraid to make a joke despite the call being recorded. Her kinda gal.

She had an idea.

"Hey, you!" Sarina yelled at the freezer door. "If you're Jaxon Quinn, what movie did you star in when you were fourteen?"

"*Armed and Dangerous.*" He snickered. "Tragically ironic, circumstances considered. That's not what I am now, though I kinda wish I was."

"You just looked that up," Sarina said. "Nice try."

"Ask me something I can't look up."

"Okay. What was your favorite memory as a kid?"

"Zip-lining in Costa Rica," he said without pause.

Oh shit. That was right. As former president of the Jaxon Quinn Fan Club (New Jersey branch), Sarina knew everything about him. Including this little nugget of info she'd gleaned from a teen magazine, bastion of truth that it was. It had long since gone out of publication and likely wasn't something that would've been transposed to the internet.

Sarina racked her brain for something else non-Googleable she knew about Jaxon Quinn.

"It's really cold in here," he said. "Can you please let me out?"

She turned away from the door and whispered into the phone. "Um, just out of curiosity, how long does it take someone to freeze to death? I'm not trying to go to jail for murdering someone."

"If he's an intruder, you're fine. Self-defense. If he is Jaxon Quinn, you won't have to worry about going to jail, because his fans will get you first."

"You're funny," Sarina said. "You should let me know next time you're coming in. Coffee on me."

"Coffee? Did you say coffee?" the man called out. "I could go for some hot steaming java."

Ah, yes. She knew what to ask.

"If you're Jaxon Quinn, then you'll know what Kelsey Grace puts in her coffee."

"Three shakes of cinnamon and a squirt of honey."

Double shit. It was unlikely the internet would have gotten word of that weirdness.

"She reads *Sense and Sensibility* every summer," the man continued. "She's terrified of Styrofoam peanuts, loves baby sloths, and is allergic to papaya. Oh, and she owns stock in Ben and Jerry's."

Sarina whipped open the door of the freezer.

And there he stood.

She gazed up into his jade eyes. Her heart flipped like it used to all those times she kissed his posters. Now, as the adult 3D version of her teen crush stood before her, with the insanely adorable addition of ruddy cheeks, purple lips, and early onset frostbite, there was no mistaking it.

She was staring up into the perfect face of Jaxon *Freaking* Quinn.

Colton

COLTON CURSED HIMSELF AS HE JUMPED IN HIS TRUCK. The last thing he wanted to do was chase after someone who'd accused him of being a shallow, heartless, money-grabber who'd let fame go to his head. She should know better— he wasn't that kind of guy. And her comment about him not having a job to return to was simply cruel.

But...he couldn't let her bike home in a thunderstorm.

He didn't mean to be a jerk about the arts center land, but if working on that property was what killed his dad, the last thing he wanted was to keep it and be reminded of that on the daily. Selling would give Colton a way out—the ability to flee Cape May and all it represented. The loss of his family. His career. Kelsey. Being with her had only stirred that feeling of rejection from everything that once mattered to him. In a classic case of fight or flight, the latter was his only option. He had no fight left.

His heart snapped when he finally came upon Kelsey, battling wind and driving rain as if her life depended upon getting as far away from him as possible. He understood the need to escape, and realized they weren't that dissimilar. Mr. Star Quarterback and America's Sweetheart—both cast into public personas that were misaligned with their true selves.

"Get in the truck," he yelled over the crashing thunder as he jumped out, grabbed the handlebars, and tried to ease the bike from between her legs.

"I'm fine, I'm going home."

"Not, you're not," Colton insisted. "Don't be foolish!"

Mere feet from them, a deafening crack ripped a huge section of tree away from its base, sending it crashing to the road, blocking it.

Kelsey turned, her eyes the size of the hail falling to the ground around them. Clearly shaken, she relinquished her bike. Colton tossed it into the bed of his truck with one swift movement as she scrambled into the front seat of Colton's pickup. He slammed into reverse and sped back to his place, unwilling to risk another tree losing its footing in the saturated ground.

Colton pulled the truck as close as he could to the porch, and they made a run for it. He opened the screen door and ushered Kelsey in ahead of him as the wind nearly tore the old wood-framed screen door from his hands.

She paused inside the door. "I'm not sure you want me coming in any further," she said, holding up the skirt of her drenched sundress, dripping into a puddle at her feet.

"It's only water," Colton grumbled as he reached for a dish towel, trying hard not to look at those perfect legs of hers, toned and tanned from the California sun and glistening. He'd always had a thing for her legs. And, well...everything about her.

He thrusted the towel at her, and their eyes met.

She gave him a teasing glance through raindrop-kissed lashes. "Do you have anything smaller?" she joked.

An unwitting smile tugged at his lips. He couldn't help the tiny ember of hope in his heart sparked by her playful comment, that she wasn't still mad at him. He'd always hated it when Kelsey got mad at him when they were kids. Rare, but when it happened, it cut him to the core. Still did, apparently. He felt the hardness in his heart softening as he retrieved a beach towel and wrapped it around her shoulders.

"Let me get you something dry to wear."

He found an old t-shirt and a pair of basketball shorts from childhood that would fit her. After they both changed, he threw their soggy clothes in the dryer.

"I put on some coffee to warm us up," he said, as he ushered her to the booth at the kitchen bay window and wrapped a blanket around her. Colton felt their previous tension wash away with every fat raindrop pelting the window.

"Thanks for coming for me," Kelsey said. "That was pretty scary."

"Yeah. I'm glad I got to you when I did. That tree—"

"I would have been right in its path." She shuddered. "Sorry to have made you go out in this. And...for the other stuff."

"It's no problem," he said, giving her a lopsided grin. "It's what friends do. Even ones with inflated football heads." Colton raised an eyebrow at her. He hadn't quite recovered from the sting of her words, but he wanted her to know he still had a sense of humor.

Kelsey winced through her smile. "Sorry for that. I know you've been through a lot. I guess I understand why you want to leave. It can't be easy being back here, with your parents gone."

"No, it's not. Among other things." He paused before sharing what he'd learned. "My dad was working on the arts center property when he had his heart attack."

Her face fell. "Oh, Colt..." She placed her hand on his. "I'm so sorry. I didn't know that. No wonder you want to sell."

Her soft skin sent an instant surge of electricity through him, and he almost forgot what he was about to say. He wondered if she felt it, too, because she flashed him a look of surprise.

Out of respect for Kelsey and her *prince*, he pulled his hand away.

The power flickered on and off, then went out altogether. Using their cellphone flashlights, they went in search of candles and a lighter. Once swathed in the glow of candlelight and the rich aroma of freshly brewed coffee, Colton poured them each a cup and settled on the bench next to her.

"Perfect timing on the coffee, getting it done before the power went out."

"I live to serve."

"*Mmm.*" Kelsey moaned as she took a sip of the familiar flavor. "Is this Sarina's brand?"

"It is," Colton said. "Only the best."

"Definitely better than *Jolt!* I can't stand their coffee. I'm morally opposed to chains moving in on the Cape, and not just because of my sister's business."

Colton merely nodded, hoping the developers weren't

planning to bring in businesses like the popular *Jolt!* coffee chain. He'd have to inquire tomorrow at their meeting.

Suddenly, Max came in from the barn, his eyes widening when he saw her. "Oh, hey Kelse!" He glanced at the lit candles, then at Kelsey and Colton, his eyebrows rising and a cheesy grin sneaking across his face. "I hope I'm interrupting something."

"It's not what it looks like," Colton assured him. "The power went out."

"Well, enjoy. I'll be in my room if you need me."

"No, Maxie-baby," Kelsey said. It was the nickname she'd given him as kids. "Come sit, have coffee with us. Tell me about your life."

He looked to Colton for approval, who waved him over as he got up to pour him a coffee.

They discussed Max's plans for the future, then segued into the past, reminiscing about the time a large batch of horseshoe crabs washed up on the beach. Kelsey and her sisters had thought they were army helmets with horns, but seven-year-old Max set them straight with a mini-lecture on the creatures.

"I knew back then you had a calling," Kelsey said.

"Speaking of memories, I found something the other day I think you'll both enjoy," Max said as he got up.

Returning with a small box, he lifted the lid to reveal a stack of photos inside. The top photo featured two toddlers holding hands as they entered a building.

"Wow," Colton whispered as he ran his thumb over the photo of him and Kelsey at age three. "I'd forgotten Mom took these pictures every year."

His heart warmed as he flipped through the pictures.

"I'll let you guys reminisce," Max said, making to leave. "Kelse, are you going home tonight or...?"

"She's staying," Colton said. "She was on her way home, but a tree fell on Seashore Road, and we can't get past it."

"Oh, right," Max said, his tone revealing he didn't believe them.

Colton picked up on his disbelief. "It was on Smith's property, so no way to get through."

Max shrugged, a grin on his face. "Hey, I didn't say anything."

"Should we take him out and show him?" Colton asked Kelsey, loud enough for Max to hear. "We don't need rumors going around, you know."

"I believe you, bro," Max called out as he headed for the stairs.

With Max gone, they turned back to the photos, both silent as they sifted through the stack.

"I can't believe how tiny we were," Kelsey said.

When they got to the photos from third grade, Colton groaned. "Oh, my— I remember my mom made me wear those gray pants with that gray shirt," Colton said. "Bobby Schmidt called me a rhino that day. I never wore them again."

"Bobby Schmidt is a jerk," Kelsey said. "I heard he went to jail for tax evasion."

They reached a photo taken in sixth grade, and Colton joked, "Although, maybe Bobby *was* on to something. That must have been the summer the ice cream man started coming around twice a day. Remember seven pizzas in heaven?"

They were at a classmate's birthday party, and the kids were playing an innocent version of seven minutes in heaven. Being middle school kids, they didn't know the real meaning of the game. In their innocent version, someone spun a bottle on the ground, and whoever it landed on would join them in a closet for seven minutes, during which time they'd come up with a joke or a skit to do when they emerged.

When Colton spun the bottle, it landed smack dab between Kelsey and Ashley. Colton argued it had landed on Ashley, but others insisted it was Kelsey. He'd just started growing feelings for his friend and was terrified to be with her in such a setting. Even though they were best buddies, he had no idea what he'd say or do and was afraid he'd make the wrong choice. Ashley was safer, because he really didn't care what she thought of him.

The group agreed it had landed closer to Kelsey. Once in the closet, she suggested they work on their secret handshake. He was relieved.

When they'd emerged, one of the class bullies cried out, "Look, he's even bigger than when he went in!"

"What did you guys do in there? Order pizzas?" another asked.

"Seven pizzas in heaven!" a third had proclaimed.

Colton recalled the humiliation he'd felt at being taunted about his weight. Even though he got jacked the summer before sophomore year, and the insults turned to accolades over his football skills, the hurt nevertheless remained.

"I still feel like that chunky kid some days," Colton said softly.

Kelsey nodded. "I know what you mean. For me it was my awkward lack of self-esteem. It's like the wounds heal but scars remain."

Colton looked at her in surprise. "I never took you for someone with low self-esteem."

"Dude, I've struggled with it my whole life."

"But you're...you."

"Colt, I hardly know who I am anymore. I feel like an imposter."

He couldn't believe she felt that way. She certainly hid it well.

"You've just summed up my whole adult experience," Colton said.

Kelsey laid out all the photos, snapped a picture of each on her phone, then sighed as she looked at them. "The irony of it all," Kelsey said. "Look at us now. Those kids never would've believed what we'd go on to do with our lives."

"Yeah, now who's laughing?"

Except they weren't laughing.

"SARINA, IS EVERYTHING OKAY?" THE 911 OPERATOR, still on the line, asked as Sarina let Jaxon out of the freezer. "Are you in danger?"

"No." Sarina laughed nervously. "Sorry to bother you. Turns out it was a friend, playing a practical joke. You can call off the cops."

She hung up.

"I think I'm dying," he said through chattering teeth. "How about that coffee?"

"Jaxon Quinn," she said, still shocked to see the man standing before her. She crossed her arms and narrowed her eyes at him. "What are you doing in my freezer?"

"I take the fifth."

"You'll take a fifth of whiskey to the head, if you don't come clean."

Jaxon laughed. "So, you're Sarina. Kelscy said you were the feisty sister, but she didn't mention your murderous tendencies. This must be your café I've heard so much about."

"What are you doing in my freezer?" she repeated.

"Mustn't you give Miranda warnings before questioning me?" the perp asked teasingly, essentially lawyering up with a raised eyebrow.

"Only if you're in custody," she said. She'd taken Criminal Law 101 as a freshman in college. She knew a thing or two. "Which you're not. You're free to go."

Sarina gave a grand gesture towards the door but lowkey hoped he wouldn't take her up on it. The storm was whipping up outside, with rain beating against the windows like a high-powered car wash, and it wasn't safe out there for man, machine, or Hollywood icon.

"Except," Jaxon said, holding up a finger. "I was being illegally detained in an ice box, so...once in custody, always in custody. *Davis v. The State of California.*"

"Oh, so now you're a lawyer, too?"

"No, but I played one on TV," he joked. "I was under duress, being chased by a pack of crazed women. I needed a place to hide."

So far, his story tracked. Sarina had witnessed the mob of screaming females in hot pursuit of Jaxon Freaking Quinn. Couldn't say she blamed them.

"The door was open, so I came in, seeking refuge before I was unlawfully trapped. I nearly froze to death."

"Objection."

"Grounds?"

"The defendant is being overly dramatic."

"It's what I do," he said, flashing his eyebrows. He, too, seemed amused by their exchange.

"Got anything else, Quinn? Being chased by a mob of women is not a legally recognized defense in the State of New Jersey."

"It is in New York."

"You're over state lines and outta luck."

Sarina was secretly delighted he was playing along. She'd always suspected he was more than a superficial, two-dimensional Hollywood type, and his quick-wittedness proved her right.

"Kelsey doesn't know you're in Cape May?" she asked.

"No."

"Until your rabid fans break the news."

She'd seen the ravenous looks on the women's faces, witnessed firsthand their collective take-him-dead-or-alive mindset. It wouldn't be long before the whole town heard about the gorgeous movie star being in their midst.

Sarina had to admit, Jaxon was far better-looking in person than in posters and movies. The scent of his aftershave wafted into her nostrils, threatening to commandeer all her senses. There was a kindness behind the sexy half-smile that had made him so famous. She felt the outrageous desire to flirt with him, act like a silly girl, toss her hair or wrap a curl around her finger like Molly probably would.

Except for two minor things. She wasn't silly, and he wasn't single.

Make that three things. He was her sister's boyfriend.

But tell that to her racing heart.

JAXON SECOND-GUESSED HIS DECISION TO COME TO Cape May without his usual entourage of security—a boneheaded move of epic proportions.

Maybe his New York friends were right when they said nothing good ever happens in Jersey.

Jaxon knew he'd made a mistake running into this place when he felt the first *thwack!* of a hard object against his arm. While he was relieved to have eluded the mob of screaming fans, he'd merely traded that carnage for a broom attack. But then, when he heard his attacker say her name, he was shocked. How could he have been so lucky to have unknowingly found shelter in Kelsey's sister's freezer? A definite sign he was meant to come to Cape May to sweep Kelsey off her feet. Broom attack aside.

As he'd listened to Sarina joking with the 911 operator, he started to worry he'd freeze to death. He reached in his pocket for his phone to google how long before death set in, but it wasn't there.

Fuuuuck. He must have tossed it in his duffle bag just before he'd emerged from the car and was chased by a throng of eager fans. He'd taken off in a sprint, leaving his driver, his duffle, and his iPhone behind.

He was thankful she'd finally sprung him from solitary frozen confinement. What he hadn't expected when she'd opened the door was for time to stand still. Her pale-green eyes were wild with indignation. Icy stare aside, he felt himself defrosting from the inside out. Heart first.

Oh boy. Was he in trouble.

She was gorgeous. There was no mistaking she was Kelsey's sister—same cute dimples, same pretty features, but her coloring was lighter. Her flaxen hair, kissed by the sun, fell in waves and brushed the top of her tan shoulders, and she had a smattering of freckles across her dainty nose. Her eyes were the most fascinating shade of green he'd ever seen, a sea of blended colors—jade, aqua, champagne—all acting in concert to produce a beautiful sea-glass effect. She was shorter, more petite than Kelsey, which made her slug fest even more impressive. She was the epitome of his perfect physical type, and on top of that, she had quick wit and playful banter. He didn't stand a chance—instantly feeling a *zing* go through him like nothing he'd ever felt before.

How he would've liked to work his charm on her...

But she was Kelsey's sister. And he'd effectively exited his F-boy era at 12:01 on the morning of his thirtieth birthday. Now that he'd embarked on a mission to woo his costar into being his one-and-only, he needed to stick to his script.

If only Sarina would stop looking at him with those eyes.

"Okay," she said. "I'll give you a pass this time."

"Whew," he sighed in jest. "About that coffee...I heard it's the best in town."

Kelsey had told him about Sarina's coffee, and how she'd opened the café on a wing, a prayer, and a shoestring budget. When Kelsey had offered to financially back her, Sarina refused. Jaxon had been impressed by that.

"Butter me up all you want, Quinn," she tossed over her shoulder as she walked away. "You're still on probation with me."

He decided it was safe to follow her, now that she was unarmed. He tried to keep his eyes straight ahead, willing himself not to take a gander at what promised to be a very fine ass, reminding himself he wasn't allowed to ogle other women if he was going to take on a full-time bae. Especially when it was her sister. Fortunately, the stainless-steel shine of industrial-sized appliances caught his wandering eye as they entered the kitchen where a high-top prep table was situated in the center of the room, featuring a cutting board, carrots, and a sharp knife.

A very sharp knife.

Hopefully, this wasn't the scene where Jaxon Quinn met his ultimate demise, eviscerated by the wicked enchantress.

He really needed to stop being so dramatic.

She pulled a hoodie off a hook on the wall and tossed it to him. "My ex-boyfriend's. Looks like you could use it."

"Thanks." He pulled on the Eagles sweatshirt, swallowing his rising bile. As a die-hard Rams fan, he felt like a traitor. Being in the early stages of frostbite as he was, Philly's phanatical team merch would have to do, as long as he didn't start chanting *E-A-G-L-E-S Eagles!*

She told him to have a seat as she turned and left the room. *Don't look. Don't look.*

Epic fail, as he watched (more like leered at) her retreating backside. He liked the way her cutoff jean shorts accentuated her perfectly shaped ass, and her cropped t-shirt clung to her in all the right places. Her body was slamming.

She returned with a mug of coffee. Her fingers grazed his as she handed it to him and he felt a zap of electricity hotter than the steaming mug around which he wrapped his frosty fingers.

"Wow," he said after he took a sip. "This is delicious. What flavor is it?"

"You tell me. It's a new blend I'm trying out for this upcoming fundraiser, and I'm curious to know what flavors you detect."

Jaxon took another sip. "Mmm. I'm getting notes of coconut. Vanilla. And something else—bourbon, maybe?"

"Wow. None of my staff were able to figure it out. I call it Drunken Snowball Fight."

"I like it. Huge fan of flavored coffee."

"So, you're here to surprise my sister. Are you heading there now?"

"Not 'til tomorrow. I want to surprise her after opening night curtain call."

"Opening night isn't until Friday."

He looked up from his coffee. "You're shitting me."

"I shit you not."

"Why did I think it was Wednesday?"

Sarina shrugged. "Does this mean you'll move up your big reveal?"

"I dunno...I really wanted to do it after her show."

"Well, good luck with that. You do know Kelsey hates surprises, right?"

"Of course I know that."

He didn't know that. There was apparently a lot more he had to learn about his costar. Maybe Sarina could help him get to know Kelsey better. Although, right now, he was more interested in getting to know *her*.

Take several seats, Jax.

What was wrong with him? This just wouldn't do if he planned to make a go of something real with Kelsey.

"Where are you staying in the meantime?" she asked.

"I booked an Airbnb on Perry Street. I was getting out of the car to go inside when the women spotted me and chased me here."

"Dude, they're probably camped out there, waiting for your return."

Sarina whipped out her phone to check social media. "Shit. Someone on Insta just posted a photo of you." She began reading aloud. "'I'm pretty sure I saw Jaxon Quinn get out of a car on Perry. It had to be him, with Kelsey home.'" She looked up at him in dismay. "Ruh-roh. Looks as if your cover's been blown." Suddenly, her eyes widened with an apparent idea. "Wait!"

She dictated her post as she typed. "'False alarm! I ran into the same guy at the fish market. Coulda SWORN it was JQ, but he's just a vacationer who says he gets this ALL the time. Trust me, if he was in town with my sister, you'd all know!'"

"Wow. Brilliant," Jaxon said as she hit send. "Coming from you, it's more legit. I appreciate you doing that."

"Comes with the territory. Having a famous sister teaches you the art of subterfuge and deception in order to properly dodge paparazzi. You probably wouldn't know anything about that."

"I don't…tell me more," he said, cupping his face with his hands as he feigned rapt attention. Although he was legitimately impressed by Sarina's quick thinking and social media bluff. "Seriously, though, I could use you on my team."

"You couldn't afford me."

Her tone was light, friendly. Good. For some reason, it mattered that she liked him. Again, something new. He'd never cared about that before—maybe because he had yet to meet a woman who hadn't liked him, as far as he knew.

"I'm guessing this thing must be real between you and Kelsey," she said, her eyes sparkling with humor. "I was pretty sure it was one big publicity stunt."

"Oh, um...no," he said, laughing nervously as he stuttered his denial. "It's...real."

Oh boy. No one had ever accused them of their relationship being fake. She must be pretty smart if she was doubting it. That, or Kelsey had spilled the beans...

Nope, Kelse wouldn't do that. They were under contract, she was a rule-follower, and she easily went along with whatever their publicist suggested.

"Truth is, I miss her." Jaxon was relieved his impeccable acting skills kicked in, allowing him to think quickly on his feet.

Sarina laughed.

"What?" he said, laughing along with her. "Don't you believe me?"

"Of course I do. It's just that I didn't take the illustrious JFQ to be such a softie. A lovesick one-woman man, to boot."

"Well, believe it," he said, hoping she would.

The question was—did *he*? It had all seemed so clear a few days ago when he'd shared his game plan with Taco. Even the tiny mutt agreed, the way he yipped and yapped in obvious excitement as Jaxon had packed his bags. But that was when neither he nor his furry friend knew someone like Sarina existed, who would set his whole *Kelsey Grace: Girlfriend* mission on its ear.

"BT dubs, what's the F for?" he asked. His middle initial wasn't F.

"Whatever you want it to be."

"Fabulous? Fun?"

"Full of himself," she suggested. "If you'll excuse me, I have to make this salad for tomorrow."

Leaning up against the counter, Jaxon watched in awe as she quickly chopped the carrots like a pro.

"Need help?" Jaxon asked.

"Can I trust you with a knife?"

Her teasing glance cut through him like the cleaver she wielded.

"I pose the same question to you. You certainly can't be trusted with a broom."

"It was a mop, and his name is Carl," Sarina said. She nodded her head in the direction of a mop leaning up against the wall.

He looked at her with a puzzled expression. "Why Carl?"

She crossed the room to pick it up. Instinctively, Jaxon ducked.

"Relax, Quinn, Carl's off duty," she said, chuckling as she shook the moppy end in his direction. She pointed to the word *Carl* burned into its wooden handle. "He's made by a company called Carlton, but the *ton* wore off. So...I present to you...Carl."

"Pleased to meet you, Carl." Jaxon acknowledged his foe with a bow of his head. "You make a formidable foe."

"I've trained him well," Sarina said. "It would behoove you to keep that in mind."

"I most certainly will. He definitely got my attention."

Carl wasn't the only one.

Stop it, Jax. You're here for Kelsey.

If only his racing heart believed it.

Colton

IT WAS GETTING LATE, SO COLTON AND KELSEY BLEW OUT the candles and navigated their way upstairs.

"The sheets are fresh, and there are new toothbrushes in

the medicine cabinet. Feel free to use the shower and...I'm sorry for the things I said earlier."

They entered the spare bedroom, and she turned to him. "Me too."

"I read the article about you and *what's-his-name*. I'm happy for you and all, but I don't understand why the media feels the need to—" He paused, hoping he wasn't about to insult her again. "To make it sound like you need saving. That you're somehow more desirable now that you have him. What's that all about?"

Kelsey sighed. "Yeah, the media likes to portray me as the lucky one to have landed him."

"When *he's* the lucky one."

She held his stare and gave him a slow smile before her eyes shifted to the shelf behind him. "That's a nice photo of you two lovebirds."

She crossed the room and picked up a framed photo of Colton and Ashley at the San Diego Zoo, posing with a gorilla in the background. "And Ashley doesn't look too bad either."

"Oh." Colton laughed nervously. He'd forgotten it was there. "Ashley insisted on giving that to my dad for Christmas. You know how he liked primates."

"Aww, that's not a nice way to refer to your girlfriend."

He laughed out loud, her comment taking him by surprise. He'd forgotten how funny she was.

"Sorry, that was rude," she said. "You know I love her."

He couldn't tear his eyes away from Kelsey as she continued to look at the picture. The dark chocolate messy bun she'd expertly twisted as they'd looked at pictures earlier revealed her graceful neck. He was overcome by her scent, hinting of coconut and peaches.

Setting the frame back on the shelf, she suddenly spun around. "Oh!"

Her face was so close, he could feel her sweet breath on his cheek.

Giving a nervous giggle, she backed up. "I didn't realize you were..."

"Sorry...I'll just..." He made his way to the door.

"Colton?"

He turned to find her smiling at him.

"Thanks for saving my life tonight. It was really stupid of me to try to ride home in this storm."

"Anytime," Colton said. He was afraid to say too much, lest she hear the yearning in his voice. "Sweet dreams."

He closed the door behind him and leaned his forehead against it, heart pounding. It was all he could do to keep from flinging the door open and taking her in his arms, telling her the truth about him and Ashley. Other than Max, he hadn't told anyone else about it. It was too humiliating, having to admit his girlfriend left him and flew into the arms of his so-called friend within days of his injury. He didn't want Kelsey seeing him as more of a loser than he already was.

But on some level, he knew she wouldn't judge him like that. His confession could help alter her belief that fame had gone to his head. It hadn't. He was telling the truth when he said he still felt like that kid in the photo. She was always a trusted confidant, and he longed for the support of her friendship. She'd know all the right things to say to comfort him and make him believe everything was going to be okay. His dad's death, the injury, the breakup, the feeling of being in purgatory before his next life began. It was all too much to handle at once.

In truth, his relationship with Ashley had been over for quite some time—he just hadn't realized it until she finally yanked off the Band-Aid and announced she was moving out. Fortunately, she didn't take his heart, because he'd never truly given it to her. It had always belonged to the person standing on the other side of the door.

Suddenly hit with an overwhelming desire to tell her the

truth, he raised his knuckles to knock. It had to be worth the risk, putting himself out there.

But...for what? She was with Jaxon now. What would be the point in telling her about the breakup? Did he hope she'd flee her relationship and jump into Colton's arms? The thought almost made him laugh out loud. No way she'd want him now. After everything that had happened, he had nothing left to offer her. She hadn't wanted him back when his star was rising, so why would she want him now, after it had fizzled and fallen?

He lowered his hand and turned away from the door.

Kelsey

BREATHE. JUST BREATHE.

Kelsey leaned her forehead on the door after Colton closed it behind him. She felt like she'd been holding her breath since he'd commented on Jaxon and the article about her life. He was right about the media portraying her to be somehow more desirable now that she'd landed Jaxon. It was ridiculous.

She put her hand on the knob, ready to whip open the door, desperately wanting to tell him the truth. How it was all a facade, that she's nobody's sweetheart, and her life wasn't what it was made out to be. However, not only was she prohibited from disclosing the truth, but the photo of Colton and Ashley, floating in her periphery, served as a poignant reminder that Colton wasn't free.

If she'd had any idea their relationship would last as long as it had, she might not have suggested Colton get with Ashley when he told her he was seeking a good-looking girlfriend.

But Ashley had followed him to the same college, and they'd stayed together afterwards. After all, who would walk away from a first-round draft pick who'd been promised millions? Kelsey assumed their engagement would be next.

Nope. Tonight was not the night for confessions.

She headed to the shelf and flipped the photo of Colton and Ashley face-down before crawling into bed.

But in the dark, as lightning lit up the night sky, she kept seeing visions of him. The look on his face when he jumped out of his truck to stop her from riding her home—a mixture of worry, care, and determination. The way he grabbed her bike and tossed it in the back like it was made of plastic, his muscles straining against his wet t-shirt. Later, at the table, seeing the sweet smile of nostalgia tug at his lips as they went through their old photos together.

She remembered that middle school party all too well, and the bitter disappointment she'd felt when Colton insisted the bottle had landed on Ashley. Then again, who could blame him? Ashley was the first girl in the class to sprout boobs—*of course* he'd want to go into the closet with her. Meanwhile Kelsey, flat as a board, never attracted the salacious glances of her male classmates, including Colton's.

She was surprised tonight when Colton said he'd never lost that feeling of being the kid who was taunted by others, despite how they'd both turned out. It was a perfect lesson in not judging a book by its cover. Except, in her case, people still did. While Colton's coverage was all about his game, maneuvers, and skills, most of the attention Kelsey drew was about her appearance. How great she looked in her swimsuit as she splashed in the waves with Jaxon. How she'd mastered the art of the smoky eye when she went out at night, or what designer she wore as she shopped Rodeo Drive. Less was said about her acting skills—after all, it didn't take Streep skills to play the part of a silly girl looking for love, ad nauseam.

Which was one reason she wanted to play more serious roles—the ability to showcase her true acting talent and express emotional depth in a way her imposter life didn't allow.

But the biggest reason she wanted to break out of her America's Sweetheart mold was that she simply didn't fit the bill.

Sarina

SARINA'S WASN'T SURE IF HER STILL-RACING HEART WAS A lingering effect of her guy-in-the-freezer scare, or the fact that her teen heartthrob was standing within inches from her, cutting veggies.

Sister's boyfriend or not, she couldn't help her biological reaction.

She leaned over to grab a wayward carrot slice and accidentally brushed his smooth, toned arm, sending a shot of something through her. She tried to ignore the fact that the air between them frizzled with electricity. At least, she thought so. Maybe it was just static from the storm.

The fact that Jaxon didn't know Kelsey hated surprises wasn't lost on Sarina. She couldn't help but wonder what else he didn't know about her. Like her past with a certain NFL football player, also now back in town, and how they couldn't seem to keep their eyes off one another.

Kelsey's decade-long crush still seemed to smolder beneath the surface. That was one reason Sarina was surprised her sister was dating her dazzling costar. Jaxon and Colton couldn't be any more different. But all was fair in love and lust. Relationships didn't always make sense to those not directly involved.

"What led you to open a café?" Jaxon asked as they chopped away.

"I'm an artist, and food is art to me. Mixing ingredients is like mixing the colors on your palette."

"As in painter's palette, or taste palate?"

"Both," she said, giving him a smile. "Interesting, I'd never thought of that word being appropriate for both. I love creating new dishes, adding a touch of something you wouldn't expect. It's the element of surprise I enjoy so much."

Like finding a hot guy in my freezer.

She continued. "The café is a way to legitimize my art into a profitable venture."

"How's the business end going? Kelsey said you've been providing free coffee and meals to volunteers and those affected by the storm."

"It's going," Sarina said, hoping her tone was convincing.

"I sense a *but* coming."

"Can I trust you with my truth?"

"Can I trust you not to stab me with that thing?" he said, gesturing at the knife in her hand.

"Stand down, Quinn. My murderous tendencies toward you have waned."

"Then yes. You can trust me with your truth."

"I think I've been *too* generous. I wanted to do my part. I just hope I still have a café when this summer's over."

"You're doing the right thing, in my book. I'm sure Kelsey would help with the financial aspect."

"Oh, heck no. I don't ask for help, especially from family. They were totally against me opening the café in the first place, because they didn't think I could do it."

"There's nothing wrong with asking for help. Some of the shrewdest businesspeople have to do it. The trick is knowing when asking will pay off bigger than not asking."

A loud clap of thunder cracked above them, shaking the

building and flickering the lights.

"You're not gonna want to go out in this anytime soon," Sarina warned. "It's supposed to last all night."

"Damn. I left everything with my driver. Oh, wait…"

He patted his pockets and pulled out a business card.

"He wrote down on his card he's staying at…" Turning the card over, he read, "Congress Hall. Would you mind texting him to let him know where I am?"

She messaged the driver, who responded to let them know he'd made it to the hotel, but a tree limb had since fallen behind his car, blocking it in.

Reading the text aloud, she looked up at Jaxon. "I have an extra room in my apartment upstairs. You're more than welcome to crash here for the night."

"I think I'll take you up on that," Jaxon said. "Just 'til tomorrow."

"It's probably best. Let's get this all put away, and then I can show you the accommodations."

They packed up the salad ingredients and she led him into the cooler. The door closed behind them just as the power cut out, casting the room into pitch blackness. Sarina yelped.

"I got you." Jaxon grabbed her hand.

"I'm terrified of the dark," she admitted.

He squeezed her hand and pulled her closer. His other hand brushed against the bare part of her stomach between her cropped top and shorts, sending a shiver through her.

"Sorry about that," he said in haste, giving a nervous titter as he found her other hand. "There you are. It's so dark, I can't see a thing."

He slid his fingers between hers. Despite the cool air, his touch was fire, and she struggled to find her breath as she condemned herself for the involuntary tingles running through her. She was surprised by her body's physical reaction to his proximity, her heart threatening to beat out of her chest as sexy thoughts ran amok through her head. Thoughts no decent sister should be having. This was way too close for comfort, and the sheer intimacy of the moment was too much to take. She withdrew her hands out of respect.

"Where'd you go?" he asked, sounding panicked.

"I'm right here," she giggled and put her hand up, accidentally flicking his face.

"Ouch!"

"Sorry. The lights should come back on in a minute."

"I may not last that long."

Sarina giggled. "Don't tell me you're afraid of the dark, too."

"Yes, if you want to know the truth. It's just that— AHHHHH!!! WHAT WAS THAT?" He began jumping around in a maniacal jig.

"What? What?" Sarina yelled out as she joined him in the jig, uncertain what the hell she was jigging to avoid.

He grabbed her hands again. "I swear I felt something run up my leg!"

She burst out laughing.

"It's not funny," he said with a humorous whine.

"Oh, no...it *is* funny."

"Whatever it was is still in here..." he whispered, as if *it* could hear him.

"Yes. It's called your imagination."

Or so she hoped. Sarina had no idea what he thought he'd felt, but what if he was right about something running up his leg? She constantly monitored the café for rodents and had never found one. She had an irrational fear of them, which was why she kept the café in pristine condition at all times. So much so, she could easily invite customers to eat off the floor and still score three Michelin stars and a James Beard Award without breaking the health code. She just hoped one hadn't followed Jaxon in during the storm.

"We should get out of here," he proclaimed. "Where's the

door? I can't see a thing. I don't want to freeze to death."

"There will be no freezing to death," Sarina said, chuckling. "It's a cooler, not the freezer. It automatically locks when the power goes off, to keep it cold. I have a generator, and it should come on any sec—"

Suddenly, the lights flickered as the generator hummed to life.

Sarina exhaled, laughing nervously as she found his aqua eyes trained on her, the warmth from his firm grasp shooting right through her. "Whew."

"Whoa." Jaxon leaped backwards, whipping his hands into the air like he was under arrest. "Sorry, didn't mean to grab you like that," he said, his tone a mixture of remorse and humor as they let themselves out of the cooler. "I'm not usually that needy."

"It's okay." Sarina gave him a reassuring smile. "I thought it was cute."

Really, Sarina? Cute? You're going to hell.

She turned away so he wouldn't see her cheeks flush. She wasn't sure what would kill her first—humiliation over her inappropriate thoughts, or Kelsey, if she ever found out about them.

Still, she knew her sister would be happy she'd offered to put him up for the night—as long as she kept herself from acting on her lustful teenage dreams.

Molly

MOLLY DECIDED TO CHECK HER EMAIL ONE LAST TIME before she called it a day. A familiar name in her inbox caught her attention, a pharmaceutical sales company she'd sent her résumé to on Sunday.

Her eyes bugged out as she read it. She'd finally scored an interview.

She called Brennan, excited to share her news, but it went to voicemail. She had to tell someone, but neither Kelsey nor Sarina answered, either. So she called Max.

"I got an interview!" she exclaimed before he'd even finished saying hello.

"Who is this?" he teased.

"It's finally happened!"

He congratulated her and asked what the job was for.

"Pharmaceutical sales," she proudly announced.

"Oh."

"What, you're not excited to hear I'm about to blow up the Ozempic market?"

Max laughed. "Of course, I am. The pharmaceutical industry better prepare for all its money to end up in your Kate Spade purse."

"I'm impressed you know that designer."

"I have a few of her bags myself. So…sales? Pretty cool."

"You sure? I've come to know your various tones, and this one seems…disbelieving or something."

"No, no, I totally believe in you. You're gonna kill it. As long as this is what you want."

Record scratch. "It is."

His silence was pierced by the ding of an incoming call. It was Brennan calling her back.

"Gotta take this. Talk tomorrow," she said, a bit peeved Max didn't sound as excited as he should be as a friend. But Brennan would.

"Yay, I knew you could do it!" he exclaimed after she told him the good news. He seemed genuinely happy for her. "When and where is it?"

"Next Monday, in Manhattan."

"Perfect. Why don't you come up on Friday and spend the weekend?" His voice dropped to a hushed tone. "I'm really missing you, Molly."

She was happy to hear he was missing her and excited to have an invitation, something that hadn't happened for a while. If only she could accept it.

"I can't. The fundraiser's on Saturday."

"Oh. Right."

"Why don't you come down on Friday and help me? We can go back up to New York on Sunday."

"That sounds nice. Let me see what's going on, make sure I can leave then."

"Don't forget my birthday's Saturday."

"How could I? I'll definitely be there for that. It's just Friday I'm not sure about."

After ending their call, Max texted to apologize for not seeming more enthused about her interview. Good. For some reason, she cared what he thought.

As she curled up in bed, she could barely contain her excitement—not only for her job interview, but for the future she'd long envisioned. She was confident she'd ace it and would be moving to New York by the end of next week.

Ozempic, here I come!

"COZY LITTLE LAIR YOU GOT HERE," JAXON SAID AS Sarina led him upstairs to her apartment.

"Emphasis on little," she joked.

Her diminutive apartment gave boho chic, with walls covered in her art, an abundance of mismatched throw pillows adorning the overstuffed couch, and a few trinkets she'd picked up from her travels through Europe.

"It's perfect for me, though. Just enough space. Two bedrooms, one of which I use one as my office. Don't worry, there's a bed in there, for those random occasions when guys break into my freezer and I have to put them up overnight."

"Good that you plan ahead for such things." He crossed the room and stared at a large painting above the couch, a watercolor she'd done of the cove and lighthouse. "This is beautiful. Whose work is this?"

"Local artist, world-renowned. Ridiculous talent beyond measure."

"*You* did this?" Jaxon asked, sounding incredulous. "Tell me about it."

"I love to surf and wanted to capture the ocean's various hues on canvas."

"You nailed it. Most people don't see the way the light reflects on ocean water, casting it in different shades, until they're out on a surfboard. What else you got?"

Sarina gestured to the rest of the walls where oil, acrylic, and watercolor paintings hung. "Everything you see."

As he walked around looking at her paintings, she tossed two oversized pillows on the floor and sat cross-legged on one of them.

"Tell me something about yourself I wouldn't know from the tabloids," she said as he joined her on the other one. "Tell me who the real Jaxon Quinn is. Seeing as you're dating my sister."

"Why do I feel as if I'm about to be interrogated again?" He gave her that half-smile.

"Because you are. I want to make sure you're good enough for her."

"Open book here. What do you want to know?"

"Umm...if you had to choose one profession other than

acting, what would it be?"

"A chef," he said without hesitation.

Sarina raised her eyebrows. "Are you any good?"

"I'd like to think so."

Scrambling to her feet, she held out her hand and yanked him to a standing position. She led him to the kitchen and gave a Vanna White wave.

"Cook for me, Quinn."

Jaxon laughed. "You serious?"

"Yes, I'm serious. I wanna see what you can whip up with what I have here."

"Challenge accepted," Jaxon said, and he began rummaging for ingredients. After she showed him where she kept everything, he placed his hand on her shoulders and guided her out of the kitchen. "It's time someone else cooks for you. Go relax. I'll let you know when it's ready."

Sarina could tell he knew what he was doing from the sounds coming from the kitchen, soon followed by notes of curry. They made idle chitchat until Jaxon finally emerged with two bowls and handed one to Sarina. "I present to you... my famous tikka masala."

How could he know this was her favorite dish? It was a complicated recipe calling for uncommon ingredients, like Greek yogurt, ginger, garam masala. She had them on hand because she often made the dish for herself, but it shouldn't have been his first idea upon seeing the contents of her fridge and cabinets.

They sat on the floor and began eating.

"Wow," Sarina emoted through a mouthful of food. She shook her head in disbelief. "Jaxon, you have no idea. I thought my tikka masala was good, but yours is even better."

His eyes gleamed with pride. "I'm humbled."

"Can I be so bold as to ask what the secret ingredient is?"

Jaxon gave her a teasing smile. "Try to guess."

Oh, she liked a tasting challenge.

She swirled the velvety chicken around her mouth and made guesses, all of which were wrong.

"Okay, don't tell me. I'm gonna figure it out." She licked the bowl, then caught him watching her. She laughed. "Sorry. I was raised by wolves."

It was the downside of living alone—the tendency to eat like a wild animal without having an audience to keep you human.

"No apology necessary. Love it when people devour what I have to offer," he said, his voice husky.

She tried to ignore the tingle his words sent through her. "Please tell me you have more dishes like that up your sleeve."

"Oh, there's plenty more where that came from," Jaxon said. "And I bake."

I'm dead. Tell me you're the perfect man without telling me you're the perfect man. "Kelsey's a lucky girl, to have a man who cooks *and* bakes. What's your specialty?"

"Brownies, for sure."

"Yum, I could go for some right now."

"Do you have the ingredients?"

They searched through Sarina's kitchen and found everything they needed. No surprise there, since Sarina stockpiled baking ingredients like a squirrel with nuts.

Jaxon shuffled Sarina from the kitchen as he went to work. Before long, the apartment once again filled with the scent of Jaxon's culinary crafting. This time, dark chocolate decadence.

When he handed her a sample of his warm gooey treat, Sarina took a bite and almost fell over.

"Oh, my God," she said, licking a dollop of melted chocolate chip from her lip. It was the most incredible treat she'd ever had.

Okay, if I can't have him, Kelsey better snag him up and good.

Life was too short not to have this tasty treat—the man

and his dessert—in their world. Even if, for Sarina, it meant as a future brother-in-law.

JAXON GOT CHILLS WATCHING SARINA CLOSE HER EYES and lick her lips as she ate her brownie. It was the most enticing thing he'd seen in a long time. It took all the reserve he could muster to keep from reaching over, cupping her face and kissing the chocolate off her lips.

When she opened her eyes and caught him looking, he quickly shifted his gaze.

He cleared his throat. "You mentioned having an ex-boyfriend. Are you dating anyone now?"

"Hell no. Nor do I plan to, for some time. Running this place takes all the energy I have."

"What if you meet somebody? Say a customer wanders in one day..."

Or a guy hides in your freezer...

"Maybe I'd consider it then, but he'd have to be someone pretty special."

"Of course. Nothing but the best, right?"

Despite embarking upon his *Kelsey Grace: Girlfriend* campaign just a couple of days ago, he couldn't help second-guessing himself. He was getting lost in Sarina's emerald gaze, looking up at him as she licked brownie off her fingers. The old F-boy Jaxon would have flashed his sexy smile and suggested she give him a chance. But he wasn't that guy anymore. Only a douchebag would come on to her when she believed he was her sister's boyfriend.

He could have stayed there all night, sitting on the floor,

getting to know the beautiful Sarina by candlelight, but he was beginning not to trust himself. Scared by his lustful thoughts, he knew it was time to exit stage left.

Faking a yawn, he told her he was getting tired.

"I'm sure. Fighting off all those women as you have."

Or just thoughts of one woman.

She led him to the spare room and gave him a new toothbrush. "I'm sure I have a t-shirt from my ex lying around if you want something to sleep in."

"No thanks, I'm good. I don't wear anything when I sleep."

Sarina's eyebrows shot up as she giggled. "Okay, then, I'll leave you to that."

"Honey," he said to her retreating back.

She spun back around, a smile tugging at her lips. "What did you just say?"

"Honey," he said, matter-of-factly. "You asked what the secret ingredient was. It's honey."

"Yep." Nodding, a slow smile spread across her face. "That's what it was. I can't believe I didn't guess it."

"G'night, Sarina," he said, but not because he wanted to. Because if he didn't, he might truly overstep his boundaries, thereby destroying any chance he had with her.

I mean, with Kelsey.

Jaxon stared at the ceiling as he lay in bed, trying to get Sarina out of his mind. He had no idea what had just happened in the past few hours, but he felt like he could see more clearly than he ever had before. For the first time ever, he felt as if he'd met his match. No—someone better than him.

He didn't even know this girl, but something about her made him feel some kind of way that was completely foreign to him. Maybe it was because she didn't fall all over herself like other women did. She wasn't easily impressed, he could tell, and that made her all the more interesting. Kind of like her sister. But unlike sweet, vulnerable Kelsey, Sarina was feisty and strong-willed, apparently driven to succeed on her own instead of relying on family money to bail her out. There was nothing sexier than that.

But more than her outward beauty and her drive to succeed, there was a level of chemistry between them that he'd never felt before with another woman. Including her sister—the one whose heart he'd come to win over.

SARINA AWAKENED BEFORE DAWN TO THE SMELL OF chorizo coming from her kitchen. She found Jaxon cracking eggs into a bowl.

"I figured you must leave super early for the café, so I wanted to fill your little belly before you had to take off."

"Wow," she said, bowled over by his gesture. No guy had ever done something so sweet for her.

Grabbing two candlesticks they'd used last night, Jaxon waved them toward the stove.

"And now," he said in a perfect French accent. "I invite you to relax, as the kitchen proudly presents...your breakfast."

Sarina chuckled with delight over his spot-on impersonation. "Thank you, candle guy."

"Name's Lumière." Jaxon smiled, breaking character. "I played him in our middle school musical. I hope I nailed it."

"Ten out of ten. Only thing missing is the mustache."

"Dammit! I knew I'd forgotten something."

"To what do I owe this incredible act of hospitality in my own home?"

"You asked if I had something else up my sleeve. Let me introduce you to my famous chorizo omelet."

"Wow," Sarina said, breathing in the aroma. "I'm so lucky you chose my freezer to hide in last night."

"I'm the lucky one," he said, his eyes gleaming as he broke another egg into the frying pan.

"How did you sleep?" Sarina asked as she padded over to the stove and leaned against the counter to watch.

"Like this." Jaxon dropped his head, closed his eyes, and mimicked a sleeping position. "How about you?"

"Like this." Sarina did the same.

They both laughed. She was amazed at the similarity of their humor and wished he could stay a little longer. He was fun to have around.

With the expertise of a seasoned chef, Jaxon flipped another omelet.

"If you're not careful, I may put you to work downstairs."

"That would be fun," he said.

He reached for something and accidentally brushed against her. Jumping out of the way, she knocked a pepper grinder off the counter.

"Sorry, didn't mean to *grind* up against you like that," he joked.

"You're so *dash*ing, I didn't mind," she said, going right into pun mode, hoping he could keep up. There was nothing she loved more than punning around with people.

"You can *pepper* me with compliments all you want."

"I take it you're a *seasoned* pro at this."

"Better not tell Kelsey. I wouldn't want to *shaker* up."

"*Ooo*-kaayy!" she exclaimed, nodding her enthusiastic approval, offering two high fives, which he reciprocated. "Excellent punsmanship. You've just passed my 'sister's boyfriend' test."

"I certainly hope so," he said, giving her another one of those looks, that sexy half-smile of his. He shooed her away playfully. "Now I need you to leave me alone so I can finish preparing your meal."

She snuggled up on the couch and delighted in hearing "Be Our Guest" whistled from the kitchen.

A couple minutes later, he appeared, holding two plates. "I present to you, your omelet," he said once again in his French accent.

And that's when she noticed he had something on his upper lip.

She looked closer. "Is that a—"

"Oui, une mustache pour mon ami."

There was a fried onion plastered to his upper lip.

Laughing, she shook her head in disbelief. Could he really be this perfect? Looks, smarts, silly sense of humor, and a fried onion for a mustache. How could a girl want for anything more?

Meaning Kelsey, of course.

She still had a hard time believing her sister was down for someone like Jaxon. Yes, he was universally appealing, but she wasn't one for effervescent crowd-pleasers. Someone broodier was more her style.

"This is amazing," she said, as she took a bite.

Next to the omelet was a swirl of red apple skins. "What's this?"

"My ill-fated attempt at a rose garnish, to go along with the *Beauty and the Beast* theme."

She shook her head. "Not ill-fated. It's beautiful."

All she could think was: Where did you come from, Jaxon Quinn? It was one of the best breakfasts she'd ever had. She was going to have to get the recipe for this dish as well and add it to the café's offerings.

"Thanks, Jax. You really didn't have to do all this."

"It was nothing. I love cooking, I just don't get a chance to do it very often. I'm also guessing you have a long day ahead of you and thought it would be nice if someone provided *you* with sustenance for a change."

"I'm not joking about putting you to work." It would be fun to have a celebrity sous chef who knew his way around a kitchen and could dole out puns along the way.

"It would literally be a dream come true for me."

His eyes locked with hers for a moment, and he bit his lip before shifting his gaze. A tiny chill went through her.

"I appreciate you letting me stay here last night, but I don't want to put you out. I can have my assistant book me somewhere else incognito so I can get out of your hair."

"Are you kidding me? You've cooked two meals since you arrived. I usually charge by night, but I think you've paid your debt."

"It's been my pleasure. Do you think it's weird for me to wait until opening night to surprise Kelsey? Should I do it today?"

"No!" Sarina was surprised by her emphatic denial. "I think it's nice you want to surprise her when her show opens."

And, I wouldn't mind having a live-in chef for a couple more days.

"If you're sure..."

"Don't make me beg, Quinn. Mi casa es su casa for as long as you need."

"That's mighty kind of you, ma'am," he said, lowering his head as he took a bow.

She grabbed the top of his head. "Oh, Jax..."

"What?" he demanded as he yanked out of her grasp, a look of alarm crossing his face.

She gave him a teasing glance. "Aren't you a bit young to be turning gray?"

"Shit! You saw that, too? Oh my God. Kelsey told me it wasn't a gray hair, but I *knew* it was. She lied to me!"

Sarina just laughed. Kelsey had told her the story of him freaking out over turning thirty. Jaxon didn't have a stitch of gray on his head. She just wanted to have some fun with him.

"Pluck it," he demanded.

"I'm flattered, Quinn, but I don't pluck someone I just met."

"I promise I'll call you in the morning," he said, instantly getting her innuendo. "Believe me, I'm not a one-pluck kinda guy."

"That's not what the tabloids say."

"Ouch."

"If you think that hurts, wait'll I get my hands on those gray hairs of yours."

"There's more than one?" he asked, sounding alarmed again.

"I'm afraid you're aging out of the rom-com scene, Zaddy. You're gonna have to start seeking different roles."

"Ha *ha*. And what roles would that be? Playing Kelsey's father?"

"I was thinking more like *Old Man and the Sea*. Maybe a couple denture commercials on the side."

"You're very funny, Grace," he said, his tone wry. "Ever consider doing stand-up?"

"I would, but I'm too busy running a café," she said, "into the ground."

"*Ba-dum-dum*. Speaking of which, when do you have to be there?"

"Pretty much now." She stood and gathered their dishes.

"Can I come help you?"

Sarina glanced at the clock. "Sure. My staff won't arrive for another forty-five. We'll just have to get you out of there before then."

It was fun having someone there to help with the pre-opening set up. Before Sarina tossed the beans into the coffee grinder, she had Jaxon smell and guess the flavors—all correctly. She poured two coffees for them, and they sat in the back chatting until the tinkling of the front doorbell alerted them to the first reporting staff member. They grabbed their coffees and hustled up the back steps.

"If you're sure you don't mind me hanging out here today, I'll have my driver drop off my bag. I may try to do some online interviews, if that's okay."

"Perfectly fine. The Wi-Fi's free. I left a spare key on the counter for you in case you need to run out. I'll be back midday to bring you lunch."

"I'll be here."

Sarina was relieved to have a full house for breakfast again, but as much as she tried to concentrate on her customers, she couldn't stop thinking about all the fun she and Jaxon had had over the past twelve hours, laughing more than she had in months, maybe even years. Her life had been all business, no pleasure, since she opened the café. She welcomed the friendly distraction. Even if he was there for her sister.

Colton

COLTON WAS HEADING OUT EARLY WEDNESDAY MORNing when he heard Kelsey's voice behind him.

"Where are you sneaking off to so early?"

"Philly." He gave her a sheepish grin. "Meeting with Luke and the developers. I wanted to hear for myself what their plans are for the arts center land."

"I reiterate my offer to buy it."

"I'll talk to them and see if I can get them to back off from wanting both parcels," he said. It seemed important to Kelsey that he at least try.

"Thanks," she said, throwing her arms around him.

He instinctively burrowed his face into her neck, and she leaned into it, like it was the most natural thing in the world. Their hug lasted longer than a simple friendly hug would.

As Colton careened down the Atlantic City Expressway towards Philadelphia, he couldn't get Kelsey out of his mind. He turned up the stereo volume to drown out his thoughts, until he realized the song that was playing was Bruce Springsteen's "Jersey Girl." He flipped to a heavy metal station instead.

He kept his promise to Kelsey and tried to dissuade the company from purchasing the arts center land, but they were adamant about wanting both plots. The farm, for a condo complex with affordable housing to encourage new residents.

The arts center land, for a strip mall to stimulate local economy and encourage small businesses to thrive. And next to the shops, a community green space.

"When we saw the garden your mom planted, we decided it would be nice to recreate it on the arts center land, replant the seeds of her perennials and name it after her. Maybe even add some meandering paths and benches so people can enjoy her beautiful green thumb."

Oh, man. Did they know how to work him. Still, he'd made a promise to Kelsey.

"You've given me a lot to think about," he said as the meeting drew to an end. Realizing he'd never shared with Max the offer Kelsey had made to buy the arts center land, he added, "I'd like to talk to my brother first."

"Absolutely." The reps exchanged looks. "How about we give you until Saturday to think on it?"

Invigorated by the development company's vision as he drove down the Atlantic City Expressway, he inhaled the future. Resolution. Redemption. A new beginning—for the Cape, new families, and him. Once the sale was complete, he could walk away, head to Montana, be united with his pup. Exactly like he'd planned. Anywhere but Cape May and the painful memories it held.

Except...being back here wasn't really all that bad, he had to admit. Now that he and Kelsey were beginning to reconnect, his main reason for wanting to flee the Cape had somehow lost its umph.

Before going home, he drove to the arts center. He hadn't been there since he returned to Cape May, and certainly not after hearing his dad's work on the property led to his heart attack. Something compelled him to go.

He was crushed to see what had become of the building. What was once a charming historic barn, with several additions added on over the years, was now a dilapidated half-structure, roofless and splintered.

Yet the treehouse he and his dad had built remained standing, seemingly untouched by nature's wrath.

He was filled with memories of that summer, working side-by-side with his dad as he'd taught Colton tricks of the building trade. His dad had big shoes to fill once their mom died and he had to take over both roles. He made it a point to spend time with both boys—with Colton, tossing a football and building things together, and with Max, gardening and the aquarium. It was as if Roger Banks knew his days were also numbered and wanted to do all he could to prepare his boys to follow their passions.

God, how Colton missed him. The pain he felt was palpable. Nostalgia melted into sadness, knowing how disappointed his dad had been when Colton's injury permanently took him out of the game. He'd never said as much, but Colton knew how proud his dad was of him playing pro ball, and how devastated he was when it ended.

A gust of wind ushered in memories of another day—he and Kelsey in second grade, spinning around on the lawn as blustery wind blew.

"I bet I can blow that building right down," Colton had bragged. "Just like the Big Bad Wolf."

"How you gonna do that?" Kelsey asked.

"I'm gonna huff and puff and—"

"Blow this place down," Colton now whispered as another tear broke free, overcome with the sentimentality of yesteryear. The good old days, when their greatest fears dwelled only in their minds, like fictional monsters in the closet. Only this fear had come to fruition.

From his salty tears emerged visions of a post-development Cape, as a new housing complex promised to swell the population by thousands. What a zoo the place would become once condos and convenience stores went in, and emissions from vehicles increased exponentially. Wildlife would be displaced, as fields and wooded areas were destroyed to add buildings, roads, and parking lots.

His heart ached as he recalled Kelsey's words to that effect. If he let it happen, the blood of this land would be on his hands.

Envisioning the building Kelsey had described, his architectural brain began working on the design, using her wish list as a blueprint. It stoked his passion for building things, which had laid dormant for too long. He'd never taken on such a complicated structure before, but after majoring in architecture and summers working in construction, he knew some things. His heart picked up its tempo as he began imagining all the improvements he could make.

The decision to move forward with the sale to the developers rested solely on his discretion. No one was forcing him to sell—it was driven only by his burning desire to leave Cape May.

Yet something was giving him pause. Maybe it was the offer to coach youth football. Or knowing the devastation he'd leave in his wake if he went through with the sale. Perhaps it was the way Kelsey had gazed up at him with those dark, soulful eyes last night, pleading with him not to sell.

He looked skyward.

"I don't know what I'm gonna do, Dad," he whispered as a tear rolled down his cheek. "I need you to give me some kind of sign, point me in the direction I need turn next."

He waited for a sign. None came.

Molly

MOLLY WAS BACK AT MAX'S FARM EARLY THAT MORNING to pick him up for their errands. While she waited for him, she received a text from Becca, asking her if she wanted to join the girls for drinks that night. She agreed, anxious to meet up with her old friends.

Max hopped into the golf cart, holding his arm. "Anyone know where I can get some oxy? I think my arm's broken."

"Funny guy. I'll be a pharmaceutical rep, not a narcotics dealer."

"Aren't they one and the same?" he joked.

"Ouch."

"Where are we off to today?"

"Higbee Beach, to find some shells and driftwood the kids can use for crafts."

"I love Higbee. They say you can find a lot of sea glass there, but I've never found any."

"Maybe today will be your lucky day."

"It already is. Hey, we should take kayaks. It's a perfect day for it, and I have two in the barn. What do you say?"

Molly considered his offer. She'd accomplished much of her to-do list ahead of schedule, thanks to Max's help, and didn't have as much to do today.

"I guess it would be fun to have some play time," she agreed.

"All work and no play makes Max a dull boy."

He hopped out and headed to the barn with Molly in tow.

"There's nothing about you that's dull," she said, mostly under her breath.

He must have heard her, as he turned and gave her a smile that made her heart go *zing* for a split second.

Max lifted the kayaks with ease, as if they were made of Styrofoam, his muscles drawing her attention. She grabbed a handle to help, accidentally brushing her hand against his. Another *zing*!

They carried the kayaks to the golf cart, assessing the physical challenge that lay before them.

"Now what?" Molly asked.

They laughed as Max admitted he hadn't quite thought it through. "When there's a will, there's a kayak," Max assured her.

Molly wouldn't have believed it if she hadn't seen it for herself, but five minutes later, she was puttering down the back roads with two kayaks strapped to the roof of the golf cart, and one Maxwell Banks lying across both to keep them secure. Thank God there was no other traffic.

"I'm so going to jail for this," Molly called up to Max. "We have to be committing fifty different moving violations right now."

"Kayaking is a lot more fun when it ends in a court date!" Max yelled back. "Gotta live a little, girl."

"Sounds fun," she added, swerving to avoid a pothole. "One last hurrah before we head to solitary confinement."

"Whoa!"

Oops, she'd taken the turn onto the beach road a little too quickly. She could sense Max and the two kayaks shifting to the side, followed by a loud crash of plastic, then a second, larger, thud.

Molly jumped out to find two kayaks lying face up on the side of the road, with Max sprawled inside one of them.

"Oh my God, are you okay?" Molly called out as she rushed over, hoping she hadn't broken her new friend.

"Cause of death: kayak-alanche."

Molly tried to contain her amusement as they hoisted the vessels back onto the cart. This time Max sat in the cart with his arm holding the side of one against the roof, while Molly held the other. A minute later, after several gut-wrenching dips and divots in the dirt road, they made it to Higbee Beach.

Once they'd portaged the kayaks to the bay, Max helped her into one, pushing her out beyond the calm waves before sliding into his own with impressive agility. They paddled in silence before Max stopped and placed his finger on his lips.

"Dolphins," he whispered.

Molly was amazed at their grace as they swam by. One dove above the waves a few feet from them and she gave a little scream.

"It's okay, they won't hurt us," he said.

"Yeah, but isn't it true that where there are dolphins, there are sharks, too?"

"Not always. Besides, we're in kayaks. We're safe."

"Ever seen *Jaws*? They've been known to eat helicopters."

"Only in the..."

Molly expected him to say movies.

"Carolinas."

Molly laughed. "Cause of death: shark-nado."

"You'll be fine. You're with me."

"Somehow that doesn't make me feel any better," she teased.

"That's because you don't know I'm reigning Shark Wrestling King of the East Coast."

"I stand corrected."

Her trepidation soon turned to fascination as the dolphins swam around, appearing to entertain them.

"I don't know if you know this, but I'm fluent in dolphin," Molly said.

"I had no idea."

Molly threw her head back and gave her best whistle-clicking dolphin impression.

"What did you say?" he asked, laughing.

"I told them this is the guy who saved their friend Bob."

"Was that his name?"

"Yes. Shame you can't speak dolphin like I can." Molly leaned her ear toward the water, as if listening for their responses.

"Now what are they saying?" he asked, amused.

"They don't know a Bob."

When the pod finally moved on, he asked if she'd in some way offended them.

"You never know with dolphins. They offend easily."

As they continued floating around, he pointed out other passing fish and their varieties, including a few turtles. It was eerily silent out beyond the waves, but so peaceful. Molly felt completely at ease as she and Max bobbed in silence, not feeling the urge to fill it with conversation. A first for her.

"I can see why you love this," Molly finally said. "It's amazing."

"I'm glad you like it."

"So why marine biology, and specifically, cetology?" she asked. "I get it, being out here, but what do you hope to do with it? What's your dream?"

"Nobody's ever asked me that," Max said. "These guys out here are totally defenseless, yet every day we come into their world—the ocean is their world, not ours—and we kill them. Knowingly and unknowingly. For food, sport, trash disposal, for our own entertainment, and beyond."

He was right. Humans were pretty selfish, even if they didn't intend to be.

"I guess my dream is to save the animal kingdom. I know it sounds ridiculous, but they, along with our planet, need people like me who are informed about what's going on. We're all part of one big food chain. Any one of us goes, we all go. It sounds dramatic, but that's how it'll happen. We all need each other to survive, and we need each other to be at our best. At all times. Call me a major geek, but that's my dream."

Molly was speechless for a moment. She'd never known anyone so passionate about something other than themselves.

Finally, she found her words. "You are *not* a major geek. I'm so impressed by you. We should all be living like you do, helping others."

She truly meant it.

Kelsey

KELSEY BREATHED IN THE SALTY AIR AS SHE RODE HER bike home from Colton's that morning. The shade of passing trees provided respite from the scorching sun, as she thrust her legs out to coast, just like she and Colton did when they were kids. Her heart felt light, and she laughed as the puddles she purposely hit splashed cool droplets onto her legs. She thought about last night and how good it felt to sit at the table with Colton, reminiscing over photos of their youth. Still surprised by her own spontaneous offer to purchase the arts center property, she hoped Colton would be successful in his bid to take it off the negotiation table.

She'd just parked her bike when her agent called. Sitting on the front steps of the porch, she answered.

"Got another rom-com for you, Kelse. It's yours if you want it."

Kelsey was about to blanketly accept as she always did, but the agent's last four words gave her pause. *If you want it.*

Choice implied.

Did she want it? It was risky passing up a guaranteed role. An actor never knew when the next would come along, and refusing could prove fatal to her career. The past called out to her. *Be a good girl, take the role.*

But...no. She wasn't doing that anymore, going along with things out of fear and duty. This was her chance to determine what type of role would be best for her authentic self.

"I need to think about it," Kelsey said, hoping she wasn't making a mistake. "As you know, I'm looking to pursue more serious roles."

"Okay. Let me know. In the meantime, I'll keep my eyes open for something in that vein."

After hanging up, Kelsey sat back and looked up at the sky, which felt higher than it ever had. A limitless cerulean backdrop against passing white puffs.

She was proud of herself for not jumping at the opportunity. The freedom of choice felt foreign to her, liberating, knowing it was well within her right to decide her next steps. She could either take the movie and continue down the same rom-com path, which had served her well. Or not and see what waited on the other side of the clapboard. Either way, she finally felt as if the choice was hers to make.

A feeling of excitement swept through her as she contemplated her life taking a slightly different turn, at least for a few months. If Colton agreed to sell the land to her, she'd be a Cape May landowner. The prospect of taking time off from acting, staying in Cape May and helping with the design of the new arts center, was intriguing.

She wondered if there was any world in which Colton might stay and rebuild it with her.

Molly

"I COULD DEFINITELY DO THIS MORE OFTEN," MOLLY SAID as they continued to kayak. "It's nice to get away from the to-do lists and the event planning stuff."

"It's nice to have someone to do this with."

Molly found it hard to look away from his gaze. Especially the way the sun danced on his tan, sea-sprayed arms, the wet parts of his t-shirt clinging to his notably toned torso. His smile seemed even brighter out here with the water's reflection, or maybe that was just because he appeared to be happier than she'd ever seen him. She wasn't sure if it was the sea air or what, but Maxwell Banks was becoming increasingly more attractive by the day. In all ways.

Molly dragged her paddle through the water, splashing Max to disrupt his magnetic pull.

"Just for that…"

He returned the spray. Droplets landed on her, instantly cooling her scorched skin.

"Oh, you don't want to take me on," Molly joked. "I was captain of our Paddle Splashing Team in college."

"Me too!" Max exclaimed. "I knew there was a reason we got along so well."

"Staring contests, kayak splashing, and saving the planet. What other amazing skills don't I know about?"

"I was captain of the paper airplane folding team and spent some time on the competition pencil sharpening squad, but I didn't see the point in that."

She nodded, smiling. "Well done."

"I was a walk-on for the chess watching team, but they were only using me as a pawn."

Molly giggled. "You're funny, Max."

"Funny-looking."

Molly shook her head. "No, just funny. You're actually—what's the word I'm searching for?"

"Beastly?"

She shook her head. "Nope."

"Nerdy."

"Not that either."

"I know—perpetual member of the friend zone."

Suddenly, she gasped. She'd forgotten about Becca and her crush on Max. "I bet I can change that."

"Why, Molly Grace, are you asking me out?"

Molly laughed out loud. "Not me. Becca Barnshaw. Remember her?"

"Uh, yeah. She was on my math team."

"I ran into her the other day, and your name came up. I told her how you've been clinging to the back of my golf cart. Fun fact—she had a crush on you back in school. Must've been your amazing pencil sharpening skills."

"I hate it when women want me just for that."

Molly laughed. "Anyway, Becca really wants to get reacquainted with you. Interested?"

"I dunno..." He paused, squinting into the sun. "Should I be?"

"Of course," Molly said a little too quickly. Max would be an awesome catch, and Becca would be a lucky woman to have a shot at him.

"Okay, if you insist," Max said, splashing her once again.

"Good, because I already gave her your number."

"Hey, speaking of getting reacquainted," Max said, "we had an overnight guest last night. I bet you can't guess who!"

"Captain Blackbeard?"

"That was last week. Terrible house guest, making a ruckus at night with his wooden leg. I'm talking last night."

"J-Lo."

"She was here with Blackbeard. Cute couple."

"Okay, I give up."

"Your sister."

"Kelsey? But why—" Molly widened her eyes as it dawned on her. "Oooh!"

Max nodded, his eyes bright. "Right? That's what I said."

"Because of Colton."

"I'd like to think it was because of me."

"That goes without saying, of course. But since you're practically engaged to Becca, I guess she'll have to settle for your brother."

"They were pretty cozy. And when I say cozy, I mean they had candles lit, she was wrapped in a blanket, and they were sitting really close."

"What about Jaxon?"

"Colton's not into Jaxon anymore."

Molly laughed and splashed Max with her paddle again.

"All I know is Colton had a major crush on Kelsey in high school."

"Kinda like you did on me?" Molly cocked her head to the side and gave him a flirtatious smile. She knew she was on the edge of inappropriateness, having a boyfriend and all, but there was a part of her that wanted Max to confirm it.

"Oh, man. Was I that obvious?" Max laughed, as he turned his kayak around in a circle. When his back was to her, he answered. "Affirmative."

"What's that?" Molly sang out, her hand to her ear. "I didn't hear you."

Max turned his kayak back around to face her. He was smiling from ear to ear, blushing.

"Why are you doing this to me?" he asked, sounding vulnerable. Sweet. It tickled her heart.

"Because," Molly said, teasingly, "I always saw you looking. I just didn't know if it was me or Brennan you were looking at."

"All you. Guilty as charged." He tossed his oar into the water where it quickly bobbed away. "I throw myself on the mercy of the court."

"You better throw yourself on the mercy of that paddle, or you're not getting back to land."

"Just as well. Now that you know my dirty little secret, I won't be returning to Cape May."

"Of course you will," Molly said as she wrangled in his

paddle and handed it to him. "It's not a secret, because I suspected it. And it's really not dirty. I think it's cute."

"That's me, being cute and stuff," he said as he began paddling to shore. "And now, my queen, I must banish myself in utter humiliation."

"Not so fast," Molly said, feeling tingly over her new title. Max turned his kayak around to face her.

She paddled toward him, trying to look serious. Just as she got beyond him, she called out, "Last one to shore buys ice cream!"

"No fair!" Max yelled out as he began paddling furiously.

A few seconds later, he caught up and zoomed ahead. Molly didn't mind; she enjoyed the show of strength in front of her. Very much.

When she got close to shore, Max pulled his kayak onto the beach and waded out to waist-deep water. Taking her paddle from her, he tossed it onto the beach. She was about to thank him for pulling her in when he let go of the rope. She started drifting backwards.

"This is for being such a tease," he said.

"Max, no!" she screamed. "Pull me in!"

Max reached out and pulled on the rope, pulling her kayak towards him. And then he let it go again.

"I'm serious!" she said, laughing.

"Why should I pull you in, after you outed me so shamelessly?"

She drifted away until he finally swam out to her, resting his crossed arms on the side of the kayak, his body floating in the water. He looked so eager.

"Why didn't you ever ask me out?" she asked.

"Because you were Molly Grace, and I was Maxwell Banks."

"What does that even mean?"

"You were the most popular girl in the school. And you

always had a boyfriend. You wouldn't have given me the time of day."

He was right. Molly felt bad about that.

"High school girls can be pretty shortsighted," she said. "Had I known you'd go on to reign as Shark Wrestling King, I would have been all over that shit."

They were drifting farther from shore.

"Can you even touch the ground?"

"No," he said. "We're floating out to sea. Now you're really stuck with me."

"Max! Stop!" she giggled through her nervousness. She began paddling with her hands. "Get us back to shore!"

Grabbing the rope, Max swam toward the beach with one arm, pulling her and the kayak with the other. Molly watched in amazement as his muscularity powered through the strong current. Soon they were back on sand.

After returning the kayaks to the farm, they headed into town for ice cream, passing the lighthouse on the way.

"Anyone up for a little race to the top?" Max asked as they passed the towering structure.

"You really think you can beat me, don't you?"

"Oh, I know I can."

"Did you just throw down the gauntlet?"

"You bet I did!"

Without warning, Molly yanked the wheel of the golf cart and drove toward the lighthouse. "I'm tired of all these empty threats. Let's see what you got."

"I forgot to tell you I was the lighthouse racing champion of the Ivy League," he said as she parked.

"I came in second during the Olympic trials," Molly said over her shoulder as she walked towards the lighthouse. "You've met your match."

His eyes twinkled with a smile. "That I have."

Jaxon

Jaxon was happy Sarina had invited him to stay at her place as long as he wanted. Not only was he enjoying their banter and compatibility, but hiding away in Sarina's little apartment offered the perfect escape, a refreshing break from the outside world.

After he'd finished his video interviews that morning, he took a nap. He wasn't exactly being honest when he told Sarina he slept well the night before. He couldn't get her out of his mind. The charge of electricity he'd felt the first time he laid eyes on her was overwhelming. The feeling of her hands in his when the power went out was like nothing he'd experienced before—exhilarating, terrifying, arousing. The way she looked up at him when the lights came on simply took his breath away.

He should feel guilty, having such feelings for Kelsey's sister, until he realized there was nothing to feel guilty about as far as his costar was concerned. Theirs was nothing more than a fake romance, a publicity stunt. Any future relationship only existed in Jaxon's mind. If he changed his mind about pursuing her, no one—including Kelsey—would be any wiser.

Except they'd done such a stellar job convincing the world they were a couple, he'd have a shit ton of public explaining to do if he suddenly went for her sister. He was pretty convinced Sarina, of all people, wouldn't go for it, regardless of whether his thing with Kelsey was real or not.

Guilt ate at him over lying to Sarina. But he and Kelsey were in it together, bound by a contract, and it wasn't his secret to tell unless Kelsey agreed and they did it together.

He'd come to Cape May fully intending to make things real with Kelsey, but he hadn't counted on meeting someone like Sarina. He wondered if it was his brain's last-minute way of distracting him, letting him know he wasn't ready to commit to one woman. Perhaps Kelsey wasn't The One, and he'd misjudged the situation. He didn't believe in destiny but found himself wondering if his plan to come to Kelsey's hometown to sweep her off her feet was really just the universe's way of introducing him to her sister.

He finally fell into a deep sleep, carried away by erotic dreams of a certain café owner, and all the things he wanted to do to her. With her. For her.

DURING A LULL IN THE MIDAFTERNOON RUSH, SARINA snuck up to her apartment with a bagged lunch for Jaxon. She didn't see him at first and he didn't answer when she called his name. She pushed on the slightly ajar guest room door and gasped at what she saw.

A fully naked Jaxon was sprawled on the bed, sunny side up, a raging erection practically waving at her like a blow-up tube man in a used car lot. Meanwhile, he soundly slept, seemingly unaware of the party raging on in front.

Jumping back in stunned horror, she could barely catch a breath for how it was sucked right out of her lungs.

Close the door, you lech!

Right. The door.

She tried to avert her eyes in her furtive attempt to pull it closed. But no matter if she looked again or not (in this case, not), she'd never forget the sight as long as she lived.

Holy. *Fucking.* Shit.

She backed down the hallway, her mouth dropping open in a silent scream, shaking out her hands in the universally recognized sign for *WTF?* Retreating to her room, she paced about, her heart rattling around her ribcage in a desperate attempt to be freed.

"Stop it," she hissed to herself.

Holiest of all fucks. The mental image was now seared into her brain for all of eternity. He was humongous, perfectly shaped. The Cape May Lighthouse had nothing on him. It was an absolute thing of beauty, standing tall and proud. Jaxon Quinn in all his natural glory. If only there was a way to transpose her mental image into a photograph, she could wallpaper her apartment with it. Hell, sell it! Assuring café prosperity for all of eternity.

Oh...but right. She wasn't a complete asshole. Creep, maybe. A horrible host, certainly. Despicable sister, yeppers! A direct descendant of Beelzebub himself.

She had to do something to wash away the image of his beautiful nakedness and flush her nasty thoughts down the drain. That's it. A shower should do it.

After cleansing her body (and her soul, assuming she still had one), she wrapped a towel around herself with plans to dash to her room before Sergeant At-The-Ready awakened from whatever sexy dream he was having. But her plans were foiled when she emerged from the steamy bathroom and careened right into Jaxon's bare chest.

He grabbed her by the elbows to steady her, wearing nothing more than a towel, a smile, and a head full of bed hair.

"There you are." He let go and stretched, yawning.

She couldn't believe his tone, all casual and shit, as they stood there facing each other with nothing but Turkish terry between them. She had a death grip on hers, hoping she'd successfully covered all her bits.

"I thought I heard you," he said. "How was your morning?"

"Huge."

Wait, *what?*

"I mean, not huge, just big. Good! It was...good."

Not as good as yours, apparently.

He chuckled. "You sure about that?"

"Yes! Yep. It was good. You know. The usual. I mean, not that it's usual. It's—*whew!*—wow." *Good God, girl. Get a grip.* "And yours?" she asked.

"Excellent. Did a couple interviews, took a nap, had great dreams."

She sucked in her breath.

"Are you done for the day?" he asked.

"Nope, nope, still have work to do," she said, averting her eyes as he slipped a thumb into the waistband of his towel skirt, presumably to scratch an itch, followed by another long, leisurely yawn-and-stretch. It was as if he were taunting her, seeing how far he could go before she ripped off his white towel and waved it in defeat.

"Do you often take showers in the middle of a shift?" he asked, cocking his head, his eyes gleaming with humor.

"Oh." She laughed nervously, tried to come up with something. "Only when I spill grease all over myself."

He smiled as if he didn't believe her.

"Well, I'd better—" She pointed to her bedroom.

"Yes, of course."

She passed him in the narrow hall, careful not to brush a single inch of skin against his.

"Oh, and Sarina?"

"Yes?" she asked, turning.

He flashed her a half-smile. "Hope you enjoyed the view."

Sarina gasped from sheer mortification as she slammed the door behind her, uncertain whether he meant the view of him wearing only a towel just then, or his one-gun salute earlier.

"Go to jail. Go directly to jail," she ordered herself, as she banged her forehead lightly against the wall.

When she finally descended from Mount Humiliation, she found Jaxon in the kitchen, rummaging through the bagged lunch she'd brought.

Taking a bite from his sandwich, he turned and pulled her into a one-armed hug. "Thank you for this. It's delicious."

She breathed in his freshly showered scent as he held the sandwich out for her to take a bite. She accepted.

Damn. It *was* delicious. She most certainly had every right to open a café. Hex on her family.

"I was wondering. Are there any secluded beaches where we could catch some waves together?"

"There are," she said, choosing not to linger too long on the words *secluded* and *together*. "I know just the place."

Years ago, one of the older local surfers showed Sarina a place most people didn't know about. It became her favorite place to surf.

"We can go after I close. After that, would you like to help bake desserts for the event?"

"I'd love to."

"Great, I'll see you at three."

She turned to leave but left him with these parting words. "Oh, and I did."

"Did what?"

She flashed him a cheeky grin. "Enjoy the view."

It was official. She was going to hell.

Max

MAX DIDN'T WANT TO ADMIT IT, BUT HE WAS FULL OF false bravado about beating Molly to the top of the lighthouse. The two stretched at the base, smack-talking each other until, finally, it was go-time.

"Ladies first," Max said as he ushered her towards the steps.

"You're right," she said, stepping aside and ushering him forward.

He gave a hearty guffaw, and Molly was off to the races.

Max took the steps by two. The staircase was wide at this point, and the two of them raced neck and neck until he overcame her.

"Not fair, your legs are longer!" she yelled as she grabbed onto his still-damp t-shirt.

Max let her pull ahead of him. He waited, then took the steps by two again. Just as he was about to pass her, she jumped in his path and spun him face-first into the stone wall. He let her lean into him, holding him against the wall, until she was off again.

"How much farther?" Max huffed as he raced to keep up, the staircase narrowing with each step.

"I lost count after seventy-five steps," Molly said, breathlessly. "Time for a break."

She stopped in Max's path again, arms stretched across the stairway to keep him from passing.

"I've been thinking," she said. "I may let you win this one. I don't think I'm up for it."

"Really?"

"*No!*" she screamed, as she pivoted and dashed up several steps.

Max was struggling. God, how he hoped they were close to the top. He'd forgotten how taxing it was to climb a lighthouse, especially at clip speed. He finally passed her as the stairwell narrowed to one-person wide.

"I'm taking you down!" she yelled, clamoring up the last few steps. She grabbed his legs, causing him to trip, and she fell forward on top of him.

"Wait," Max said, turning faceup beneath her and grasping her tiny waist. "Let's catch our breath first before we climax."

They burst out laughing. She sank into him.

"Cause of death," she said into his shoulder, "lighthouse challenge."

The sound of children's laughter below broke the moment.

"We'd better—"

"Yeah," he agreed as they disengaged and crawled their way to the top.

Declaring a tie, Max held open the door to the narrow outside walkway at the top of the lighthouse. They gazed out over the sparkling water and stunning vistas of the southernmost tip of New Jersey.

"Beautiful," Molly said, looking at the ocean as she leaned up against the railing.

"Best view I've had all year," Max agreed. Only he was looking at Molly.

Standing behind her, he placed his hands on the railing, enclosing her. It was a bold move, but it felt right in the moment. His heart pounded, and he hoped she wouldn't tell him to buzz off. Instead, she leaned back into him, resting her head on his chest. He resisted the urge to brush her hair aside and kiss her neck.

Her backside pressed against the front of him, and he hoped she couldn't feel what it was doing to him. He almost lost it when she placed her hands on his and wrapped them around her waist. There they stood, both looking out at the water as Max hugged her from behind. His breath ragged, his heart racing.

"Max," she whispered as she turned in the circle of his arms to face him.

She gazed up at him, the setting sun reflecting in her eyes. Max let out an involuntary grunt as he bit his lip, his heart about to burst from years of built-up passion, wondering if he was about to make every dream he'd ever had of kissing Molly Grace come true.

Until she put her hand on his chest. "I'm sorry. I...can't."

Max suddenly felt like the biggest asshole on the planet. Of course, she couldn't. She was about to be engaged to someone else. What was he thinking?

He pulled back. "I'm sorry, Molly. My bad."

"No, *my* bad. I really like you, Maxwell Banks," she said, gazing up at him. "But...as a friend. Because...you know. Brennan."

Max's heart deflated as humiliation flooded his cheeks. He turned away so she wouldn't see the hurt in his eyes, or the sheer remorse for his actions.

He had to save face. Say something funny.

"Cause of death: morbid shame."

Molly

MOLLY'S HEART WAS ABOUT TO BEAT RIGHT OUT OF HER chest as she pulled back from Max. She was blown away by the urgency coursing through her, practically begging her to kiss him, before she came to her senses. She couldn't help her powerful yearning, not after spending such a beautiful morning on the bay with him, taking in his silent strength, their teasing banter, the looks he gave her when he thought she wasn't looking. Simply intoxicating.

What was she thinking? Becoming so intimate with him when she was about to be engaged to someone else? She was a terrible human being. Not just because she'd come on to a man who wasn't her soon-to-be fiancé, but because Brennan was the last thing on her mind. The first thing: the sweet boy descending the lighthouse ahead of her in silence, who'd used humor as a shield against what looked to be crushing disappointment in a desperate attempt to save face. If anyone should die from morbid shame it should be her. What she'd done to Max was wholly unfair, playing with his feelings like that, knowing he'd once had feelings for her. And probably still did, the way he leaned into her, the warmth of his embrace, the way his breath caught as he looked at her.

At the base of the lighthouse, she reached for his hand. "Hey," she said, stopping him. "I really am sorry for that. I don't know what I was thinking. You're a great guy, and if I wasn't in a relationship…"

"Thanks, Molly. That's sweet of you to say."

But the look on his face didn't look grateful. Disappointment, shame—whatever he was feeling—appeared to have hardened into something else.

He let go of her hand and started to walk away, before turning back to her.

"You know what, Molly? You were right about the crush I had on you in high school. Unfortunately for me, it's only gotten stronger, spending this time with you. But after what just happened up there, I don't think I can keep doing what we're doing."

"What do you mean, 'doing what we're doing'?"

"I don't know," he said, looking at her pointedly. "You tell me."

Molly didn't know what to say. She had no explanation for her actions, only that she really liked Max. Perhaps in a different time and place, whatever it was between them—she could no longer deny that there *was* something—could be more than platonic. But her heart was too invested in Brennan. They were going through a rough patch, but he was her high school sweetheart, and they were in it for the long haul.

"Does this mean we can't be friends?" she asked, fearing his answer from the look on his face.

"I don't know what it means. Maybe I just need some time to reset myself after…" He motioned to the top of the lighthouse. "After all that."

"Can I at least give you a ride home?"

"No thanks. I'll walk."

"But it's a long way," she objected.

"It'll do me good."

Molly watched as he walked away, wishing she could say something to change his mind.

Suddenly, he stopped again, turning back toward her. "Can I just ask you one question?" His tone sounded argumentative.

"Sure," she said, not certain she wanted to answer.

"What is it you see in him? Besides *looks* and *money*."

Molly's thoughts tumbled around in her head as she tried to find reasons to defend her choice in Brennan.

Max cut in before she could answer. "You have to think hard before coming up with something, don't you? When I asked you this question earlier, you said he was kind of funny, kind of nice, kind of smart. But I don't believe it. Because if he was funny, you would've been smiling and laughing when you guys talked, not angry and frustrated."

Her back went up as she felt the urge to defend her relationship. "That was one conversation, Max. Unfortunately, not a good one."

"I hate to point out the obvious, but he's making it clear he won't make room for you in his life. Is that what you want for yourself?"

She recoiled at his verbal bitch slap. "He *has* made room for me in his life."

"Has he? Where's he been?"

"Why are you doing this?" Molly said, her voice wavering as tears threatened.

Max forged on. "If he's so nice, why he hasn't been here with you, helping with event planning?"

She was about to point out the obvious—his job—but Max was unrelenting as he stepped closer and lowered his voice.

"And now for the million-dollar question. If he was as smart as you say, then why isn't he here, making sure some other guy isn't falling for his girlfriend? Some guy who has liked you so hard from the beginning of time, he won't even *look* at another girl. A guy who adores you, cherishes you, worships the very ground you walk on. But you're too hung up on his *looks* and *money* to see it. Or maybe I'm just not good enough for you."

Molly's mouth flew open, and her heart pounded as she was caught in a windstorm of emotion. Sheer anger over the fact he had the audacity to say these things to her when he didn't know anything about their relationship, except for what she'd told him in the heat of the moment, never believing he would turn it against her. Defensiveness over wanting to protect her relationship. Protect Brennan, and her choice in him. Profound sadness that they'd gone from laughing and flirting to ruining what might have been one of her favorite days of all time.

But what shook her most of all was his bared-soul confession. His words, raw and stripped of pretense, slammed into her heart and exploded in a feeling she'd never experienced before. A mixture of euphoria and grief, outrage and empathy. More emotion than she'd ever allowed herself to feel since the day her dad walked out on her.

Amidst the maelstrom of emotion, she was overcome with

a crazy desire to grab his face and kiss the living shit out of him. But outrage won out.

"How dare you stand here and rip my relationship apart when you know nothing about it?" she demanded. "You've probably never even *been* in a serious relationship, so how the hell can you profess to be some sort of expert?"

Max dropped his head, and Molly knew she'd won. She'd gotten him right where it counted. She should feel elated, but instead she felt awful.

He turned to leave.

"Wait, Max—that was unfair. I'm sorry."

"Not as sorry as I am," he said, head still hanging as he walked away. "It's been nice getting reacquainted with you, Molly. Good luck with the event."

Tears streamed down Molly's face as she watched him walk away, down a dirt path through the woods, wondering if this was the end of them.

She took her heavy, sorrow-filled heart and climbed into the golf cart, not knowing what hurt the most. Losing Max... or realizing that maybe—just maybe—he was right. About Brennan. About her. About everything.

Max

MAX'S HEART POUNDED AND TEARS STUNG HIS EYES AS he walked away from Molly. He had no idea what had come over him, coming at her like he did. He just hadn't been able to take it anymore. He couldn't take being with a woman who had his whole heart, while she freely handed hers off to some schmuck who didn't seem to give a shit about her.

She was right about one thing—Max certainly wasn't an

expert in relationships, but it didn't take a PhD in romance to know how to love someone, how to treat them with kindness and respect. The fact that she was choosing to cling to someone who didn't seem to want her around caused Max to question not only her motives, but Molly herself. He'd always seen himself with someone who was strong, smart, independent. He'd once thought of her that way, but had he been delusional? Had he projected an aura of perfection upon her she didn't deserve?

As he made his way down the wooded path (a strategic move to avoid *cause of death: golf cart*), he thought about the things he'd learned about her over the past week. When asked about her boyfriend's attributes, looks and money were the first two on her list. She had to be shallow for that to be her focus. Putting up with his bullshit excuses screamed of low self-esteem. It was entirely unfair of her to tease Max into admitting he had feelings for her, eliciting his deepest, darkest secret. To come on to him, knowing she didn't reciprocate his feelings, then push him away and dangle her future fiancé in his face. It wasn't the work of a good person. It was self-serving at best, cruel at worse.

Back at his house, he climbed into bed and tried to get to sleep but couldn't. Despite all the energy he'd just expended vilifying Molly, he couldn't get the look she'd given him at the top of the lighthouse out of his mind.

He pulled the sheet over his head and pronounced his own demise.

"Cause of death: unrequited love."

Jaxon

"THIS IS SO PLEASANT OUT HERE," JAXON SAID AS THEY coasted on their bikes through the shady backroads of the Cape. "It's not often I'm in a place by myself with no one around."

"Should I leave?" Sarina joked.

"No," he said, probably a little too quickly. "Being with you feels natural. Like being alone, but in a good way."

Sarina chuckled. "Oddly enough, I know exactly what you mean."

Deciding it was too nice a day to drive to the beach, they'd taken Sarina and Luke's bikes, both outfitted with surfboard racks.

"You're sure your ex won't mind me riding his bike and using his board?" Jaxon had asked as he eyed up the old beach cruiser.

"They're mine now. I got them in the split."

"Good deal. What'd he get?"

"Pain and sorrow."

Jaxon laughed. He understood how the poor sap would feel that way.

They leaned their bikes up against a tree and walked through an overgrown trail to the beach.

"It's my favorite place to surf," she said. "The tourists don't know about it, and the locals prefer other beaches, so I usually have it to myself. Especially at this time of day."

Jaxon tried not to ogle her as she whipped off her t-shirt and shorts to reveal a tiny turquoise bikini that highlighted her golden tan, fitting her perfectly in all the right places.

He tried to keep his eyes averted as she squirted sunscreen and rubbed it on her body. Epic fail. Her abs were toned and tight, and what he imagined existing in those cute little cutoff shorts was a thousand times more juicy in the flesh. When she bent over to do her legs, he struggled to keep the old F-boy inside him from reincarnating and grabbing her from behind.

"Here, let me do your back," he offered.

She squeezed lotion onto his hand, and he took his time working it into her hot skin. She offered to do the same for him, tantalizing him with her soft touch.

Guiding their boards into the water, they jumped on their bellies to cruise over the waves, finally making it beyond the breakers. The swells were still impressive after the previous day's storm.

Lying on his stomach, Jaxon ran a hand through the water. "The water's so green."

"I thought you said you've surfed before?" she teased.

"First time surfing the Atlantic. The Pacific is bluer."

"You're shitting me!" she exclaimed, amazed he'd never surfed the East Coast before. "I'm honored to be sharing this first with you."

He rested his head in his hand and took in the sight of her—tan legs, straddling the board, dangled in the viridian water as she ran her hand back and forth, making little waves. Beads of sea water clung to her lashes, and her eyes reflected the glimmering greens of the water. She was simply stunning.

Another first dawned on him then. First girl he'd ever surfed with.

"Sarina..." He said her name as barely a whisper, hoping she heard him. He had to tell her the truth. About Kelsey, about the fauxmance. About how utterly taken he was by her.

But she was already down on her belly, paddling like her life depended upon it.

"Hold that thought!" she called out as she positioned

herself for the oncoming wave.

He watched, mesmerized, as she caught the swell at just the right moment. Her body moved in sync with the rhythm of the ocean. The sun glinting off the rolling wave highlighted her strength and poise as she executed a perfect bottom curve. Gliding effortlessly, she nailed a sharp top turn with the fluidity and precision of a world-class surfer in a stunning display of athleticism.

Sexy. A.F.

"Nice!" he yelled.

"Your turn, Quinn!"

Jaxon waited until he spotted a good wave. Turning, he paddled out and caught it just in time with an equally impressive bottom turn, if he had to say so himself. Focusing on the wave's momentum, he shifted his weight to harness its power and made a gnarly cut that even he was dazzled by. He hoped she enjoyed the show as much as he enjoyed giving it.

She was waiting for him in the shallows when he jumped off. Wading over, she high-fived him.

"Duly impressed, JFQ. Now, if only you could act as well as you surf, you might actually make the big time."

He laughed out loud and dredged his leg through the water to douse her. She responded in kind, and soon a water fight was underway. He got off a couple great shots until she retreated. Caught up in the game, he tackled her, and they tumbled into the water, both laughing so hard they struggled to get up. He managed to stand first and held out a hand.

"How can I trust you won't yank me back down?" she asked.

"Believe me, if I'd really wanted to take you down, I already would have."

"You don't stand a chance."

He gave her a shy smile. "You're probably right about that."

She flicked water at his chest. "C'mon. Show me what you got, Quinn."

They bellied down on their boards to paddle out when he was struck by something.

It was the same thing the woman in his dream had said to him.

He stopped paddling and watched as she lifted up on her board to top the crest of the wave. Her glistening skin, her perfect ass, the sound of her laughter as it carried over the water weren't all that had him mesmerized.

It was the fact that it was her. The woman in his dream.

"What are you waiting for?" she yelled back at him.

You. Dream girl.

She was already sitting on her board beyond the breakers when he finally caught up to her.

"You good?" she asked.

"Never been better." He grinned. "Thanks for this. I'm having the time of my life."

She gave him a slow smile. "Me too."

They took turns riding their last waves as the sun began its descent into the horizon, casting a pinkish hue across the crashing waves. They sat on the beach, wrapped in towels to dry off.

"I hope you're up for our baking challenge tonight, JFQ. We've got a lot to do."

"You were serious about putting me to work?" he joked, even though the thought made him happy.

"Absolutely. I always make my houseguests work off their stay."

They were silent for a moment as they looked out over the water.

"So weird not to see the sunset out there," Jaxon said.

"That's right, Pacific Ocean boy. Here, we watch our sunsets over the bay." She pointed to their right where the sun was about to dip below the horizon.

Another first or him.

Sarina

SARINA AND JAXON WATCHED THE SUNSET IN SILENCE when he leaned into her, bumping his shoulder against hers.

"I've been thinking about something."

"Should I alert the tabloids?"

"I already have. It's not very often it happens."

"I'm glad I get to witness it."

"After we were joking around this morning about you doing stand-up, it got me thinking. Have you ever considered offering entertainment at night? Like a coffee house vibe."

"No, I haven't. The café's really just a breakfast and lunch place."

"What if you opened one or two nights a week? Hear me out—it may help bring in more money. Especially if you offered different types of entertainment. Comedians. Poetry slams. Local singers. Didn't Taylor Swift play in a coffee shop in Stone Harbor back when she was twelve? I remember Kelsey telling me that once."

"That's right. She played at Coffee Talk."

Jaxon's words got Sarina thinking. It wasn't a bad idea. She was surprised she hadn't thought of it herself. But then she heard Grand Lillian's voice, telling her she didn't have common sense and was *taking on too much*.

She wondered what the cost would be to open at night. For one, she'd have to cover staff wages and possibly offer different food and drinks. Speaking of drinks—

"I don't have a liquor license."

"Who said you need one? Your coffee is fantastic. People love hanging out at night, especially in summer, and it would give them an option that isn't a bar. You can't go wrong with dessert, coffee, and entertainment. I'm thinking you could have different theme nights, like trivia and board game nights."

The more he spoke, the more excited she became over the idea. "Keep talking."

"You can offer specialty desserts and drinks with fun names. Like Open Mic Macchiato. Local Singer Latte." He laughed at his own brilliance. "See what I did there?"

"I saw," Sarina said, her eyes lighting up over Jaxon's plethora of ideas. "You're good, Quinn. You may have to help me write the menu."

"I'm here for it. Seriously, Sarina. Think about all the extra money you'll draw in. It wouldn't have to be every night, just like every Thursday, or on the weekends."

Sarina nodded. "That could work. I'll have to give it a try one night after the fundraiser."

"Why wait? What if we were to throw something together for tomorrow night, as a kickoff to the fundraising event?"

"That's...actually brilliant. I like the way you think, JFQ."

He waggled his eyebrows at her. "You should see what else I can do."

Oh, I bet. But...that was between him and Kelsey.

As they rode their bikes through the backroads, dusk settled in, and the cicadas serenaded them. They discussed possible names for the event, settling on *Café Au Late Night*. Sarina decided she'd make a few specialty desserts for the event. She did a mental inventory of the ingredients she had, and they decided on three offerings: a blueberry cobbler ("Sing Me the Blues"), a key lime pie ("In the Key of Lime"), and Jaxon's decadent dark chocolate brownies, à la mode ("Rapsody in Chocolate").

Back in her apartment, Sarina tossed him a fresh towel. "Shower up, dude, and then it's time to show me what you got."

His eyebrows shot up as he gave her a salacious glance.

Oh, shit. That came out wrong.

Flustered, she quickly added, "I mean, time to put your money where your mixer is and go bake some goodies."

He gave her a crooked smile. "Okay, Grace. Game on."

AFTER SHOWERING, JAXON SAT ON THE COUCH, WAITING for Sarina to finish. Flipping through a magazine, he glanced up every so often, hoping to catch another glimpse of her in her towel. So excited was he by the prospect, he wasn't paying attention to what he was reading until he focused more closely. It was the article about him and Kelsey. He tossed it aside as if it were on fire, not wanting to think about that right now.

Hearing a noise, he looked up to see Sarina scurrying down the hall, wrapped in her towel, just before she slammed the door behind her.

Damn. Missed it.

His eyes rested on the magazine again, where Kelsey's photo face was looking up at him.

"I'm sorry, Kelse," he whispered. "I know I'm a pig, but I can't help it. Your sister is..." He exhaled, his eyes rolling back. "*So* damn fine."

Kelsey's face continued to stare.

"I'm in big trouble here. We gotta do something about this."

"Who are you talking to?" Sarina asked, her tone playful.

He startled to find her standing in front of him, wearing a loose sundress. "Oh, just myself." He tossed a pillow over the magazine so she wouldn't see it. Too late.

She nodded toward the hidden magazine. "Nice article.

You guys make a cute couple."

Her tone had shifted, edged with a touch of sarcasm. He caught the smirk tugging at her lips and wondered if she saw right through their facade.

"But for tonight, you're mine," she said over her shoulder as she headed for the door.

Leaping up like a lapdog in heat, he followed. "*All* yours."

In more ways than you can imagine.

Down in the café, Sarina put on her favorite playlist and assembled the ingredients they'd need for their desserts.

"I'm thinking that, while we're down here, I'll make and freeze cakes for the fundraiser and decorate them later."

After a quick discussion of what they needed to accomplish, they began their dance around the kitchen, Jaxon on mixer and oven duty, while Sarina added ingredients and supervised. When they were making Jaxon's brownies, he got a charge out of playing it up like he was a professional baker. He rarely had time to pursue his interest in the culinary arts, so being able to work in an industrial-grade kitchen with a fellow foodie was exhilarating.

This one in particular.

"This is the most fun I've had since I can remember," Jaxon said over the music. He loved her eclectic taste, which matched his own random and varied interests. Prince, Etta James, Sabrina Carpenter, and more. He was having so much fun, he was shocked to find it was three in the morning when they finally loaded the cooled desserts into the freezer.

"Tomorrow morning's gonna hurt," Sarina said as she closed the door. She looked up at him, her pale-green eyes wide with wonder. "Can you believe we've been at this for six hours?"

"Time flies when you're having fun. And this, my friend, was amazing. It makes me feel alive to be here, doing this."

"Me too."

"Especially with you."

He couldn't help but add that last part. It was true. He just hoped that wasn't too forward of him. He needed to keep his head straight, not follow his instincts. Because, facts: it was getting harder and harder to be in Sarina's presence and not sweep her into his arms. Kiss her luscious lips. Do everything he'd been dreaming of doing with her ever since he got there.

He had until Friday to sort out his feelings and his plans, decide how he was going to approach Kelsey and what he'd ask of her.

One thing was certain. The intended target of his Cape May visit was no longer his costar. It was her sister.

Molly

As MOLLY GOT READY TO GO OUT WITH HER FRIENDS, she couldn't stop rehashing her argument with Max. The more she thought about it, the more defensive she became. He had no right to question her relationship and paint her in such a bad light.

She *had* to focus on his biting words. Something, anything, to keep his other words from echoing in her heart.

Adores you, cherishes you, worships the very ground you walk on.

Despite her anger, that sentiment took her breath away.

She was relieved to have something to do that night to keep her mind off it. She met up with her friends at the Rusty Nail beach bar, and after a round of typical awkward reunion comments—how long it had been, how fast those four years had gone by and how none of them had changed—they settled at a table.

Molly was surprised at just how little her friends seemed

to have changed, at least on the outside. They still wore their hair in the same long bobs they'd all gotten the summer they'd graduated, when they'd collectively decided to ditch their long locks in favor of something sophisticated for college. While Brennan had thought she looked hot, he'd often commented on how he missed her long hair, so she grew it out again and hadn't changed it since.

As they caught up with each other's lives, Molly was happy she'd gone out. It was good to see her friends again. But as the wine eased the bitter edge she'd felt earlier, her mind drifted to sadness over the fallout with her friend. The one she really wanted to hang out with, despite everything that had happened.

Before long, Molly realized the conversation was mostly being carried by Justine and Ava, centered around the tea they couldn't wait to spill on their classmates.

"Have you seen Maria Tobias?" Ava asked the group as she blew air into her cheeks and made a large circle with her arms.

The three of them chortled while Molly looked on, confused.

"She blew up," Becca explained. "Fat as fuck now."

Molly flinched from the cruelty of her words, as if she'd been physically slapped. She was shocked that Becca, who'd been overweight in high school, would judge others for their size.

"Not me! Thanks to my gastric sleeve, I've lost forty pounds," Becca exclaimed, pointing to her now-flat stomach.

While Justine and Ava cooed their approval, Molly wondered if she'd also lost her humanity.

"While we're on the subject of people who went downhill..."

Molly scrunched her face. "Were we?"

"Gigi Smith," Ava said. "Four DUIs and counting."

"Don't forget that girl, Nina something or other, can't remember her last name," Becca offered.

"Oh, the one with a botched nose job? She looks like one of

those sea creatures—" Justine let out a guffaw as she snapped her fingers. "What did you call her the other day?"

Becca, wheezing with sudden onset laughter, struggled to get the word out. "Blobfish!"

"Aww," Molly said, pouting as the others cracked up. "That's not nice."

"Sorry," Ava said. "You're right. We're lucky to still look the way we look. We should be nicer to those who don't."

It pained Molly that her friends had become so cruel. Or had they always been that way—mocking others for their worst traits or misfortunes—and she just hadn't realized it? No wonder she'd felt the need to lie to them back then about her dad, pretending he was traveling around Europe. For self-preservation.

She and her college friends never poked fun at others. Their conversations were more thought-provoking and productive, pro-female, and supportive of one another.

She regretted having given Max's number to Becca. Hopefully, she'd lose it along with her forty pounds.

Molly was thankful when their focus shifted to weddings. Finally, something she could relate to. Preparing for the inevitable proposal, she'd already started a vision board and hoped to get additional ideas.

She was about to ask when Becca jumped in.

"Y'all can have that shit. I want to sample all that's out there. Our twenties are when we're still figuring out who we are."

"You don't have to do that if you find the right person," Justine said. "Derek helped me figure out who I am."

"True," Ava jumped in. "I had no idea what job to do until Jason helped me find one. Not exactly what I want to do, but who cares? Soon we'll have kids, and it won't matter."

Their words were uncomfortably familiar to Molly.

"Oh! My wedding video is in," Ava said, holding up her

phone. They all crowded in to watch, but then Ava's face fell and she turned it off. "Oops. I'm so sorry, Molly. All this talk about marriage. How insensitive of us."

Molly looked at her, perplexed.

"We heard about you and Brennan," Justine explained.

"What did you hear?" Molly asked.

"That you guys broke up."

"But...we haven't."

"Caroline Andrews was in New York, and she ran into Brennan on a date with someone," Ava blurted out. "She just assumed..."

"Wait, back up," Molly said, holding up her hand. "When was this?"

"The weekend of July Fourth. She went to visit her boyfriend. They were at an outdoor bar on Saturday night and saw him there with a woman who wasn't you...and, well, it being a Saturday night and all..."

Molly quickly sorted through her conversations with Brennan about that weekend. There had to be an explanation, a business meeting of some sort.

Justine gave her a sympathetic look. "Sorry, Molly. I'm guessing you guys are—"

"Going to be engaged soon," Molly stated, matter-of-factly. "So do let Caroline know, whatever she thinks she saw, she didn't. It was probably one of his clients, who often request informal meetings to discuss their investments."

And then Molly put on the tried-and-true *Who, me? Worried?* smile she'd worn so often, ever since she'd become a fatherless child. Even though she had no idea if what she'd said was true. She just had to save face somehow.

After a brief awkward silence, the women went on to discuss other matters, but Molly no longer cared to listen. She waited just long enough for the conversation about Brennan to be a thing of the past, then excused herself, claiming an early café shift in the morning. While true, College Molly would have been able to survive on two hours of sleep. Funny how, two months out, already she was carrying on like an old head, claiming she needed eight hours.

Or maybe it was just the company she wished to escape.

"Aww, thanks so much for joining us," Justine said in her squeaky high voice. "It was so great seeing you."

"Yes," Ava said, going in for a hug. "It's nice to see you haven't changed at all."

Oh, but I have. In ways you wouldn't begin to understand.

As Molly walked home, fear over Brennan being seen with another woman rippled up from her chest, while her rational brain fought against the current, knowing there had to be a plausible explanation.

She was tempted to call and confront him, but it was late, and she'd had drinks. She wanted to be thoughtful about how she brought it up. Their discussions were far more productive when she gave herself a cooling period, thought through what she wanted to say, and did so with a clear mind. It was probably best to hold off until the weekend when they could have the conversation in person, and she could gauge his reaction.

Lying in bed that night, she thought about Justine and Ava's assertions that they didn't need self-discovery. They seemed all too happy—proud, even—to have the men in their lives defining them. Coming from someone else's mouth, the idea of someone giving up her agency to a man seemed preposterous. Yet, as much as Molly wanted to judge the women, hadn't she been doing the same thing? Looking in the proverbial mirror, she saw the reflection of her own dependent self.

For twenty-two years, she'd let the men in her life dictate who she was. Eclipsed by their larger-than-life personalities—first her dad's, then Brennan's—her life had never really been about her. She'd graduated with honors and a degree in economics, but since then, she'd let her boyfriend make important decisions about her life. As if she were a chess piece, and he, the master. His schedule dictated when they saw each other. He decided whether she'd continue to live here in Cape May, or whether she would "get" to move in with him. Not to mention when, or what jobs she should go after to prove herself a worthy roommate, a solid financial partner.

When did she get to just be Molly, making her own decisions? She didn't have to ask. It was when she was with Max.

Sweet Max, the only male in her life who'd given her the space to be herself without label or judgment. Without asking anything in return, except her company. He was whole, self-actualized.

His friendship had sparked in her a passion to do something important. That had always been her goal when she was younger, back when she wanted to be someone who helped others. Just thinking of Max, her heart began beating to the rhythm of the words she couldn't forget.

Some guy who has liked you so hard from the beginning of time, he won't even look at another girl.

Words she'd give anything to hear coming out of Brennan's mouth, but never would. Not because his feelings for her weren't of that magnitude (at least she hoped they were) but because Brennan was a different kind of guy. He wasn't sentimental, good with words, deep and thoughtful like Max. But was that what she wanted, to spend her life assigning excuses for why he couldn't give her what she wanted? Which, above all, was...

Longing. What she'd felt every second she'd spent with Max. And not because she needed him to fulfill her, but because she knew she was worthy of a man who felt that way about her and never let her forget it.

She couldn't stop replaying the scenes from their day together, before their ugly fight. Max's animated explanations of the marine life out on the bay, the expression of joy on his face as he talked about his favorite subject. Bobbing peacefully on the waves as silence fell between them, and the calm that came over her, no urgent need to fill the silence tugging at her tongue. Racing up the steps of the lighthouse and the way her heart beat wildly as she lay atop him on the steps.

An aching sadness creeped in, thinking about how she'd prodded him to admit his crush and the vulnerable way in which he'd exposed his feelings, like a puppy showing his belly. Just to satisfy the longing for male attention she'd only recently realized she craved. She felt horrible for using his confession for her own benefit. She had no right to do that to him.

Maybe she owed it to him to consider his point. Really hear what Max had to say, and instead of deflecting his accusations about her relationship, pay them heed. She didn't need to agree with him but should probably test his accusations against facts to make certain her defense of Brennan held up in the court of love. It was the least she could do. As much as she wanted to hate Max for speaking those words, she knew they came from a place of caring.

She was too tired to think anymore. Too much had happened that day, and she needed to sleep. She recalled Max's parting words, wishing her luck on the fundraiser. It sent a shiver of fear through her. She hoped his words didn't mean their friendship was over. She couldn't let that happen.

Just as she was about to fall asleep, she recalled why she and Brennan weren't together on the July Fourth weekend. He'd told her he was going on a golf outing.

In North Carolina.

IT WAS ONE IN THE MORNING WHEN MAX'S PHONE RANG with a number he didn't recognize. Fearing it may be a marine mammal stranding emergency, he answered—only to find it was Becca Barnshaw.

Great. Just what he needed.

Without apologizing for the time of her call, she rambled on. "I ran into Molly Grace the other day, and she told me you were in town."

His ears perked up when he heard Molly's name, until he remembered their fight.

"Let me get to the point of my call." It sounded like she was slurring her words. Even better—a drunk dial from someone he'd barely known in high school and hadn't seen in years. "I was wondering if you'd like to meet up sometime?"

"Uh, sure," he said. Maybe it would be good to have another friend in tow, someone to take his obsessive mind off Molly for five minutes. "That would be nice."

"Good! I was hoping to see you sometime this summer. I actually asked Molly to invite you for drinks tonight."

"You guys went out for drinks?"

"Yeah. Sorry you couldn't make it. Molly said you were busy."

Well, that was a bold-faced lie. The only thing he had going on that night was a staring contest with his phone, alternating between hoping she'd call and wondering if he should call her.

"What's your schedule like tomorrow?" Becca asked. "We could meet for brunch or dinner."

He wasn't sure. His heart was too damaged to think of starting something with someone new—although, really, the woman was just asking if he wanted to share a meal. He considered whether Molly might need him for something, but...

Fuck it. After what happened earlier, she was on her own.

"How 'bout we meet for brunch tomorrow morning?" Max suggested. The sooner he moved on from Molly, the better.

"That would be great. Sunrise Café sound good?" she said.

He wondered if it was a good idea to parade another woman around Molly's sister's café. He contemplated suggesting another restaurant, but what the hell. Hadn't Molly basically pushed him into this? She'd given Becca his number. After touting *my boyfriend this* and *my boyfriend that* all week, it seemed deserving. Maybe seeing him with another woman would...

Would what, Max? Make her jealous? Make her want you? Get over yourself.

"It's a date."

Max cringed as he hung up. Was it a date? Then again, maybe it *was* time to give someone else a chance. Someone who was actually interested in him.

It would be nice to know what that felt like, for a change.

IF SARINA THOUGHT SHE WAS GETTING ANY SLEEP THAT night, she was wrong. Not after the night she just had with Jaxon. She'd worked in many kitchens before but had never worked alongside someone so fun and easy to be with. They just jived with one another—from their unspoken choreography as they moved around the kitchen together, to the occasional jokes and puns they tossed around. It felt as easy and as natural as being with a best friend.

While her unintentional guest had given her a nice respite from financial worriment, her lurking debt still loomed. Wednesday's crazy busy rush had certainly helped, but it hadn't solved everything. She still needed to grovel for help.

Swallowing her pride, she planned to talk to Kelsey first thing in the morning and ask her for a loan, hoping her funds weren't tied up in some sort of screw-you-if-you-need-it-sooner investment scheme. Maybe they could meet up at the bank and do a transfer...

Wait. Another option *did* exist.

Sarina recalled that when she'd taken out the initial bank loan, the officer suggested she also open a line of credit. She explained that while the loan would be a lump sum payment up front, the line of credit would allow her to borrow against it going forward, if the need ever arose. She'd dismissed the idea outright, as she was generally against extending her credit too far. She'd made a practice of saving and managing her money well, so she never had to rely on, or be indebted to, anyone else. It's why she'd never had a credit card or borrowed money from people.

Her money wizardry had, up until that point in her life, paid off. She'd not only traveled around and lived in Europe, but called it quits when her money ran out. She'd also pulled a business plan out of her ass and started a café from scratch. All before the age of twenty-five. She couldn't be that much of an irresponsible buffoon, as her fam seemed to believe.

In the end, she'd decided, if it ever got bad enough that she had to borrow more money, she'd throw in the dish towel and move on to another venture—

Oh, boy. Maybe there was some legitimacy to Kelsey's concerns.

Sarina began to see her plan-to-bail-when-things-get-tough philosophy in a new light. While it sometimes served her well, she'd worked hard to make this dream of hers happen.

She couldn't bail on her café. A tough first year didn't make her a failure at business.

She decided to forgo asking family for money and open that line of credit, only taking out the bare minimum she'd need to get through the next couple weeks until the coffee house evenings project kicked into gear and cash flowed more freely. It wasn't the best option financially, as family loans would likely come without interest. But this way, she could get it from a cold-hearted banker who wouldn't force her to admit defeat. As with every part of her life, it meant she could do it all on her own. Just the way she liked it.

As the sun peeked through her blinds, she was surprised to hear a sound coming from the kitchen, certain as she was that Jaxon would be sleeping in after being up so late. Instead, she found him standing at her kitchen island, looking at his laptop.

"Morning, sunshine!" he exclaimed as he looked up at her with a bright smile. He turned his screen to face her. "Check it out. I made a flyer for tonight's event."

His impressive design included coffee house clipart and photos of the café. "That looks great, Jax. I appreciate you doing that."

"If you have a printer, I'll run off some copies for you to hang. I also created an Insta post. Oh, and this..." He turned and pulled something from the warmer. "I made you a grab-and-go breakfast burrito."

"What are you doing for the rest of my life?" she blurted out. "I could really use a breakfast chef to start my day."

"You couldn't afford me," he teased, using her line from earlier.

After printing the flyers, Sarina took a stack to the back room, where she assembled her staff to let them know about the coffee house event.

"I know it's super last minute, but the desserts are baked

and ready to be served. Would any of you be interested in picking up an extra shift? I only need two of you. It'll go from seven to ten."

All five staff members raised their hands.

She laughed. "All of you?"

Shoot. She hadn't planned on paying more in wages than she'd bring in.

"If we work, can we also perform?" asked James, her most senior server. "I play a pretty mean guitar."

"Yes. I'd love it if you guys would participate."

Each staff member admitted to a hidden talent. Impersonations. Stand-up. Poetry.

"Count us in, boss," James said. "Hell, I'll even work it for free."

The others joined in too. Sarina promised to give them paid time off in exchange.

Café Au Late Night was officially in motion.

Molly

MOLLY COULD BARELY CONCENTRATE ON THE ORDERS she was taking that morning during her café shift. She'd awakened in a panic, thinking about Max, hoping their fight didn't mean their friendship was over. As soon as rush hour abated, she vowed to find him and apologize.

As she wiped down a table, her thoughts shifted to Brennan and what he'd been doing out with a woman on a Saturday night. While she wanted to talk to him in person, the conversation couldn't wait until the weekend.

She was relieved when the morning rush died down, ready to wipe the bubbly waitress smile off her face and get down to business. First, find Max. Second, call Brenan.

She was about to wrap up her shift when Max entered the café. Elated to see him, she waved, but he didn't see her. He was too busy looking at the woman he'd just entered with.

Becca.

"Ooh, looks like Maxie has a date," Sarina whispered to Molly as she glided by.

Molly fought the urge to run over and tackle him before Becca could get her claws in him. How did that happen so fast? She'd just dropped Becca's name yesterday. A pang of protectiveness pierced her heart. She wished she'd never given her his number.

"Can you seat them?" Sarina asked as she rang someone up.

Shit. The last thing she wanted to do was engage with them, especially now that Becca was looking up at him, batting her eyes. He said something and they both laughed.

"Hey, guys, you can grab that booth in the window," Molly called out. "Sarina will be right with you."

"Hello to you, too, Molly," Max said, his voice formal, but his smile teasing.

Seriously, they had to come *here* for their date?

She asked Sarina to drop off menus for them before fleeing to the back, where she paced to calm her gnarled stomach.

Sarina popped her head in. "Moll, we just got slammed with a large party. I need you to cover table five."

"But that's Max's table."

"And that's a problem...why?"

"He's on a date."

"So?"

Molly sighed and dropped her voice to a whisper. "He told me yesterday he had a crush on me. How awkward would it be if I waited on them?"

"Why? Are you jealous?"

"Pssht!" Molly recoiled, waving her off. "There's a greater

chance I'd run off with Carl the mop."

"Okay, just checking." Sarina smiled. "Play nicely. We wanna show them a good time."

"Do we?"

Molly felt flustered as she approached Max and Becca, the complete opposite of how in control she felt yesterday. Especially when he'd admitted to his crush, the way he'd looked at her, their playful race up the lighthouse steps together. There was a heady feeling that went along with knowing someone had a thing for you. Intoxicating. But then she'd blown it, and now here he was, with someone else. Molly had no one to blame but herself.

She couldn't let Max know how their fight had gutted her. Nor should she make the situation any more awkward than it already felt by acting all sad and pouty. She flashed her usual smile and decided to have some fun with Max and his little date.

I'll show them a good time, alright.

Max

HAVING BREAKFAST WITH BECCA SHOULDN'T HAVE BEEN a big deal, until they entered the café and saw Molly. After the way she'd toyed with his feelings like a kitten with a toy mouse, he didn't expect his heart to leap into his throat when he saw her. But there he was, ogling her, thinking how cute she looked as she flashed that dimpled smile, her infectious giggle dancing across the room, tantalizing him. Her long curls were swept into a messy bun, and her tennis skirt swished from side to side as she walked away, just like her cheerleading uniform used to all those years ago, capturing his rapt attention.

Suddenly she turned, her eyes sweeping the room before her golden gaze locked in on his. He tried not to notice how the sun, cascading through the large front windows, sparkled in her champagne eyes, just like it had at the top of the lighthouse.

When she directed them to a table, he quickly looked away out of respect for his date. It wasn't fair to her, but he couldn't help it. The heart wants what the heart wants.

Molly bounced over to their table with two menus and a coffee pot in her hand, looking as fresh-faced and happy as ever. Which was surprising, given the last time they'd laid eyes on each other, she was shooting daggers through him.

"Sarina's busy. Looks like you guys are *stuck with me*," she said, enunciating the last three words.

She flashed her eyebrows at Max as she poured their coffees. A smile tugged at his lips over their inside joke. Her exuberance was delightful, sweeping away any residual hard feelings he'd had from the night before.

"We have a couple specials today I'd like to tell you about. One is called The Kayak. Scrambled sea turtle eggs sitting atop a pork roll kayak with hash browns on the side."

Becca grimaced.

"That sounds interesting," Max noted as he prepared to match her humor. "What species of turtle eggs did you say?"

"Oh, I don't believe I did. That would be Black—Bay—Diamond Back—Sea Turtles, I believe. I'll double-check with the chef."

"Do that, if you don't mind. I'm allergic to Black Bay Diamond Back Sea Turtles, but I could probably do Leatherback or Loggerhead if you have any."

"Oh, I get it. Marine biologist joke," Becca said, looking from one to the other.

"Got anything else?" Max taunted.

"Of course, we do. Our other special is the

Lighthouse Challenge."

"Can't wait to hear this one," Max uttered through a smile as he looked down at his menu.

"High stack of pancakes, topped with a puff of whipped cream and a very special surprise at the top."

"Oh, that sounds yummy," Becca said.

"And there's a challenge involved?" Max asked as he hooked an eyebrow at her.

"Yes. You have to start from the bottom, saving the succulent surprise topping for the end."

"I couldn't eat all that myself," Becca said. "Wanna share?"

But Max's eyes were on Molly. "What do you get if you finish the challenge?"

"You'll have to try it and find out," Molly said.

He turned six shades of purple. "I'm actually not that hungry," Max said, taking a hard swallow of coffee. "What smoothies do you have today?"

"You're in luck. Our smoothie of the day is called Orange Crush. It's utterly delightful."

Max almost spit out his coffee.

"I'll let you guys mull over your choices. Becca, it's good to see you again. And you, Max. How are the kids?"

Max shot Becca a look. "She's joking."

"Oh!" Molly threw back her head and laughed. "I didn't mean human kids. I meant that tank of mice you keep to feed your boa constrictor."

"Ew, mice and snakes? My two least favorite things," Becca said, squinching up her face.

"Remember at cheerleading camp, when our cabin was invaded by both?" Molly asked, her devious smile suggesting she'd intended to give Becca the ick.

Molly turned to him. "Max, does the snake have a name?"

Max looked at her in amused disbelief.

Game on.

"Brennan," Max said, cocking his head slightly to the side as he stared at her. "The snake's name is Brennan."

Molly laughed out loud, her eyes sparkling. "How original!"

"Just like your—*oh*! I get it," Becca said, joining in. "Last name Sloane?"

"Exactly," Max said, then quickly broke character. "I'm just kidding. Me and Brennan are tight. Right, Moll?"

"Tight as ever. All joking aside, I'll give you time to look over the menu. In the meantime, can I interest either one of you in a Crush?"

"I'm in," Becca said.

"And you, Max?"

He leveled a look at her. "No thanks. I'm good."

ONCE AGAIN, THE CAFÉ WAS PACKED THAT MORNING, and Sarina's heart was full. Between baking with Jax the night before, and the anticipation of their first evening event, she felt confident in her decision to keep the café going. She just needed to make sure she could pay off her debt. One line of credit, coming up.

As soon as the morning rush died down, she flew to the bank.

She was dismayed to learn her original loan officer was off that day, so she had to meet with someone else. Not ideal, having to recount the entire history. Even less so upon learning it had been too long since she'd made her original application, and her credit would have to be run again.

"When will I find out if it's accepted?" she asked.

"You should know by close of business tomorrow. Once

you sign the official papers, you'll be able to draw funds."

Perfect. Plenty of time to meet her Monday deadline.

Just in case, she called the management company to ask for an additional extension. Four more days should do it, just to be safe. The more time she had to fill the café with customers, the less she'd have to borrow.

"I can assure you the money will be in your account, including August's rent, by close of business on July 31," she told the landlord rep.

She was surprised when he agreed. She felt a renewed sense of hope and couldn't wait to tell Jaxon.

After checking in with her staff to make sure they had a handle on things, she went up to her apartment, half hoping to see him in his naked state again.

Stop it.

Instead, she found him in her kitchen, making a PB+J.

"Another one of my specialties," he said, holding it out for her to sample. "I'll warn you. It's life-changing."

Taking a bite, her eyes bugged out in mock surprise. "OMG, how did you ever come up with this idea? Marrying a creamy peanut spread with a fruity gelatinous substance?"

"There's a lot you don't know about me, Sarina Grace," he said. "Let me make you one."

Gazing at her, he ran his thumb along the blade and slowly sucked the remaining peanut butter off. If he was looking for a reaction, she sure as hell gave it to him when she gasped involuntarily.

Quick. Make a joke.

"I wish I could make a sandwich that good. I'm *jelly*."

"Food porn is my *jam*," he said, catching on.

"You certainly know how to *spread* it on."

"Keep *buttering* me up. I'm a *Smucker* for compliments." Jaxon broke first, laughing as he finished making her sandwich. "Okay, that one was a stretch."

He held up a half for her to take a bite. Their eyes met as she sank her teeth into the soft bread, her tastebuds bursting with delight from the salty sweet center.

"Wow," she whispered, eyes closing.

He continued feeding her the sandwich until she'd eaten the very last bite. She briefly considered licking his fingers.

Three strikes! You're out. Enjoy the trip to hell.

She felt guilty for her impure thoughts, but who could blame her? It wasn't every day a storm blew one's teen idol into their freezer. Like every normal girl with a celebrity crush, she'd spent years fantasizing that he'd somehow fall off his star and into her life, declaring her to be the girl of his dreams. Now here he was, in a slightly modified version of the wild dreams she'd had about him in her youth.

The biggest modification—he was her sister's boyfriend.

So what if he just fed her a sandwich? How was that a crime? It was no different than if she were a goat at a petting zoo, eating a carrot from his hand.

Minus the zoo, the goat, and the carrot. And respect for her sister.

She needed to change the subject, and fast.

"The coffee house is a go. My staff offered to work in exchange for a day off and the chance to perform."

"Awesome," Jaxon said. But neither his tone nor his expression matched his apparent enthusiasm. "I just wish I could partake in it."

"What, and cause mass pandemonium?" she joked. "You know, we have a few hours before the event begins. You could always surprise Kelsey now so your presence here is out, then come together. That way, you can be free from all this," she teased.

Yet as soon as she said the words, she regretted them. She enjoyed having him around and wasn't ready for him to leave.

"Who said I wanna be free?" he asked.

The affirmation in his tone, the steadiness of his gaze, gave her tingles. She'd better get out of here before she did something stupid.

She fled to the cafe, where she found Molly in the back, looking as pale as Greek yogurt.

Molly

*N*O THANKS, I'M GOOD.

Max's comment when Molly had asked if he wanted a crush hit hard. Probably to let her know he was over her and on to someone new.

As fun as it was bantering over inside jokes, Molly was surprised at how rattled she felt seeing Max and Becca together, despite having no right to feel that way.

She was in the back making Becca's smoothie when she received an incoming text from Hugh just as Sarina walked in.

"Oh my gosh," she said, almost dropping her phone into the blender. "Hugh fell off his roof yesterday and broke both his legs."

"Oh no!" Sarina said.

"He says he's okay, all things considered." She sank into a chair. "But I'm not."

"Wow, Moll. Seems a bit dramatic when you hardly know the guy."

How could she admit to her sister that she wasn't only bummed about Hugh? Telling Sarina how upset Max's date made her would be admitting to having feelings for him. And sharing the news that Brennan had been seen with another woman would make him look even worse to her sisters. Especially if it turned out to be a misunderstanding.

Focus on Hugh.

"The play's in two days," she said. "It's too late to find someone else. We may have to cancel it."

"Don't you think that's Grand Lil's call?" Sarina asked. "I'm sure a local actor could fill in last minute."

True. Their grandmother, with her show-must-go-on attitude, would have a solution.

"Can you take care of Max and Becca? I need to go deal with this." And, bonus—not deal with Max and Becca.

"Yes. Go."

Kelsey

KELSEY WAS SHOCKED TO HEAR ABOUT HUGH'S ACCIdent. She'd just arrived at the theater when his text came through. Before she could process the news, Molly rushed in.

"It's horrible," Molly said, eyes watering. "I worked too hard for this day to have the main attraction go wrong."

"Hugh's the main attraction?" Kelsey asked with a smirk.

"No, you are—the play is. But Hugh's also my Santa. Without him, we're doomed!"

"And I thought I was the dramatic one," Kelsey teased as Colton approached them. "Everything's going to be okay."

"How are we going to find a fill-in, so close to opening night?"

"Gee, I don't know…" Kelsey turned to Colton with a teasing smile. "What do you think, Colt? Any brilliant ideas?"

Colton looked her dead in the eye. "You'll figure something out."

"Colton—"

"No," he said emphatically.

Grand Lillian came in just then. "I sense drama, and not

the stage kind," she said, thrusting her bony fists on narrow hips. "What's going on?"

"Hugh broke both his legs!" Molly wailed, just as Colton made like a felon and absconded backstage.

"I've heard," Grand Lillian said. "Looks like we need a plan B."

"If you mean B as in *Banks*, don't bother," Kelsey said. "He already shot us down."

Grand Lil smoothed her coiffed hair and thrust her chin in the air. "Clearly, you have a lot to learn about acting. Take note."

With that, the family matriarch disappeared behind the curtain, returning less than five minutes later with a contrite Colton following closely behind.

"I'll do it," he said, looking like he'd rather be pecked to death by wild chickens.

As Grand Lil handed him a script, Kelsey wondered what she'd said to convince him to take on the role.

As if reading her mind, her grandmother patted her on the arm as she passed by. "Kiss to be determined."

Seeing the gleam in her eye, Kelsey couldn't help but wonder whether the old bat had something to do with Hugh falling off his roof.

"Wait, Grand Lil, I have some questions about the event," Molly said, following the matriarch, leaving Colton and Kelsey alone.

"I'm touched by your change of heart," Kelsey teased. "What ever happened?"

"Not funny, Kelse."

"I think it's hilarious, you being tortured into playing my leading man again. Oh, the humanity!"

"I didn't say anything about being tortured."

"The look on your face does."

She didn't miss the slight tug of a smile as he turned to

walk away.

"Don't worry, I won't fall in love with you this time," she muttered to herself.

He spun back around. "What did you say?"

Shit. She didn't realize she'd said it that loud. "Nothing."

He sauntered over to her with a half-smile. "No, I'm pretty sure I heard you say something about falling in love. Or was that just wishful thinking?"

The oxygen was suddenly sucked from the room, rendering her speechless.

Swallowing hard, she found her voice. "What I said was, 'you'll fall in love with this play.' Like you did last time."

His gaze was unwavering. "I certainly hope so."

Max

MAX WAS STILL LAUGHING TO HIMSELF ABOUT MOLLY'S inside jokes when Sarina approached their table.

"Hey, guys, your food should be right out," she said.

He raised his eyebrows. "Where's Molly?"

"Tending to an emergency."

"Is she okay?" Max blurted out.

"She's fine. Just a fundraiser thing."

He and Becca ordered their food, but Max had lost his appetite. He couldn't stop wondering whether Molly needed his help. Despite their argument, he still wanted to be of assistance in any way he could.

Not only that, but he wanted to apologize for the things he'd said to her the day before. He was relieved when she'd come out that morning, sucker punches and snappy humor swinging, happy she hadn't written him off completely as a friend. He felt bad for excluding his date with their banter, but the conversation between him and Becca had felt forced from the moment they met up.

"Do I have some tea to spill," Becca said after Sarina walked away. She wasted no time jumping in with gossip about how one of their former classmates had seen Brennan out on a date with another woman. She recounted how they'd told Molly about it last night. "She acted like she didn't care, but I know she did. You could see it on her face."

It pained him to hear that. If he were a lesser man, he would've leaned across the table and encouraged her to go on, soaking it up for his own twisted benefit. But he wasn't wired that way. Before long, it became clear it wasn't just tea she wanted to spill. It was blood. Molly's blood.

Not on his watch.

"Listen, Becca, I'm not big on gossip," he said. As rude as it felt to cut her off, it was worse to let her go on.

"Oh, me either."

"Great. How 'bout you tell me what you've been up to since high school?"

As she regaled him with stories of her recent life, Max's brain glazed over. He tried to ask questions that wouldn't elicit long responses, but it seemed the woman was incapable of short answers. By the time they'd finished eating, there wasn't a thing he didn't know about Becca Barnshaw. Including the fact he didn't care for her very much.

"I'm also looking for an apartment," she said. "Know of any available?"

"No, but we've been working with Luke Martin to sell our farm. Have you reached out to him?"

"*The* Luke Martin? The one who graduated three years ahead of us?"

"I'll give you his number," Max offered.

After he paid the bill, they left the café. At long last. The experience reminded him he wasn't interested in casual dating—at least not with someone like Becca.

Strolling through the outdoor mall, Max tried to come up with an excuse for why he needed to break away. All he could think of was finding and helping Molly.

"Oh my God!" Becca suddenly exclaimed, grabbing his arm. "It's him!"

Just as he was about to ask who, Luke emerged from a storefront.

"Max!" he exclaimed, clasping his hand in a firm manshake. "Good to see you, friend."

Luke did a double-take, his eyes resting on Becca. "Well, hello there," he said, flashing her his billboard Realtor smile. "Max's girlfriend, I presume?"

Becca emitted a tinny laugh. "Oh, no. We're just friends."

"Just friends," Max enunciated, hoping to drive the point home.

"Becca Barnshaw," she said, offering him a limp hand. "We went to high school together."

Max looked on, amused, wondering if this wasn't the most fortuitous meet-cute ever.

"We were just talking about you," Max said. "Becca's looking for an apartment in Cape May."

"Got anything to offer?" Becca asked.

"As a matter of fact, I have a few. Would you have time to check them out today? I'm actually on my way to a vacant studio that just became available. I don't want to interrupt—"

"No!" Max and Becca proclaimed at once.

Max wondered if she was as relieved as he was to end their date.

"You sure I'm not taking her away from you?" Luke asked.

Please. I'll pay you.

"Not at all. Becca, it was great catching up. Good luck on your apartment hunt."

Becca barely looked in his direction as she waved him away, so taken she was by Luke.

Walking away, Max chuckled over the unmistakable spark he saw between Becca and Luke. As soon as they were out of view, Max pulled out his phone and called Molly.

Molly

Now that Colton had agreed to fill in for Hugh, Molly could breathe easier about the fundraiser. She still needed to find a Santa, but that should be easy enough. Worst-case scenario, she could probably get Max to do it.

Max.

She wondered if he and Becca were still on their date, and if it was just a brunch thing, or a day-long date. She hoped the former, although it shouldn't matter to her. It just did.

She felt lonely riding around town without him. He'd made fundraiser prep fun, and she'd enjoyed the time they'd spent together. A feeling of panic swept through her, wondering if the fight yesterday meant their friendship was over.

All because of her.

Molly went to the beach she and Max had gone to a couple days ago. Wanting solitude for the phone call she was about to make, she found a deserted section and dialed Brennan's number. It went right to voicemail, so she left a message.

Sitting on the beach, she wrapped her arms around her knees. The water, now sparkling and still, reflected what she felt inside—a calm before the storm.

Finally, her phone buzzed. Without looking, she answered, expecting it to be Brennan.

"Hello, yes," a male voice started. "I'm from the Society for the Protection of Black Bay Diamond Back Sea Turtles. I've been told you've been harvesting the eggs of these precious sea creatures for your culinary pleasures. You must cease and desist, or I'll unleash the sharks."

She laughed. "I plead the fifth."

"That's what they all say."

"How was that long walk home yesterday?" she teased.

"Pretty good. I took the road less traveled by—"

"Did it make all the difference?"

He laughed at her reference to the Robert Frost poem they'd had to memorize in ninth-grade English.

"*All* the difference. And a great opportunity to ponder my ridiculousness." He took a breath. "I'm so sorry for what I said to you, Molly—"

"No, Max. I'm sorry. For…everything."

"You did nothing wrong. But I definitely crossed the line with all I said. It was cruel and unwarranted."

"No, it was your truth. I'm glad you were honest with me." She dug her toes into the sand. "How was that date?"

"Oh, well…you know. We're eloping tonight."

"I figured as much. Do I know how to match-make, or what?"

He was silent for a moment before he let out a soft chuckle. "Or what."

She breathed a sigh of relief. "Now Imma trust you with my truth," she said. "You're right about a lot of what you said. My relationship with Brennan is far from perfect. *He's* far from perfect, but so am I. You've definitely given me some things to think about."

"I had no right to challenge you about your relationship. As you said, I haven't been in many, so…"

"Hey, it doesn't take a marine biologist to know what a healthy relationship looks like. Oh wait, maybe it does…"

"I only want the best for you, Molly."

"I know that."

She was tempted to tell him about Brennan and the woman, ask for his advice, but she knew he'd tell her to talk to him about it. There were too many questions for her to ignore the red flags anymore.

"So...friends again?" Max asked.

"Looks like you're stuck with me."

"I hope so. No, I pray so. You're an amazing person, whose playful, bubbly nature brings a light to my day whenever I see you."

"Cause of death: extreme flattery."

After their call ended, she breathed a sigh of relief that they were back on good footing. Despite only connecting a few days ago, she couldn't imagine them not being friends.

Unwilling to wait any longer, she dialed Brennan's number again. This time he answered.

"Hey. What's up?" His tone was terse, businesslike.

"Oh, nothing much," she said, trying to sound casual. "Just...a funny story to tell you."

"I'm all ears."

Although it didn't sound that way. He seemed preoccupied.

Damn. This wasn't starting out great. Since she'd heard the news last night, she'd wrestled with how she could bring it up without making him defensive or mad. As if she were in the wrong for wanting answers.

But suddenly, she was hit with a tsunami of clarity. It wasn't just this issue. She'd been tapdancing around Brennan throughout their entire relationship, trying to be smart and cute and funny. Treating him as the main character in her life, hoping to prove her worthiness, never wanting to piss him off or make him think twice about her. Trying to be "enough."

Something in her snapped. She *was* enough. She deserved the truth.

She took a breath. "Who were you out with on Saturday

night of July Fourth weekend?"

All she could hear was the *whomp-whomp-whomp*ing of her heart. The longer his silence went on, the more she knew.

Finally, he took a breath. "Who told you—Caroline?"

Busted.

"If it was Caroline, yeah," he continued. "I ran into her at a bar."

"Who were you with?"

"Just...a friend. From work."

"What's her name?"

"Sheila. She's a coworker. A friend. That's all."

"Oh yeah? Then why haven't you ever mentioned her before?"

"Why are you doing this?"

"Why am I doing *what*? It's a simple question, Brennan. Why haven't you told me about this so-called *friend* of yours?"

"What, am I not allowed to have female friends now?"

"Oh, you can have all the friends you want. But when you start sneaking around and not telling your significant other—"

Well now. Wasn't this ironic. As if she hadn't been doing that herself all week. But...this wasn't about her. It was about Brennan. About their relationship.

Her voice took on an eerily calm tone. "It's not about you having female friends. You know I'm not like that. The issue is, you were supposed to be out of town that weekend, remember? Does golfing in North Carolina ring a bell? Was that a lie?"

"No. That trip just—fell apart at the last minute."

"So instead of calling me so *we* could hang out, you called your 'work friend' to go to a bar with you?"

"It's not like that. Trust me."

"I *have* trusted you, Brennan. I trusted you wanted me to move to New York and start a life together. Yet here I sit in Cape May, alone. I'm getting the feeling you don't want me there."

"I do want you here, Molly...it's just that..." He was quiet for a moment before his voice dropped. "Remember that conversation we had in sophomore year?"

She knew what he was referencing. She'd caught him flirting with a woman at a party and confronted him, demanding to know if he wanted a break. They'd been dating for four years and had often talked about the fact that they'd never dated anyone else. Her offer wasn't born from benevolence, but her own curiosity—wondering what it would be like to date other guys. She'd suggested they break up for a month to test their commitment.

But both had chickened out the next day. She hadn't thought about it since, but apparently, he had.

"We've been together a long time. I care about you so much, so I'm not gonna lie." He took a breath. "Truth is, I'm ninety-five percent sure I want to spend my life with you, but that five percent...I dunno. Again, brutal honesty, but I'm lowkey wishing we had broken up back then like you suggested, just to test the waters."

"Did you test her waters?" she demanded. If so, game over.

"Absolutely not."

Foolish or not, she believed him.

"But you lied to me about your plans that weekend," she continued. "Even if it was a last-minute cancellation, you never told me."

"I'm sorry, Molly. If it's any consolation, I feel horrible. After I went out with her, I realized I don't need to test anything. I love you, and...I do wanna to spend my life with you."

"But only ninety-five percent of you."

He didn't answer. Again, his silence allowed her to hear her own thoughts. She recalled Max's words. *He's making it clear he won't make room for you in his life. Is that what you want for yourself?*

She didn't want to be someone's afterthought. Someone's ninety-five percent. She wanted someone who was all in, nothing less than a hundred percent.

A guy who adores you, cherishes you, worships the very ground you walk on.

Max's friendship, his confession, her friends needing a man to define them...it all swirled together in one perfect storm.

"We need a break," she blurted out, her words surprising her.

"What does that mean?" he asked, sounding panicked.

"It means I think we should cool it. At least for a while. If you feel the need to sneak around behind my back because you're 'not sure,' then I'm pretty sure I'm not the one for you."

"Wait, Molly! I didn't mean that—"

"But I do."

Because I've kinda been doing the same thing.

This wasn't where she thought this conversation would go, but hadn't they been on an unspoken break already? Living in different states for the first time in their lives. Doing their own thing. Hanging out with other people and, at least in her case, enjoying it.

She wasn't sure where her calm resolve and strength came from. Maybe it had always been inside her and she just never gave herself credit for it. Like Justine and Ava, she'd been too willing to seek acceptance and belonging from the guy in her life rather than find it within herself. For the first time ever, Molly felt herself shining outside of Brennan's spotlight, and it felt pretty good. She owed it to herself to keep exploring this part of her.

"Look, I should be honest with you too," she said. "I've run into an old friend from high school, and I've been spending time with him—"

"Who?"

"That's not important. He's also just a friend."

Who I almost kissed.

"It's a temporary break, Brennan," she said into the awkward silence. "Just to see how we do."

"I don't like it."

"Sorry, this time it's not your decision to make. Let me get through this fundraiser, think about what I want to do with my life, and I'll get back to you. If it's meant to be, this is the only way I'll know for sure."

Jaxon

JAXON HAD JUST FINISHED UP A TELEPHONE INTERVIEW when Sarina returned again.

"I'm gonna take a nap," she announced. "Too much drama for one morning and I hardly slept last night. Can you make sure I'm up by five?"

"You got it," Jaxon nodded, his eyes softening. "Sweet dreams."

Jaxon played around on his laptop while Sarina napped. When it was time to wake her, he tapped on the door, which was slightly ajar. He waited for signs of life before he pushed it open and walked to her bedside.

God. Even in sleep, she was gorgeous.

She was stretched out on her back, one arm over her head, one leg bent at the knee. She was wearing tiny sleep shorts and a tank top that had ridden up to just below her breasts. He hadn't noticed it before, but she had a small sun tattoo centered around her pierced belly button. Major turn-on for him. As was her badass attitude and snarky sense of humor. But now, lying here in peaceful slumber, she was pure angel.

It was all he could do to keep from climbing into bed with her and kissing her sweet, succulent lips as he slipped his hand beneath the waistband of her shorts.

He had to get a hold of himself.

"Hey, sweetheart," he whispered as he lightly touched her shoulder.

She rolled toward him, hugging her pillow. Eyes still closed, her voice was so soft, he barely made out her words. "I love you, Jax," she said.

He gasped.

Did he hear what he thought he heard? Hard to know over the ringing in his ears. She could have said "Thank you, Jax" or even "Fuck you, Jax," for all he knew.

He traced the tip of his forefinger along her shoulder and down her arm. "Wake up, sleepyhead," he whispered, this time a bit louder.

Still in apparent REM sleep, she rolled closer and reached for his hand. He was tempted to straddle her and kiss her into consciousness. Then again, he wasn't a Disney prince. Or a pervert.

"Hey, sweet girl," he sung softly. "Time to get ready for your big night."

Moaning slightly, she rolled onto her stomach. He tried to avert his eyes from her sleep shorts, now ridden up, revealing a perfect set of apple cheeks.

"Oh, fuck," he groaned, turning away and biting his hand to keep his arousal from springing to life.

What the hell was going on? He'd seen many beautiful women throughout his life, in all forms of undress. In barely there bikinis. Push-up bras and thongs. Wearing nothing more than fuck-me pumps. He'd witnessed them sleeping, dancing, riding him on waves of pleasure. But never had a woman captured his heart, and his libido, like this one had. Doing absolutely nothing. Not strutting around, trying to be hot. Not fucking his brains out.

Just. Sleeping.

Her eyes peeked open. "Hey," she murmured. "Come sit."

He wasn't sure he could trust himself, so he perched on the

edge of the bed.

"I just had the best dream," she cooed, eyes closed again as she went into a fetal position, her knees almost touching his back.

"About what?" Jaxon's voice cracked from dryness. Possibly panting.

"You."

His breath caught, wondering if it was the kind of dream he'd had about her during his nap the other day.

"You were making sandwiches and tossing them out my window."

Hmm, not exactly what he'd hoped for.

"Not a dream, sweetheart. That's what I was doing while you were napping."

She smiled. "I was outside, and we were playing a game, seeing how many sandwiches I could catch with my mouth, like a dog with a flying disk."

Jaxon laughed out loud. "How'd you do?"

"I lost count after seventeen."

He feigned seriousness. "Sarina, I believe the record was fifteen. We should call Guinness."

"I already texted them."

He laughed. "So you're just as much a nut in sleep as you are awake?"

"Hey, I can't be blamed for what goes on in my head when I'm sleeping. At least it wasn't pornographic—"

Oh, but what if it had been?

"I'm sorry. That wasn't appropriate." She suddenly shot up to a sitting position, her face mere inches from his. "I hope you know I'm not a bad sister. I respect what you and Kelsey have, I just sometimes take shit too far."

"You've met your match," he said, meeting her gaze head-on. "I do the same thing. And you're not a bad sister."

She didn't look so certain. "I should get ready."

He rose from her bed. "Since I can't be there, why don't you send me photos and videos, and I'll post them on the café's Insta. I'm hoping you'll be too busy to be on social media."

"Sounds good. Now get out of here, so I can change."

Sarina

SARINA WAS BLOWN AWAY BY THE TURNOUT FOR THE event. Before they even opened, there was a line out the door, and they sold out of their special desserts within the first hour.

What impressed Sarina the most were the performers. She had no idea how much hidden talent existed in Cape May and was thrilled when people demanded to know when the next *Café Au Late Night* would be. Jaxon had certainly been on to something.

Jaxon. The thought of him huddled upstairs, alone, made her sad. She wished he could be here, enjoying the event, but it was best he wasn't. Kelsey, not wanting her presence to take focus away from other performers, had declined to come. Sarina wondered if there was another reason, noting Colton wasn't there either. What if they were together? She didn't want Jaxon to get burned by the embers of their smoldering torches for one another.

Before she knew it, the night was over. Sarina sank into a chair in the back room, elated over the night's success. She texted Jaxon the all-clear and invited him to join her in celebration. No sooner had she hit Send than he came bounding down the steps with two glasses, a bottle of wine, and a victorious grin.

"Success!" he cried out, grabbing her in a bear hug. "I could hear the revelry up there!"

Sarina laughed as he spun her around. "It was amazing. So many people, such great talent. I just wish you could have been there."

"Maybe for the next one," he said, his tone optimistic as he opened the bottle, poured their drinks, and offered a toast. "Here's to your café. You really have quite a thing going here."

He was right. After the fun night she'd just had, she couldn't believe she'd considered quitting. Even for a second.

"Speaking of next ones," she said, "we got some cake decorating to do for Saturday. Before that, though, I just wanna sit and enjoy this moment."

He gave her a tender smile. "You deserve it, girl. I'll cue up some tunes."

The velvety voice of Sade oozed from Bose speakers, bathing them in auditory sensuality with the song, "Kiss of Life."

"Love her." Sarina closed her eyes as the singer seductively sang of an angel leading someone special to her. "My favorite artist to listen to when I want to be mellow."

"Me too," Jaxon said, sounding surprised. "That's actually uncanny."

"Seriously?" She lifted her head. "How can we have known each other for two whole days and not known this about each other?"

"I don't tell just anyone about my Sade obsession."

Closing her eyes, she returned to her meditative state as the song played on. "How long are you sticking around?"

"All depends."

There was something about his tone. She opened her eyes to find him gazing at her over his wine glass.

"On what?"

"How long I'm...wanted here."

Her heart stopped. He must have meant by Kelsey.

"I'm sure she'll want you to stay as long as you can." Rolling her head in a slow circle, she rubbed her shoulder to ease the knotting tension.

"Here," Jaxon said, setting his glass down. "I'm well known around Tinseltown for my massages. May I?"

Sarina nodded. He rubbed his hands together to create heat. The feeling of his strong fingers as they grasped her shoulders was simultaneously painful and orgasmic. Her eyelids drooped to half-mast as his kneading fingers pushed deep into her tight muscles.

"Ahh," she exhaled involuntarily as her head collapsed into her chest, her words coming in whispers. "That. Feels. So. Good."

"I'm glad," Jaxon said, his voice husky. "That's what I was going for."

Sarina was in absolute heaven as Jaxon manipulated her aching muscles with his magic fingers. He wasn't kidding. It was the best massage she'd ever received, even from professionals.

Next up on Jaxon's playlist was Sade's "Smooth Operator."

"Appropriate song choice," Sarina joked. "Being all cool as you work your magic on me."

She could hear him laugh softly. "You're on to me."

"Jaxon Quinn. Smooth operator." She was only partly joking.

"Nah," he said softly. "There's so much more to me than this."

She still wondered how her sister had fallen for someone with such a track record with women, when, up until recently, Kelsey had probably only loved one boy her whole life.

Jaxon released one hand from her shoulder. "Sip?"

She nodded. He leaned into her as he held the glass up to her lips. It was such a subtle, non-sexual gesture, but it felt intimately sensual at the same time.

"Here's an idea," she said, clearing her throat to keep her voice from sounding too suggestive. "Why don't you skip your next shoot, and I'll put you to work. Chef Quinn by day,

Magic Masseuse by night."

He chuckled as he looked down at her with his sexy half-smile. "That could be arranged."

Her head rolled back, and she let out an involuntary groan. Looking up at him, she found him gazing at her with an intensity she couldn't be imagining. The air around them suddenly felt charged as the music built to a slow, seductive crescendo.

This wasn't right. She shouldn't be sitting here, enjoying his physical touch as much as she was. She didn't want to, but they had to stop.

"Okay. We'd better get to work."

"You're the boss," he said, deepening his thrusts, now working her shoulders with the heels of his hands as he built to the finale. Talk about a happy ending. He lightly karate-chopped her shoulders to end the massage. "How's that?"

"Orgasmic." Her eyes bugged out, and she clasped her hand over her mouth at her accidental sexual innuendo. "Sorry, that just came out."

He laughed. "Exactly the reaction I was hoping for."

Colton

It was against Colton's better judgment to agree to undertake the role of Kelsey's romantic interest, but the Grand Dame of Cape May theater had cornered him backstage—literally and figuratively—and slipped him a well-mixed cocktail of reason, praise, and guilt, with some good ol' fashioned bribery thrown in.

With the play opening tomorrow, they had to find someone fast (reason). He'd nailed the role before, making him the obvious choice (praise). If they didn't find someone good, their donations would be lacking (guilt).

The clincher: no one else would be as good a match for Kelsey. "Especially if I decide to add in that kiss," she'd added (bribery).

"Sure, I'll do it," he said hesitatingly, feeling as if he didn't have a choice.

He tried to convince himself his willingness to step in had nothing to do with the possibility of another onstage kiss. But if he couldn't kiss Kelsey in real life, an onstage kiss may quench his thirst, douse his flames, and allow him to move on. He refused to entertain the notion it could further ignite his already smoldering desire for her.

Until he remembered Prince Quinn, who probably wouldn't appreciate Colton living out his fantasy, even if in character. Then again, being a fellow actor and all, Jaxon should understand.

Colton laughed to himself. *Fellow actor.* He hadn't acted in ten years. Although...he had spent years pretending football was his passion. Impersonating a professional athlete. Feigning a perfect relationship. He'd been so good at it, he deserved an Oscar.

At home after rehearsal, he was making a sandwich when someone knocked on the door.

"Mr. Banks?" the postman asked, reading from the label on a box he held in his hand.

"Yes?"

"This box you mailed to an address in California was denied delivery. Unfortunately, it got lost in our system and we just discovered it had never been returned."

Accepting the package, Colton examined the label. It was from his father, sent to his old address. When he opened it, he was shocked to find a letter with his dad's handwriting inside, dated a few days before his death.

KIMBERLY BRIGHTON

Dear Colton—

As you know, I'm not great with my words, but you need to hear them now more than ever. I'm sorry about your injury, but not as sorry as I am about pressuring you to pursue a career in football. You did it for me, and for that I'm grateful. You've made me proud on the field, but even more so for what you've done off the field. Like earning your architectural degree. Building things has always been your passion, and I've loved the time we've spent working on projects together. In this box are just some mementos of what we've built. I'm sending them to inspire you to get back to making things with your hands, a reminder of the bright future ahead of you in that regard.

I also wanted to tell you I purchased the Cape May arts center. The city couldn't keep up with maintenance on the property, and I feared it would be sold to someone who wouldn't keep the program running. I'm hoping it will continue to run under the direction of Lillian Grace. Selfishly, I didn't want to see the treehouse we built get torn down. I couldn't let that happen, not with the memories you boys have of growing up there. I don't know where life will take you, but I have an idea for a project that will allow you to put all your talents to good use. I look forward to the next time you're home so I can share my ideas with you.

I know you're dealing with so much right now. Not just the long road to recovery for your physical injury, but the emotional fallout too. This, my son, is when you'll discover who your true friends are and those who aren't. Take care of your heart and only give it to those deserving. I think you know what I mean. I love you with all of mine, and I'm here for you. Always.

Love, Dad.
P.S. – Come home soon.

Colton was sobbing by the time he got to the end. As if his dad's words gave him permission, he finally released everything he'd kept bottled in for so long. What really got him was his dad's promise—*always*—a promise he couldn't fulfill. Yet Colton knew he was there in spirit, in the skills he'd helped Colton develop and the memories they'd made together.

Climbing into bed, he cried until he had nothing left, eventually passing out from emotional exhaustion. He was awakened hours later by a simple question: what project had his dad intended for him?

Unable to get back to sleep, Colton pulled the shoebox from his closet, the one Max had found in the barn. He gingerly lifted the top and stared at its contents. Mementos of Kelsey. Ticket stubs of movies they'd seen together. Notes they'd passed in classes to each other. And more.

Including the letter he'd written to Kelsey that night after the gazebo incident—all the words that had been rattling around his chest for some time, clamoring to get out, but couldn't because he was dating someone else. Even though only expressed on paper, for his eyes only, writing it all out had given him temporary relief.

But not completion.

Seeing the words now, as raw and as real as they were the day he wrote them, brought tears to his eyes. Each sentiment he divulged still rang with the same painful truth as the day he'd written it, his first and only love letter to Kelsey.

He tucked the painful memories away and slid the box back under his bed. But as hard as he tried, he couldn't get them out of his mind.

There was only one person he wanted to talk to just then, as he lay there trying to piece together the shards of his re-shattered heart. Unable to resist the gravitational pull of her, he took a breath and dialed her number.

Kelsey

KELSEY WAS LYING IN BED, LOOKING AT THE SCRAPBOOK she'd made for Colton at the end of their senior year. It was intended as a high school graduation gift, but she'd thought better of giving it to him after he and Ashley became an item.

It started with childhood, photos of them making snowmen, building sandcastles, playing at the arts center. Next, Colton's football career throughout high school, including clippings from every media source she could find.

She felt wistful, wishing she'd gone to one of his games to see him play after high school, but she'd been too stubborn. She remembered a time in college when Colton texted her and invited her to attend a game, the first and only time she'd heard from him since that night in the gazebo. She refused, citing a conflict. There wasn't one. The thought of watching him play, knowing Ashley was there on the sidelines, was too painful. Instead, she watched the game on TV with Devin, one of her guy friends.

Just before the game began, the camera panned to Colton warming up prior to kickoff. Turning to the lens, he held his fingers in the shape of a heart, in what would become his trademark gesture throughout his career.

For you, he mouthed.

"Oh, sweet Jesus," Devin had exclaimed, grabbing her hand. Professing Colton to be the second coming of Christ, he asked Kelsey why she hadn't gone to the game. The camera then showed cheerleaders. Focusing on Ashley, the announcer referenced her as Colton's girlfriend, saying what a lucky guy he was.

"That's why." Kelsey gestured to the TV.

"Ah," Devin had said, disappointed. "Thus, the heart gesture. For her, I assume?"

Kelsey confirmed his suspicion, launching into the whole ugly story, including the character-driven kiss and the last time she saw him in the gazebo.

"Rejection the first time around is bad enough," he had said. "But...I have thoughts."

"Share them."

He'd hesitated. "Could it be that you rejected him first, before he could reject you? Shoving Ashley at him, pretending you didn't have feelings for him. You're shockingly insecure, but so much better than you give yourself credit for. You're gorgeous and talented beyond words. *Own it*, girl. Even if you have to fake it till you make it. I promise you...someday, you'll run into this Adonis, and you'll have him eating out of your hands."

Kelsey had taken Devin's advice, throwing herself into her major and taking on the role of a self-confident woman, a star in her own right. Boy, did she fool everyone. Including the media, leading them to nickname her America's Sweetheart.

Everyone...but herself.

Devin's words came back to her. What if he was right? All these years, she'd believed Colton had rejected her without considering one important fact: she'd been the one to suggest he date Ashley in the first place.

She was mulling it over when her phone rang.

"Hey," Colton said, sounding sleepy. "Sorry. I know it's late."

She inhaled sharply as her heart skipped several beats.

Breathe.

"It's okay, Colt," she said, giving a nervous giggle. "I can't sleep either."

"Good." She could tell from his tone he was smiling. "So... there are some things you need to know."

Kelsey's heart pounded, fearing the worst. He and Ashley

were engaged. They were already married, or worse—she was pregnant. She winced in fearful anticipation, deciding to rip off the Band-Aid before he did.

"You and Ashley are—"

"Done," he said.

"Done what?"

"We're done. Over. Kaput. Fini."

"Wait....*really*?" Joy coursed through her and spilled out in laughter. "Sorry. I mean, I don't understand. Can you use a few more adjectives to paint a clearer picture...?"

"Disbanded, split, going separate ways, she's now sleeping with a friend of mine..."

"Oh, Colt." Kelsey's face fell, her heart breaking for him. "I'm so sorry to hear that."

"It's fine. We hung in there long after we should have."

"When did this happen?"

"A couple months before I came back."

So, all this time...he'd been single? "Why didn't you tell me sooner?"

"I didn't want you to think I was a loser."

"Why on earth would I think you're a loser?"

As good a friend as she once was, Ashley had to be the loser. Seriously. Who walks away from someone like Colton Banks?

"I assumed you were in a rush to wrap up your dad's estate so you could get back to her," Kelsey said.

"Nope. We sold everything, including our house. Time for greener pastures."

"Where are you going?"

"Probably Montana. At least, that *was* my plan. I don't know what I'm supposed to do next."

He told her he'd found a letter from his dad. After he summarized it for her, he said, "I'm not sure what project he was talking about, and that has me confused. On top of that, I feel pressure as to what to do with the arts center land."

"Let me buy it," she whispered. "I'll take it off your hands."

Colton sighed. "The developers want both parcels, Kelse. Their offer's kind of contingent on them being a package deal. That was the other thing I wanted to tell you."

Although it wasn't a surprise to Kelsey, it still hurt to hear he was leaning toward selling to soulless developers. "So they can destroy both. And the Cape, in the process."

"I know," he sighed. "At first, I was so anxious to sell, I could give two shits about what happened. But now..."

"What if I bought both the arts center and the farm?" she countered.

Colton laughed. "What?"

"I'm serious. That way you can go off to wherever you're going, and I can preserve both parcels."

"Kelsey, I don't know—"

"I'll offer whatever they're offering. Doubled. Just give it some thought."

He was silent for a moment. "I will."

She was relieved he was willing to consider her offer. "Or you can, you know...just stay," she teased.

"Actually, there's something else—"

A beep interrupted him.

"Darn it, it's Ashley," he said, sounding annoyed as he exhaled. "I gotta take this. Our dog had surgery, so I need to—"

"Go take it," Kelsey said. Now that she knew they'd broken up, his cutting off their call to talk to Ashley didn't sting nearly as much as it otherwise might have.

When they hung up, she stared at her phone in utter amazement, elated over his news. Colton Banks. A free agent.

She needed to end her ridiculous charade with Jaxon. Regardless of whether anything might happen with Colton, she needed to do what was right for her. Live her life honestly. Keep her heart open to someone new.

She'd call Verna first thing in the morning.

Pulling up their first-day-of-school photos on her phone, she thought about the words Colton had written on the picture frame of their first-day-of-school photo. *You'll never walk alone.* Yet as they entered the threshold of adulthood, they'd dropped each other's hand.

An idea came to mind. Opening a browser on her phone, she created a photo gift online and placed an order with expedited delivery. It would be for Colton, a combination closing night and going away gift, assuming the latter happened. She wanted to get it to him before he fled Cape May—in reconciliation of their broken past and hope for future redemption.

Jaxon

JAXON COULD HAVE STOOD THERE ALL NIGHT, RUBBING Sarina's shoulders, listening to her soft moans. Knowing the pleasure he was giving her as he worked her tense muscles into submission and eased her pain. But in his wildest dreams, he wouldn't have stopped there...

Now, decorating duty called.

"Come with me," she said, interrupting his X-rated thoughts as she pulled him into the freezer to retrieve the cakes they'd made the other night. She assembled mixing bowls, utensils, and ingredients and showed him sketches she'd designed for the cakes and cookies, featuring Cape May scenes with touches of holiday flair.

"I spy with my little eye, another sleepless night," he joked.

"Yeah, we better get started. Ready, Chef?"

"Ready," he said. Loving his new nickname, he tossed a chef's kiss her way.

Sarina began making frosting while Jaxon looked on, all

the while fighting the urge to come up behind her, put his hands on her waist, and lean into her.

Suddenly, she stopped piping icing onto a cake and turned to him. "There's no standing around in my kitchen," she teased, waving him over. "Time for you to get to work."

"Tell me what you need, boss."

She handed him a bag of frosting and, guiding his hand with hers, showed him how to swirl it. Her proximity, the feel of her soft hand on his, made his head swoon. Or maybe that was the wine. They worked side-by-side for the next hour, Sarina making beautiful icing art on the sheet cakes with impressive speed and precision. Singing along with the music, they occasionally broke into dance as they maneuvered around the prep table like a well-orchestrated machine.

"I had no idea how great a decorator you'd be, Jaxon Quinn," she said. "If I'd known this back when I had a crush on you, I'd have hunted you down."

He stopped piping and looked at her. "You had a crush on me?"

"Uh, yeah? So did every girl in America? Well, except Kelsey."

"Of course. That goes without saying."

"I was also the president of your fan club. Well, the New Jersey branch."

"You're shitting me!" Jaxon said, laughing. "They actually had state fan clubs?"

He was thrilled to learn she'd had a crush on him, given how cool she was with him. The fact that she treated him like a regular guy was part of her allure, though, allowing him to act like a regular guy. One who cooked breakfast for her. Who screamed like a baby when the power went out. Who sprouted a raging hard-on at the very thought of her.

"You didn't know that?" Sarina asked.

"Dude, I was protected by parents who knew the business and kept me away from it all."

"So, it *wasn't* you signing all the headshots you sent?"

"Nope."

"What about the personalized letters?"

"Publicists. All of it."

Sarina feigned outrage. "What a load of crap."

"Show biz isn't all it's cracked up to be. Lots of smoke and mirrors."

"You're forgetting I'm closely related to an insider. I've heard all about it."

Not all of it.

"That means you've got a shit ton of signing to do before you leave."

"How's this for a start?" He plunged a finger into the pink icing and wrote "JFQ" on her arm, encircling it with a heart.

She smiled. "I'll never wash this arm again."

It was two a.m. when they finally loaded the decorated cakes into the freezer.

"They'll stay fresher this way," Sarina said. "We'll move them to the cooler to defrost tomorrow."

He noticed she had a tiny blob of pink icing on the tip of her nose.

"Hey, Rudolph," he said softly as he took her arm. "You have a little—"

He gently wiped it away with the tip of his forefinger, holding it up for her to see.

Looking up at him, Sarina parted her lips. With the tip of her tongue, she licked the frosting from his finger. A jolt of electric desire shot through him.

"Missed some," she whispered as she wrapped her lips around his finger and pulled it in with a soft, gentle suck, rendering him helpless as his knees went weak and his breath came in jagged waves. An involuntary grunt escaped him as she pulled away, her teeth gently scraping his skin. It only lasted a second, but there was no mistaking her intent as she gazed up at him with teasing eyes. It was all he could do keep from smashing his lips down on hers.

"New recipe," she said, her tone husky. "Just wanted to make sure it's good."

He found his breath. "Must be delicious."

"It was, but…sorry. That was wrong." Turning away, her voice frosted over. "We should go."

God, how he wanted to stop her, pull her into him, tell her she had nothing to worry about. That the crazy chemistry they were feeling was real—after that move, he knew she was feeling it too. The only thing wrong with the whole fucked up mess was that he and Kelsey had fooled Sarina and the world into thinking they were a couple when they weren't. He needed to make this right. If not…

He had no choice. He needed to leave Sarina's place. Tonight.

SARINA AWAKENED WITH A START FRIDAY MORNING, wondering what had shocked her from a deep slumber. And then she realized what it was.

Silence.

For the past two days, she'd been awakened by the sounds of Jaxon in the kitchen. Not that morning. Memories came drifting back of sucking on his finger like a tart.

"You *ass*hole," she hissed as she flung her forearm over her eyes.

She had to be, coming on to her sister's boyfriend like that. Have wine, will flirt. Still, no excuse.

Jaxon's door was open, and he was nowhere to be found. Maybe out for a walk. Or a protection order. Either way, it gave her time to collect her thoughts. She'd apologize profusely when he returned.

Until a note on the counter caught her attention.

Sarina, I cannot thank you enough for your wonderful hospitality, but I think I've overstayed my welcome. I'll be in Cape May until after the play but wanted to get out of your hair as you prepare for the fundraiser. I hope to catch up with you before I leave.

Sincerely,
JFQ—President, Sarina Grace Fan Club (New Jersey branch)

As much as the last line made her smile, she was mortified about her actions of the previous evening. Of course, he'd felt the need to flee after she'd taken something way too far.

Again. While they were both natural flirts who thrived on witty banter, it wasn't an excuse for coming on to him like that. Sarina knew where her heart was, and it was not with her teen crush. It was with her sister. She was Team Kelsey, through and through.

She wondered if Jaxon had appeared in her freezer for a reason other than the dangling carrot he presented as. He'd certainly helped her realize it wasn't the end of the world to ask for help, pushing her to think outside the lunchbox and envision more for her café.

Perhaps his cameo in her life was to show her the type of man who could steal her heart. Someone who excited her, challenged her, and made her feel the way Jaxon did. Not him per se, just someone like him. She shouldn't settle for anything less.

Molly

WITH ONLY ONE DAY LEFT BEFORE THE BIG EVENT, Molly was up at the crack of dawn, excited to put the final pieces in place.

She had offered to set up resource tables for businesses and nonprofits to share information about their services. She made several stops to pick up brochures and other materials before ending up at the Stranding Center, where a job posting caught her eye, advertising the need for a part-time fundraiser.

Molly found her way to the director's office, where she inquired about the position.

"We're looking for someone with extensive fundraising experience," the director explained. "What are your qualifications?"

Molly opened her mouth to speak but heard a voice behind her.

"Why, she's the Unsinkable Molly Grace."

Twirling around, she laughed to find Max there.

"For the past week, she's worked tirelessly on a fundraiser to help rebuild Cape May after the devastating storm," he said. "You'll never find someone more passionate than Molly. She'll bring that same verve to the Stranding Center. She's organized, dedicated and, rumor has it, fluent in dolphin. You don't find that in every applicant."

"Thank you, Max," Molly said, then turned back to the director. "I didn't pay him to say that. Max is my good friend, so he may be a little biased. But if you're willing to take a chance, I'd love to prove myself to this organization."

"That she will," Max said, setting a stack of folders on her desk. "Here are those files you requested."

The director nodded and turned to Molly. "Well, Unsinkable Molly Grace, we've known Mr. Banks for years. We trust him. We're hoping to do a fundraiser next month. How soon could you start?"

"In my mind, I already have."

The director sized her up. "Max's word is respected, but you'll need to prove yourself. How about this. I'll visit your event to see how you do. If I like what I see, the job's yours."

As they left her office, Molly exhaled. "I don't know what came over me. I saw the job posting and hunted her down without even thinking it through."

"I guess that's what happens when you know what you want. But...*do* you know what you want? What about New York?"

Molly shrugged. "New York doesn't seem to want me, and not one single finance position I've applied for has excited me as much as this fundraising one does."

"Maybe this means you've found your passion."

"You may be right." She shook her head in disbelief. "Now

I'm really excited for Saturday. I believe I'm gonna kill it."

"Of course, you will," Max said, chuckling. "You're the Unsinkable Molly Grace."

"I love your unsinkable faith in me."

"Hey, come with me. I have someone I want you to meet." He led her through the halls and into a giant room containing a dolphin tank. "Molly, this is Babette. Babette, Molly."

"Wait, is this—"

"Our rescue. But plot twist—she's a she."

"No wonder the other dolphins didn't know who I was talking about," Molly said as she rubbed the dolphin's head. "I got your name wrong."

"She forgives you."

"Does this mean you're fluent in dolphin now, too?"

"I've been taking night classes," Max said.

She smiled, so glad to be in his presence. "When's your shift over?"

"In an hour. Wanna meet up when I'm done?"

Yes, please. "I do. I believe I owe you an ice cream."

Kelsey

KELSEY HAD PLANNED ON PHONING VERNA FIRST THING, until she remembered the time difference. Good girls didn't call people on the West Coast that early, no matter how anxious they were to put an end to their fauxmance.

As they ran through their final rehearsal, Kelsey noted a perceptible shift in Colton's attitude. He was softer, more like his old self, cracking jokes and occasionally holding her hand as Lillian made last-minute blocking changes. When they finished, he hugged her.

"Feels amazing to be back on stage with you," he whispered.

"The feeling's mutual." She gave him a coquettish glance through her lashes, the *gaze lovingly* stage direction she'd perfected on screen but never utilized in real life.

"I'm sorry we were interrupted last night. I'd love to talk some more. Are you free for dinner after the show?"

"Yes," she said, going a bit breathless. "I'd love that."

Kelsey dialed Verna as soon as she left the theater, but the call went straight to voicemail. She declined to leave a message, wanting to talk one-on-one. If she spun it the right way, Verna might agree that a real-life friends-to-lovers plot twist might do more for box office enticement than pretending she and Jaxon were in love. Assuming that's how things between her and Colton would go.

She could only hope.

Jaxon

JAXON RAN HIS HAND THROUGH THE EMERALD WATERS of the Atlantic as he bobbed on a surfboard. He felt bad leaving Sarina the day before the fundraiser, but it was too dangerous to stay near her, if what had happened between them the night before was any indication. Feeling the way he did about her and not being able to act on it resulted in a physical ache like nothing he'd ever felt before.

After his assistant booked him a new Airbnb, he had his driver rent him a surfboard and take him to the same secluded beach where he and Sarina had surfed. He spent a rare day in solitude, just him and the waves, thinking. He needed to separate feelings from facts, to make sure he wasn't making any rash decisions as he grappled with how to free himself from the tangled web he'd weaved. And potentially start a new one.

At first, the fauxmance ploy had seemed innocent enough. A simple publicity stunt hinting of a blossoming romance between costars, designed to drive box office sales. It wasn't the first time such a farce had been perpetrated upon the public and certainly wouldn't be the last. But it was no longer innocent. Not since he'd fallen for his fake girlfriend's sister.

They needed to end it, but first he'd need Kelsey's agreement. He also needed her blessing to pursue Sarina. Because he wasn't sure he could go on without doing so.

Facts: no one had ever captured his attention and his heart as Sarina had. The spark he'd felt the moment he laid eyes on her hadn't fizzled in the days he got to know her. It had only grown. He could bob on his surfboard and contemplate it all he wanted, but there was no denying the truth.

Jaxon Quinn had found his person.

Molly

MOLLY AND MAX MET AT THE MARINA WHERE THEY ORdered cones from her favorite ice cream shop. Finding an open slip on the dock, they kicked off their flip flops, dangled their feet in the water, and laughed as they speed-licked their cones to stop the melting flow.

"I love looking at boat names," Max said as he pointed to a yacht in the next slip. "*Tax-Sea-Vasion.* Pretty funny."

"*She Got the House,*" Molly said, pointing to another.

"What are you naming your boat?"

"Lemme think." She glanced around for inspiration. "So much pressure..."

Max smiled and playfully pushed her away. "How about *Pier Pressure?*"

"Yes!" she laughed. "What's your boat's name?"

"*Fishful Thinking.*"

"*Yeah, Buoy!*" Molly said.

"Good one!" Max laughed and gave her a sticky high five.

"No, wait. I know exactly what I'd call my boat. *The Unsinkable Molly Grace.*"

"Now you're talking."

"Okay, next question," Molly said. "Most romantic setting for a first date."

"Easy. A rest stop on the Garden State Parkway."

"And you say you're not a hopeless romantic."

"What's yours?"

"A beach picnic, at dusk, with fireworks."

"Nice," Max said. "Ketchup on a hot dog—yay or nay?"

"Team Ketchup, all the way."

He made a gagging face.

"Don't tell me you're one of those mustard snobs?" she teased, giving him a shove.

"Next question. If you could live anywhere in the world—except New York, of course," he said, rolling his eyes, "where would it be?"

"Here."

"Really?"

"Yep. I've always dreamed of living in a city, but my heart will always be in Cape May. I envision having a cottage on the water, with a lavender-colored door, and window boxes filled with flowers. It'll be my escape, a place I come on weekends to relax and rejuvenate."

"That sounds nice."

"Unless, of course, I get the job at the Stranding Center. Then, my cottage-by-the-sea will be my permanent home."

There was no mistaking the twinkle in Max's eye. She

longed to tell him about her break with Brennan, but needed time to adjust to her new situation without bringing someone else into it.

"My turn. If you could have dinner with anyone throughout history, dead or alive, who would it be?"

"Easy," Max said as he laid back on the dock. "My mom."

She should have known better than to ask that question. "I'm sorry," she whispered. She lay down and faced him, making a pillow with her hands. "What would your conversation be about?"

As Max told her all the things he'd love to discuss with his mom—things she missed from his childhood, his college years, his dreams for the future—he got choked up.

"I'm sure she's so proud of the man you've become."

He wiped at his eyes. "The year she died, it was all we could do to get through each day. Soon, my dad and Colton began focusing on his football career, and it consumed their lives. I was always on the sidelines, looking in. I felt like nobody could see me, standing there, just beyond the glow of his fame. I felt completely alone and lost."

Her heart broke, thinking of young Max in that situation. She reached for his hand. He turned his palm up and slid his fingers between hers.

"But then I walked into eighth-grade science lab, and I was paired with you. You smiled at me, joked around with me, made me feel seen for the first time since Mom died."

Molly rolled onto her back and blinked at the sky, salty tears stinging her ears. Her breath caught in a sob and her chest heaved.

"Oh, Moll, I didn't mean to make you cry," he said.

They sat up and Max put his arm around her as she shed more tears. She'd never felt such compassion for another human. He didn't try to shush her, talk over her, tell her how she should feel or act nervous like Brennan did when she showed her emotions. He let her cry it out, patiently waiting, his quiet strength filling the space between them until her chest heaved its final sob.

"I don't know where that came from," she said, laughing softly, while Max ran his thumb under her eyes to wipe her tears. "I just feel so bad for what you've been through, losing both parents. Yet you seem to have so much love to give. To everyone, creatures great and small."

"I was so loved in those early years, it's all stored up in here." He tapped his chest. "In reserve, for anyone who needs it."

She pouted as his eyes teared again.

"Geez, woman, how did we go from naming boats to this sob fest of ours?" he asked as he wiped a tear from his cheek.

Molly looked up at her friend, this gentle soul, the kindest person she'd ever met. He never asked her for anything, just quietly stood by, ready to help in whatever way he could. Being around Brennan and his frat-boy friends for as long she had been, she'd forgotten nice guys like Max existed.

"Despite all you've been through," she said, "I know they're both still with you."

"Funny you say that. She wrote me a letter, right before she died. In it, she said she'll always be with me, in my heart, and the flapping of a butterfly's wings. And guess what? As soon as I finished reading the letter, I looked outside and there was a butterfly just outside the window."

Molly wrapped her arms around herself. "That gives me the chills. Sometimes the universe provides what you need, just when you need it."

Like Max. He was just what she'd needed this week, as she planned this event and struggled with doubts over her life situation. He came along right when she needed a friend, a helper, a good laugh. He'd given her space to be herself, no filters or pretenses. To see her own strengths, to shine on her own, and in so doing, find her passion.

Whatever happened with her and Brennan, even if they were done, no longer mattered. Because in the process of losing him, she'd found a friend.

Even more importantly, she'd found herself.

Sarina

ONCE AGAIN, A LINE HAD FORMED OUTSIDE THE CAFÉ Friday morning. Social media reaction to the previous night's events had gone viral.

Throughout the morning, Sarina checked her phone periodically, but there was no news from the bank. What could be taking so long? She had excellent credit. Shoulda been a slam dunk.

Worry grew as the day wore on. Not just about the bank's eerie silence, but about Jaxon, whose departure had left a hole in her heart. She struggled not to think about the lovers' reunion that would go down that night.

The café was so busy, she almost missed report time for the show. As she rushed to the theater, she called the bank and left a message, then waited until the last possible moment before turning off her phone for the show. Hopefully, good news awaited her afterwards.

Max

"REMIND ME WHAT WE'RE DOING HERE AGAIN?" MAX asked as they crossed the debris-scattered lawn to the arts center.

"Taking photos so I can share them on social media and remind everyone why we're doing this fundraiser."

Shit. He wondered if Molly knew he and Colton owned the land and that they were in negotiations with a development company. Standing by nervously, he waited until Molly got her shots. When she was done, she suggested they sit in the treehouse.

"I can't believe it's still standing," she said as their feet dangled off the edge of the platform. "It's a wonderful gift from your dad for all us kids. I have such great memories of playing here."

"Me too."

She looked at him with a nostalgic expression. "I remember you vaguely back then. I thought you were weird."

Max laughed out loud. "I thought you were a crybaby."

"You'd be right about that. Funny how our siblings were so close, but we didn't really become friends until—"

"Eighth-grade science lab," Max said.

Molly chuckled. "I was gonna say last week."

"Oh," he said, blushing.

"Just kidding. We did become friends in science that year. Why did we ever drift apart?"

Max knew, but didn't want to say it. Somehow *because you became popular, and I was a total dweeb* didn't sound right. Instead, he went with, "We just had different interests."

They sat in a comfortable silence, occasionally interrupted by a shared memory. Like the time Sarina had won a contest for the most realistic painting of the very treehouse in which they were sitting.

"That's one reason, among many, why we have to keep the arts center here on this property," she said.

"Molly...there's something I haven't told you."

"If it's that you and Becca are expecting your fourth child, I already know."

He laughed. "It's more serious than that."

"Your fifth?"

He paused. "Apparently, my dad purchased the arts center property just before he died."

"I know." She looked up at him, sighing. "Kelsey's trying to convince Colton not to sell."

"Oh, I...didn't know you knew. I've left it up to him, but he's not sure what he wants to do."

"What do *you* want?"

"Honestly? I'd like us to keep it. But with me going away, it's not fair to impose that on him. He wants to move away."

"Want my two cents?"

"Absolutely."

"Let Kelsey buy both," she said. "She and I discussed some possibilities over breakfast this morning. We'll rebuild the center here, and split the farm into three parcels, one for each of us. Kelsey will keep the farmhouse, Sarina, the vegetable garden and greenhouses, and I would take the bayfront part."

Max smiled. "To build your cottage?"

"You got it."

Great. A cozy place for you and Brennan.

While he was happy Molly would have a piece of his family's property for her dream cottage, knowing she'd be sharing it with *my boyfriend* made Max feel sick. Oh well. At least he would be living on a distant coast and wouldn't have to see them. Assuming a distant coast would have him.

"To whatever extent you can, please, *please* convince him to let us buy the property," Molly said. "For my family's sake, and yours."

"I'll try." He really would.

She glanced at her phone. "Wow, almost time for the play."

"How 'bout I drive tonight for a change?" Max offered. "We can drop off the golf cart and maybe grab a pizza after the show?"

"You had me at pizza."

Climbing down from the treehouse, Max saw a couple pieces of trash in a pile of broken branches. Always environmentally conscious, he picked them up and shoved them in his pocket to throw away at home.

Suddenly, he became aware that Molly was no longer walking with him. He turned to find she'd stopped dead in her tracks.

"Max?" she whispered.

She pointed to her chest where a butterfly clung. Just above her heart.

Kelsey

KELSEY AND COLTON PLAYED TO A SOLD-OUT CROWD that night, bringing the house down as they took their final dramatic bow. Grand Lillian had deferred decision on the final act kiss until closing night.

"You still got it," Kelsey teased Colton as the curtain fell. She wasn't kidding—he was as natural onstage as he was on the football field.

"You too, my leading lady," he teased as he linked his fingers with hers.

Kelsey wondered if his comment was intended to be as flirtatious as it sounded.

"We still on for dinner?" he asked.

"Absolutely. I'm just gonna shower and change."

"Me too, but first I need to deliver the tables Max and I built, and help set things up for tomorrow. Pick you up at nine?"

After parting ways, Kelsey gathered her belongings. As she

walked up the aisle of the now-deserted auditorium, she saw a man standing in the back, waving to her. His long curly hair was tamed under a bandanna, and his unruly beard, tie-dyed t-shirt, and John Lennon sunglasses gave Grateful Dead. Then, he stepped from the shadows, jade eyes twinkling.

One sweep of his long lashes, a nibble of his supple lip, and she had no choice but to...gasp.

"Betcha didn't expect to see me here," he said, flashing his all-too-familiar dimpled smile.

Colton

COLTON COULDN'T WAIT TO HAVE DINNER WITH KELSEY and catch up, just the two of them. He had to keep reminding himself she had a boyfriend, but he couldn't help but wonder what lurked behind her teasing glances, the way she bit her lip when she looked at him. If all she was feeling was nostalgia for their past friendship, he'd take it—certainly better than a decade of silence.

After he collected his things from backstage, he headed up the aisle toward the exit—and that's when he saw them. Two dark figures standing at the back of the auditorium, locked in an embrace. She, gazing up at him, as she was in the magazine photos. It only took him a second to realize who she was with.

Her prince.

He came to a dead stop. Pivoting, he endeavored to exit stage left before they saw him.

"Colton?"

Too late. He turned back. "Hey," he said.

"Colton," Kelsey said, "this is Jaxon Quinn. Jax, this is Colton, my...friend."

"Hey, man," Colton said, clasping Jaxon's outstretched hand, even though it was the last thing he wanted to do.

"Not good enough, bro. Bring it in." Jaxon laughed and pulled him in into a man hug. "Big fan of yours. Big, huge fan."

Colton internally cringed at his over-the-top friendliness but appreciated Jaxon's use of the present tense.

"Big fan of your getup," Colton joked, indicating Jaxon's disguise.

"It was either this or a bearded priest. This way, I only attract old stoned hippies. No one's asking this dude to hold babies or offer blessings."

Colton was surprised at how down-to-earth Jaxon seemed. He'd been around enough alpha males to spot a boastful phony from miles away, but Jaxon seemed different. He was treating Colton as if *he* were the megastar. It warmed him to Jaxon a bit.

Just a bit.

"I'll never forget that Hail Mary pass you threw against Notre Dame," he said. "Man, you saved me from losing my house."

"Glad I could help."

"Just kidding. I never bet on games. I just bet on you, winning for us. Thanks for that."

And...he warmed a bit more.

"Listen, I gotta run," Colton said, wanting to get outta there before his emotions showed through. "Nice meeting you, Jaxon."

He hightailed it out of the theater, not wanting Kelsey to see his bitter disappointment. And his confusion. Had she invited Jaxon to the show, or had he just shown up? Maybe she'd only agreed to dinner to be polite. Either way, what did it matter? There was no way she'd leave her "prince," who'd obviously flown a great distance to see her, to have dinner with Colton. She'd probably insist on bringing him along.

Hard pass.

Molly

AFTER THE PLAY, MAX AND MOLLY PICKED UP A PIZZA AND went back to his house. Sitting at the old wooden table outside, Max blared a playlist of old standards through an outdoor speaker and poured wine. Fairy lights strung from a pergola twinkled as dusk fell around them. Digging into their pizza, Molly rattled off everything on her to-do list, including the assignments she'd made for volunteers, while Max added his recollection of things she'd talked about. She was amazed at his attention to detail. It was great having someone to talk with about the event, especially someone who'd been with her through it all.

When they finished, Molly slid her notebook aside, rested her chin in her hands, and gazed at Max.

He laughed nervously. "Why are you looking at me that way?"

"You are an old soul, Maxwell Banks."

"What gave it away? My top hits from the 1940s?"

"No, you just have such a calming effect on me. I thought I'd be a nervous wreck tonight, but I'm not. It's as if you've lived this life before and nothing rattles you because you know it's all gonna be okay."

"That's really nice of you to say."

"It's true. I want you to know I really appreciate all you said to me at the lighthouse. It took a lot of guts to trust me with your feelings."

"I meant everything I said."

Molly nodded. "I know. I feel it."

"I hope—"

"Brennan and I are on a break," she blurted out.

He stopped short. "What?"

"I told him last night I couldn't do it anymore. You were right, he's been making it clear he really doesn't care about seeing me, much less starting a life with me."

He paused, looking truly sad for her. She appreciated his reaction, the expression of a true friend. Not gloating, not lunging at her. Just being there for her.

"I'm sorry, Molly. That must have been hard to do."

"In the end, it wasn't. You've helped me see what true friends are. Turns out, I've never really had one, at least not one like you. I didn't tell you this, but I went out for drinks with the girls."

"Yeah, Becca told me. Too bad I *couldn't make it*," he teased.

"Sorry I lied, but you didn't miss much. Despite being each other's ride-or-die in high school, I have nothing in common with them anymore."

"What changed?" he asked.

"Me," she said, matter-of-factly. "I'm not into the surface-level shit they're into."

"Yeah, five minutes with Becca and I can see why."

"I just need some time to process everything with Brennan. We're not officially over, but I can't make a final decision until after the fundraiser."

"A wise move. Make sure it's what you want. Just...promise me, whatever happens, we'll always be friends."

"I promise. Otherwise, it'll be 'Cause of death: losing Max's friendship.'"

Kelsey

Kelsey's heart sank as she watched Colton bolt from the theater. She wondered if they were still on for dinner, but he was gone before she could ask.

The bigger question...

"What on earth are you doing here?" she demanded of Jaxon.

"Well..." he said, looking at her with an expression she couldn't quite place, despite knowing each of his expressions—both real and dramatic—as if she were inside his head directing them. "Originally, I came with an ulterior motive."

"What, to send Cape May women into cardiac arrest?" Kelsey joked.

"I didn't come for *their* hearts. I came for *yours*."

Oh, God. His words took her breath away, nearly causing her heart to stop. Was this really happening?

"I really dig you, KG. You're, like, my best friend. Now that I'm thirty, it's time for me to get serious. I'm done with this playboy lifestyle. I want a girlfriend—someone sweet, funny and real." He paused and squeezed her hands. "Someone just like you."

Never in a million years could she have expected this. To have the likes of Jaxon Quinn stand here and tell her he'd gotten the *real* feels for her? This couldn't be her life.

Her heart fluttered, but not in the way she'd expect after years of searching to find real love. Casting 11:11 wishes, blowing on dandelion fuzz, gazing at shooting stars as she wished for a bona fide romance. In real life, not on a movie set.

There he stood, in the flesh, as if dandelion fuzz had taken root before her.

But the fluttering in her heart wasn't excitement. It was dread. She was scared shitless, wondering if she was about to make a mistake in passing up this opportunity of a lifetime. Terrified to hurt someone she cared deeply for. Of course, she loved Jaxon Quinn, not only as the dashing and talented actor. As a dear friend. But...as much as she willed herself to, she just couldn't make her heart feel something it didn't.

She gazed up at him as she took a breath. "Jax...you're the sweetest, kindest—"

"I know," he said with a sheepish grin. "I finally found my person, Kelse, but...it's not you."

She laughed out loud. Ah, yes, that was more like it. History repeating itself with the good ol' one-two punch, just like back in high school with Colton. Once again, casting her in a familiar role. The friend-zone girl. The one no one wanted.

Not that she wanted Jaxon to want her in that way.

"But she's *like* you," he continued. "Very much so."

"Let me get this straight. You came to win my heart, but along the way you found someone else? Who...a flight attendant? An Uber driver? A screeching fan?"

"Your sister."

Kelsey laughed out loud. "That's actually a good one."

Knowing Jaxon as the prankster he was, this sort of joke was right up his alley.

"Seriously, who are you—"

"Dude, it's Sarina. She's been sheltering me for the past three days."

"Wait." Kelsey held up her hand. "How do you even *know* my sister?"

"I was chased by a pack of she-wolves into her freezer. She let me crash at her place until opening night, when I was gonna pull a stunt as part of the fauxmance, but also to ask you for a *real*mance." He chuckled. "See what I did there?"

Kelsey tipped her head to the side, trying to hide her smile as the vision of Jaxon hiding in her sister's freezer played in her head.

"But as we got to know each other, I realized how incredibly well-suited we are to one another. She shares so many of the great qualities I love about you, but—and don't take this the wrong way—she makes me feel things I've never felt before."

Wow. Kelsey had not expected that. But the more she thought about it, the more it made sense. Jaxon needed someone with a little edge, and Sarina had edge for days.

"So..." he said. "Is it okay for me to date Sarina?"

"I think you have to ask *her*. I'll warn you, she does have good taste..."

"Ha *ha*, very funny. What do you think?"

As much as she wanted to protect her sister from a self-described reformed F-boy (she'd believe it when she saw it), she knew Sarina would not only hold her own with him but hold his feet to the fire as well with her quick wit and strong self-esteem. Maybe they would be a good match.

"Okay, but under one condition."

"Name it."

"We're done with this charade. Obviously. We're calling Verna right now and telling her we're done."

"Deal."

Kelsey pulled out her phone and FaceTimed Verna. As they waited for her to answer, Jaxon jabbed her with his elbow. "Colton Banks, huh?"

"What?" Kelsey shot him a look.

"The guy who's had your heart all along."

She sighed. "Was I that obvious?"

"No," he said. "But he was."

"Who has your heart, Kelsey?"

She startled to hear Verna's voice coming through her phone, unaware the woman had answered.

"Oh, um...no one..."

"Did I hear Colton Banks?" Verna teased. "I recall you guys grew up together."

"We're just friends."

"Not what it looked like to me," Jaxon said, ducking in anticipation of the arm slug Kelsey delivered.

"Interesting..." Verna's voice trailed off. "So what's all this urgency about? I see you tried to call a few times."

"We've decided to end the fauxmance," Kelsey said.

"Facts," Jaxon chimed in. "We're both interested in other people."

"This was supposed to go on until the movie release," Verna said, tapping her long fingernails on her chin as she appeared to give it some thought. "Hmm. A breakup before your movie release over other people? That's some spilled tea right there."

Kelsey and Jaxon exchanged a look.

"Okay," she said. "Done deal."

"Just like that?" Kelsey asked. Had she known it was that easy to get out of a contract, she would've asked a lot sooner.

"You know Hollywood romances. Here today, gone tomorrow. This is some juicy shit, so we don't need the fauxmance anymore."

Now you tell us.

"How are we gonna spin this?" Kelsey asked. "I don't want our fans to hate us."

"You leave that to me," Verna said.

After they ended their call, Kelsey turned to Jaxon. "Are you serious about dating my sister?"

"Dead ass."

"Listen, Quinn. If you hurt her or pull any of your F-boy shit—"

"Not gonna happen, Kelse. I'm crazy about her."

From the look in his eye, she knew he was serious.

Amazing. Jaxon and Sarina. The more she thought about it, the more it made sense. But she couldn't help the guilt niggling at the back of her mind.

"She's gonna be pissed when she discovers we've been lying to her," Kelsey said.

"I know. I'm hoping you'll tell her first, before she reads whatever Verna puts out there."

"Sure. Make me do your dirty work." But he was right. Better the confession come from her than Jaxon.

"Let me know once you've talked to her. I don't want to say anything until I know she's heard it from you."

"Are you still staying with her?" Kelsey asked.

"No. I'm in an Airbnb."

Good. That gave her time to find Colton first and break the news.

She decided to wait until they went out for dinner. Both conversations—with Colton and Sarina—needed to be in person. She'd tell Sarina after she told Colton over dinner.

If she thought lying was complicated, getting out of a lie was starting to feel way worse.

Colton

COLTON JUMPED IN HIS TRUCK AND THREW IT INTO Reverse. He had to get out of there, away from the theater, away from Kelsey and...*him*.

As hard as he tried, Colton couldn't erase the visual of the famous couple hugging in the back of the theater. No wonder they'd ended up together, beauty attracting beauty. Even Colton had to admit they were fire together. The more he thought about it, the more the visual became etched in his brain, as if to remind himself that no matter how close he and Kelsey might have gotten that week, however carefully they'd worked to repair their damaged bridge, she still belonged to someone else.

And a pretty decent someone else, if first impressions were accurate. Colton hadn't expected to find Jaxon so down-to-earth and friendly. Which only made matters worse. If he were an asshole, it would be easier for Colton to denounce the two of them, cast judgment against Kelsey for choosing such a loser, and put the ridiculous notion of somehow ending up with her to rest. Permanently.

Another vision came to mind. Kelsey and Jaxon, shacked up together in his family's farmhouse. Teaching kids to act in a newly rebuilt arts center, on land once owned by *his* family. If he sold the land to her, it could happen. The beautiful Grace-Quinn duo building a family on the backs of his own.

He could feel his brow draw together at the thought. *Not gonna happen.*

Whipping out his phone, he texted the development company and asked if he could meet with them first thing in the morning. They agreed. Of course they would—they were as desperate to own the Banks properties as Colton was to offload them. He'd seal the deal, finish packing up, and hopefully be gone by the end of the week.

The thought that he'd soon be reunited with his beloved dog, Cadence, was the only thing that gave him hope.

But then, shit. He'd forgotten about the fundraiser, where he and Max were tasked with putting together the smaller tables they'd built to achieve Molly's vision of the Whoville fest. Sighing, he knew there was no way out of staying through the weekend to fulfill his promise. Oh well. He'd feel better after he signed papers to put the land sale in motion, knowing the wheels were in motion and there was light at the end of his Cape May tunnel.

He packed a duffel bag and booked himself a room in a hotel on the outskirts of Philly. Not only to have a shorter drive in the morning, but to get the hell out of Cape May before the buzz of Jaxon's appearance drove the townsfolk into a frenzy. The last thing he wanted was to face the two of them parading around town, dining together, kissing under the moonlight, making a spectacle of their love to the delight of their fans.

The thought reminded him to cancel with Kelsey. While it was a total dick move, he had to do it, for his own sanity. He texted to let her know he couldn't make dinner, that something had come up. After messaging Max to let him know where he was going, he turned off his phone so he wouldn't be tempted to check if social media had gotten wind of Prince Quinn's arrival.

Max

"THANKS FOR TONIGHT," MOLLY SAID AS MAX PULLED into her driveway. "I needed this nice, calm evening to mentally prepare for tomorrow."

He was sad the night had to end and drove as slowly as he could. He even took a couple wrong turns on purpose.

Thanking him for the ride, she hopped out of the truck but only made it halfway across her lawn before returning. Max rolled down the window.

"Thank you for all you've done this week," she said. "You've been a great help. I couldn't have done it alone."

"It was my pleasure."

"No, it was mine. Goodnight, Max."

She walked away but turned back. "I'm gonna miss you when you leave for school."

His pulse thrummed. "Me too."

She nodded. "Okay, goodnight again."

This time she got a little further before coming back.

"You really didn't like Becca?"

He shook his head. "She's not my type."

"Okay," she said, walking away.

Max laughed when she turned back again.

"For future reference, what is your type?" she asked.

"You've hung out with me for the past few days. What do you think?"

Molly crossed her arms on the window well. "You need someone nice, quick-witted, smart, and fun."

"There's your answer."

"Okay. I'll do better next time." She turned, then swiveled back. "Do you even want me to fix you up?"

"Not really. With grad school coming up, I don't want to be tied down."

She hesitated. "Is that the only reason?"

A beat passed. "Yeah, that's about it," Max said, swallowing his truth.

"Okay. Goodnight. This time for real."

But she didn't get far before turning back again.

"Molly, do you wanna just get in and talk?"

"No, I should go. I just...hope you fall in love with someone who deserves you."

"I'll keep that in mind."

This time she made it inside.

He exhaled. "I already have."

SARINA SCOOTED OUT OF THE THEATER BEFORE THE CURtain fell, knowing that's when Jaxon planned to surprise

Kelsey. Watching her sister perform onstage, she was struck by her breathtaking beauty, her wholesome appeal. No wonder Jaxon traveled so far to witness her live performance.

She popped into the café to check on the status of tomorrow's desserts after having moved them to the cooler to defrost.

When she arrived, she was met with the sound of gushing water.

"No!" she screamed. A sprinkler was going off in the hallway.

She rushed to the back room where she kept her emergency numbers and called the sprinkler company, who instructed her on how to turn off the main water valve. Once the water stopped flowing, she demanded to know how this had happened.

"It's hard to say," the representative said. "Looking at our records, it appears you were supposed to schedule an annual inspection but are way overdue."

Shit. That's right, she'd decided to put it off until after the weekend.

The man promised he'd get someone to look at it tomorrow. Great, just in time for the fundraiser. But she had no choice. She couldn't risk losing the café if an actual fire were to break out.

But that didn't mitigate the damage that had already been done.

She opened the cooler, hoping against hope it had been spared, but was devastated to find the sprinkler in there had also gone off. The desserts she and Jaxon had lovingly made and decorated were now oozing from their shelves, as cake and icing dripped and blended in with the murky floor water.

"Oh, no!" she cried, instinctively cupping her hand under a section of sheet cake that toppled from a shelf. Although she desperately tried to save the desserts, her efforts were futile. Nothing was salvageable.

"Oh, God. What am I going to do?"

Molly was going to be devastated. There'd be no desserts for the event.

She pulled her phone from her pocket to call her, and that's when she saw a voicemail from the bank, igniting a spark of hope—which was instantly snuffed out when she played the message.

Her line of credit had been denied.

Sarina sank to the floor, deflated and sobbing. In one day, all her hopes had been eviscerated. She couldn't take any more. She sat and cried until her ducts ran dry.

Heaving a last sob, she looked around at the mess she had to clean up. Fortunately, her natural instinct was to clean when she was stressed, allowing her to shut off emotion and become a robotic cleaning machine. Donning rubber gloves, she shoveled the destroyed desserts into a large trash bag and brought out her Shop-Vac to suck up the standing water before turning on oversized fans.

Then it was time to break the news to Molly, who answered on the first ring.

"Oh, my gosh, Sarina! I'll be right over to help clean."

"Already done. I just don't know what we're gonna do about desserts tomorrow."

"We'll figure it out. Let me call in Grand Lil and Kelsey so we can come up with a plan."

"Don't bother Kelsey, she and—" She stopped herself before she said Jaxon's name. "She's...busy with the play."

"Okay..." Molly drew it out as if she were confused over Sarina's concern. "Hang up. I'm gonna group FaceTime you and Grand Lil."

A moment later, her phone signaled the incoming video call.

"How bad is the damage?" Grand Lillian asked as she came into view.

"Mostly just water," Sarina said. "I got here in time before the place was totally flooded, but the desserts are ruined."

"They're replaceable. How are you?"

"Fine," Sarina said, her tough-girl persona taking over. "All good here."

"Why aren't you more upset about this?" Molly asked suspiciously.

"Because I'm done. Not doing this anymore."

"Not doing what anymore?" Grand Lil challenged.

"The café." She looked around the place, feeling weirdly disengaged from it. "It's a money drain, and now I'm going to be hemorrhaging even more. So…I'm out."

"I thought you said you were doing fine financially?" Grand Lillian asked.

"I lied. I didn't want to come crawling to you for help, because I didn't want to hear 'I told you so.'"

"'Told you so' about what?"

"That I had no business opening a café and, of course, it would fail," Sarina accused. "Oh, and that I'd probably quit. I tried not to, because that's what you all were expecting of me, but a person can only take so much…" Her voice wavered as more tears threatened.

"Now, now…" her grandmother warned. "No need to be snarky, child. I wouldn't have offered help if I didn't have the ultimate faith in you."

"Faith in my certain demise."

Grand Lillian laughed. "I don't know where you've been, but the café had a full house of eager new customers on Thursday night. That little place of yours has gone viral on local social media, and your popularity is growing. I see nothing but success there."

"It's all a facade," she said. "I'm two months late on rent, and August is due next week."

"You should have told me," Grand Lil chided.

"I don't want handouts. I'm only doing this if I can do it on my own."

"I'll offer you a loan, not a handout."

"Take her offer, Sarina," Molly said. "I want to see you succeed at this."

Sarina mulled it over. It would be so easy to walk away at this point, see if she could get *Jolt!* to take over. But it had felt so great on Thursday night, to see her little passion project thriving...

She recalled Jaxon's words, that even the most savvy business people sometimes have to ask for help.

"Okay," she finally relented. "I'll take you up on that. I promise I'll pay you back as soon as I can."

"I'll make sure you do."

She was relieved to find asking for help wasn't as painful as she'd imagined.

"Okay, ladies, we need to figure out desserts for tomorrow," Molly said.

Sarina had an idea. "Let me reach out to some of my contacts and see if I can get donations."

"I'll do the same," Molly said.

"Are we all set, then?" Grand Lillian asked. "It's late, and I need my beauty rest."

"Yes. And thanks again, Grand Lil," Sarina said. "I appreciate your offer of financial assistance, and I promise it'll get paid back as soon as I can, but so you know, I want to do this on my own, no silent partner shit. Deal?"

"Child, if I wanted to be a café owner, I'd have been one by now. I'm lending you money, and of course, I'll always be here to lend you my grandmotherly advice. That's not stopping anytime soon. But this is your café to run as you see fit. I think you've been doing a fantastic job of it so far, and I'm not going to step on your toes."

And just like that, Sarina Grace was back to owning a café.

Kelsey

Just as Kelsey arrived at home to get ready for their date, Colton texted her to say something had come up and he couldn't make dinner.

Her heart sank. She hoped it had nothing to do with the Jaxon thing. She texted back, asking him if he was okay. After a half hour with no response, she dialed his number, but it went to voicemail. She left a message, telling him she needed to talk to him in person and to call as soon as he could.

Exhausted, she crawled into bed and waited, struggling to keep her eyes open. She must have drifted off at some point, because she was startled awake by a call from Molly, telling her about a flood at Sarina's café.

"Oh no. Does she need our help with cleanup?"

"No, you know Sarina. She did it all herself."

After their call, Jaxon texted to ask if she'd talked with Sarina. Shit, she'd forgotten. As much as she'd wanted her newsflash to be in person, she decided she'd better call and break the news to her sister before someone else did.

Sarina

Sarina was relieved the fundraiser would soon be over and that her life could return to normal. Including the ability to get more than three hours of sleep. She was also relieved that the financial strain was, for now, somewhat lifted. Now that Grand Lil had expressed her belief in her all along—the surprise to end all surprises—Sarina felt silly having gone through all the gyrations she had this week to avoid asking for help.

Speaking of help—she needed desserts. She turned to social media and posted a message to her followers, explaining the sprinkler issue and asking if people could donate a box of cookies or a store-bought pie. After posting, her phone rang.

"Sarina, are you okay?" Kelsey asked. "Molly just told me about the café."

"I got here just in time to turn off the water before it totally destroyed the place."

"That was lucky. Sorry to hear about the desserts."

"Yeah, we put a lot of work into those. What are you doing up so late?"

"I've been waiting to hear from Colton. He and I were supposed to have dinner tonight, but he canceled. You...haven't seen him, have you?"

"No?"

Why was she so jacked about Colton when JFQ was in town? Maybe he hadn't surprised her yet...

"That's not the only reason I'm calling." Kelsey's tone dropped as she took a deep breath. "I wanted to tell you this in person. There's something you need to know about me and Jaxon. My fake boyfriend."

"What do you mean, fake?" Sarina was incensed at Kelsey's assessment. "He seems pretty real to me."

Kelsey laughed out loud. "I don't mean fake that way. I mean, the thing between us was fake. A fauxmance, a publicity stunt. We're nothing more than friends. Don't hate me."

"Wait, really?"

"Yep."

"I knew it! He's so not your type. I mean...not that I would know..."

"Chill, girl, *I* know. And he's all yours."

Whoa! "Who said anything about me wanting him?"

"Just...don't hold it against him. He's a good guy."

Sarina was in shock. She should be mad at both of them for lying to her, but she knew how Hollywood worked. No need to be precious about it because...

Jaxon Quinn was a free man. Holy. Fucking. Shit.

As much as this news excited her to the core, she had no idea if he was even interested in her. She could swear they'd shared a couple moments, but who's to say he didn't share moments like that with every woman he met? For all she knew, he was already on his way back to LA, looking for his next victim.

And anyway, she wasn't one to date her sister's ex. Oh...but not really an ex. It was hard to wrap her head around it all.

Breath in. Breath out. *Jaxon is free. Shut up.* Breath in. Breath out. And so it continued, until she finally fell into a deep state of blissful unconsciousness.

JAXON SPENT FRIDAY NIGHT HOLED UP IN HIS AIRBNB, waiting for Kelsey to let him know she'd spoken with Sarina.

He thought about the play and how much he'd enjoyed sitting in the back row of the theater in complete anonymity, watching his costar perform on stage. She was amazing, no surprise there.

But what really impressed him were the acting chops of his man-crush, Colton Banks. Jaxon knew Kelsey was childhood friends with his football idol, but didn't know he was also a thespian. Kelsey never talked about him much, even when Jaxon grilled her for details about his life. It was obvious after seeing them together, their romance was fire. Onstage, and off.

Jaxon was relieved to know she was as eager to end the farce as he was, and even more so to know she didn't object to him pursuing Sarina. But, out of respect to their relationship, he wanted Kelsey to be the one to break the news.

So there he sat, awaiting the signal from Kelsey that it was okay to talk to Sarina. The more time went by, the more nervous he got. Which was so out of character for him. Jaxon ordinarily never got nervous about women, but there was nothing ordinary about this one.

Finally, his phone dinged with a text from Kelsey.

She knows.

Sarina

SARINA WAS AWAKENED BY A LOUD SOUND COMING from her kitchen. Startled, she shot up in bed when it hit her. Right in the nostrils.

The smell of freshly baked brownies. Followed by the faint sound of someone whistling something familiar. "Be Our Guest."

He was back.

She leaped from the bed and ran to the living room, which was basked in the soft glow of candlelight. Rose petals were scattered around the floor and in the middle of it all stood Jaxon, holding a heart-shaped brownie.

She stopped dead in her tracks, grinning like a lunatic. "What's this all about?" she asked.

"A peace offering, for what I'm about to tell you. Hoping you won't be mad."

"I'm gonna be mad if you don't let me have that brownie," she teased.

He tore off a tiny piece and held it to her lips.

"Mmm." Eyes closed, she moaned her approval as she swirled the dark chocolate delight in her mouth. Opening her eyes, she met his intense gaze. "Is this a real brownie, or just another publicity stunt?"

He shook his head and sighed, a sheepish grin on his face. "I'm sorry for lying to you. It's not who I am. You asked who the real Jaxon Quinn is? I'm just a normal guy. An honest guy, who likes helping people and wants the best for everyone. I go out of my way not to hurt others. I've never killed a bug in my whole life."

"What about mice?"

"Never stick around long enough."

"I gathered that."

"I'm not all good. I burp and fart and sometimes get things stuck in my teeth. I once returned something to Amazon I'd already used. I'm terrified of big dogs. I know...to be a cool guy, you need to love big dogs. Not me. I love little ones that I could carry in my man purse if it was still the '90s. Like my housekeeper's dog, Taco. My spirit advisor."

Sarina smiled up at him. "Everyone needs a Taco. The food, and the animal."

"I know I come across like a player, and...I *have* been a player. In my defense, I've never met anyone who inspired me to settle down. Someone who makes me laugh, who gives me tingles, and makes me want to take her in my arms and dance to Sade with her all night long. Until now."

"Do I know this woman?" she asked.

"I'm looking at her."

Her pulse galloped. "Jax," she whispered as he moved in closer.

"It's you, Sarina." He closed his eyes as he shook his head in disbelief. "I'm just sorry for starting on the wrong foot. I hope we can have a do-over."

He set down the plate and that's when she noticed a rose stem lying next to the brownie, with one single petal clinging to the top.

"I see you went all out on the roses," she said in a playful tone.

He laughed. "As you may have guessed, I'm somewhat obsessed with *Beauty and the Beast.*"

"Because you played the candle guy in middle school."

"He has a name. It's Lumière."

"Ah, yes. What's the significance of the rose? I forget."

"An old woman came to the castle, offering the prince a rose in exchange for shelter but he turned her away because she was hideous."

"*Hmm.* If only I'd known that was an option."

"Very funny. Anyway, she warned him not to judge her based upon her looks, but he did. She cast a spell on him, turning him into a beast and giving him a rose. She warned him that, if he didn't learn to love, the rose would die. Belle came along, and you know how that ended. There was one petal left just before he fell..."

"Fell?" Sarina raised her eyebrows. "into what?"

"Into...culinary shenanigans. You know, entertaining people with kitchen utensils and stuff. Kinda like...you 'n' me."

"So wait, are you Lumière, or the Beast in this scenario?"

"Both."

"Who am I in this story?"

"A dancing spoon. But that doesn't matter."

She laughed out loud.

"You're Belle. Maybe a bit of role reversal, but you gave me shelter. You made me laugh, and I've loved getting to know you. Before you, my rose was dying, but you brought it back to life. You've made my heart feel things it never has. It took me thirty years to find you, and I'm not going anywhere. So..." Jaxon held up the rose. "Before this final petal falls off, let me tell you what I've been dying to tell you."

She was breathless as she looked up into his jade eyes.

"Sarina Grace, I'm falling so hard for you."

She giggled.

Pulling her in, he lowered his lips to hers. "Is it okay if I kiss you?"

"Be my guest."

Max

MAX WAS EXCITED TO JOIN MOLLY FOR THEIR BIG DAY. Pulling on his jeans, he felt something crumple in his pocket. It was the ball of trash he'd picked up at the arts center. He'd forgotten to throw it away.

He was about to toss it out when something caught his eye—handwriting that looked vaguely familiar. He unfurled the ball to find the three torn shreds of blueprint paper.

He pieced them together, a heading emerging. *Colton's Woodworking Shop*. Beneath it was a sketch of a room and notes about where equipment would go.

It had to be the project his dad had referenced in his letter—an annex that would become a woodworking shop for his brother. What an utterly random and fortuitous find, almost as if his dad had arranged for him to find it from beyond the grave.

"Colt!" he called out frantically.

Max ran to his room, but it was empty. Glancing out the window, he noticed Colton's truck was missing.

Max pulled out his phone and called him, but it went straight to voicemail. He texted him to call him as soon as he got the message.

And then he paced, waiting for Colton's call. He wasn't going to believe this. He just hoped it wasn't too late.

Keeping his phone close, he gathered his supplies and prepared to leave for the café, where he'd be meeting Molly and the other volunteers. As he loaded up the truck, his mom's wildflowers waved to him in the breeze. He smiled, knowing just what he'd do with them. Cutting a bunch, he organized them into a big, beautiful bouquet. Perfect gift for the birthday girl.

Just before he left, he decided to try Colton again. This time, he answered on the first ring.

Colton

AFTER CHECKING OUT OF HIS HOTEL, COLTON HEADED to the development company's office—a man on a mission. A mission to sell.

He navigated his way to an already crowded I-95—not unusual for a Saturday in July, when shoobies headed to the shore for their week-long vacations. Stopped in traffic at one point, he checked his phone to confirm the meeting time, and realized he hadn't turned it back on from the night before. As soon as he toggled the switch, notifications began dinging in rapid succession. Texts from Kelsey and Max flooded his screen, but traffic was moving again so he wasn't able to read them.

Until his ringtone filled the cab of the truck, signaling a call from Max.

"Colt!" His brother's voice was frantic. "Please tell me you haven't met with them yet."

"I'm on my way. Why?"

"Look at the last text I sent you."

"I can't. I'm driving. Just tell me what it is?"

"Pull over. You have to see this for yourself."

The urgency in Max's voice frightened him. He found a wider section of the shoulder and pulled over. Consulting his phone, he found Max's text—a photo of a blueprint.

"What is this?"

"It's a blueprint Dad made."

He zoomed in. Tears flooded his eyes as he read the heading.

"Molly and I went to the arts center yesterday," Max explained. "I found this paper, thinking it was trash, but I just looked at it and realized what it was. It must be—"

"The project he referenced," Colton whispered.

"Say no, Colton. Call off the meeting and let's talk this out. If Dad bought the land to build you a woodshop, you owe it to him—to me, to *us*—to think this over. I know you wanna get out of here, but I'm begging you..."

Sighing, Colton looked skyward, trying to determine his next move, when a billboard looming above him captured his attention. It featured a construction worker holding a cup of coffee with a familiar logo and an announcement in bold letters.

Putting Jersey Shore on the coffee map. *Jolt!* **Coming to Cape May this fall.**

Squinting, he read the smaller line on the bottom of the sign:

Milton Developing Company, bringing Cape May into the 21st Century.

"You've got to be kidding me!" Colton slammed his hands on the steering wheel, enraged to see that the company was apparently forging ahead with their plans to commercialize the Cape before he'd even signed the agreement.

What did he expect, selling his precious land to a company that only cared about making a buck? The fact that they were already advertising their plans meant a fast-moving wildfire of development. It would have to be, if the coffee chain planned to open in the fall. A huge detriment to Sarina's business, and a shocking change in the inner Cape's landscape. There was no way Colton could let that happen.

"Kidding you about what?" Max's question broke through Colton's rage.

He told Max about the billboard, and agreed he would call off the meeting.

"You're doing the right thing," Max said. "Maybe you can stick around a little longer, and we can talk about whether selling is really what we want to do."

"I thought you were on board with selling?"

"I was...but, I don't know, now I'm not so sure," Max said. "And, you know, these are just my thoughts, but maybe it's time you stopped running. Your passing game was always your strong suit. Why not sink back and wait for an open opportunity before you throw it away? I'm sorry if that analogy is painful—"

Colton laughed. "I love you Max. Rest assured, I'll call a time-out and hold the ball so we can decide together how to get it down the field."

"Sounds good. When will you be back?"

"Turning around as we speak."

"Great. Could you swing by the café to help set up the tables? I'll meet you there."

SARINA HAD NO IDEA HOW MUCH TIME HAD PASSED since Jaxon began kissing her. Or how incredibly sexy it felt to be kissing a guy she not only had a crush on as a teen but had quickly developed feelings for as an adult. Her head felt swimmy, as his kiss catapulted her to another dimension.

But then, reality crept back in, reminding her they had a fundraiser to do. Molly was having event volunteers meet at the café that morning, which would serve as the hub of the event, to receive their assignments.

"I'll be here, waiting," Jaxon said, squeezing her hand.

"Why don't you join me for a little celebrity chef gig? You can help dole out goodies and dazzle our guests with your presence."

"That would be fun!" he said.

"Although, is it safe?" she joked. "I saw those crazed women the other day. They're likely to tear the place down, once they get wind you're here."

"Nah, the hype is usually temporary. If not, I know you and Carl will protect me."

"Facts."

Sarina headed down to the café, leaving Jaxon behind to clean up from brownie-making. Turning on the lights, she heard a loud rapping on the front door. As she approached, she saw a crowd gathered outside.

"What's this?" she asked, opening the door for them.

Everyone held a dessert in their hands—cakes, pies, trays of cookies, and more.

Sarina laughed as they filed in, giving hugs and telling her they were sorry to hear about the sprinkler fiasco.

Turning to the crowd, she wiped the tears threatening to break free. "Thank you so much. I'm overwhelmed."

"Aww, honey. Don't cry!" one woman sang out as she pulled Sarina into a hug. "You've taken such great care of the community, and now it's our turn to pay you back."

"This means the world to me."

"We'd do anything for you," another woman gushed.

"I baked all night," a third said. "And I never bake!"

Max came in just then, holding a bouquet of flowers under one arm as he balanced a birthday sheet cake in the other.

"Molly should be here in a few minutes," he said. "I was hoping we could do a little impromptu surprise."

Shit. Between the fundraiser and Jaxon, she'd completely forgotten it was Molly's birthday.

Suddenly, the room grew silent, mouths gaping. A single shrill scream, followed by more blood-curdling ones, broke the dead-ass silence.

She didn't have to turn around to know Jaxon Freaking Quinn had entered the building. But she did because she couldn't get enough of looking at him.

"Hey, everyone." He smiled shyly as he waved. Turning to Sarina, he leaned down and whispered. "I'm sorry. I didn't realize you'd opened."

"It's okay," she said, her tone hushed as she smiled up at him. "They were going to see you sooner or later."

The crowd was still in a frenzy as people whipped out their cell phones, snapping pictures and taking videos as they called out his name.

"Hey, folks!" she called out, but the hubbub continued.

Jaxon gave a loud whistle, and the room fell silent again.

"As you can see," she continued, "we have in our midst Jaxon Quinn, our celebrity chef of the day. Jaxon, do you want to say a few words?"

"Uh, sure." He held out his hands to the crowd. "Welcome to Sunrise Café!"

Everyone cheered.

"I'm honored to be here with you and our esteemed host, Ms. Sarina Grace. We both thank you from the bottom of our hearts for your generosity, providing desserts for this event. The reason we're all here today is to raise funds to help rebuild what was damaged. I'm told that, in the wake of the storm, Sarina and the café provided food and coffee for volunteers and those who were displaced. How 'bout we show her some love with a round of applause?"

Jaxon and the onlookers applauded.

"Thanks, everyone," Sarina said, blushing. "It's been

my pleasure to serve the community, and I look forward to continuing to do so. What do you say—shall we get this party started?"

As the crowd cheered, Max leaned into Sarina, whispering that Molly should be there any minute.

"One more thing!" Sarina called out to everyone. "Many of you know my sister, Molly, is the reason this event is taking place today. It's her birthday, so please help us surprise her when she comes in."

She turned down the lights and ushered everyone towards the back of the café, waiting for Molly's arrival.

Kelsey

Kelsey was beyond worried when she awakened Saturday morning to find Colton hadn't responded to her texts. She had a strong suspicion Jaxon's appearance in Cape May was the reason he canceled dinner. Not only was she sad he'd canceled the date, but she was hoping to convince him to let her purchase the land. Maybe there was still time. She texted him one last plea, hoping she wasn't too late.

Especially once she remembered it was Molly's birthday, and she'd promised Max she'd help surprise her. She grabbed the bag of party supplies she'd picked up for the occasion and headed out the door.

Kelsey was shocked to see how many volunteers were already at the café when she arrived. Molly had done an amazing job rallying people for the cause.

"Look at all this," Sarina said, waving at the counter, covered with homemade desserts of all kinds. "So many people donating desserts after I posted about the flooding."

"A testament to what you and the café mean to this community, Sarina. I'm not surprised."

Kelsey helped Sarina move some of the desserts to the back room, where Grand Lillian cornered her.

"You've got some explaining to do," the matriarch said.

Uh oh. She had a feeling she knew what was coming. Sarina must have told her about Jaxon.

"I can explain everything. Jaxon and I—"

"Not about the fauxmance," Grand Lil said. "You forget I've been around the Hollywood block a few times myself. Even went out with Rock Hudson a few times as a front. A mustache, they called me...or some nonsense."

"Then what must I explain?"

"Why the world was told about your little crush before I was."

Her grandmother held up her phone to show her a social media post.

Reading it, Kelsey felt the color drain from her face.

Fuuugh. Her secret was out. How could Verna have done this to her?

And...to Colton. He didn't deserve to have his name dragged into her drama. She knew how the social media mentality went. All someone had to do was make a mere suggestion, and suddenly it was fact. It was the price one pays as a celeb, and Kelsey was accustomed to it. She'd grown a thick skin, able to cast off rumors and accusations.

Likely not the case for her sweet friend, despite his own fame. Colton was going through a rough time, and he had enough on his plate to worry about without being tethered to Kelsey's alleged romantic mood swings. Jaxon one day, Colton the next. While Jaxon knew the truth, Colton didn't.

She certainly had some explaining to do, but it wasn't to her grandmother.

It was to Colton.

Molly

FINALLY, THE BIG DAY. FIRST UP ON THE AGENDA: HEAD TO the café and scarf down a huge cup of coffee. Next: meet with volunteers to go over assignments, then make sure everything was ready. Finally: start the event.

Somewhere during all that, she'd have to find a way to celebrate her birthday. She was reminded that this was the day she once thought she'd get engaged and was surprised by how fine she was, knowing it wasn't happening. Instead of the soul-crushing disappointment she would have imagined she'd feel, she felt a sense of awakening. Turning twenty-two, with a freshly minted college degree and newly discovered passion, she felt the world was hers to make of it as she wanted, with or without a ring. Or a trophy husband.

Max texted as she was getting ready, asking her if she could pick up an extension cord he'd accidentally left in the barn. She agreed, even though it would make her late.

The café seemed eerily dark and empty when she arrived, which was surprising, as the volunteers should have been arriving by then. Just as she opened the front door, the lights came on.

"Surprise!"

She almost fell backward as a large crowd of people blew on party favors and twirled noisemakers, singing to her. Someone emerged from the crowd, hiding behind a huge bouquet of wildflowers.

"Hey, girl," he said as he handed them to her.

Giggling from sheer surprise and delight, she went up on her tiptoes and hugged Max. "Are these from your mom's garden?" she asked as she gazed up at him.

"They are. Nothing but the finest in stemware for my bestie."

Molly knew this party had to be Max's idea. Of course, he wouldn't let her birthday go by without celebration. "You're so sweet. I really appreciate this."

"I have another surprise for you later. I just need you to meet me on the beach in time for the fireworks."

She smiled at him, wondering if he remembered her idea of a romantic date. "I'll be there."

Molly gathered everyone, thanked them for the surprise, and doled out assignments. Max went to hang lights on the pergolas he'd built for the Washington Street tables, and Molly jumped on the golf cart to make her rounds. After checking in at the various stations scattered throughout town, she returned to Washington Street Mall, where most of the event's festivities would take place. It was where people would gather to eat the box lunches offered for sale at the café. Throughout the day, local musicians and street artists would stroll through town, entertaining the crowds. Then there'd be the community Christmas dinner, the play, and fireworks on the beach. The mall shops and restaurants would stay open late for those who wanted to shop or have ice cream after fireworks.

"How you feeling, girl?" Max asked as he joined her.

Molly looked at him, eyes wide with disbelief. "I can't believe I'm about to say this, but I think we're good to go."

He held out his fist for her to bump, which she did.

"Let's do it."

Colton

When Colton arrived at the café, Max was nowhere to be found.

"Hey, Colt," a familiar voice came from behind him.

It was Jaxon.

"Max is tied up. I've been sent to help you set up the tables."

Great. Had he known he'd be paired with Jaxon, he'd have stayed in Philly.

The men found the unassembled tables in front of the café, awaiting final construction. Colton showed Jaxon how to assemble them, and the men worked together in silence, only communicating when necessary.

"Sarina said you and Max made these tables?" Jaxon asked.

"Yep."

"Impressive. I wish I could do something like this."

"Not hard, if you have the right materials and tools."

Colton's phone buzzed in his pocket. Max was calling again. "Yo."

"I need you guys to go back to the farm when you're done there," Max said. "There's some donation boxes we need you to deliver to Sunset Beach."

Colton agreed, even though driving in an enclosed space with Kelsey's *prince* was the last thing he wanted to do. But duty called.

They'd just arrived at the beach to drop off the boxes when Jaxon laughed at something on his phone.

"What's so funny?" Colton asked.

"Oh, man. The comments section of our publicist's post is blowing up."

"About what?"

"The fauxmance. People are losing their shit over—"

"What do you mean, fauxmance?"

Jaxon gave him a sheepish look. "Oh, um...I'll let Kelsey explain."

"Except she's not here now. Can I see the post?"

"Don't kill the messenger," Jaxon said, running his hand through his hair nervously as he handed Colton the phone. "Kelsey's gonna want first dibs."

> *After six months of dating, America's Sweetheart, Kelsey Grace, and her dashing costar, Jaxon Quinn, have called it quits. The couple had starred together in several rom-coms before taking their on-screen love to the streets. The split was amicable, as rumors have been circulating that Grace, starring in an off-Broadway play this weekend, may have found a new leading man in her longtime friend, former NFL quarterback Colton Banks, while Quinn has set his sights on a new mystery woman. Grace and Quinn, who've remained good friends, are looking forward to releasing their new rom-com,* **Falling for You,** *set to hit movie theaters in September.*

Colton had to read it a couple times before he found his voice. "Is this true?"

"Yeah, dude," Jaxon said. "There's more to the story, but I'll let her tell you."

Colton was speechless. Not only over the fact they'd broken up, but that his name was being floated as her new love interest. His heart rattled around in his chest as his pulse quickened.

"Do what you want with that tidbit of info," Jaxon said, tapping the screen of his phone. "I know what I'd do."

Colton shot him a look. "You'd be okay with me asking out your ex?"

Jaxon sighed. "She's not my ex."

Confused, he asked for clarification.

Jaxon chuckled. "Dude, we were never really dating. The whole thing was a publicity stunt."

"Are you serious?" Colton said, flabbergasted by this news. Surprise didn't begin to describe the flood of emotion Jaxon's confession unleashed. Shock, was more like it.

"Sorry, man. I can tell there's something between you guys. Again, I know what I'd do, given this info."

Colton didn't have to think twice.

"You handle the donation boxes—I've got somewhere to be," he said to Jaxon as he leaped from the truck and took off on a sprint down Sunset Boulevard in the direction of Kelsey's house.

A minute later, still running at a pretty good clip, he heard the squeal of brakes. He turned to see his truck on wild approach, with Jaxon at the wheel.

"Watch it!" he yelled as he jumped off the road.

"Forget something?" Jaxon held out Colton's phone.

"Two hands on the wheel!" he cried as Jaxon brought the truck to a screeching halt.

"That was fun," Jaxon said, laughing. "I've had drivers my whole life. I've never driven one of these myself."

"No shit."

"Hell, I've never driven on actual roads. Other than in *My Trucker Romance*, and even then, it was a movie set."

"Loved that movie," Colton said as he opened the driver's side door and pulled Jaxon out. "But you can't drive for shit. Get the fuck outta my truck."

"And go where?"

"Passenger seat, Quinn. Let a real man show you how to drive."

"I'm here for it!"

Colton peeled out as soon as Jaxon jumped in.

"You've had drivers your whole life?" Colton asked.

"Facts."

"I thought you were just gonna unload the donation boxes. What made you think you should drive my truck?" he teased.

"A. You left your keys in the ignition, running. B. Your stats have shown that, while you can throw a ball like a badass, your running game isn't stellar. And C—"

Colton shot him a look. Only a real fan would have known his stats.

"What?" Jaxon asked. "I wasn't joking when I said I've watched every one of your games, from college days on."

Colton was taken aback to hear that. "What's C?" he asked.

"C. While I don't know much about cars, I do know about running from crazed fans. I've found motorized vehicles make you go a lot faster."

Colton laughed and gave the Oscar-winning actor a playful punch in the arm. "You know what? You're a lot smarter than you look."

Jaxon's expression grew serious, his tone dropping a couple octaves. "I may not be a driver, but I play one on the screen." Then, in his own voice, he added, "And I'll take that as a compliment."

"Exactly as it was meant."

Molly

MOLLY WAS EXHILARATED TO SEE HOW MANY PEOPLE had shown up for the event. The love for Cape May, from residents and visitors alike, came pouring into town to replace what the storm had taken away. Molly's heart was full, knowing she was responsible.

"How's it going?" she asked Sarina as she and her volunteers buzzed about, doling out boxed lunches.

"We can't restock them fast enough," Sarina said. "Come here."

Stepping away from the table, Sarina gave Molly a hug. "I know I was less than enthusiastic when you first floated this idea, but you killed it, Moll. I'm so proud of you. You have a true talent."

Molly was pleased to receive the rare compliment from her older sister. As she pulled away from their hug, she heard a woman's voice.

"If it isn't the Unsinkable Molly Grace."

Molly spun around to see the Stranding Center director standing before her.

"Max was right. The name suits you."

"Thank you, Ms. Peters."

"Please, call me Angie. I'm beyond impressed. If you can do all this as a volunteer, I can't wait to see what you do as our next fundraising director."

"Are you serious?" Molly asked, excitedly.

"Of course, I am. If you're still interested, the job's yours. Be in my office on Monday at nine."

"In my mind, I'm already there."

"I have a feeling you're not joking about that."

As Angie walked away, Molly had to pinch herself. It might be only been part-time, but it was a job. Doing something she had come to love, a passion she'd discovered for herself rather than one born from someone else's expectations.

Looking around, she couldn't help but beam with pride. Several groups were seated at the tables, enjoying their boxed lunches as they chatted with one another. Kids gathered at craft tables, making ornaments, while others ran through the open spaces, waging candy cane battles. Others meandered through the summer wonderland, dropping envelopes—hopefully filled with cash—in the donation boxes scattered around, while shoppers took advantage of sidewalk sales. In the distance, a jazz quartet played a sultry version of "It's Beginning to Look a Lot Like Christmas."

It was beautiful. It was everything she dreamed of and more. She burst into tears.

"Hey," Max said, enveloping her in a strong hug. "I hope those are happy tears."

She had no idea where he'd come from, but it didn't surprise her. He was always right there, whenever she needed him.

"Max, I got the job," she whispered into his chest.

Pulling back, he smiled. "Of course, you did. Congratulations, but I'm not surprised."

"I just—never envisioned it being this successful. It's truly magical."

"It's Christmas in July. Of course, it's magical. I can't wait to celebrate with you tonight."

Colton

COLTON DROVE THE BACKROADS OF THE CAPE LIKE A fleeing felon. Taking the steps to Kelsey's house by two, he called out for her but soon discovered no one was home.

"She must be at the café, helping with the fundraiser," he said as he threw his truck into reverse, tires squealing as he peeled from the driveway.

"Ever thought about being a stunt double?" Jaxon joked.

"No, but I am looking for a career change."

A short time later, Colton careened into a space in the lot behind the café.

"Where's Kelsey?" he demanded as he ran through the back door, followed closely by Jaxon.

"She went to home to get ready for the play," Sarina said.

"I just came from there."

"Then I don't know where she is. Maybe the theater—isn't it almost call time?"

She was right. He was cutting it close, timewise. He still had to get home, shower, and finish a gift he'd been making for Kelsey. It was their tradition, during the four years they were involved in the plays together, to give each other something special on closing night.

As anxious as he was to talk to her, it would have to wait until after the show.

Kelsey

KELSEY ARRIVED LATE TO THE THEATER TO A WHIRLWIND of activity. She'd been hoping for a chance to talk with Colton, but after makeup and a minor wardrobe malfunction, it was go-time.

She found Colton on stage as they were about to take their places.

"Hey," she whispered. "I'm sorry about…everything. Jaxon. The social media post, bringing your name into it—"

"I'm not," he said, smiling.

Whew. "We need to talk," she said, relieved to hear his reaction. "I have a lot of explaining to do."

"We have all the time in the world."

Music poured from the speakers, signaling the beginning of the play. She assumed her opening stance.

"Kelsey," he whispered.

She looked over to find him making a heart with his hands, just like he did before every game.

"For you," he said. "It was always for you."

So shocked was she to hear his confession, she almost forgot her opening lines. Fortunately, she recovered quickly, jumping into character as only she knew how.

When they came to the scene where the two characters dance around the subject of falling in love, Colton forgot his line. She was about to prompt him when he cleared his throat.

Turning to her, he took her hands in his. "One of the first rules of theater is to never break character," he said. "But this past week has taught me a lot of things, including that rules are meant to be broken."

Kelsey looked around nervously, wondering what he was up to.

"Like the rule that you're not supposed to fall in love with your best friend. Seems I've been breaking rules for over a decade. Because, the truth is, I've been in love with you for as long as I can remember. The kiss we shared back in our senior year, when we acted in this same play, was the kiss to last a lifetime. As you know, the script didn't call for one, but my feelings for you at the time did. So I went for it. Later, too shy to tell you how I truly felt, I let you get away, but I'm not about to make the same mistake twice. I don't know what the future holds for us, but I can't wait to find out. That is, if you'll let me."

She smiled through flowing tears, her voice cracking with unbridled emotion. "Of course I will." It was only a whisper, but being mic'd up for the play as they were, the entire audience heard it.

Grasping her waist, he leaned into her as he kissed her with a ferocity she'd only ever seen in the movies—and not any she'd been in. It was as honest, pure, and passionate as the kiss back in high school, only a thousand times better.

The audience members jumped to their feet with deafening cheers. The curtain fell and time stood still as Kelsey and

Colton gazed at one another.

"Wow," was all she could say.

"I know..." he whispered. "I've been holding that one in for a long time, girl."

The *clackety-clack* of approaching heels and her grandmother's barking voice broke the moment.

"Your meet-and-greet starts in five minutes, so you need to get going."

As Grand Lillian ushered Kelsey offstage, the unmistakable gleam in her eye matching the smile on her face, told Kelsey she was pleased with the ending. Or...maybe the beginning of what could be.

"Wait!" Kelsey spun away from her grandmother's guiding arm and yelled to Colton over the chaos. "The gazebo. Meet me there in an hour."

Max

THE DAY FLEW BY IN A WHIRLWIND OF ACTIVITY. MAX ARrived at their beach early to set up the picnic he'd planned for Molly. He laid out the blanket and set up faux candles for ambience before unpacking a basket filled with treats—a bottle of champagne, two glasses, and a variety of charcuterie items, including chocolate-covered strawberries. He'd even baked a tiny cake last night with an icing inscription: *Cause of death: extreme celebration.*

He knew she wasn't looking to start anything with someone new. He respected her desire to take some time for herself, and he supported that. He just wanted to treat her to something she said she loved—a romantic beach picnic. He'd give all the disclaimers once she got there, but she deserved to have someone treat her to something nice on her birthday.

His heart was pounding with excitement as the first firework exploded above him, signaling her anticipated arrival time. She should be there any moment.

Molly

MOLLY WAS PRACTICALLY SKIPPING ON HER WAY TO MEET up with Max at the fireworks. Now that she'd put out the last fire—finding a second replacement Santa after the first was hit with a stomach bug—her work for the night was done.

She was jubilant over the enormous success of the Christmas in July event, thanks to the help from her partner in crime. She couldn't wait to celebrate—the success of the event, her birthday, their friendship. Which, she had to admit, was feeling like something more.

Molly had gained all the clarity she needed as she skirted around town that day, watching all the happy merry makers coming together to celebrate their town. She wasn't a Manhattan socialite, no matter how glamorous it seemed. She was a Jersey girl at heart. She belonged in Cape May, cruising around in a dilapidated golf cart, not a Lincoln Town Car. She needed to be surrounded by ocean waves, sea breezes, and lush greenery, not a concrete jungle. She wanted to lick ice cream cones on a dock at the marina, not dine on caviar from a swanky uptown restaurant.

Most of all, she needed to be surrounded by family and friends. One friend, in particular.

She made it to the beach just as the first firework exploded above. Dodging bodies, she was searching through the crowd for him when someone tapped her on the shoulder.

"Molly."

She turned and gasped.

It was the last person she expected to see.

"THANKS FOR DOING THIS," SARINA SAID AS SHE HANDED Jaxon his costume. "I know Molly appreciates it."

An hour earlier, Molly had come to them, panicked, after the replacement Santa had fallen ill.

"No problem," Jaxon told Molly in response to the favor she'd asked. "I played Santa once. It'll be fun to reprise the role."

"I can't thank you enough," Molly had said. "Although this isn't exactly a movie role."

"Neither was that. It was Naughty Santa."

Molly looked shocked. Sarina was intrigued.

"Just a little striptease act I did back in college to make some extra bucks."

Sarina guessed there was nothing "little" about it. IYKYK. Molly, blushing, turned to Sarina. "Will you be Mrs. Claus?"

There was very little she'd like less.

But then, Jaxon said, "Yeah, Sar. Be my wifey."

Which was very hard to argue with. So she agreed.

"Thanks, guys," Molly had said, giving them each a hug. "I'm off—a few more errands to run before I meet Max for the fireworks."

"Sounds romantic," Sarina teased.

Molly smiled. "I hope so."

As she left, Sarina looked at Jaxon wide-eyed. "Oh, my God. I think my little sister may have a crush. Plot twist—it's not her boyfriend."

"She wouldn't be the only one," Jaxon said as he grabbed Sarina around the waist.

Now, as Sarina buttoned his last button, she tapped him on the ass. "Come on, Kris K. It's showtime."

"Wait. Am I playing Santa, or Mrs. Kardashian?"

"Very funny, Mr. Claus."

"Just to be clear—we're going for a nice Santa vibe, not naughty?" Jaxon asked as they left the café.

"You do you," Sarina suggested.

In costume, they headed to Santa's throne, where a long line of kids had already formed—nothing compared to the line of grown-ass women snaking around the block.

"He's here!" someone yelled, while others screamed.

"I hope I come out of this alive," he whispered to Sarina.

"You will. It's not the kids you'll need to worry about. Remember your audience, and don't break into your naughty routine."

"Don't blame me if I do, Sar. That comes more natural for me."

"Save it for a private viewing later."

"Promise?" Jaxon asked, sending a thrill down her spine, before he made his way to the throne.

"Hey, everyone," Sarina called out. "Santa and I are spending our summer vacation in Cape May, and he wanted to see you before he heads to the beach. Are you ready, Santa?"

Jaxon ho-ho-ho'd as Sarina rallied the kids, handing each a candy cane after they made their pitch. When the women insisted on making their own wishes on Santa's lap, Sarina just laughed as she looked on.

After the line finally died down, Jaxon grabbed Sarina and pulled her down onto his lap. "What can Santa bring you, little girl?"

"Got anything to get rid of pesky house guests?"

"What kind are we talking about?"

"The kind that show up in your freezer and just. Won't. Leave."

"I'm afraid you'll never get rid of that kind."

She smiled. "Good. I was hoping you'd say that."

"Now I have a wish for you."

"Lay it on me, old man."

Jaxon pulled his fake beard down and gave her a vulnerable smile. "Will you be my girlfriend?"

She giggled.

"Sorry, did that sound weird? I've never asked a girl that question before."

"No, Jax, it was perfect."

It *was* perfect. With his filming schedule, Sarina would have the independence she craved to focus on the café and stay in touch with her creative self. Whenever they found precious time together, they'd savor it even more.

"Yes. I'll be your girlfriend."

It was official. Sarina Grace finally believed in love at first sight.

Max

AS FIREWORKS EXPLODED ABOVE HIM, MAX STOOD UP from the blanket and peered through the crowd of spectators on the beach. Molly should have been here by now. Maybe she'd gotten hung up somewhere. He double-checked his texts to make sure she hadn't written to let him know she was running late.

Nothing. He typed out a message.

> Hey girl, hope you're okay. The celebration has started :D

In between two loud explosions, he heard people cheering down the beach from where he stood. It was too soon for the grand finale, so something big must have been going on.

He took a few steps forward and looked toward the water. And that's when he saw her, silhouetted against the fiery sky.

Molly. Her hands covering her mouth.

And before her, a man.

On one knee. Holding a ring box.

Kelsey

KELSEY COULDN'T GET AWAY FROM THE THEATER FAST enough once the meet-and-greet was over. She raced to the gazebo, where she found a waiting Colton.

"Hey, America's Sweetheart," Colton said, his tone warm as he grasped her waist and pulled her in.

"Not anymore," she said, gazing up at him. "I want a new nickname."

"How does 'girlfriend' sound?"

"It sounds perfect."

Colton lowered his lips to hers, and they kissed for what felt like an eternity, making up for lost time. When they finally came up for air, he cupped her face.

"I never should have let you leave the diner alone that day. You were supposed to leave with me."

"I didn't think I stood a chance. You had girls like Ashley hanging all over you. Remember what you told me the recruiter had said? 'Get yourself a good-looking girlfriend.'"

"Kelsey, I wanted that to be you. Here."
He pulled a note from his pocket and handed it to her.

Hey, good-looking! Will you be my girlfriend?

Kelsey's eyes darted up to Colton.

"That's the note I had in my pocket that night I asked you to meet me at the diner," he said. "I was about to give it to you when you told me I should ask Ashley out instead."

"Oh, Colt…" A fat tear rolled down her cheek as she considered how much time they'd lost. How much heartache they could have avoided. "I had no idea."

"*You* were the good-looking girlfriend I wanted. I could kick myself for not making that clearer. But then you called Ashley over—"

"I truly thought you liked her."

"And here I thought it was your way of letting me down easy. As in, 'Sorry, Colton, I'm not into you, so here, date my friend.'"

"But you hung in there with her for ten years. That's a long time to be with someone. There had to be something there."

He shook his head. "She was in it for the fame, Kelse—obviously, because the moment I was hurt, she was gone. For me, she represented home. We started out as friends but, in the end, that's all we ever were. I think she knew on some level I wasn't fully in it. I kept trying, because I was hoping I'd get there with her, kept hoping my feelings for you would go away, but they didn't. I guess when someone else has your heart, you don't have it to give to another."

"I wish you'd told me," Kelsey whispered.

"I tried. That night in the gazebo, before you took off. When you asked if I was in love with Ashley, I hesitated because I was afraid to admit the truth, that I was only dating her because you wanted me to. When I got home that night,

I wrote it all down on paper." He fished in his pocket. "Here. You can read it later. I just wanted you to see it, in case you had any doubt about the depth of the feelings I have for you—have *always had* for you. I have something else for you, too."

He walked to a bench and picked up a wooden box. "In keeping with our closing night tradition, I made you a little gift."

The box had a beautiful heart-shaped carving around her initials. Opening it, she found another wooden carving, this one of two hands in the shape of a heart.

Just like Colton's pre-game signal.

"I did that before every game, hoping you were watching. Hoping you knew you had my heart."

She couldn't believe it. She'd witnessed him doing it several times on TV, but never in a million years would she have guessed it was for her. "This is gorgeous," she said.

"It's carved from one of the original beams at the arts center. So you'll always have a piece of it."

"Oh my God, Colton," she whispered, clutching her chest. She was blown away by the beauty and sentiment. "I also have something for you. A combination closing-night-going-away gift."

Reaching into her bag, she pulled out a blanket, the one she'd ordered the other night. Holding the corners, she let it fall open to reveal its design. Their first-day-of-school photos were printed on the soft fabric, framing the edges of the blanket. In the middle was a quote: *You'll Never Walk Alone.*

His eyes filled with tears as he studied it. "I'm speechless."

"Regardless of what door you go through next, I wanted you to know you'll never do it alone. I made that mistake once, but never again."

"What if I don't leave?" he whispered, pulling her close. "Can I still keep the blanket?"

"Does that mean...?"

"I'm not going anywhere. I'm thinking maybe I'll stay, look for an arts center to rebuild."

Kelsey gave a little clap. "Are you serious?"

"Yes. I've called off the sale so I can stay in my hometown. *Our* hometown. I know you'll be returning to LA, but just know I'll be here waiting for you."

Kelsey smiled up at him. "I can't wait to come home again."

Max

BOOMING EXPLOSIONS CAME IN RAPID-FIRE SUCCESSION, heralding the end. The end of the show, the end of hope. Max's chest tightened as each deafening crack pierced his heart. Unable to take it, he took off running. He had no idea where he was heading, just anywhere but there.

With every ragged breath, reality sunk in. Brennan had proposed to Molly. It's what she'd wanted all along. That's probably why she initiated their break, knowing the ultimatum it would deliver. And it worked.

Blocks later, he sank down on an empty beach. The smoky sky, still ablaze from the grand finale, fell into pitch black, matching the darkness in his soul. Facing the ocean, he clasped his arms around his knees and stared at the churning waves, tears streaming down his face. There was nothing left of his shattered heart but shards of bitter disappointment.

Once again, he was right back on the sidelines. Alone.

The distant sound of the jazz quartet playing "Blue Christmas" lulled him into numbness. At some point, he fell back on the sand and wept. Eventually, he succumbed to sleep, not even caring if the tide came to claim him.

Awakening hours later to the morning sun peeking above the horizon, Max was disappointed to find he was still on the beach and not at the bottom of the ocean where he belonged. He sensed the tide was rising. It was only a matter of time.

Closing his eyes, he felt a smattering of sand hit his cheek. He opened one eye and turned his head to find a pink flip flop lifting sand and flipping it onto his chest.

"Cause of death: buried alive."

He looked up to find Molly standing above him. Scrambling to a sitting position, he ran a hand through his sandy hair. She might be engaged to someone else, but he didn't want her seeing him looking like a real-life beach bum.

She sank down next to him. "Most romantic thing you can think of," she said. "You go first."

He thought for a moment. "A live burial doesn't seem so bad right now." Then, so she wouldn't think he was such a morose spoilsport, he added, "I saw it all. I guess congrats are in order."

"Thanks." Somber, she nodded. "They are."

His heart deflated. It wasn't a bad dream. It was real as shit.

"I'm guessing if I asked you that same question, your answer would be a beach proposal under a sky of fireworks," he said.

"You'd be right about most of that."

"Most of it?"

"You're missing one crucial element."

"What's that?"

"Fireworks going off above, handsome man kneeling before me, ring box open..."

Why would she torture him like this?

"And then," she said, "along comes a butterfly. She lands right on the ring box, looks at me, and says..." Her voice dropped to a whisper. "'Don't do it.'"

He shot a look at her.

She met his gaze, holding it as a slow smile spread across her face. "Or maybe she said, 'do it.' I can't be sure, I'm not exactly fluent in butterfly just yet. In any event..."

He held his breath, hoping she would say what he was dying to hear.

Leaning her head on his shoulder, she hugged his arm in hers. "I said no."

His heart raced so fast he thought it might beat right out of his chest. "You're kidding me?"

"Well, I'm kidding about the butterfly. I just said it because I thought it sounded cute. Truth is, I don't need a beautiful creature, or another person, telling me what I already know."

"What's that?" Max asked, grinning.

"That Brennan's not the one for me. Congrats are order because I said no."

"I thought it's what you wanted?" he asked, simultaneously confused and elated.

"I did." She smiled up at him, her voice barely a whisper. "Until you."

Resting his forehead against hers, he closed his eyes. His breath caught as he lowered his lips to hers, his heart exploding with anticipation for what was about to happen.

And then, Maxwell Banks did something he'd dreamed of for years.

He kissed Molly Grace.

One year later...

THE SCENT OF FRESHLY BAKED CINNAMON BUNS FLOATED into Sarina's room as the sun peeked through her blinds. She opened an eye to find Jaxon pushing the door open with his toe as he balanced a tray of breakfast treats, coffee, and flowers.

"Mornin', sunshine," he sang as he placed the tray on the bedside table. "I present your breakfast. But first..."

Sarina yawned and stretched, her eyes gleaming with anticipation as Jaxon set down the tray and crawled into bed next to her. Sliding his leg between hers, he linked their hands and slid them toward the headboard, kissing her before they made slow, sweet love.

Jaxon was taking a much-needed break from filming to spend the summer in Cape May with Sarina, and the two had fallen into a daily routine. After awakening early to a little morning delight, they'd head to the thriving café where they'd work side-by-side, allowing Jaxon to live out his dreams. Later, they'd surf until sunset and enjoy a beach picnic featuring JFQ's special concoctions. Nights consisted of backyard bonfires, outdoor movies on her apartment's rooftop deck, or game nights with Molly and Colton as they anxiously awaited Kelsey and Max's return. Occasionally, Grand Lillian would make a cameo with her new beau, Ralph.

The only downside of the otherwise perfect summer was knowing Jaxon would soon be off for his next movie shoot. Funny how the woman who loved her independence loved being with him more.

"Ready for today?" Jaxon asked.

"Ready as we'll ever be."

It was the day of the grand opening for the new state-of-the-art Cape May Arts Center, and Sarina and Jaxon were in charge of providing appetizers and drinks.

On the other side of town, Molly waited on the dock for her ship to come in—the one carrying her boyfriend, returning from a week-long class at sea. Halfway through his master's program, Max was spending his summer working at the Stranding Center's high school camp for future marine biologists. The two had no problem maintaining a long-distance relationship while he was in school, but there was something about this week that made her miss him more than usual as they approached their first anniversary of dating.

She bounced with excitement as the ship approached, nearly bursting as the crew secured the lines. Ushering the kids off the boat to their awaiting parents, Max glanced around expectantly until their eyes finally met. He jumped off the boat and broke into a sprint toward her, scooping Molly up as she leaped into his arms and wrapped her legs around his waist. Their lips crushed together.

"Oh, my God," he whispered when they came up for air. "I've missed you so much."

"Not as much as I've missed you."

Setting her down, he leaned into another kiss, this one more passionate than the first.

As they made their way along the dock, Molly skipped beside him, asking questions about his trip and catching him up on the things that had happened in the week he was gone.

"I'm just glad you made it back for the party today," she said.

"I wouldn't have missed it for the world."

It seemed appropriate that the grand opening celebration was to be held on July 25th—the first anniversary of the Christmas in July event, and Molly's twenty-third birthday.

"Happy birthday, sweetheart," he said as he squeezed her hand and leaned down to kiss the top of her head. "I have a special gift for you."

"Ooh, can I have it now?"

"In a little while, I promise."

"I can wait. You being home is all the gift I need," she said as she went up on her tiptoes and kissed him on the cheek.

Max jumped in the shower once they were back at the farm, as Molly performed a final inventory of the silent auction donations she'd received for the event. Minutes later, she felt his strong arms around her waist as he approached her from behind, ready to make up for time lost at sea.

"Wow," she whispered as she stood back and took him in. "Are you a sight for hungry eyes."

And not just on the outside, either. It was his soul, his personality, that made him desirable. Molly was grateful he'd hung in there with her, or she'd be missing out on the love of a lifetime.

He picked her up and laid her on the bed.

"Just the sight of you..." His voice was gravelly with lust as he removed her sundress. "I'm about to burst."

Moving deliciously slowly, he kissed his way up from her navel. She, too, felt ready to burst from pent-up passion. Unable to wait any longer, she curled her fingers around his strong shoulders and pulled him into her.

"I'm home," Max groaned, eyes rolling back as he entered her.

Their session, which didn't last too long, culminated in cries of pleasure as Max, once again, took her to places she didn't even know existed.

"My God," she whispered as they came down from their high. "You do things to me I never knew were possible."

"I've had lots of practice."

"Yet you were still a virgin when I got my hands on you,"

she teased. "Where'd all this practice come into play?"

Talk about going places she'd never been before. There was nothing like the thrill of indoctrinating a twenty-two-year-old man who'd been waiting his whole life to experience mind-blowing passion.

"All in my mind, girl," he said, smiling. "When you spend years dreaming of all the things you want to do with a person, you get quite good at it. I'm just glad you gave me a chance."

Gazing up at him, Molly sobered. "Thank you for waiting for me."

Max trailed his fingers down her arm and clasped her hand. "I was gonna wait and do this tonight, but I can't hold off any longer."

Molly's eyes grew wide with excitement, wondering what new trick Max had up his sleeve, assuming it was something sexy. Instead, he pulled her out of bed.

"It's time for your birthday surprise."

Minutes later, they were on Molly's golf cart. Max steered them to the far corner of the Banks' farm, overlooking the bay where a wooden structure, surrounded by bayberry and sea grass, revealed itself through the scrubby pines.

"What's this?" Molly asked.

Silently, he took her hand and led her to the bare-bones building—really just a frame, yet to be completely built. But in the center, a door, painted lavender, had been attached to a doorframe.

She gasped. As they got closer, she noticed a sign hanging on the door.

Max and Molly's Cottage by the Bay.

Standing behind her, Max wrapped his hands around her waist. "Our future home," he whispered in her ear.

Tears sprung to her eyes. "Are you serious?"

"Colton's been helping me build it since I returned in May,

but I wanted to surprise you on your birthday. We should have it done by end of summer."

"Oh, Max. This is the most amazing thing anyone has ever done for me."

"Molly, you're the best thing that's ever happened to me," Max said as he touched his forehead to hers.

Max walked her around the structure to show her the layout, which incorporated every design element she'd told him she wanted in a house, ending with a small room on the corner of the house with a large window overlooking the bay.

"And this will be the home of Grace Consulting, your office, where you can gaze at the water as you dream up your spectacular fundraising ideas."

In the past year, Molly had expanded her fundraising business beyond the Stranding Center to take on other clients, mostly nonprofit organizations that existed for the protection of the Cape's natural resources. Since then, she'd successfully raised over a million dollars for various clients, providing a healthy income for her and Max.

"I love this. I can't wait to play house together."

Max smiled. "Cause of death: spending the rest of your life with me."

"Consider me dead."

At twenty-three, both agreed they were too young for marriage, but knew they were each other's endgame. Molly was convinced beyond all doubt Max was her person, something he'd known since he was thirteen. They were excited for their future, with no need to commit to marriage just yet.

They discussed plans for the cottage grounds, including a pergola with a swing by the water's edge and a perennial wildflower garden.

"I've already transported some of the seeds from my mom's garden. By next summer, they should be thriving."

"Just like us," she whispered.

"I guess we better get going," Max finally said. "Party's gonna start soon."

"You're right. I just don't want to leave. It's so peaceful here."

Down the road at the arts center, Sarina and Jaxon were setting up the refreshment stand when Max and Molly arrived.

"Are Kelsey and Colton here yet?" Molly asked as she helped Sarina with the appetizers.

"Just left the airport. They're on their way."

Kelsey was returning from filming an anticipated blockbuster drama. After turning down the rom-com her agent had offered her and following her own script, her reward was being cast in a role she'd once only dreamed of.

After kissing Colton in the arrivals thru-way of the Philadelphia airport, she handed him her bag, which he threw in the back.

"I can't wait for you to see the finished product," Colton said. "The arts center is beyond what we imagined, all thanks to your vision."

Cars lined the road leading to the center, where a party was well underway. Guests milled about on the lawn, enjoying cocktails and appetizers, as a jazz quartet's soothing notes were carried on gentle sea breezes.

Emerging from the car, Kelsey's jaw dropped in awe of the building before her. Colton had salvaged part of the original structure and creatively infused it with a contemporary design. The photos he'd sent her over the past few months simply didn't do it justice.

"So glad you're back for this," Sarina said as she and Jaxon gave them hugs. "You're gonna be amazed when you go inside. It's everything you wanted and more."

"Especially since Sarina did the interior design," Jaxon said. "Another talent unearthed in this remarkable woman."

"Don't underestimate your part," Sarina reminded Jaxon. "Turns out my man here has quite the eye for design."

He gazed at Sarina. "I know a thing of beauty when I see it."

"Well, what are we waiting for?" Colton asked as he ushered them to the building.

The two couples joined Kelsey and Colton and gave her a tour. A two-story lobby, encased in glass, led to two dance studios, a performing arts theater, and an industrial-sized kitchen for cooking lessons. The upstairs loft featured multiple art rooms for pottery, sculpting, painting, and more, where artists were currently demonstrating their crafts.

"In addition to giving tours today, we'll also allow guests to participate in various demonstrations," Sarina explained. "The acting class is doing a puppet show, and the music you hear outside is by a student quartet."

"So cool," Kelsey said as she admired Colton's contemporary, sleek design elements and Sarina's tasteful décor, including several pieces of her own.

"We're giving recitals to showcase the different types of dance classes that'll be offered, everything from ballet to hip-hop," Molly said. "I'm teaching some classes as my latest volunteer project."

"There's my sweet granddaughter," Grand Lillian's voice came from behind them. She gave Kelsey a warm hug. "Magnificent, isn't it?" she asked, beaming with pride. "All of you have made my dreams come true. I cannot thank you enough."

"Bring it in," Molly said, initiating a group hug.

"Enough of this sentimental stuff," Grand Lillian announced. "Time for the ribbon-cutting ceremony."

She led the group to the front entrance, where a ribbon stretched between two railings, beyond which milled a large crowd.

Tapping a microphone, she summoned their attention. "Welcome to the grand opening of Cape May's new arts center. We'll commemorate our opening with a ribbon-cutting ceremony, after which you're invited to tour the building, participate in demonstrations, and enjoy our new space."

She turned to Sarina. "Today's refreshments and drinks have been provided by my granddaughter, Sarina, and her wildly popular café. As you know, Sunrise was recently named Cape May's Best Café. Please give her and her hunka burnin' love boyfriend a round of applause for all they do to keep this community well-fed."

The crowd erupted in cheers.

"For those of you who don't know the history of this program, let me fill you in. One day, long ago, a group of moms were reminiscing about our high school years, discovering that each of us held a hidden talent. For me, it was acting. For others, it was dance, ceramics, painting, and more. We decided to host a monthly event where we'd teach our children those skills. Once word got out, other talented artists came forward, as well as parents who wanted their kids to have an opportunity to learn about the arts. The town allowed us to use the barn as a meeting place. Over the years, volunteers helped build it out to include various classrooms, a theater, a kitchen, and more. Sadly, the original structure was destroyed by last year's storm.

"I've been running the center for the past forty-five years, beyond blessed to get to know each and every child who came through here. But no children were as special to me as my own granddaughters, Kelsey, Sarina, and Molly. You've gotten to know them over the years for their talents—Kelsey for acting, Sarina for visual and culinary arts, and Molly for her big heart and ability to raise funds for nonprofits that keep our Cape alive and well. At the end of the day, I am just a proud grandmother—not only to these three, but to all of Cape May's children."

She laughed. "Okay, enough about me. Let's get this party started. Is everyone ready?"

Ralph handed her an oversized pair of scissors. As she was about to cut, she paused.

"Actually, there's more I'd like to say. While I'm proud of the work us founding mothers did to create this program, nothing makes me prouder than the way in which my love for this program has been instilled in my granddaughters, beyond their artistic abilities. As noted, Molly's impeccable fundraising skills are the reason we're here today. Sarina's interior design is what makes the new Arts Center the beautiful, bright space that it is. But it was Kelsey and her boyfriend, architect Colton Banks, who were the driving forces behind bringing this center into the twenty-first century—with Kelsey's vision for how the building should be designed, and Colton's amazing skills in bringing her vision to life. Were it not for this great team, we wouldn't have an arts center today. Therefore, I feel it's most appropriate that they do the ribbon-cutting. Can you two please come forward?"

Kelsey, baffled, hadn't expected to take a starring role in the grand opening. Colton led her up the steps to where Lillian waited.

"Colton, why don't you say a few words about your design?" she asked, handed him the mic.

"Oh! Um..."

Kelsey's heart lurched with empathy, knowing how much Colton hated public speaking. Always wanting to make things better for him, she was about to take the mic to spare him his agony, but he turned to her.

"I can do this," he said, giving her a tentative smile. "When I think back on my childhood, one memory always gets me. It was Valentine's Day, and Kelsey and I were four years old. We were here at the arts center for a finger-painting class. Our teacher asked us to make a heart and showed us how to spell the word 'love.' Later, I went home and asked my mom what love was. 'It's when someone makes your heart happy, and you can't imagine your life without them,' she said. As my toddler brain mulled this over, she asked what I loved and if I wanted to paint it on the heart. When I told her, she took my finger and, dredging it through paint, helped me spell my love. I still have it."

Reaching into his pocket, he unfurled a paper and held it up for the crowd, who gasped. He turned the paper toward her.

"Kelsey," he whispered.

Tears sprung to her eyes when she saw her name written on the heart.

"There were other things I'd learn to love in this lifetime. Football. Building things. Most of all, growing up in Cape May with you, and having a world of culture at our fingertips through this beloved program." He turned to the crowd. "We wouldn't be standing here today if it weren't for her convincing me to rebuild the center, which is why I'd like to have Kelsey do this honor."

He handed her the scissors. "Help me count down, everyone. One...two..."

Positioning the scissors over the ribbon, Kelsey waited for "three."

Before she could cut, the crowd gasped again.

Colton had dropped to a knee, sparkling diamond held high. "Kelsey Jean Grace, you've been my best friend since infancy. You've made me the man I am today. I wasn't kidding about giving you my whole heart when I was four, because you've had it ever since. Will you do me the honor of marrying me?"

"Yes!" she cried out, dropping the scissors as he swept her in an embrace and leaned into her for a kiss. Laughing through tears, she whispered, "I love you, Colton Banks."

"I love you Kelsey," he whispered into her hair. "I can't wait to spend my life with you. Because from this point on..."

Pulling back, they both spoke the same words. "You'll never walk alone."

Acknowledgments

FIRST AND FOREMOST, I'D LIKE TO THANK MY EDITOR EX-traordinaire, Emily Ohanjanians. Since the day we met, you've been one of the most inspirational and encouraging people in my authoring journey. My stories wouldn't be what they are without your guidance in storytelling, your expertise in love, your wealth of knowledge and your awesome humor. Now, it's my turn to support you as you jump the desk from editor to author this year with the release of your debut novel, *The Book Tour*. I look forward to cheering you on in every way you've done for me.

Thank you to the rest of my team who helped make this book a reality. Thank you, illustrator Diane Meacham, for your beautiful cover artwork, and Jessica Kleinman for your interior book design (not to mention endless book therapy sessions:). Thank you, Shannon Cave, for your proofreading skills. I've so enjoyed working with you all! You're *chef's kiss* in your respective fields of expertise and I feel blessed to have had you on my team for this project.

To my family...you guys have been and always will be my biggest supporters. You've given me strength to keep going when things got tough, and made me feel as if I was meant to do to this book writing thang. Your unconditional love is truly the wind beneath my wings. Special thanks to my parents, who've read each of my books from beginning to end (even the spicy parts) and have given me constructive feedback (but thankfully not on those! :). Thank you to my hubs for showing me what real love looks like, and for my daughter who is my greatest source of love, joy, and motivation as I forge ahead following my dreams. I love you all for your support, your humor, and your hearts—more than you will ever know.

I also wish to thank the booksellers who've given my books precious space on their shelves. I am so appreciative of your support, and quite charmed that you wanted to stock them. When I first started writing these books, I figured the only way I'd get them into the hands of readers was to walk up and down the beach handing them out for free. Thanks to you, I didn't have to do that. I've loved working with each and every one of you, doing fun events with you, and getting to know your loyal customers. Meeting your readers has been the absolute best part of the authoring journey, and I'm honored that you've opened your space to me and my books.

Last, but certainly not least, I thank you, readers, for giving this newbie writer a chance to share her stories with the world. Without you all, there would be no reason for people like me to write. I'm blown away by the incredibly viral reading community, especially those of you who've made it a passion (and in some cases, a profession) to share your reading experiences, give reviews, and keep us authors wanting to write for you. You are the reason we do this. Thank you for letting us pour our hearts and souls out to you, and for helping to make our dreams come true.

XOXO, Kim

Reader's Guide

INSPIRATION FOR
THIS BOOK

BOOK CLUB
QUESTIONS

Inspiration for this Book

IF *CAPE MAY CHRISTMAS IN JULY* FEELS ODDLY LIKE A Hallmark movie to you, that's because it started out that way. I originally wrote this book for a Hallmark Publishing contest, back when they published books. Alas, it wasn't selected as a winner, so it sat on a shelf behind me, looking wistfully on as I wrote and completed my Cape May series. With an endless litany of ideas for future books, I was trying to decide what to write next, when I sensed my CMCIJ manuscript practically jumping from the shelf, hoping I'd notice. As it was already fully written, I decided to brush it off, spice it up a bit, and make it my fourth novel. (But hey, Hallmark...I'll be happy to unspice it for future film-making consideration! I'll even write the screenplay!)

The setting (Cape May). If you can't tell from my first three books, I'm somewhat obsessed with Cape May. Make that Cape May County, which consists of eight coastal towns. From north to south, they are: Ocean City, Strathmere, Sea Isle City, Townsends Inlet (not an official town, just a part of Sea Isle that maintains its unique identity). Across the inlet is Avalon and Stone Harbor, which comprise "Seven Mile Island." Beyond that lies "The Wildwoods" and, finally, at the southernmost tip of Jersey, Cape May.

Like many families who visit this region in summer, my family would visit each of these towns during our annual summer vacation. We'd stay in Sea Isle, but we'd head to Ocean City for its family-friendly boardwalk, Strathmere for beachcombing, Townsends Inlet to dine at Sunset Pier,

Avalon to walk the dunes, Stone Harbor to shop 96th Street, Wildwood for its wildly entertaining boardwalk, then finally Cape May to shop Washington Street Mall, climb the lighthouse, and watch the sun slide into the bay at Sunset Beach as we searched for Cape May Diamonds. It truly is a magical place, this southern coastline of New Jersey, and will always be my biggest inspiration for writing. If you'd like to learn more, check out my blog at *TheShoreBlog.com*, a travel website dedicated to this beautiful coastal area.

The storylines. It's been a minute since I first drafted this novel, so I'm not sure exactly how I came up with the storylines for each of the characters. Suffice to say, they've evolved over several years and were inspired by real-life events, a wild imagination, and random middle-of-the-night thoughts.

What I do know...

For Kelsey and Colton, I wanted to explore what it must be like for celebrities whose public images don't align with their own self-beliefs—due to low self-esteem, a lack of confidence, mental health issues, past trauma, or other inner turmoil. I wondered what it would feel like for Kelsey to be adorned with a label like "America's Sweetheart" when she's never seriously dated someone. Or what it feels like to be Colton, a professional athlete whose entire identity has been wrapped up on a sport they can no longer play.

But more importantly, I wanted to explore the fact that Kelsey and Colton were once kids who were bullied and taunted yet rose from the ashes of childhood trauma to make something of their lives. It's a good reminder not to judge a book by its cover, or a person by their outward appearance. Especially our youth, whose covers have yet to be designed; their books, yet to be written.

With Sarina's story, I wondered what it would feel like to have your childhood crush "fall off his star" and into your life (or, in her case, fall off her wall and into her freezer). To have every one of your teen crush fantasies come true—how he gazes at you, yearns for you, even gives you the chills through his very touch—yet is untouchable to you. I love the tension that situation creates, which was tricky because I had to keep them both at bay, not acting on their impulses even though both felt compelled to do so. I hope I accomplished that, and you're shipping Sarina and Jaxon as much as I was when writing their story. (PS, I'm pretty sure Jaxon could play Sam if my Cape May series ever hits the big screen. IYKYK)

And then there's Molly and Max. With them, I wondered what it would be like to run into someone you knew in high school and had nothing in common with, but upon reuniting, all those high school differences melt away as you discover you're more similar than you realized. Maturity, life experiences, and face-to-face conversations tend to reveal we have more in common with our perceived "opposites" than originally thought. Seems the world could use a bit of this as well.

The Characters. When I decided to create a wildly popular actress local to South Jersey, my inspiration for Kelsey came from two real-life actresses with connections to Cape May County: Grace Kelly and Anne Hathaway.

Grace Kelly was an actress in the 1950s whose family owned a summer home in Ocean City (that still stands today). As a teen, she worked summers at the locally-famous Chatterbox Restaurant until her acting career took off. At age 26, she met and married Prince Rainier III of Monaco and gave up her acting career to tend to royal duties. As Princess of Monaco, she continued to vacation in Ocean City until her death at the age of 52 in 1982. It later dawned on me, after I finished writing the story, that Kelsey was said by the media to have "met her prince," just as real-life Grace had. Fortunately, for Kelsey, it didn't signal the end of her acting career.

Another "prince/princess" connection I just realized: Anne Hathaway, whose physical attributes were the inspiration for

Kelsey, starred in *The Princess Diaries* trilogy. Anne, who was born and raised in New Jersey, has strong family connections to Cape May and often visits this area. I recall a local article reminding readers that she and other celebrities who visit this popular destination deserve to enjoy their vacation without being hounded by fans. I may have given Kelsey a bit more free-range-chicken-about-town than real celebrities enjoy, but I loved the idea of someone famous returning to their hometown, shedding the glitz and glamour, and getting to just be the person they were before stardom. Getting to just...*be*.

While Anne was the model for my character's physical attributes, I later learned that it's her mom's story that resonated more with Kelsey's plot, which I didn't know at the time I wrote it. Turns out, Kate McCauley Hathaway is a star in her own right, having acted in local Cape May productions since childhood. Like Kelsey, she met her true love during a production as teens, but both moved away and led separate lives until, ten years later, they returned to town. Unable to resist their feelings for one another, they married—but not to the surprise of their friends, who knew they'd been in love all along. Again, a discovery I made reading an article (assuming it's true) after the fact. Kismet? Or maybe there's just something in the Cape May water.

Finally, I named my character *Kelsey Jean Grace* after wanting to play upon Grace Kelly's name. Kelly Grace seemed too obvious (as Jaxon would say, "see what I did there?") so I went with Kelsey. At first, her middle name was going to be "Jane", but then my beloved nephew and niece-in-law had a baby girl during the writing of this novel who they called Kelsey Jean, not knowing the name was similar to the character I was creating. She's the first grandchild of my brother and sister-in-law, my parents' first great-grandchild, and the star of every family gathering. With big beautiful dark chocolate eyes and silky brown hair, she remarkably looks like the childhood version of my character, lighting up every room she toddles into as her bubbly belly laugh fills our ears. She has captured all our hearts in ways we didn't know were possible. So...Kelsey Jean it was. And always will be.

No shade to the rest of the characters, but they just evolved from the topics I wanted to explore.

Sarina, for the struggles faced by small business owners. Also, to represent people whose dreams don't make sense to those around them, but who forge ahead regardless of that—sometimes finding support was there all along. I wanted her to be feisty, independent, and with a strong sense of self as a survivor of family trauma.

Molly, for her career confusion—and the many young people who, like her, are either unable to find jobs in the fields in which they've been educated (and degrees for which they spent way too much money for), or who are uncertain about what career path to follow. I wanted to let folks know...it's okay to not know what your passion is at 18. Even 81. You'll eventually discover it, right when you need to. She also represents how personal growth and maturity can affect your choice in life partners. After all...we have to know ourselves first, before we can know another.

Colton, for his sweet vulnerability, and the idea that while people may appear tough and strong on the outside, we never know what inner struggles they may be dealing with on the inside. Not just the result of childhood bullying, but when life takes swings at us. He also represents the need to pivot and make the best of our situations when our dreams are thwarted.

Max was created in honor of the truly good guys who do exist, but who are often passed over. Like Molly discovered, once you give a guy like that a chance, you will discover a true gem (same goes for women!)

Lastly, Jaxon was created because I wanted someone fun, full of himself, but who was no match for true love. I wanted him to be taken down at the knees upon meeting his person—at long last, humbled by an unexpected love.

Themes. As noted, this novel includes lots of human relationship themes: friends-to-lovers, second chances, celebrity crushes, missed opportunities, career fulfillment, sister love, brother love, love for one's hometown. Love for small businesses, especially those who brew coffee.

Touching upon the theme of small business, I wanted Sarina's café to be the go-to place for coffee and sustenance, but to be faced with the real-world threat of corporate businesses taking over the small guy. The best part of the shore, in my opinion, are the small businesses that serve residents and make visitor's trips here so enjoyable—bookshops, coffee shops, ice cream parlors, restaurants, boutique stores. So please, when you're here, support them the best you can, and give them positive shout-outs on social media, word-of-mouth, and review sites like Yelp. Without these little businesses, the shore just wouldn't be the same.

As for the Christmas in July theme, I wanted to infuse a bit of holiday revelry into the story, especially since it occurs after a damaging storm. Most people have probably heard of this made-up holiday, typically celebrated on July 25. It's a tradition that dates back to 1933 when Fannie Holt, co-founder of Keystone Camp in Brevard, North Carolina, decided to bring Christmas cheer to her summer camp with activities like a gift exchange, a Christmas tree, and a visit from Santa. The concept gained further popularity with the 1940 movie "Christmas in July". At the Jersey shore, many towns make a big deal of this summer holiday, often with celebrations, parades, bike and boat decorating, and family-friendly events. Santa makes appearances, usually wearing swim trunks and a Hawaiian shirt. Holiday revelers can be found in bars along the coast wearing festive garb, ranging from Santa hats to ugly sweaters, and everything in between. I wanted to capture the local "down the shore" spirit of Christmas in July by centering Molly's fundraiser around the theme.

Lastly, there is the most important theme—the reason for a Christmas in July fundraiser to begin with—and that is the devastating storms that have ravaged our coastlines over the past few years. I purposely didn't use the term "hurricane" in this book because so many people along the Jersey coastline suffered devastating losses during Sandy and other such events. The truth is, it doesn't take a hurricane to cause coastal flooding and demise. And it's happening more and more.

The Marine Mammal Stranding Center. Guys, this place is for real. Although not located within a golf cart ride from Cape May, as in my story, this non-profit agency is located in Brigantine, New Jersey, 50 miles north of Cape May. I wanted to keep its real name in here (even if the location is fictional) to highlight the amazing work they do. Along with (and shout out to) the real people like Max—scientists, biologists, legislators, volunteers—who are dedicating their lives to protecting these beautiful creatures. To learn more about this center and donate to their cause, visit their website at https://mmsc.org/

Book Club Questions

1. Which couple—Kelsey and Colton, Sarina and Jaxon, or Molly and Max—did you find yourself rooting for the most?

2. Have you ever been in a situation, like Kelsey and Colton, where you weren't able to express your feelings to someone you were crushing on? How did you handle it, and do you have any regrets over not voicing it (or voicing it?)

3. Did you agree with Sarina's decision not to ask family for money to help her with the café's financial issues? Should she have swallowed her pride and asked earlier, or do you understand her decision not to be judged by them and to want to do it on her own? Have you ever embarked on a risky project and later regretted it? What did you do?

4. Is there anyone from your high school who you wish you'd gotten to know better? Why?

5. For many, including the author, Cape May is a favorite vacation destination. Have you ever been there? If so, what do you love about Cape May? If not, would you ever want to visit?

About the Author

KIMBERLY BRIGHTON IS AN AWARD-WINNING ROMANCE AUthor, incidental humorist, and asparagus enthusiast from the Philadelphia area. *Cape May Christmas in July* is her fourth novel. Her first three books comprise the Cape May Series, including *The Way to Cape May*, *A Cape May Kind of Love*, and *Cape May Ever After*. She studied satirical writing and screenwriting at The Second City and is the author of *The Shore Blog* (theshoreblog.com), a travel website focusing on the Jersey Cape, and *BlaBlaBlog* (BlaBlaBlog.org), a humor website. When not dreaming up swoony romance plots, she spends her time searching for food expiration labels and sitting at red lights. Married for 25 laugh-filled years, she's discovered the key to a lasting marriage: takeout.

To stay in touch and learn more about her upcoming releases, sign up for her newsletter at KimberlyBrighton.com or visit her on social media @KBrightonAuthor.

Made in the USA
Middletown, DE
08 July 2025

10196783R00241